The Hunter of the Dead

And The Kiss of Persephone

For Mark, Doug, and Kirk, who was like a brother to me.

And also with thanks for 'ChaCha' who vetted this project for me and gave me the thumbs up.

First edition 2009

A Relentless Endeavor

Courtesy of Lulu.com

978-0-9789507-9-8

(Paperback edition only)

THE HUNTER OF THE DEAD

And the Kiss of Persephone

By Maria Aragon

Author of *Deus Ex Machina: a Divine Comedy*

DRAMATIS PERSONAE
(who is who: a handy dandy list)

Aidoneus Zagreus Hades, Lord Hades – Lord of the Underworld: Tartarus, Erebus, etc; brother of Zeus, Hera, Poseidon, etc.

Cerberus – his three-headed dog, who guarded the underworld.

Persephone-Kore – daughter of Demeter; depending on the source, father is either Zeus, Iasion, or even Poseidon, reluctant consort and Queen of Hades.

Zeus – Sky God, Leader of the Olympian Gods, father of many.

Hera – Unhappy Consort of Zeus, also his sister, Goddess of women, marriage and childbirth.

Demeter- goddess of the fields, agriculture, protected marriage and domesticity, Kore's mother.

Dionysus- Twice born, ancient bull-horned god of fertility, vegetation, wine, god of liberation from societal constraints.

Ariadne –Minoan Princess betrayed by Theseus, became Dionysus' wife instead – he set her crown among the stars after her death, immortalizing her.

Hermes – trickster spirit, herald/messenger god, led souls to the Underworld.

Hecate – goddess of witchcraft, magic, wilderness, crossroads, childbirth, ghosts,

Apollo- Phoebus, Paeon, Pajawone, which may be his earliest name, god of the arts, music, poetry, an ideal figure who was also god of light, archery, healing, prophecy, possessed the power to cause and cure plagues and illness.

Aphrodite – goddess of sexual love, beauty, desire, fertility, also a sea goddess, predates Zeus, has enigmatic associations with Dionysus according to some traditions.

Eros – God of sexual love, brought Gaia and Uranus together, lethal, potent 'son' of Aphrodite, but according to Hesiod's Theogony, was present when Aphrodite set foot on Cyprus after her birth in the ocean, guardian of marriage, protector of love between men..

> *Consort: Psyche, mortal beauty turned goddess.*

Ares- god of war and the spirit of battle, son of Zeus and Hera.

> *Sister: Enyo – who is bloodlust and violence personified.*

> *Daughter: Eris – who is Strife, and is sometimes called Ares' sister as well.*

> *Son: Deimos – dread.*

> *Son: Phobos – fear.*

Athena – Atinija – her earliest name > from Crete, goddess of arts, war and wisdom.

Artemis – virgin goddess of chastity, forests, wild animals, the hunt, childbirth and fertility.

Medusa – a beautiful priestess of Athena, punished by her for being raped by Poseidon and thereby desecrating her temple, rendered monstrous by Athena who later sent Perseus to take her head. She symbolizes the death processes and death.

Helios – frequently combined/confused with Apollo, the original ancient Greek sun god, who drove a chariot, like Sunya across the sky.

Hephaestus – god of fire, blacksmiths, craftsmen, metallurgy, neglected consort of Aphrodite.

Gaia – an ancient Earth goddess, primordial creator of the world who created the world with her son the sky god Uranus.

Heracles – originally the mortal son of Zeus, rendered immortal by his father.

Poseidon – God of the oceans and of horses and earthquakes.

Ganymede – exceedingly good looking young Trojan prince, probably a teenager, when Zeus kidnapped him and, immortalizing him, then kept him as his cupbearer and lover.

Osiris – ancient Egyptian god of the Underworld, god of vegetation.

Nepthys – Osiris underworld consort, mother of Anubis.

Isis – Osiris' consort, mother of Horus, protective mother goddess, 'great of magic'.

Anubis – jackal or jackal headed god of the mummification wrappings, assoc. with Funerary rites, assisted in the Judgment of the Dead and led the Righteous to Osiris, his black fur represented both death and fertility.

Horus – hawk-headed god of the sky, patron of sun and moon, son of Osiris and Isis.

Hel – Norse goddess of Death, rules the Underworld, over those who did not die in glorious battle, also a name for the underworld.

> *Garmr – her bloody dog, guards the underworld.*

Freyja – Norse goddess of love, battle, war, fertility and magic, patron of crops and spring, half of all slain warrior souls went to her hall Sessrumnir in Asgard.

Wotan – or Odin, leader of the Norse gods, creator of both the world and its people, god of war, wisdom, magic, poetry, prophecy, victory, hunting, and death.

> *Two Raven companions: Huginn and Muninn.*

Thor – Norse god of thunder and lightning, son of Wotan, volatile temper and loved battle, watched over the common man, welcomed slaves to his hall after their deaths.

Tyr – Norse/Germanic god of single combat, military justice, treaties, self-sacrifice.

Yamaraja – or simply Yama, a Vedic god of death and lord of the underworld, the first man to die and find the path to the underworld/afterlife.

Asclepius – son of Apollo and Coronis, god of healing, medicine, doctors.

Immutef – or Imhotep, apparently a real architect who worked for Djoser and high priest, a reputation as a sage and physician gathered after his death to the point that he became sanctified. His tomb site was a place of pilgrimage for people seeking cures.

Dhanvantari – Like Imhotep, a real person it seems, who was a talented healer who came up with Ayurvedic medicinal practices and one of the world's earliest surgeons, later elevated to divine status as a healer to the gods and god of Ayurvedic medicine.

Vrinda Devi – according to what I could find: goddess of devotion to the Supreme, also physical health and wellbeing, also is associated with Radha and Krishna.

Shiva - Hindu god of destruction and also regeneration.

Parvati – Shiva's Consort, divine Shakti and mother goddess, reincarnation of Shiva's first wife Sati, mother of Skanda and Ganesha.

Durga – the warrior aspect of the Divine Mother - DEVI, the fiercer, demon-fighting aspect of Parvati, according to one reading, an aspect of Kali.

Kali Ma – goddess of time and change, figure of annihilation, redeemer of the universe – the one who finishes, her black appearance concerns her associations with war and corpses.

Surya – the Supreme Light, solar deity, drives a chariot drawn by seven horses.

Tumatauenga – Maori god –the fierce fighter, originator of wars.

Anu – aka Anann the personal name of the Irish goddess Morrigan, personification of death, predicts death in battle.

Lord Ogoun –Haitian and Yoruba assoc., presides over fire, iron, hunting, politics, and war.

Hadak Ura – Hungarian war god, metal smith, forged the Sword of God.

Perun – Slavic, highest god of their pantheon, god of thunder and lightning and war, like Thor, has a hammer.

Parashuram – or Parashurama, a martial Shraman ascetic, sixth avatar of Vishnu.

Skanda – six-faced son of Shiva and Parvati, also Lord Murugan, war god.

Takemikazuchi – Japan, god of lightning, sword and bows are his weapons.

Huitzilopochtli – a sun god and a war god of the Aztecs, legendary wizard.

Mextli – Aztec warrior god, of the moon and of storms.

Teoyaomicqui – Aztec god of dead lost souls, esp. from battles.

Tezcatlipoca – 'smoking mirror' - Aztec god of hurricanes, night winds, the earth, divination, sorcery, strife and war.

Trebaruna – Spanish/Portuguese goddess of protection of home and families, a war goddess.

Babd – Irish goddess of war who took the form of a crow or a wolf.

Kukailimoku – Hawaiian god of war.

Resheph – Canaanite god of war and plague and lightning.

Andraste – Anglo-Celtic goddess of war, battle.

Cernunnos – god of the underworld, but also of produce and fertility.

Archangel Michael – field commander of the army of God, patron saint of warriors.

1.

Where or when did love stories begin?

Did they begin with Aphrodite and her illustrious paramours Ares and Adonis?

Or did they begin with the rapacious Zeus and his many hapless, helpless conquests?

Perhaps they began with Inanna...

Or did they begin one beautiful, balmy, and fateful day when Hades ran afoul of Eros and that fearsome hunter ever so calmly notched a golden arrow in his dreadful Scythian bow and released it. No one was immune from the power of Eros, not even the Lord of the Underworld...

Hades recoiled from the impact, his hand grasping the lethal shaft. Eros' sudden, efficient violence startled him. He met the young man's terrible, knowing glance. "You bastard!"

Eros smiled and it was terrible to see.

Hades looked down. His own hand laid pressed flat against his chest. The accursed arrow was gone, but a mark bloomed all red and purple, looking as inflamed and tender as it felt to his touch.

Hades looked up. "Do you realize what you've done?"

Chuckling lowly, Eros turned his smiling gaze toward the meadow.

As though hypnotized, Hades followed his glance to where the sunlight danced across the wildflowers and softly waving blades of grass.

A most splendid sight greeted his feverish gaze: light, lithe figures draped in gossamer gowns that wafted in the breeze whenever they idled or threatened to fly away whenever their wearers rushed about. Maidens or nymphs, not that it mattered much to Hades, it mattered only that they were near enough for his eyes to drink their fill of their beauty. His spirit warmed as they rushed every which way exclaiming over the goddess Flora's wild, beautiful bounty.

Hades moved a step closer.

Eros chuckled again.

Hades ignored him, but in the back of his mind he wished mightily for a Zephyr to seize Eros and dump in the Himalayas. A touch of frostbite might cool his heels for a little while.

As colorful as the blossoms they gathered in their soft arms or into the aprons they improvised from their raiments, the troupe of maidens scattered further and farther a field. They called to one another over each wonderful new find.

Hades had seen them all, but he watched only ONE. They were each lovely and bright, but this *one* ... She shone the brightest in his dazzled sight with her sun-kissed golden red hair and skin so pale and translucent he knew that the slighted touch would bruise her.

Already he envisioned his umbre-toned hands touching her soft skin, caressing her delicate boned hands and slender arms…and then closing about her wrists with their purplish blue veins. In his arms she would abide, so warm and supple to hold. Even her rich hair, he knew, would be as fragrant as honeysuckle, as night blooming jasmine, and he would close his eyes as he buried his face in that radiant hair and simply breathe.

Such thoughts carried him forward.

This incident the Fates had decreed.

The Zephyr Hades would have invoked to blast Eros all the way to Shambala did the winged one's bidding instead. It stirred the leaves and the sea of grass, muffling the voices of the maiden's companions.

"Kore. Kore. Come see…"

Half-stooping, *she* raised her head.

The Zephyr tossed the ends of her hair, carelessly, knowing how it made the Lord of the Underworld's heart ache.

Eros smirked, leaned against the cypress tree, and folded his arms over his lean, muscular chest. No one could escape his power, not even the King of the Dead.

"Kore…Kore…" But the Zephyr made certain to carry their cheerful voices the other way.

Her friends waved to her, beckoning to her to rejoin them among the pure white and yellow blossoms that grazed against their knees.

Wildflowers overflowed from her improvised apron. She had plenty. She had more than enough to delight in. Smiling at her fragile treasure trove, she heaved a great sigh and stood erect.

His breath stolen, Hades moved but three swift soundless steps forward.

The sun-dappled shadows conspired to conceal the dark lord just a little longer beneath the stooping tree boughs.

What a brave, bold creature was this Kore. Hades admired her straight strong back and the fullness of her form filling out that simple summer garment. The impudent Zephyr made certain to give him a sound appreciation of her figure by tugging at her gown until it pressed close to her flesh.

Hades wanted to slap that Zephyr for taking such liberties with her innocence.

She began to turn away.

Hades faltered in mid-step.

Eros' smile widened.

Something yellow caught her eye. She stopped to look again and then to look closer still. She caught her breath.

Such a flower she had never seen in all the days of known existence. This yellow bloom she had to possess. How her mother Demeter would adore it! She stooped once more and stretched out her hand to take it. The shadows covered her from the meadowlands.

"Kore? Kore? Where are you?"

At the leafy border between the vast bright meadow and the dark whispering forest, Kore's companions found a great pile of flowers and no other trace of their friend

Invoking fierce Artemis' protection, a stalwart trio braved the restless shadows in the forest to search for Kore.

They did not trespass far.

Not ten paces in, they encountered the formidable winged god Eros twirling a luscious yellow flower between his fingertips. They froze at once and dared not move. Perhaps he had not noticed them.

As though reading their minds, Eros turned an amused glance their way. Intent glowed dark in his amber brown eyes.

The maidens fled to the safety of greater numbers out upon the meadow. His laughter, full of scorn and daemonic delight, sent them all running as far and as fast as they could go. It was the only sensible thing to do.

None of them dared look back.

Delighting in the chase, the Zephyr blew upon them, stampeding them, even as Hades rumbled in the opposite direction aboard his ebony chariot.

Already as powerful as an elemental force, passion gave Hades unyielding might. In one hand, he gripped the reins and with the other he clasped his destiny, his hand firmly pressing against her belly.

The entrance to his realm lay but a short stretch away. His three black destriers knew the way, only his impatience compelled them to rush headlong this time. He had to rush, for she struggled with tremendous vigor and shouted and screamed enough to shatter the celestial ceiling if he lingered for too long in the open.

Their sudden descent from the sunny world of the Living into the valley of the shadow of Death caused Kore to falter. A tremor went through her. A sob jolted from her and she trembled as she passed into the darkness of the Underworld.

Hades pulled her close against him. How she shook. How wildly her heart raced. "Fear not this realm, fair Kore, for here I am King and here shall you be Queen."

Kore buried her face in her sleeve and all but choked on her tears.

Her legs would not bear her, so he carried her from his chariot. He breathed in deep. She smelled of warm soil, sunshine and all the things that flourished in its grace.

She was in no state to assume her place on the royal and divine dais beside him, so he carried her into his chambers behind the dais.

The spirits of the dead rippled in their wake from the force of his desire and her anguish.

Neither food nor drink could tempt her. She had appetite only for grief, so he bid her lie down and rest.

She collapsed upon his bed.

His love wound bled anew into his heart. Hades could not bear to leave her side. As invisible hands drew down the curtains surrounding their retreat, Hades stretched out beside her and stroked her hair...for there was nothing else to be done.

Afterwards – a potent word 'afterwards' – when her tears had dried and the last echoes of her cries had faded even into the bleakest recesses of Tartarus and Erebus, Hades consigned the torn and spoiled remnants of his bride's once splendid maidenly gown to the pyre that forever blazed between the dais and his private chambers. She watched him sacrifice its softness to the greedy flames and understood what it was to be a sacrifice herself – a virgin sacrificed upon an expedient marriage bed. Her own blood bore her ordeal witness.

"My Mother will be mightily aggrieved," she said.

Hades turned and gazed with frank and scarcely sated love upon her pale and bruised beauty. Her hair shone golden in the firelight as it hung full and loose all the way to her thighs. She did not attempt to veil her nudity with it. There was no sense in concealment or modesty, however vulnerable she still felt. He knew her entirely.

No one would save her now, she realized. Once she was lost to the sun's sight, there would be no going back to the life she had enjoyed. So she gazed into the fire and felt her heart expire along with her lovely dress.

"Do not think of leaping upon this pyre," Hades said in a low, but gentle voice. "These flames would not dare to so much as singe your hair."

"And if I tried anyway?"

"I would catch you and hold you fast and keep you near; besides these flames are for purification. They are dangerous only to the 'unclean'."

She would not meet his gaze even when he climbed the stone steps toward her and stood before her again. Instead she gazed into him, seeing that terrible bruise over his heart. "I am cold."

He smelled of the incense from all the flames burnt in honor of the Dead in all of the world. "Then I shall warm you."

When at last she emerged again from the curtained chamber, Hades with gentle hands attired her in Queenly raiments: a gown of white silk that glowed like a moonstone and sparkled with a multitude of small, faceted clear quartz beads, slippers made of embroidered silk of the softest shades of blue Hades knew of, a gossamer blue veil that floated about her on the softest of whispers, and at last an embroidered corselet both very light and very strong, which was studded with gemstone cabochons. He combed and arranged her hair with his own hands and with great care, before arranging her veil just so.

Everywhere she moved the most delicate chiming emanated from her person. She felt like a precious temple ornament when Hades brought her forth upon the dais.

"Kore no longer," Aidoneus Zagreus Lord Hades announced to the Sacred Court of the Underworld, "henceforth are you Persephone for your beauty is such that it destroys the light."

She murmured, "My Mother will surely hear of this."

2.

In the Underworld realms, all was quiet and as calm as an undisturbed lagoon. There Persephone reigned beside Hades, his Queen of iron, haughty towards him and resentful towards all.

Other than a steadily growing trickle of souls driven emaciated out of mortal existence, all was as it ever was in the Underworld.

In the upper realms of Earth and Sky, all was in tumult until at last Life itself hung in the balance.

Demeter held the Earth itself hostage until Zeus bestirred himself to retrieve her abducted daughter and restore her to her mother. She was still grumbling ominously as Hermes sped off to the Underworld. "Bring her to me at Eleusis first."

Zeus sighed and rubbed his brow. He knew better than to meet hers or Hera's glances. He could feel Hera simmering. When she was truly, deeply, fiercely angry, she tended to smell like sandalwood, oddly enough. He hated that smell.

"For someone who purports to concern himself about the maintenance of the law and the social order itself, you are the epitome of indifference when it suits you," said Demeter.

"That is not entirely true," Zeus said.

"Thank you for qualifying that," Demeter snapped. "Your words give me such consolation."

The instant Hermes crossed into the realm of Hades and Hel, Persephone took one look at his frown and sat forward with a smile. She gave Hades a bright, defiant look. "I shall be Kore again."

As Zeus was Lord of the Skies, so was Hades Lord of the Underworld, therefore, Hermes paused to incline his head to him upon the dais.

Hades inclined his head in return.

Breathless, Persephone stood up.

Hermes observed her impatience, but he couldn't help by observe also the pain that turned Hades' gaze inward. Sometime there was nothing he hated more than being a messenger. "You know why I have come."

Hades grunted. His brow furrowed. He reached into the bowl of fruit beside his throne. He chose a pomegranate.

"My mother," Persephone said, her chin held high and her eyes flashing bright. "You have come to escort me home."

"This is true?" Hades looked Hermes hard in the eyes.

Hermes nodded.

Hades regarded the great round bruise colored fruit in his hands…and tore it open with focused violence.

Hermes almost winced at the sound it made. "Your presence is not unwelcome on Olympus, Aidoneus Zagreus."

He smiled tightly. "Oh, of that I'm damned sure." He began to eat of the pomegranate.

At that moment, Hermes doubted that Lord Hades tasted anything other than his own bitterness. He frowned and tilted his head for a better look. "What is that blemish on your chest?"

Hades glanced up toward bright-eyed Persephone. "It's a wound. It'll be a scar soon enough." Anguish welled up in his face again.

Hermes avoided Persephone's scowl. "I don't recall seeing it before."

"I acquired it recently, very recently."

Already his consort behaved as though nothing had happened and that he didn't exist.

"If you have come to take me away," she said, "then do so. My Mother will be impatient to have me at Home."

"Coming, my Lord?" said Hermes.

Hades bit into the heart of the Pomegranate's wound and would not look up at either of them.

Hermes sighed. "Ready, Kore?"

"Yes! Let's go," she snapped.

Hermes inclined his head toward Hades again and to Anubis and Hel off to the side, where they had observed everything, and turned away from the dais. "Let's be off then. Olympus is in high dudgeon over you."

Persephone stepped from the dais.

"Wait!" Hades' voice thundered across the vast chamber.

In mid-step, Hermes flinched and risked a look over his shoulder.

Persephone froze in place, but quickly busied herself with removing her veil. She did not look back.

Hades stepped into her path. "You can leave that readily?" he said very lowly.

She arranged her rich garments and tried not to see him or that purplish red scar over his heart. "Yes, of course."

"After everything that has happened between us?"

"Particularly after what has occurred between us," she said, cool and curt.

"You may indeed leave, but you shall never forget." Hades took her face in his hands and kissed her.

Persephone gasped and tried to push him back, but he closed his arms about her. Every moment of ardor combined with grief he poured into his kiss. She tasted the pomegranate seeds on his tongue and then in her mouth. Her eyes widened, staring into his dark eyes. Then she closed her eyes...and swallowed.

His lips brushed hers in parting. Then he peered into her face for some sign of compassion.

Her eyes opened, but she looked beyond him to Hermes, who pretended, poorly, not to have witnessed anything.

His arms fell away from her and he resumed his place on the dais. Shifting his back toward her empty throne, Hades took up the pomegranate and picked at its remains seed by seed.

Hermes could not get Kore away to Eleusis fast enough.

From Eleusis, Hermes had the dubious task of escorting Demeter and Kore to Olympus to see Zeus. At Olympus, Hermes took one look at all the tense and angry faces and decided that he couldn't clear out of there fast enough either. Hermes tipped his shining winged helmet to all present, pivoted and fled to Sicily to wait out the drama.

Demeter could not caress and pet her Kore enough. "Where did you get these garments? So fancy. Too formal. Never mind. I shall get you fine new gowns." She took one look at the darkness in Zeus' face and decided that she wanted her precious daughter well away from him. Turning away from the Olympian thrones, she ushered her darling one away ahead of herself. "Your friends have missed you so much..."

"Bear with our presence a moment more," said Zeus. His voice rumbled everywhere.

Mother and daughter looked back. Kore's face shone. Demeter's clouded over.

"Kore?" he said.

"Sky Pater," she replied.

"That is no longer your name, am I correct?"

She looked down. Her regal garments shone as could the full moon behind the thinnest veil of cloud, soft and pure and cool.

"It is best to answer the great Pater Familias," said Hera.

"You have another name now," said Zeus in the tone of one who knew all too well what he needed to know. "Tell it to us that we may know the woman you have become."

Demeter scowled.

Trembling, she lifted her gaze. A movement off to the side caught her attention. It was Eros, eyeing her over the wing he was preening. His unsmiling look of bemusement sent a chill through her. Then anger surged throughout her being. Her face reddened.

"Per...Persephone." Although gently uttered, her name carried throughout Olympus as clear, pure, and strong as a temple bell's chime.

Zeus considered her anew. "And do you destroy the light as your name proclaims?"

She shrugged. "I cannot say."

"The ruler of Hades chose that name for a reason."

"I cannot begin to fathom what inspired him so."

"Can you not?" Eros plucked a feather from his left wing without so much as a passing wince.

Zeus cast a dark look at the young man.

Blithe in his sovereign indifference, Eros began preening his right wing.

"May I leave now?" said Persephone.

"Not yet." Zeus gestured. "Those exquisite garments..."

"HE gave them to me."

"He dressed you."

"It was necessary." She blushed and lowered her gaze until she could compose herself.

"Then he was a good host to you."

"That is not how I would describe him."

Eros snorted.

"Zeus, do not torment the girl," said Hera.

"Has she not suffered enough?" said Demeter.

"There is a purpose to my inquiry, Great Harvest Mater, so bear with me." Zeus' voice, formerly calm and patient, rumbled forth from Olympus.

Demeter bit her lip and kept a firm hold on her daughter's arm.

"He dressed you in Queenly raiments. He sheltered you. Did you accept food and drink from him during your sojourn?" Zeus leaned forward in his throne.

"Ample quantities of food and drink he set before me, but I did not taste of it," she said primly, although a shadow glanced suddenly across her brow.

Zeus saw it though. "Not so much as a sip of refreshment?"

"No, Sky Pater, not one sip."

"Do you mean to say that the whole time you were in his domain you did not *taste* even the smallest morsel?"

Persephone began to open her mouth, but stopped and frowned. "The smallest morsel?" A sigh shuddered out of her. "I have damned myself," she murmured.

Demeter peered into her face as fresh lines of grief spread across her browned, careworn face.

"Persephone?" said Zeus.

Tears rolled down her cheeks. She brushed them away almost impatiently.

"Something passed your lips," said Zeus.

Eros smirked.

With a trembling fingertip she touched her lips. "Some pomegranate seeds…when he…"

"And only one would have sufficed," Zeus declared. He stood. "Persephone – for that is your name – you have tasted of Death so to its Lord you belong even as you belong also beside your Mater among the sweet blossoms of Primavera. For that reason, you must retire from the sunlight to the realm of shadows, returning when the Seasons deem it fit. Dry your tears for they are useless. It is a fair judgment as the Fates have decreed." Zeus avoided meeting Aphrodite's glance. "Now, go abroad with your Mater and bless the fields anew with your presence."

Zeus extended his great hand.

Dutifully, Persephone kissed it.

Without a glance at her, he withdrew his hand at once, for he knew in his conscience that she would have rather bit him. Zeus brushed away her tears against his purple robes as though they would burn right through his hand and strode off.

"Where are you going this time?" Hera called after him.

In a smiling tone, Zeus replied, "For a long stroll. I shall return when I return."

Hera made a short, angry sound.

Persephone looked up.

Hera was glaring at Aphrodite, who shrugged.

"He doesn't need me for motivation," the goddess of Love and Beauty said.

Hera's fierce gaze settled on Eros, so casually preening his wing. "I expect you know where he's going."

Persephone was struck by the young man's fearlessness.

"And if I do?" he replied.

Hera shook. She looked fit to spit and tear her hair. "You never apologize for anything, do you?"

"Never." He smiled.

Hera tore from the Great Throne Hall.

But for her mother fretting in the entrance and Eros, whose merciless gaze had shifted toward her, Persephone lingered alone. The rest of the Divine Assembly had prudently slipped away in all directions.

"You are to blame for this," she said.

Eros leaned toward her, perfectly serious, thoroughly earnest, and said in a lowered tone, "What I did was decreed by *another.*" Then he leaned back and said loudly, "You are what you must be, just as I am. We have roles we must fulfill. You will see."

Pivoting, Eros spread his wings and, brandishing his bow, soared high and away.

Not much later, in the Underworld, Lord Hades received the report of Lord Zeus' decree from Hermes, courtesy of Apollo, who had borne witness to all of it in Hermes' stead. A thoughtful silence ensued between the two divine incarnations.

Abruptly and decisively, Hades crushed the pomegranate husk in his fist and pitched it into the fire pit behind the dais. As he stalked past Hermes, he patted his lean shoulder.

Beyond any doubt, Hermes knew he had glimpsed a smile on somber Hades' face. In the near distance, he heard Hades whistle and the three-headed Cerberus simultaneously yap, whine and bark.

3.

There was no pretending otherwise. Everything about her had changed. More than the awkward silences, the meaningful glances that her former companions gave her, or Demeter's forced cheerfulness, Persephone felt it in her very being.

She was different. Her sojourn in the Underworld, coupling with Aidoneus Zagreus Hades, had altered her. Before, she had felt the energy of life dancing within her. That energy flowed *through* her now. She felt as though Life itself cut a channel through her, passing through her as a river rolled through a delta into the sea... and felt strangely invigorated.

To her companions and Demeter, she said nothing. It didn't seem prudent, not when she couldn't make sense of it herself, and not when the mortal world she returned to had suffered a change too.

Where everything had flourished, blossoming and ripe with abundance for all to share, Persephone found its dire opposite. Only the most stubborn leaves clung to the trees, but the north wind peeled them away one after another. Not one vibrant green blade struggled in the currents. Only dying and dead yellow and brown grass huddled against the cracked soil, barren and quick to fly to dust upon the restless winds.

For a very long time, Persephone walked in a landscape of anguish, unaware that her eyes mirrored the grief of the world. She found dead livestock beside dried up ponds and streams and blessed their bones for the suffering that had been inflicted upon their blameless souls.

Inscrutable, Demeter walked beside her at a slight remove. If she felt any sympathy, or had a moment's empathy for what her wrathful pain had inflicted upon the helpless mortals, she showed no trace of it.

They found an abandoned village and an excess of evidence of funerals recently observed of men, women, children, whole families who had perished. Persephone lingered there a moment simply absorbing the silence. Even the birds had deserted that place. She cast a look toward Demeter and saw only self-satisfaction.

"You did this. How can you be so content?"

Demeter blinked out of her musings. "How can you speak so to me? I was half out of my mind when I couldn't find you."

Persephone gestured about her. "Are all these...Is all this worth less than me?"

Demeter looked long and hard at her, as though her daughter had said something utterly imbecilic. Then she moved onward toward the near meadow, the one she knew to be sacred to Dionysus, saying, "It is of no importance; besides it all can be restored." She waved a hand at their unnaturally still surroundings.

Persephone stopped to regard the deserted village. She had never thought her mother to be anything but benevolent, benevolent in her duties and in her nature. Suddenly, she saw how hard and selfish Demeter could be. "It did not have to be this way," she muttered as though swearing an oath she was just beginning to understand.

"Come along, Kore," Demeter's voice was gruff. "There is work to be done."

She folded her arms over her breast. Her fuming gaze scraped along just ahead of her feet.

Someone already waited there in the sacred meadow. "Ah, there you are…at last."

Persephone looked up. For a moment she was surprised. Then she saw the mountain of Nysa beyond its plain and nodded to herself. This was *his* stomping ground, almost literally, for here in the meadows of his plain Dionysus carried out his especial ceremonies.

And there he stood: the Bull-Horned One, Twice-Born Dionysus. Vines entwined about his bull horns and trailed through his long brown hair. A snake rested in a lazy coil about his neck, its black eyes resting upon her just as its master's did.

Of him, she had heard more than could be proved. Certainly there was a unique aura about Dionysus. Although his handsome face belonged to a sensual young man, his kohl lined eyes had the sort of impenetrable quality and, already, a world-weariness and comprehension such as emanated from the visages of reverent, wizened sages. Dionysus struck her as somber, but that was hardly surprising, considering the dire circumstances confronting them. Those same deep, unfathomable eyes flickered slightly as he took a full view of Persephone.

Inclining his head slightly, he said in a richly accented, strong voice, "Greetings, Demeter, Harvest Mater."

Demeter bowed a little more profoundly. "Greetings, Bull-Horned Lord."

Dionysus faced Persephone and bowed deeply. "Greetings, Queen of Hades."

Persephone hesitated. That was the first time she had heard herself referred to precisely as a Queen. A random quandary arose in her, but she was mindful enough to bow most respectfully to the Twice-Born One, who was the oldest of the Olympians…if Truth be admitted amongst friends.

Was she Queen of a place or person? Or both?

"Greetings to you, Twice-Born One," she said.

Dionysus took a step toward her and extended his hand, while with his free hand, he tossed his gleaming silk chlamys over his opposite shoulder. Except for its rich, voluminous folds hanging about him, he was all but naked.

Before Hades, she would have scarcely noticed, since Apollo roamed about in the slightest and most flowing of coverings also.

After Hades, Persephone was keenly aware of the slightest of cloth barriers standing between their bodies. She kept her gaze aimed above his waist, but as she accepted his hand, she noticed its fine strength and eloquent fingers. Well adored by the sun, his skin was a radiant brown and his tousled and long hair a golden hued brown. Whereas Hades possessed all the strength of bedrock and iron, as though formed by Gaia herself, and could move with swift, irresistible purpose – a formidable manifestation of divine energy, Dionysus possessed a subtle and beguiling energy. Hades took charge. Dionysus beckoned one onward, just as he was doing then with Persephone out upon his sacred plain.

From the instant she took his hand, the energy that flowed through her flowed into him…and through him into Gaia. He was also a conduit. She caught her breath.

"We have a great task before us, Persephone," he said in a soothing, but firm voice.

Dionysus cast a brief look at Demeter. She stopped where she was, turned away, and holding her hands out over the barren ground, began uttering mantras.

Far out upon his sacred plain Dionysus led Persephone. "You and I must restore this realm. We are the only ones who can, for the Living have long since forsaken this place." Genuine sadness hung heavy in his voice. "Have you been here before?"

"No. Never." Persephone gazed about at the desolation. "Was it nice here before?"

"It was a wonderful wild place once, full of birdsong and whispering trees. Now the trees have lost their voices and the birds have gone in search of more charitable habitat."

"I wish I had seen it then."

"You shall see it rise up and grow fertile again. You shall hear my beloved birds sing and chatter. Then the people will wander back…but only if you help me restore this realm."

"What must I do?"

"I would not ask this of you if my people were still here, but we are all and, truth be told, only you and I can – this once – repair your Mother's damage. We are special, you and I."

The entire time they strolled forth side by side, hand in hand, Persephone felt their combined energy surging into one another, pooling, gathering in force and potency inside their beings. When she had been simply 'Kore', her 'self' was quite contained. Now that she had become 'Persephone' by the fated desire of Hades she possessed power, from the Underworld but also as part of her matriarchal birthright she empathized with Life's forceful resilience.

And Dionysus shared her associations in ways she hadn't considered. Perhaps, she reasoned, it was because their connection as vehicles of rebirth had never been crucial until that day.

"Yes, I can feel a connection. Strange."

"Do not be alarmed."

"No, I am not alarmed, just a little surprised when I first touched your hand." She glanced down at their clasped hands. "Startling.

"Are you well with it now?"

"I am quite well with our bond." Her eyes locked with his. "I am quite prepared to do what it is you require of me."

"It is not I who require this. I am content." Dionysus motioned toward the land and the golden-hued horizon. "The land, Life itself, requires this of us both if everything should flourish again and the people return."

"Tell me what to do and I shall do it with all of my being."

"See that circle just ahead?"

"The one marked out with stones painted with red earth? Yes."

"Stand on the northern side of it and I shall stand on the southern side."

Persephone shone in her pure colored raiments as she darted across the dry ground to her place on the circle.

Dionysus walked. There was a meditative frown on his face. His eyes remained fixed upon Persephone. He took his place opposite of her. His whole demeanor altered. The Bull-Horned One stood perfectly straight and alert with his feet placed well apart. The great snake that had been resting in its favorite place coiled about his neck slid down his chest. It coiled languorously about his waist before easing down his left leg to the ground.

Impassive to distractions, his serious face remained focused toward his partner in the ceremony.

As the snake slithered a slight distance from the circle and coiled tightly to wait, Dionysus lifted his chin a little higher. "Are you ready?"

"What are we doing?" she called across the circle.

"We dance within the circle, keeping always directly opposite of one another."

"I do not know this dance."

"Mirror me."

"There are no musicians."

"The wind shall play for us and for percussion we shall have to use our feet. Gaia the Mother of All shall not mind us using her great round belly for a drum. This time we must provide the rhythm. If we are successful, Persephone, mortal ones shall take our places next year."

"I see." Persephone straightened as he had and lifted her chin slightly. "Show me the way."

Defiant in the face of their mutual determination, a bitter cold wind rushed over the sacred circle and the two Incarnations. Dionysus smiled in its teeth and could scarcely be buffeted in retaliation. Infuriated, the wind snatched at the gossamer blue veil Hades himself had placed with such tender care over Persephone's radiant hair. She stood still, resolved to fulfill her purpose. The wind tore away the veil and tangled it and tore it against the bare tree branches.

Dionysus watched it vent its anger on that supple veil and smiled.

Persephone felt a softer breeze run through her uncovered hair. In the open, her hair shone a honeyed shade of golden red. She smiled with delight.

Dionysus regarded her again. Something kindled in his amber-hued brown eyes, causing Persephone's breath to catch in her throat. She was not alone. Gaia was there, everywhere, her heart beating beneath their bare feet. In the distance Demeter stood facing east with her hands held facing skyward from her sides, still saying mantras to heal the world of her wrath and pain. Persephone was not alone. She was well and soon she and her companion in Life and Death and Rebirth would make the world well.

Dionysus raised his arms from his sides and took one step to his right, then a swaying step to his left.

Persephone mirrored him precisely, if a little stiffly.

Then he took two steps right and one step left, then three right and one left. Each time he shifted directions he stomped his right foot.

Mirroring him from across the circle, she did as he did.

After he had counted up to seven steps right, Dionysus moved a step nearer the center and resumed the series of steps from 'one' step again. Swaying something akin to a rhythmic cobra, the Bull-Horned One moved a little faster at the conclusion of each series of seven steps.

Gradually, Persephone's motions became fluid and assured. She let the breeze toss her long gleaming hair about as she moved her head in rhythm with her body's movements.

The energy they shared, the power they embodied in that ruined place filled the circle. Their dance wove their energy behind them leaving an imprint in the ground. Their energy penetrated Gaia. As Persephone felt Dionysus' irresistible vitality, she felt Gaia's strength rising into them. They warmed the air about them and that warmth radiated from the circle of red-stained stone. Gaia sent her own tremendous warmth outward, bathing them in her energy in gratitude…and in blessing.

Closer and closer their dance brought them. Faster and faster and then the trance came upon them. Gaia's heart fires, volcanic fires, glowed in Dionysus' eyes. His hands burned when they took hold of Persephone by her arms. She gasped, so did Dionysus, for her skin had burned him to touch also.

Still dancing, hands touching, they moved in circles until they stood at the very heart of the circle. Breathless, they stopped, face to face, and looked at each other and then cast glances about themselves. The very air trembled and in the distance the land seemed to ripple from the heat of Gaia and Dionysus' circle.

Something tickled their toes. They looked down. Blades of grass sprouted all around their feet. The desolate farm fields in the distance bloomed green with such impatience that for a moment Persephone and Dionysus disbelieved their eyes for a moment.

"We did it." Persephone laughed and squeezed his hands.

Dionysus let go a great whoop and spun her about in his arms as she laughed to the skies. He set her down upon her dusty feet in the grass carpeting the circle, but Gaia was not done with them yet. She required a sacrifice of Persephone and an offering from Dionysus.

As Dionysus took Persephone's face in his hands and they gazed breathless and smiling into each other's eyes, Gaia slipped the God's chlamys cloak from about his body and let it drop carelessly in the sacred circle.

"Just this once," Dionysus whispered, "my beautiful light destroyer…my sacrifice."

Persephone shivered. Her gem-encrusted girdle fell soundless upon the grass, for all the treasures of the Earth obeyed Gaia's will. His warm hands bared her bosom and Gaia carried away the crystal beaded gown of white, flinging it atop Dionysus' chlamys.

Persephone shivered again. The Bull-Horned One's hands were cupping her breasts, his thumbs fondling her. She knew this act of sacrifice, of submission to Divine Will, knew it so well. He turned her body this way and that, running his hands across her everywhere. She closed her eyes and leaned her head back against his shoulder as he filled his hands with her breasts, where they nestled perfectly.

His breath grazed her left cheek. Opening her eyes, she turned her face towards his, closing them again as Dionysus touched her chin and kissed her half-parted lips. Breathing in deep, Persephone kissed him back as she had never kissed Hades. Her head swam as Dionysus bore down. His kiss was ravenous, but his lips were soft, tender even and so enticing to kiss.

Gaia had prepared a lush bed of grass within the sacred circle and onto it Dionysus sank with Persephone pressed close against him. They paused kissing only when Dionysus rose up and rested on his knees. His honey-brown eyes roamed across Persephone's luxuriant beauty as he removed his vine-laden bull horns, his unusual crown, and set it aside. Contemplating her in potent silence, he combed his fingers through his hair, loosening it for the breezes to play with.

Fascinated, Persephone watched his hands. He moved always with a kind of languid grace and calm purpose, which rather surprised her. He and his followers especially had a reputation for wild abandon, but he had shown her the way into his trance state. They remained in its grip, under the primordial spell of Gaia, and it was nothing like she had heard or imagined.

Alone with Hades in his realm, beyond all aid, she had been afraid.

Alone within sight of the mountain of Nysa, alone with the Twice-Born One naked upon their bed of succulent grass, Persephone was unafraid.

Dionysus lowered his hands to rest upon his knees. Her gaze followed his motions. She had avoided gazing at Hades as much as she could even to the point of averting her face and closing her eyes when he lowered himself onto her. Now, her gaze lingered upon Dionysus, his face, his shoulders, traveling downward mesmerized by his remarkable hands, and seeing his readiness for her.

Raising upon her elbows, Persephone shifted toward him and raising her knees, parted her legs.

His eyes kindled. He leaned out over her and then leaned into her.

Delight escaped Persephone's lips and she took him fully into her embrace.

Their sacred act carried them far from themselves back again into the Sea of Consciousness that Source of All Things which formed all of Life. Dionysus became whole with Persephone and together they became whole with Gaia. Her energy poured into them, flooding their minds. The couple felt and knew every sentient mind in Existence become part of them with all the force of a tsunami.

Then just as suddenly a great peace came upon them. Gaia had withdrawn, sated and invigorated by their union. Alone together, Dionysus and Persephone climaxed.

At last, in the stillness, the Fates granted Dionysus the vision his heart craved: of a maiden abandoned by a faithless young man and the island where Dionysus would find her weeping. Smiling, he kissed Persephone's neck and raised up on his elbows to look into her face.

The dreamy expression on Persephone's face unclouded and she looked surprised. "You?! How did you…"

Dionysus knew when someone was having a hallucination and he could rouse anyone from a lingering trance state. He took her face in his hands and caressed her. "It is I, Dionysus. Who did you see, Persephone? Who did you see?"

"Hades." She touched his browned face for reassurance. "You were him or he was you, but he was here. His face…"

Dionysus kissed her hands. "Come with me. The natural world has been renewed and I know of a sacred pool close by where we can bathe."

Persephone nodded.

4.

Joyous nymphs greeted Dionysus and Persephone at the sacred pool with a wonderful banquet and fresh garments for afterwards. They smiled and bowed and blessed them for their sacrificial act. As the couple stepped into the waters hand in hand, the nymphs tossed blossoms upon the water and poured sweet, fragrant essences into the water.

Dionysus had walked directly in, but Persephone hesitated just long enough to test the water with her toes.

"It's warm!"

"Umhmmm," said Dionysus. "That is why I come here when I crave a good soak."

She stepped quickly in beside him and let the water touch her earlobes.

After they had soaked in meditative silence for awhile, they moved into the shallows and sat beside the water's edge. At once, the nymphs offered them refreshments and delicacies. Dionysus leaned his damp head back against the grass and gazed up into the abundant sea of leaves rustling softly. He chewed on the olive bread and cheese he held in his right hand. Persephone savored the bread and cheese, looking happily at their restored paradise.

"Where is my Mother?" she wondered without a trace of anxiety.

"Elsewhere," Dionysus said. "She is not allowed to come near us."

"Oh."

"When you are ready, you can leave and you will find her."

"She will be busy by then," Persephone mused.

"She had better be. 'Serves her right."

"You are angry with her."

"I was, but not anymore." He smiled kindly at her and brushed a wet strand of glossy red hair back away from her brow.

"She was selfish. You think that don't you?"

"I do. There were other ways to get you back once Helios told her and Hecate what had happened. Her initial anguish and panic I understand perfectly, but she did not have to punish Life itself to get you back. Many innocent beings suffered and perished needlessly…and it just did not have to be that way."

They gazed out at the sunlight sparkling on the water for a moment.

"I think she was selfish too, when I saw what had happened."

Dionysus stroked her shoulder a moment. "Now that I have met you I understand though."

They exchanged quiet, friendly looks.

"I understand also why Hades HAD to make you his consort."

Persephone looked at the bread and cheese in her hands and frowned. "I do not. I had never set eyes on him before he carried me off. I had only heard of him. His reputation carried far beyond him, just as yours does."

Dionysus arched his brow and mused to himself for a moment. "And how do I compare to my own legend?

"I expected a wild man with crazy eyes. I expected someone deep in a narcotic haze and raving some sort of visionary nonsense."

Dionysus gaped. "Heavens, Kore!"

Persephone burst out laughing, causing the nymphs to giggle behind their hands.

"What HAVE they told you about me?" he said.

"About the wine soaked, opium addled orgies with your followers for starters."

"We all drink wine." He made a face and shook his head. "As for my opiates, whatever I apply to my purposes is for a purpose: for divination, for the attainment of greater insight into oneself and the cosmos, or as a means of transcendence from the confinements of *self* … as a means of attaining enlightenment. What you encounter with me is decided as much by what you bring with you as by what you seek. I am a means and a way. I am just a conduit for those who would follow my path."

Dionysus let her mull that over for a moment. "You yourself are a conduit and certainly, so is your Lord Hades Zagreus."

A frown flinched across her thoughtful brow.

The Twice-Born One tilted his head slightly to peer better into her face. "There is a reason why we each had visions at the peak of our union."

She seemed startled. "You had a vision too? What did you see?"

Dionysus gazed past her sat the foliage shimmering in the sunlight. "I saw a young woman upon a desolate island. She was weeping her heart out for the ship and the faithless hero aboard who had left her behind. My heart went out to her. My heart is hers…when I find her."

"Then what are you doing here? You should fly away to her."

"I would, but she is not there yet. We are deeply associated, this brave maiden and myself because of the bull who is also a man and I, the man-god who wears the bull's horns. She is not born into this realm yet, but the Fates have shown me her and where and when I shall come to her. I need only be patient."

Persephone gazed into the water. "I see."

Dionysus studied her expression. "And you saw Hades."

"Please do not..."

"There is a reason for your seeing him in my place."

"It was a bad memory, simply that."

He whispered into her ear, "You can tell yourself that all day, all night, and for years to come, but you know the truth."

She shook her head vehemently. "I cannot bear to dwell upon it."

"Dwell or not, him you must return to for you are required there just as you are required here. I think you know that."

"But I cannot accept it. I do not want to." She turned passionate eyes toward him. "I would rather have belonged to you."

"Me? A raving visionary?" Dionysus smiled. "Are you certain?"

Persephone blushed. "No. No, you are nothing like that."

"Then how do you see me?"

"I expected someone wild and almost primordial and exotic. You are exotic to be sure, but in the most beguiling manner. You strike me as being meditative, contemplative, philosophical, very compassionate, which I do appreciate particularly, and…otherworldly. One minute you are this roguish young man and the next I see this ancient sage peering out from your eyes. You are nothing I was told to look out for."

"I am pleased and frankly, a little relieved to hear that. Now, how did you see Lord Hades?"

"Before?"

"Yes, before."

"They speak so ill of him on Olympus."

"They? You mean Zeus, don't you?"

"Well, he almost never comes to Olympus, and Zeus and Hera speak so disparagingly of him."

"Yes, I know, but I also know why."

"Why then?"

"Later. Go on first."

"On the very few occasions my Mother brought me to Olympus, I have overheard Zeus grumbling about how seldom Hades responds to his summons."

Dionysus smirked and nodded.

"And apparently," Persephone continued, "when Hades does deign to appear at Olympus, he is aloof to the point that he seems indifferent. Zeus and Hera seem to find his attitude offensive."

"Believe me, they do. What else had you heard – and believed – of Hades before the Fates arranged your marriage?"

"On Olympus, Hades is described as somber, bemused, aloof, distracted, ill at ease, high and mighty, judgmental…" Persephone shrugged. "And none of them speak of his realm with any enthusiasm or respect."

Dionysus nodded the whole time. "So any opinion you had of your future consort was prejudiced by the ill-favored comments of those on Olympus."

"You have spent more time on Olympus…"

"Among other places…"

"…than myself. What is your impression of Hades?"

"What does it matter?"

"I would not ask if I was not genuinely curious. Humor me, please, Dionysus."

Dionysus gazed down through the water at his own body. He grinned abruptly and cocked his brows. "Otherworldly, philosophical, perceptive, intuitive, compassionate or merciless, depending on whom he's confronting, feared, under-appreciated, misunderstood, and not without a dry sense of humor. What? Did you expect me to denigrate him too? Did you want me to describe him as a twin-headed ogre who eats boiled babies for breakfast?"

"No, of course not."

"You wanted me to revile him so you could feed and justify your revulsion of him. Look. Anyone would understand your dislike, especially after what you went through, but you are more than what you used to be." Dionysus gestured at the burgeoning land about them. "You know that beyond any doubt. Yes?"

Persephone nodded.

"You have become who the Fates foretold you must become. The ordeal you endured was meant to transform you and it did just that."

She brushed away a hot rushing tear with her wet hand. "But why me?"

There was something to his silence that caused her to look into his face. He was rubbing his chin.

"What is it?" she leaned closer to him and laid her hands upon his shoulder and his arm. "You look troubled."

Minnows made quick work of the olive bread she dropped into the water. The cheese slice sank toward the mud.

Dionysus pulled his gaze away from the trees and returned his thoughts to her. "I am ready to come out of the water," he said loudly.

The lovely nymphs arrayed themselves along the pond. When Dionysus rose from the water, they dried him with the softest of cloths and draped him in a fine chlamys that was the color of saffron. At the very last, one of the nymphs bowed as she held out his vine decorated bull horns to him.

Dionysus accepted it in both hands, but did not put it back on. "It is time to come out of the water. We have purified ourselves long enough."

The nymphs rushed upon lightly treading feet to collect Persephone's wardrobe. They regrouped beside a pond and waited a little breathlessly.

With a sigh, Persephone left the wonderful warm waters. The instant she stepped upon the grass, a nymph wrapped her in a sun-warmed blanket.

Dionysus watched the nymphs dress her in diaphanous garments of lavender and blue that flowed wistfully upon the slightest of breezes. They dressed her luxurious golden red hair with great care and wove sweet blossoms into her braids before arranging her hair high upon her head. At the last, they arranged the ringlets and the long thick coil they let trail down her back.

Finished completely, the nymphs withdrew in unison and removed themselves a polite distance away.

Persephone held her hands up from her sides. "What do you think?"

"Exquisite work, ladies," Dionysus called.

They bowed, smiling and whispering excitedly amongst themselves.

He held out his hand to her. "Come and sit with me in the shade for I have a story to share."

Persephone took his hand and strolled into the shade.

There they settled down under a wide-spreading tree. The Twice-Born One drew the Queen of the Underworld into his arms and almost upon his lap. Immediately, the nymphs spread before them a great feast to enjoy at their leisure.

"Do help yourselves, my fair handmaidens," Dionysus said.

"Thank you, Bull-Horned One," said one for the rest.

As Persephone rested her head against his shoulder, Dionysus fed her a grape and then four more before closing his arms loosely about her.

"This is a true story," he began as the nymphs also settled about their feast to dine and to listen. "Once upon a time…"

5.

"Once upon a time there was a great god who hunted the Living, ever since Life itself began – a Reaper of Souls. Merciless and unrelenting he was and all were one and EQUAL in his terrible sight: the Great, the Obscure, the Powerful, the Humble, the Rich, the Poor, the Damned and the Blessed. Nothing deterred him from his hunt, neither tears, nor pleas, nor station, nor purposes unfulfilled, for Destiny decreed his actions.

A creature of Fate and yet, not belonging to it, he held himself apart from his prey, impervious and calm. The self-regarding, if polite disdain with which his fellow divinities beheld him passed as the slightest wisp of a cirrus cloud across his consciousness and scarcely troubled his brow. His purpose brooked no distractions and unlike them, he could sense the passage of time, an unexpected and yet not unwelcome insight he gained from the prey he captured.

It is of Aidoneus Zagreus – Hades Zagreus Lord of the Underworld I speak. Yes, HIM whose story has never been revealed thus to anyone. For, you see, the separateness of Lord Hades piqued the Sky Pater to the point that Zeus felt himself obliged to humble him. Unwittingly, Hera gave him his excuse...

'Indeed, something must be done,' said Hera, for she was in a fine temper that evening. 'He conducts himself fartoo grandly. You would think he was Master of All when he is only the Lord of the Dead.'

Now, down the banquet hall, the Olympians digested their meal in such silence that only their eyes spoke, and then only discreetly amongst themselves. With such guarded glances did the Lord Apollo communicate with us all, for, yes, lovely Queen of Hades, I was there too, enduring the ill temper of the Queen of Olympus. From Athena did Apollo communicate his uneasiness to Artemis and to Ares and then to Hermes and myself. We drank our ambrosia and I drank my soma and we all of us wished ourselves elsewhere, for the evening was as an overripe fruit fast turning to rot.

Only the lovely Aphrodite was in fair spirits still, but she is ever the minx, smiling private desires into her goblet whilst others fret. Not even the smoldering lights in the fearsome gaze of Zeus the Thunderous One could put her out of spirits. Although, I must admit, the rest of us felt Zeus staring past us all into the fading twilight and dared not meet his glance.

And Hera would go on, for she will not be content until she can provoke the Sky Pater. Sorry lady that she is, she is much neglected and if she cannot have his contentment she will encourage his dissatisfaction. There are times, sad to say, when either reaction if the same and equal to her needs:

'One scarcely hears a peep out of Hades and then up he springs from nowhere and upsets all of our arrangements. When one does expressly desire his presence at court, he can hardly be bothered to attend.'

Such is the profound justness of Lord Apollo that he spoke for your lover. 'Great Queen, please remember that tremendous obligations are his lot and they demand his attention at all times. Hermes can verify this. He has conducted a great many souls to the Underworld.'

How Hermes winced at being prodded into the conversation. He coughed and had to clear his throat as he stole an ugly look at impervious Apollo. But defend he did, saying, 'Indeed, whether above or below the sacred skin of the Earth, he is never idle.'

Hera would not relinquish the matter though, not even to virtuous industry. 'All the same, he comes to Olympus on a whim and we are expected to accommodate him.'

With the merest of glances, Apollo rallied the serene Athena to the cause and she said, 'He has always come and gone as errantly as a breeze. That is his way, and you must admit, he never makes a fuss. If anything, he has always been undemanding and objective.'

'Hades is forever holding himself apart from us, as though he was different or...'

And here Apollo attempted to forestall the inevitable. 'Do not say the word! Do not utter such a thought. There is absolutely nothing presumptuous about him.'

Then wily Hermes bestirred himself to speak, 'If anything, Great Hera, Lord Hades is guilty only of taking his duties so seriously that he neglects everything else.'

Now, here I felt compelled to address Hera. 'His purpose consumes him so utterly that everything else is an afterthought.'

Then even wild and unapproachable Artemis spoke up, 'I have never witnessed any intentional acts of rudeness and we all know the sorts of personalities with which he must contend in the Underworld.'

Even Hera's surly son Ares spoke his piece, 'He is forbearing almost to a fault, and he disturbs only the Living, which is his ordained purpose.'

And yet Hera would be nothing that evening, but unhappy. 'Would it hurt him then to be a little more sociable? We see far more of Poseidon and his whole court than we do of Hades by himself. Then, when he does appear, Hades sits in his little bubble of bemusement and scarcely says 'Boo' to brighten the conversation.'

I had a weary notion and whispered it across my cup to Aphrodite. 'Hera would not be wound so tight and spoiling for trouble if Zeus would spend the proper time satisfying her. Can you not lend her your enchanted girdle again so that Zeus will abide with her for a change?'

Sweet-smiling Aphrodite looked as though a great headache swelled upon her horizon. 'I should simply give it to her for keeps, but I fear that Zeus would become too accustomed to its magic. Then we would be right back where we started.'

Hermes prodded her as well. 'Loan it to her for a season at least so we all can have a little respite from the turmoil.'

Ares muttered his own dire admonition to his beloved Aphrodite, 'If you do, give us fair warning so that we can speed away to our remotest temples before the connubial bliss kicks in here.'

Before the Beautiful One could say 'yea' or 'nay' though, Zeus at last felt himself prodded to address the subject…and we all braced ourselves.

'I really do not think that Hades causes any difficulties intentionally, Hera. I do agree: he is a little standoffish, but, be fair, we all find him a little difficult to relate to. He is alone down there and perhaps his manners have suffered as a result.'

Hermes, who knows these matters well, had to correct Zeus. 'Hades is not alone.'

This came as something of a surprise to the Thunderous Lord. 'He is not?'

'Thanatos and Hypnos are there.'

'But they are spirits, are they not?'

Hermes tallied the names on his fingers. 'Osiris and Anubis…'

Zeus was dumbfounded. 'Osiris and Anubis?' I tell you, it was hard to say which surprised him more: their names or that they existed at all.

As Hermes did not wish to stand alone upon the field of Truth, he prodded me with his sufficiently sharp elbow. I then invoked the name of Nepthys also as a resident of the Underworld.

To which Zeus cried, 'Who in Hades is Nepthys?'

You laugh, sweet Persephone, but I tell you, it was hard to say whether he was more bewildered than irritated by these revelations.

'Why Nepthys is the Underworld Consort of Osiris and Anubis is her son,' Hermes informed him. 'Did you not know?'

How Zeus sputtered. 'No, I did not, but...'

Then an old familiar voice, laconic and quiet spoke forth, 'That is because Zeus never troubled himself to find out.' Hades stood atop the steps in his cloak and tunic the color of a moonless night.

Zeus shouted his name, such was his surprise.

Hera could only find wit enough to snap, 'You are late. Have you no sense of time?'

Your Lord bowed most sincerely. 'My apologies, Great Queen of Olympus,' he said, "I would have been here with time to spare, but the Fates decreed that the Earth should shiver and shake. The consequence was that there were a great many disoriented souls to shepherd from their startled remains into the afterlife. Quite a few refused to believe that they had indeed passed on. It took some firm persuasion on my part.'

Zeus has the disarming, except from Hera's perspective - annoying - habit of smiling to himself as though he is contemplating some exquisite delicacy for his dessert. It is a look that only leads to mischief. He pronounced, 'Even in the grip of their delusions these mortals are endearing.'

Hades took his preferred place, which is always at the farthest end from Zeus, but he said just loud enough for his closest of friends: Hermes, Apollo and myself to hear, 'Mortals are not the only ones who suffer from delusions.'

'We had thought you led a solitary existence, but that is not the case?' said Hera, who was in a foul mood that evening and needed someone to prod.

Hades allowed himself a moment's peace to partake of the soma I offered him. He likes his soma with extra honey for it can be bitter. 'The Underworld is a community like any other. I am never truly alone, Great Hera, for even my thoughts are with me always.'

Ares frowned at that moment and glanced about. Later, he revealed his suspicion that Eris lurked in the shadows, for there was a growing atmosphere at that fateful gathering.

Zeus snapped out of his reverie. 'Who is this Osiris anyway?'

'My abiding equal,' says your lover..."

Dionysus shifted a little to avoid the sunshine. "Did anyone ever tell you that Hades does not suffer fools gladly or that he can be blunt when his patience ebbs?"

"None of the Olympians have a great deal of patience from what I can tell," said Persephone.

"True enough, Loveliness, but your Lord is the only one thus far who has ever dared confront Zeus…as he did that evening for he looked Zeus in the eyes, saying…

'Frankly I am stunned by your persistent ignorance, Sky Lord. I know that you have glimpsed in passing my Cerberus romping with Garmr.'

Zeus began to lose his fragile patience. 'Who is Garmr?' How he glowered at your Lord to be.

And brave Hades would have none of it. 'Hel's bloody dog.'

'Hel?!' For indeed Zeus' mind was quick to tangle in what he could not be bothered with in the first place.

Hades let go a mighty sigh. 'I have not all the evening to acquaint you with what you can scarcely concern yourself with.'

'You complain of my ignorance…' Zeus protested.

'If you spent less time meddling with mortal maidens and making them wretched, and occupied yourself more in your true domain, you would know the things you ought.'

Now, Hades has a sense for disasters and the fresh harvest they bring him. He stood up and frowned. At that same moment a Zephyr rushed past us. It carried the aroma of fierce downpours and rushing earth. Whispers soft, whispers lost amid the Zephyr's breathless trespass that passed over the table. Then, amid the delicate chimes of our temple bells, came another ominous sound, the sound of distant multitudes in terror and grief.

Something dire had taken place and sad to say, the only two who sat indifferent to such distant suffering were Hera and Zeus, for the one was too preoccupied with simmering jealousy and the other sat scowling at Hades, whose thoughts were leagues away…

Dionysus sighed and shrugged. "Truth be told, Shining One, it happens more often than one cares to admit that the mighty Zeus and his maligned Queen bother more about their own cares than they do about those whom they claim to have charge over. Yes, shocking, I can see by your looks, Generous One, that you are appalled. Not all who occupy our realms are free of the traps of their own egos. Remember that when you sit in judgment of the Dead. Remember also that all things must end, even our blessed turbulent realm."

"What happened next?"

"Eastward we gazed as the aroma of churned earth passed over Olympus and blew our sacred incense westward. Our leisure had ended. Swift Hermes wiped his mouth and took up again his helmet and winged sandals. Great Apollo stood and frowned, for he, as we all did, heard the faint cries of distress, of terrible agony and grief.

Hades could tarry no longer. He shook out his night-colored garments. His irises turned whiter than the full moon in a winter's night. 'Ready?'

'Ready enough,' replied Hermes.

'There will be shock and confusion,' declared the Wise Reaper of Souls. 'It is best that I accompany you this time to shepherd the stragglers Home.'

Hermes nodded, for when there is grim work to attend to he is solemn and purposeful. He looks a different person then, for the rest of the time he is all Trickster. He bowed to the assembly and to the Lord and Lady of the feast, who did not bother to return his gesture, such was their irritation.

Upon his swift, light feet Hermes sprinted down the steps, caught the night wind and veered east.

'Duty calls,' Hades announced. He performed his proper courtesies. 'Thank you for inviting me. I will see you when I see you. Good night, All.'

Scarcely had we bid Hades farewell when he dissolved back into the Night, borne away upon its winds, which know him well.

Next Apollo rose and made a parting toast. 'I have a symposium to patronize and then I must journey north. There is a bardic gathering to attend, so eventually...' With a lordly flourish, Pajawone Apollo donned his golden saffron and maroon cloak and strolled forth into the deepening night, softly illuminating it.

"The wolves will be howling in the timberlands of the Americas soon,' declared Artemis. 'I have a longing to hear their voices. Therefore I must absent myself.' One polite bow and the fierce Artemis was gone off to roam amongst the wild things in her virgin forests.

Only Athena, Ares, Aphrodite and I lingered at the banquet to have our cups filled anew by fresh-face Ganymede. Athena had taken refuge in her contemplations and a platter of fresh samosas. Ares and Aphrodite, those brazen illicit lovers, simmered with mutual appreciation from a scarcely polite distance across the table."

"And you?" said Persephone.

"With all the discretion of a household feline I observed all that passed. My intuition barked as a dog in the night and I would see the evening's conclusion...

For all her planning and preparations and hopes, Hera's gathering had been ill-fated, but she could not know that this time the poison of her discontent would reach out beyond the heights of Olympus. Yes, Fated One, this is your story.

Zeus might have been Master of the lightning bolt, but there have been times when it appeared that the storms themselves in all their fury heeded Hera's moods. That evening they betrayed their tendency to answer her summons and align their wild energy with her. At last Hera had had enough of company. Accompanied by a chill breeze strong with the aroma of impending storm, she flung her shawl over her right shoulder and padded away in her silk slippers.

Left to his own devices at long last, Zeus turned his seething stare in Aphrodite's direction. She felt the full force of his thoughts and returned his regard.

Understand this: Aphrodite and her lethal son Eros are greatly respected and dreaded in the same heartbeat. Their powers come from the heart of our cosmos, the Source itself. They have the power to upend lives and affect whole civilizations. That Zeus commanded her in his silence was ominous.

I watched, as gradually and steadily as dawn's approach, Aphrodite took on a smile full of shadows. In their distant lair, the Fates, as I did, felt an alteration in the balance of all things, felt it as a terrible new day coming.

Satisfied, although still discontented, Zeus downed his ambrosia and stalked away – in the opposite direction of his Consort Hera's chambers. The Earth trembled beneath his feet. The air quivered from the force of his passage.

In the silence of his wake, Aphrodite, the Beautiful One, smiled over her cup at Ares the War Lord. 'I may be delayed, Beloved.'

Ares, who sees more and knows more than he lets on in Zeus and Hera's presence, glanced at Sky Pater's seat cooling in the night air. 'You know where to find me.' He tossed his empty cup to Ganymede and stood from the table.

Wretched Ganymede, captive pet of the Pater whom Hera scarcely tolerates in her husband's wayward affections, flinched at the War God's violence even as he caught the golden missile.

Aphrodite's hungry gaze followed her lover's departure. Then and only then did she gaze my way, for we are old and intimate acquaintances. We knew one another before Zeus roared down from the north and before Ares emerged from Conflict.

'I wonder where Eros has fluttered off to,' she mused in a manner that told me that she knew full well where the Dreaded Archer lurked at that hour.

Off she wafted, her exquisite robes of gold and burnished ruby trailing the sort of perfume that is found only upon one's pillow.

There was but one thing I dared do. I took myself to Delphi.

Now, dear Betrayed One, comes the terrible truth of how you were given over to Divine Sacrifice.

At last Hera's discontent formed an ulcer in Zeus' belly. Too long had he endured Hades and his casual indifference towards Olympus. Was not the mighty Zeus Lord of Olympus itself, land and sky? Was not Hades master only of those places the sun never penetrated? Were not his subjects only those wretched remnants of exuberant full-bodied Life? After all, what could take precedence over the Divine Court that he ruled on Olympus?

Nothing, my Persephone. Nothing.

So Zeus delayed his pleasures that evening, but only for so long as it took him to visit the Fates. He had set his retribution in motion, for even then Aphrodite bent the ear of her warrior cohort Eros to tell him where to go hunting and who his prey would be. Eros smiled. His is a most terrible smile, Innocent One, and accepted his mission, for not even Artemis enjoys her hunts as much as Eros does. None tremble more than the supposedly mighty Gods of Olympus when Eros is on the prowl.

Zeus came to the Fates at their hearth, where that feared trio sat huddled over their simple meal.

Long before Sky Pater drew near their humble abode, the skeins on their looms quivered. There had not been the slightest breeze or tremble in the earth. The three sisters felt this and sat silent for a moment.

The eldest stirred first. 'Trouble,' says she as she filled their cups.

'Indeed, for all Creation,' said the middle one with a shake of her head.

The youngest sister laid her left hand across several strands. Two of them were more substantial than the rest. Her fingers traced along them for a moment. 'Ah! I see that we have a fresh tangle, quickly forming a knot.'

'Zeus approaches,' declared the eldest with a weary sigh any matriarch would appreciate. 'As I said, trouble.'

'Whatever his original intentions,' said the middle Fate, 'what results from his meddling even he must accept. There are times when the wretched Zeus forgets that even HE is subject to *cause* and *effect,* and that which directs us directs him too. *This* was meant to happen and cannot be undone."

The youngest of the Fates grumbled, for she was hungry and their meal yet fresh and hot from the hearth, 'All the same I would rather he stayed well away and keep his impure motives to himself.'

Here did the eldest Fate crack a lean and very wry smile. 'Little does he realize that all things must pass – even for him.'

'I wish you would be so good as to inform him of that,' said the middle Fate.

'And be quick about it, for I do not care for cold soup,' said the youngest Fate.

'I shall speak,' said the eldest. 'Dine in peace and hide your smiles. He is upon us.'

Into the evening the eldest Fate sent her stern and hollow voice. 'Zeus of Olympus, why do you creep upon our threshold like a sneak-thief?'

Now, Zeus hesitated at that, for of all the entities in his territorial domain the Fates could not be controlled nor persuaded nor dissuaded. They stood...they still stand apart from everyone and everything. Zeus respected them, but then he had to although he begrudges them their infallible authority. If he thought it truly possible, he would overthrow them as he did those who reigned before him, but you cannot destroy what stands upon the threshold of Infinity and speaks from the Mind of the Source.

Before the Fates even such an incarnation as Zeus must stand humble. 'I have a question,' he said.

And the Fates cast knowing smiles toward one another.

'Make your inquiry,' said the eldest Fate, 'and know the Truth.'

Zeus would be clever and practice cunning, so he couched his question in the blandest of terms. 'An event has been set into motion and I...'

'...wish to know the consequences of your actions?' she said. Remember, Innocent One, it is impossible to hide the Truth from the Fates.

'Yes, of course,' he declared and blessed the darkness for concealing his angry blushes.

'O Mighty Zeus, Sky Pater, Divine Interloper, you thought only to interfere with the complacency of Hades Zagreus. You have done far more than deprive him of his contentment, for the world shall know such tremendous suffering as a consequence and shall never be the same. Console yourself that all is as it was meant to be. That which happens, happens. Mighty Zeus, you are but the vehicle of Destiny, so saith the Fates. Now, get thee hence about thy affairs, before thy desires immolate you entirely.'

How Zeus burned with aggravation even as he gladly withdrew far, far from the terrible Fates. He, who presumed himself Lord of Creation, King of the Mortal Realm, had been reduced to a servant of a greater Will that he chose not to acknowledge. Yes, mighty Zeus thinks most mightily of himself, Persephone.

So it came to pass that even as Zeus consoled his wounded pride by taking yet another mortal as his concubine, so did Eros lie in wait for Hades and Aphrodite speak in passing to the nymphs who were your playmates of a meadow redolent of the sweetest abundance of wildflowers. You see, whenever there has been a great tragedy amongst the living, Hades Zagreus can only calm his mind by taking a constitutional upon this mortal earth. He is not and has never been as aloof as Zeus has imagined. It is his nature, as the Reaper of the Living, to wander where Life flourishes.

Sure enough, Eros waited near that fateful site. Hades appeared. If he noticed you and your cheerful companions at all, it was only to appreciate that you were present and in wonderful good spirits. Eros he noticed right away and he was in no mood for company.

Eros knew what he was about. He menaced Hades with a smile.

Hades would have none of his mischief. 'Whatever you have in mind, spare me and go disturb another. You have no authority over me, impure Eros.'

This, of course, was precisely the interaction that Zeus had counted on and Eros' planned reaction fooled no one who heard of it later. *No one can deny the power of Eros.* He shot Hades and with a glance guided spellbound Hades to *see* you and you alone. The rest you have experienced, sad Persephone."

6.

For a long spell, Persephone sat nestled close in Dionysus's warm – oh, so warm – and protective embrace. She gazed at the sparkling water as Dionysus gazed into her face, reading her every thought's fleeting expressions on her bright face. He breathed in the scent of her hair.

At last she heaved a great sigh. "I have seen a fearsome purple and red wound in the center of Lord Hades' chest. I suspected at the time that there was something unusual about that mark."

"And now you know."

"It was the scar of Eros."

"It will never go away."

She buried her face in his neck. "I cannot bear to think…"

"Hades will love you *always*."

"I do not…I cannot love him."

Dionysus laid his hand over her heart. "I notice that you bear no such wound. You are unblemished."

"Except for what Hades inflicted upon me…"

"…And what you endured by me."

Persephone's face stung bright pink. "Other than *that*, I am unscarred."

"Then what feelings arise are your expression and responsibility alone."

"If it were not for Eros' nasty arrow, Hades would not love me? This is true?"

"Today it is true."

"Is there a way…?"

"No." Dionysus glanced about.

So did the nymphs just as warily. Then they met his gaze and shook their heads.

Dionysus sighed. "Count yourself fortunate, my Queen, that Eros did not deprive you of your Free Will with one of those arrows. I shall tell you how I came to know of Zeus' visit to the Fates." He looked about again as silent and alert as a lone stag on the edge of a clearing.

When he spoke, it was so softly that the nymphs had to sit quite still and lean a little nearer to hear him.

"The Raven told me of Zeus and his furtive visit to the Fates who told him what he wanted to know and mocked him in the same breath. As soon as Zeus departed, Raven came to Delphi in great haste where we awaited him."

"We?"

"Apollo and myself. We share the authority over Delphi and there are times we share the same mind when events are in motion. We had our suspicions. Raven confirmed them. Zeus had unleashed Chaos upon Creation and cared only that Hades bore the brunt of it." He took a breath. "Now, when Apollo left, fires of determination glowed in his eyes. He spoke of seeking out Aphrodite. I think he hoped to discover what plot was afoot. I think he hoped to put a stop to it."

"He failed evidently," said Persephone dryly.

"Great Apollo found Aphrodite. I am certain of that and he must have found out something of what she intended because she saw to it that he told no one else. Before Eros found Hades, he found Apollo."

Persephone caught her breath. "What happened?"

"As I said, you were fortunate that Eros shot only Hades and not you too. That very morning he waylaid Apollo and picked a quarrel with him about his shooting skills. Eros can put on an impressive front of belligerence when the situation requires it. He delayed Apollo upon the meadow and there he shot our Golden One too. Unlike your situation, Eros shot another: a blameless maiden enjoying the morning with her friends."

"Just like me."

"A golden arrow of Love and Desire for Apollo and a lead arrow for unfortunate Daphne so that she would run away instead and run she did. Apollo was aflame with desire and she could not outrun him. When she felt his fingers catching at the wildest strands of her flying hair, she cried out for aid, for protection, and then for deliverance."

Dionysus watched her expression. "Her father is Peneius, a River Incarnation. He heard her frantic pleas and did the only thing he could in such an emergency. Summoning all his strength, Peneius invoked the aid of Gaia. The instant Apollo's bewitched fingertips grazed Daphne's soft skinned hips Gaia seized her in a powerful maternal embrace. She cast a special arboreal cloak of her particular creation across the terrified virgin, removing her from the reach of all possible transgressions."

His voice grew softer, sadder, "For hours upon hours, day into night and back into day, Apollo knelt at the base of the fine new laurel tree that once was Daphne – and still is her – and suffered with heartbreak. He wept. He whispered to her. He implored for another chance and received only indifference. Peneius was content that Daphne should remain irreproachable. Eros was content to inflict suffering upon Apollo, and the Fates...Well, they are stoic to the bone."

Persephone looked into his face and saw old melancholy eyes gazing into the distance.

"At last, Apollo rose from his knees. He cut leaves from the laurel tree as lovers take clippings of their beloveds' cherished locks of hair. Just as lovers fashion love knots with those trophies, so did Apollo weave for himself a laurel wreath to crown his shining hair. Donning it as though it were made of the finest gold, Apollo swore in the presence of all Creation to honor Daphne thus. Then with a heavy heart, he set to wandering and found himself at last in Gandhara. He is there still, mourning his ill fortune with Love, for he is supremely unlucky. His beloved companions and consorts either suffer unfortunate ends or they betray him and then come to an unfortunate end. Love seldom is kind to him. I rather think it is because Helios and he revealed Aphrodite's infidelity with Ares to Hephaestus. Mind you, Aphrodite can charm and seduce her way out of most difficulties, but she did mind being inconvenienced while in the throes of lovemaking."

"I shall endeavor to maintain a polite distance," said Persephone. "Indeed, I have suffered from her influence enough as it is."

Dionysus smiled contemplatively as he stroked a stray curl away from her right temple.

"Honestly, I do not know who I feel sorrier for: Daphne or Apollo or Daphne's father," she said. "What a terrible fate."

Dionysus nodded.

"When must I leave this place?"

"Only when you are ready to." His smooth sure hands began to stroke her body.

Persephone smiled and laid her head back against his brown shoulder.

"Let me be reborn within you again," Dionysus' lips touched her cheek.

"Yes."

Lighting from within, Dionysus kissed her and moved upon her.

The nymphs withdrew a polite distance and dangled their lovely feet into the water as the Bull-Horned One rutted in abandon beneath the shade.

Many miles away, Demeter stood in a field of newly sprouted wheat and barley, smiling to herself. Once upon a time she had met her lover in a thrice plowed field. Iasion was his name or was it Iasios? Funny that she could not quite recall his name, but she did recall the rapture of their union in the field. How she had rejoiced to the heavens in her delight. She remembered that so distinctly that she heard the echoes of the past even then. Somewhere in the wooded valley beyond, their daughter Kore, now Persephone, fulfilled the purpose of her parents' coupling. Zeus had killed Iasion long, so very long ago and then as though not satisfied by the grief he had caused Demeter once, he caused Kore to be torn from her mother's careful side.

Kore no longer, with the Twice Born Dionysus, the Bull-Horned Incarnation of Fertility, Persephone redeemed the world Demeter's grief had devastated. Demeter hoped that Hades would ever hear the exquisite torture Dionysus was inflicting upon his stolen Queen and suffer most terribly.

When at last Persephone rejoined Demeter beyond Dionysus' domain, it took the Harvest Mother a moment to recognize her. She wore flowing, diaphanous clothes of raven's black, royal purple and forest green. A deep purple veil covered her incandescent hair, which the nymphs had restored to exquisite order atop her head. She carried a basket in her hands from which a cobra politely peered out, a parting gift from the Twice-Born One.

Her communion with the Bull-Horned One had also blessed her with a mien of such serene contentment that she radiated joy. Her very presence was a divine blessing incarnated. The wounded maiden was long gone.

In her place stood a Queen.

7.

Hades awoke with such suddenness that his eyes hurt to see. He had to close them and for a long meditative silence, his fingertips massaged his eyelids with great care. He peeked once to verify that he was still in his bed beyond the eternal fire in the pit because for a moment he had doubted. For a moment Hades thought himself in a field flooded with sunlight, warm from its touch and warmed also by his wife's naked body writhing in perfect motion beneath him.

The joy he had realized was rivaled by a pleasure so intense that it was almost unbearable. His Persephone shone in the sunshine, blinding in her beauty. She gasped and gave a great shudder. He felt her utter peace even as she panted and clasped him close. When he rose up on his elbows to look into her face, she looked startled and then horrified. She cried out in surprise.

The shock of it all forced Hades apart from her. Only then did he realize that Persephone coupled with another and awakened with a pang in his heart. The welcome memory of her pleasure lingered longer than the vision of the other lover though and with his aching eyes closed he savored his dream of her.

Hades groaned for want of release himself. He swung his left arm across the empty space beside him and gripped at the soft, embroidered coverlet. Staring up at the domed ceiling, carved directly from the bedrock, Hades whispered her name, wishing that she would hear him and have a change of heart.

Instead, a soft, shivering sound of delight echoed from someplace quite close to him. This was his domain. Nothing there frightened him, but he looked and saw a supple female figure coalesce from the darkness beside his feet. There she knelt peering up past her loose, rippling hair at him. Her eyes glowed as softly as a fog veiled moon.

"My Lord Hades," she murmured soothingly, "I serve only you." She drew the coverlet slowly downward.

"Indeed you have," he said, watching her uncover him to his knees.

The short, eager little sound that she made revealed her delight at what she had uncovered. Her electric supernatural hands she could not restrain.

50

Hades laid his head upon his left arm and gripped the edge of the coverlet with his right hand. He caught his breath and shivered once, for the succubus had a voracious appetite.

"I can help you forget her," the succubus breathed.

"You can try."

"Then I shall, Lord of the Dead, my Love." The succubus settled swiftly atop him, drawing his vitality deep inside her.

"Do your worst," Hades commanded.

"With pleasure, Lord Hades."

An ordeal that would have left a mere mortal man, especially a healthy one, an invalid and a haunted wreck left Hades in a calmer state of mind. He missed Persephone, but the succubus had taken away his terrible, painful desire, for the time being. Eventually, he would burn again for his Queen, something he knew the succubi were counting on even as this one slipped away sated and wisp-like into the Maelstrom of Tartarus.

Not even mighty Zeus could take on the full force of such an entity as a succubus and not need a very long siesta afterwards. Hades knew this only because an awed Hermes informed him of such when he stepped forth upon the dais and found him waiting, or rather, fidgeting there.

Hades paused as he adjusted his black robes. "Have you been there the whole time?"

"No," said Hermes, "but I wish I had. I had never even dwelled on the possibility of such an encounter."

Hades poured fresh water in a basin and washed his face and hands. "So I fucked a succubus, so what?"

"I didn't think it was possible to give a succubus a full on orgasm."

"Well, now you know: it is." Hades dried his face and hands.

"You don't realize at all, do you?"

Hades shrugged.

"You gave a succubus an orgasm! She was crying out for sweet mercy with you pumping away beneath her. Zeus couldn't manage that."

"I don't think Zeus would want to."

"A valid point, I guess. Still, it was an impressive spectacle."

"I would appreciate it if you kept it under your helmet. A succubus is a poor substitute for having my wife in my arms instead."

"Don't let that succubus hear you say that. She may be offended."

"Succubi are predators. She was attracted to the aroma of unfulfilled desire and we both got something out of it, which is rare, and which is why she and her sisters shall return from time to time. They cannot destroy me, but they can certainly enjoy me."

Hermes grimaced. "Now I wish I hadn't seen."

"Very well. Why are you here?"

"I figured you would want some company. Apollo is in the dumps and I figured we could go visit him."

"Ah."

Hermes gazed past Hades at his bedchamber. "Maybe he could use a little succubus care too."

"Excuse me?"

"Come on. I'll tell you on the way there."

They had not gone far, not far at all, before Hades observed the fresh shoots of green grass and leaves everywhere he looked. By the time he and Hermes alighted before Delphi, he saw an abundance of blossoms and the eager bees that tended to them. Before Delphi, Hades realized the previous absence of birdsong when he heard their melodic defiance thrilling anew among the trees and shrubs.

'Persephone,' Hades thought with a full heart, 'this is your doing.'

Hermes removed his golden helmet the instant he crossed the sacred threshold. "I hope he's here. He's been away since you both were afflicted by Eros." Peering this way and that as he rumpled his hair, the divine messenger moved deeper into Delphi's dominion.

Hades adjusted his shadowy robes and entered.

There were mortals here from every station in life, judging by the varying quality of their raiments. Lost in their own concerns, most stood oblivious, waiting their turn to visit the Oracle. A few though frowned and cast odd looks at the air beside them as first Hermes and then Hades passed them, unseen. Hermes had scarcely given them more than passing glances, but Hades surveyed his future charges in thoughtful silence.

He caught up with Hermes standing just beyond the Oracle's chamber. "Apollo has indeed returned," Hermes said.

A young girl marked out as special when she had been dedicated to Delphi, the Oracle was now a woman near her fortieth year. Her widened eyes gazed in Apollo's direction.

Enveloped in his belted tunic the color of saffron and his maroon colored cloak, Apollo gazed sternly back at her. He shone but softly, discreetly. To mortal sensitive eyes such as hers, his presence was indicated by a subtle, but distinct lightening of her darkened space and the faint aroma of exotic incense.

Just beyond the threshold waited three priests, ready to take down the Oracle's words.

"Something is different this time," whispered one of them so as not to disturb her.

The other whispered back, "Can you not feel him? In this very space? The Bright One is here."

The one waiting with his stylus and tablet nodded without removing his eyes from the Oracle.

"Is something amiss?" muttered Hades to Hermes.

The Oracle gasped and shot wild looks about her.

The three priests flinched and looked about, too, although they had heard nothing.

"Lord of the Underworld, why have you come?" the woman cried.

The priests exchanged alarmed looks, but kept their silence.

Apollo reached out of his maroon chlamys cloak and touched her chin ever so gently with his right hand. She panted and trembled.

'Sorry', Hades mouthed to Apollo.

Apollo nodded and still gently, turned her face in his direction.

Her frightened expression filled with wonder.

Hermes and Hades exchanged looks. Then Hermes caught Apollo's attention, pointed at his own eyes and then at the Oracle. Apollo shook his head. Hermes sighed.

Leaning in close, Apollo peered into her restless eyes. A flicker of interest crossed his serious face and he moved his hand up upon her left cheek and ever so softly caressed it.

Astonishment and delight mingled on her face.

Her priestly attendants held their breath. She was in communion with Lord Apollo. They hoped that it was a sign of good things to come. They hoped that the presence of Lord Hades was not the actual omen.

Apollo kissed her forehead, blessing her third eye.

The Oracle sighed and closed her eyes. Her whole body relaxed. She sank from her stone seat onto her knees before Apollo. She turned her palms toward the ceiling and waited in perfect submission. Under her breath, as soft as thought, she murmured prayers.

Hades glanced at the priests. If they didn't breathe soon, they were going to faint.

Hermes watched the priests, waiting to see if they would indeed faint.

Apollo stood straight and lordly before his Oracle. Looking both grave and kind, he stretched out his right hand again with his blessing fingers extended. He paused, his index and middle fingertips just shy of her third eye.

"Please, Lord Apollo," she gasped. "Please."

His lips curved into a smile and he touched her third eye.

The Oracle let go a sob and collapsed utterly before Golden Apollo. She lay there trembling and moaning.

To anyone outside of those sacred, secret precincts the sight of the Oracle writhing on the floor would have provoked alarm and concern. Not so to the priests, but even they looked on in a kind of intimidated awe.

Only when his Oracle lay peaceful before him did Apollo withdraw his arm beneath his chlamys and pass from the chamber.

As Hades turned to follow him and Hermes, he watched the priests raise the Oracle from the floor. While the strongest of the three supported her upon her seat, the other filled a cup with cool water and the last stood peering into her face. She opened her eyes and spoke and he wrote what she said.

Beyond Delphi's precincts the three Divine Incarnations strode purposefully, led by Golden Apollo, who, lost in thought, outpaced Hermes and Hades.

"What was all that about?" Hermes called.

Apollo paused, letting them catch up. "Just tending to my duties. It keeps me out of trouble."

"Eros has much to answer for," said Hades.

Apollo grunted and nodded. His luminous gaze kept traveling to the horizons north and east.

Hades eyed the laurel leaves crowning his gleaming hair. Eros had been crueler to him by far. Whereas Hades had had his existence upended and been coupled with a being who was a most reluctant consort, again and again Apollo suffered betrayals and abandonment, the bitterest taste of unhappy love and, just as bad in its own cancerous way, unrequited love. "Perhaps you should go away for a time," he said.

"I have been away."

"You look as though you could use a sabbatical," said Hades.

"Perhaps I should return to the east," said Apollo with genuine longing.

"What? And miss all the fun?" said Hermes.

"You obviously have a tale to tell," said Apollo. "I shall humor you."

"What do you know?" said Hades.

"In a word: Karma."

Apollo and Hades exchanged arch looks.

"Go on," said Apollo. "You're dying to speak."

"It seems that not even the fierce Eros is immune to Aphrodite's pervasive influence. While the two of you were suffering his torments, he encountered the fairest, most enchanting mortal maiden and became utterly besotted with her. Such was his desire for her that he arranged to take her for his consort in secret. No one knew that Eros had taken this maiden for his lover, not even the guileless mortal. Now, bear in mind, Aphrodite knew of this girl's unsurpassed beauty and wanted her humbled and in a sense done away with. Eros disobeyed her."

"That was asking for trouble," said Apollo as Hades nodded.

"You don't know the half of it," said Hermes. "He lavished everything upon her, except his identity. Eros came to their bed only under the cover of absolute night, so she never saw what he truly was. In her pure, good little heart, she knew only that she loved him. And, shocking as it may be to us – his past victims – Eros loves her, so much so that he would keep her apart from all of Olympus."

"She is that special, eh?" said Hades.

"Her beauty is the equal of Aphrodite's. It is a different kind of beauty, pure and luminous, whereas Aphrodite's is luxurious and sensual, but it equals hers."

"Really?" said Apollo.

"Truly. I have since met her so…you see."

"We'll take your word for it," said Hades. "Go on. What happened? Something had to happen, right?"

"The poor girl had a couple of sisters, who were fairly rotting with envy at her great fortune. They filled her innocent mind with poisonous doubt. To make a long story short, she betrayed Eros' trust; he took off in a snit; she tried to make it up to him and then Aphrodite got involved."

"Oh dear," said Apollo.

"We all know Aphrodite," said Hermes.

"Not quite as well as you do, Hermes," said Apollo.

"But well enough," said Hades.

"Supremely lovely as she is, she flies into some unholy snits herself if she isn't the fairest one of all. She also likes to keep Eros devoted to her and her needs. Suddenly, he's pining for someone else and not catering to her every whim. It didn't help that the girl came to Aphrodite herself to beg for help."

"I'll wager she did not take that very well," said Hades.

"That is putting it lightly," said Hermes. "Aphrodite tried to kill her."

"Oooooh," went Apollo chuckling as he shook his head.

"You may not have been present when it happened, Hades, but Aphrodite sent this hapless girl with a special urn to visit your Persephone. She lied to the girl about what was in it just to stoke up her curiosity, so your Queen is blameless in this plot: she knew nothing preceding this visit."

"I was not there and neither Persephone nor Hel thought it important enough to tell me," said Hades.

Apollo nodded. "They probably took one look at the lovely young thing and assumed she served Aphrodite."

"Anyway, after being explicitly and INTENTIONALLY told not to open the urn, what does she do?"

Apollo and Hades exchanged wry looks. "She opens it."

"And promptly falls into a 'death sleep', right then and there. So here comes Eros in a panic because she is his precious one and he has caught onto Aphrodite's mean little plot. He manages to resuscitate her – great relief. Knowing full well that he cannot take her home for fear of what Aphrodite will do. After all, she is still a fragile mortal - so he runs to Zeus… and well, Hera was there too. Anything that inconveniences that troublemaker Aphrodite is fine with Hera. And anything that enables Zeus to reaffirm his authority over anyone and everyone works for him too."

"Typical," said Apollo while Hades smirked.

"Thanks to Hera, Eros married his beloved Psyche, for that is her name, and Zeus rendered her immortal so they could live 'happily ever after'."

"And are they?" said Hades.

"So long as they keep a prudent, civil distance from Aphrodite for the time being. She was sulking so much that it took Artemis and Athena both to persuade her to take a tour of her temples and get away from Olympus for a little while."

"Where is she now?" said Hades. "I would just as soon not encounter her any time soon."

"Cyprus, last I heard, swanning about in the absolute adoration of her followers and supplicants."

"Did Eros suffer mightily?" said Apollo.

"I wish you had seen him. He was a wreck by the time all was said and done. When the whole thing started, we hardly saw him at all and when we did it wasn't for long. Even then he was jumpy and evasive. However, he was astute enough to make sure that Aphrodite saw enough of him to curtail any suspicions. It worked for a little while. It might have worked for much longer, but Psyche got Eros riled at her. Apollo, you would have truly appreciated the sight of him moping over Psyche."

Apollo took on a lean smile, the sort that suggested his wounds were far from beginning to heal. "Indeed, I would have been content to witness his distress. 'Not sure that speaks well of me though."

"It doesn't," said Hades, "but it's understandable. Perhaps Eros will leave us in peace for a time now.

"One can only hope. Still," Apollo turned brisk and resolute again, "he got what he deserved. Good."

For a long moment, the three incarnations stood gazing out across land unto the golden horizon.

"It is good to see all that green growing everywhere in sight again," Apollo sighed. He glanced at Hades. "I am sorry you suffered too, old friend. How are you bearing up?"

"I can cope," began Hades.

Hermes cleared his throat.

Hades pointed his finger. "Don't...you...dare."

Hermes grinned a very wide grin, not a reassuring response.

"Behave or I shall send you a 'night visitor' too," said Hades.

Hermes blinked "You win. You win."

Apollo looked from Hermes to Hades. "You must tell me how you managed that, Hades."

"He...does...not...dare...either," said Hermes.

"True." Hades shrugged. Then he slapped Hermes on the shoulder. "Some things must stay between friends, eh?"

Hermes nodded. "This time, that's for sure."

Apollo eyed the scar on his own chest and looked again at Hades.

"Someday, Enlightened One," said Hades.

"Daphne scolds me whenever I trim her hair of some of its leaves." Apollo removed the laurel wreath from his head and studied it. "She does not care that I honor her thus."

"Persephone pretends that I am not there. She will meet my gaze only when necessary and says the absolute minimum to me when I address her. When we are close she looks through me or averts her face to the shadows."

Having absolutely nothing to contribute, the trickster Hermes stood silent and looked genuinely sympathetic.

Apollo handed the laurel wreath to Hermes. "I think I shall indeed take a sabbatical."

"Where will you go?" Hermes looked somewhat disconcerted.

"Back to the east or north, or both directions. I feel a need to reconnect with the Source of All Things in a peaceful place. Perhaps I shall return to India and spend some time along the Ganges." Apollo faced east and smiled placidly.

Hermes gestured toward the sun. "So does that mean…?"

"Helios is where *he* has always been and always will be until it is time to cease *being*. Surya still drives his twelve-wheeled chariot, so I am not needed here."

"Go and restore yourself," said Hades. "Give my regards to Shiva and the rest of our fellow incarnations."

"I will do that."

"Give my regards to Wotan and Freyja when you do go north," said Hermes.

Apollo paused. "Do you have any greeting for Loki?"

"Loki knows where to find me when he is ready to talk." Slapping his winged helmet atop his tousled dark hair, Hermes folded his arms across his chest.

Apollo chuckled. "Very well, I'll be around."

A zephyr breathed upon him and the Golden One was gone.

Hades and Hermes stood gazing eastward toward the twilight gathering on the horizon.

"The world always seems a little greyer when he isn't around," said Hermes.

Hades nodded, grunting softly.

"It feels like a tranquil night ahead," said Hermes.

"It does indeed. Get some rest tonight, while Gaia herself rests."

"Where are you going?"

"Home. Where else would I be?" Hades took three steps and dissolved into shadow.

8.

There were times, nights and sometimes whole days, in the course of the Earth's annual voyage around fiery Helios when the barriers between the realms waned thinner than papyrus, and the concerned, the caring, and the restless went abroad among the Living…and were seen. One such set of nights came to be known as Samhain, and later All Hallow's Eve, and also el Dia de los Muertos. Another such blessed, or cursed, depending on one's perspective, happened in the opposite time of year. In some places, the mortals called it Beltane and in another Walpurgis Nacht. These were sacred days for Hades.

Because his realm's unsettled charges overran its boundaries just as a river sometimes overflowed its banks, Hades himself also journeyed out among the Living in his official capacity as Lord of the Underworld. Those who saw him striding past blessed themselves out of fear that he whom they dared not name would linger just long enough to claim a fresh soul.

Certainly, Hades made a stark and unforgettable appearance during those sojourns. He swathed himself in flowing black garments, a long belted tunic and hooded cloak pulled over his dark, dark hair, boots and a staff. His dark Olympian eyes turned silvery white and those mortals who glimpsed his face with his otherworldly eyes took the memory into their nightmares. They could not know that he went abroad among the Living to shepherd the Dead. There were unclean spirits seething with malignance that sometimes slipped free of Tartarus and Hell to do mischief where they could not do literal harm. Fear was their most potent weapon.

In his place, Osiris took a commanding stance upon the dais with Nepthys on one side and Anubis on the other. Hel had the management of the bitterest, darkest depths of Tartarus and Hell. Garmr and Cerberus snarled whenever some truly malignant spirit attempted to skulk out, so the Underworld was, as ever, in more than capable stewardship. If Hades ever decided to spread his essence upon the winds and become one with the Source, the Underworld would remain in fine hands.

In this truly welcome season of rebirth in spring, Hades patrolled the earth keeping an eye on the restless souls who crowded close to witness the Living honor Beltane or Walpurgis Nacht or whatever else they called that celestial time. Thoughts of Persephone accompanied him everywhere he went. He might as well have been traveling in a fog for all he cared to observe during his wanderings.

Therefore, it was a jolt of a surprise to encounter Dionysus almost directly in his path, cup in hand, snake coiled around his neck, vines gracing his long golden brown hair, and bull's horns. There was a thoughtful look on his face. He saluted Hades with his cup and remained where he was, leaning against a tree.

"I almost walked into you," said Hades.

"Do not fret over that," replied Dionysus in a low, calm voice. "I would have prevented a collision."

It was then that Hades realized he heard music in the near distance. Dionysus looked off over his left shoulder and Hades followed his glance.

A discreet distance away, lit by both the moon and their one great bonfire, male and female bodies writhed together making evocative and unmistakable sounds.

"Ah," said Hades.

"Indeed," said Dionysus.

"Why are you not in the thick of it?"

"Who says I'm not? In spirit at least," Dionysus arched his brow, "my influence is most compelling."

Hades frowned. There were 'hungry ghosts' lingering outside the sacred circle. "You do realize...?"

"Yes, I see them."

"If they cause any trouble..."

"I will summon you or Hecate immediately."

"There are some forms of possession that are particularly unpleasant." Hades moved on past Dionysus, keeping himself on the shadow side of the clearing.

Dionysus watched one particular participant and the maiden, a beauty of sixteen summers, whom he was preparing to sacrifice in their particular manner. "I know where you can find Persephone."

Hades paused. "Where is she?"

"In a sacred glen in the land of the Celts resting at the foot of a mighty oak. She has been lulled into a lovely sleep by the music of the Faerie folk. You should go see to her."

In the distance the girl cried out. The other participants briefly voiced their hearty approval as the man continued his sacred labors. Dionysus smiled and moved closer.

"She will not want to see me," said Hades.

"Later, when you get the opportunity, seek out Kama. He has some useful sutras that you might find enlightening," said Dionysus. "Now go to her."

As Hades slipped away, Dionysus took possession of the man so that he might partake of the young beauty's sacrifice. Her sounds of pain and distress gave way to deep resounding sounds of merciless pleasure.

"The Bull-Horned One is with us!" cried one of the participants.

A great rejoicing ensued, but Hades had moved leagues away already. He moved swiftly now, north by northwest, into the lands of the Celts in search of the great and now sacred oak tree where Persephone rested. If the Faeries had lullabied her, then there would be a Faerie circle quite close by. He searched both for the Faeries and their circles and for mighty oaks that stood out in their forests.

Beside a stream, he encountered the incomparable Freyja, beautiful, desire-creating Freyja, luscious golden Freyja. "My Lord of the Underworld," she said in a tone that curled and caressed the night air.

"Lady of sensual delights, Mistress of belligerent death upon fields martial, good Walpurgis Nacht to you."

"Indeed, it is, for the leaves stir more from the passage of your charges than from the breath of the wind."

"The rivers of the Underworlds overflow as do all rivers in their seasons."

"All waters rise," agreed Freyja.

One of her cats curled about her ankles, purring just as seductively as its Mistress.

"I so seldom see you in my domain in these northern realms," she said.

"My apologies for trespassing in your domain."

"It is of little matter, Hades. We all meet in the Underworld when the season is ripe. How fares Baldr?"

"Not so restful as you would have expected."

"Oh?"

"He has had cause to dispatch avatars to reincarnate in the upper realms."

"The Source is wise in all things." Freyja blessed herself and the moment. "We go where we must and in the forms most suitable."

Hades bowed his head briefly. "Indeed."

"Why are you traipsing around our night-haunted forests?"

"Dionysus…"

Freyja's face turned incandescent with a smile. "Oh? And where is the great Bull-Horned One?"

"Presiding over a fertility rite when I left him."

"Ha! I'll bet he was!"

"Anyway, I encountered him – both of us in the course of our official duties as it were – and he told me where I could find my new Consort."

"I heard about her. My compatriot Eros has been restive these past few months."

"Dionysus said that she slept in a sacred glen at the foot of a mighty oak. He said that she had been lulled by the music of the Faerie folk in the land of the Celts."

"Oh! She is west of here, many leagues away, upon the smaller of two Celtic island realms. Go west, Hades, if you would rouse your wife."

Hades inclined his head. "I thank you."

Freyja inclined her shining head back. "Most welcome and do come and visit more often."

"I shall consider it most sincerely."

They inclined their heads to one another again.

Then Hades turned and with purposeful strides disappeared into the night once more.

Crossing two seas in a thought's life span, Hades set foot on the smaller of two Celtic islands and met at once his fellow avatar Gwynn ap Nudd the Lord of Annwyn. The Lord of Annwyn summoned the owls and sent them forth across the length and breadth of the island realm looking for Faerie circles in the vicinity of mighty oaks.

It was a busy night. It took a little while for one little white owl to return to Hades and the Lord of Annwyn. Holding the owl safe against his chest, Hades followed its breathless directions back to an oak tree. Resting softly beneath its whispering branches, Persephone lay lost in slumber.

The shadows clung so to her that it took a moment for Hades to perceive her pale face and hands emerging from her dark gown and long purple veil that shrouded her form entirely. Nearby lilting, lulling Faerie music coiled from the forest. The Faerie folk were quite near.

"Thank you," said Hades as he released the owl to the night.

For a moment, a long thoughtful moment, Hades gazed upon the voluptuous goddess – his wife. His desire faltered though. There was something not quite right. When Dionysus had urged him to seek out his consort, Hades had thought it for a particular reason. As he stood frowning at Persephone's sleeping form, he realized that there had been an imperative to Dionysus' parting command 'Go see to her'.

"What mischief is this?" Hades mumbled.

Little figures rushed in the undergrowth tittering and whispering in malicious little voices.

"Pixies. Sprites," growled Hades. "You bewitched my Consort."

"Just a wee bit o' enchantment," chortled one tiny voice from the safety of the foliage as its chums giggled. "She looked like she could use some rest."

"Release her."

Howls of tiny laughter erupted from the surrounding forest. Several leaves and blossoms tumbled.

"We answer to no one. We do as it pleases ourselves," retorted another little voice from close beside Persephone's head. "And we wish it to be Spring ALWAYS"

The music grew a little louder.

Hades stared in wonder. He could actually see the music rolling tentacle-like toward him. They meant to stop 'Death' if possible.

"Infernal sorcery," he said. "Withdraw your spiteful magic or suffer the torments of Tartarus."

"You'll have to catch us first!"

Hades threw back his hood. His eyes shone a blazing white. There were ways of dealing with Nature's Imps. "Release your hold over her or suffer the consequences."

"You don't frighten us."

"Oh, really? I'll wager a touch of frostbite will sort you out. How does an unseasonably hard frost sound to you?"

Helpfully emphasizing his point, the North Wind ruffled his dark hair.

"You wouldn't dare."

"Try me."

"Spoilsport. Fine. Take her and go."

"Just like that?"

"As simple as that."

"How do I know she won't stay asleep forever?"

"Take her well away from the music and she shall awaken. I swear upon my pointy ears."

Hades knelt beside her, still glaring at the many little yellow and green eyes watching him. "If she remains unwell, January will come early."

"Take her and leave us!"

Hades lifted veil-shrouded Persephone up and rose to his full height. "Count yourself fortunate that you were not dealing with her Mater. She would have pinched your ears clean off."

Turning carefully away, Hades took three simple steps and vanished from the mortal realm.

Still attired in her rippling garments of black, purple and green, still shrouded beneath a veil the soft, yet rich color of clouds in fading twilight, Persephone lay atop her bridal bed with her lovely hands arranged over her breast.

While Hades stood keeping vigil, Anubis took a few other associates out to insure that there were no malingerers among the Living when dawn crept over the world. Anubis could be a fearsome shepherd, if need be. The spirits hastened back well ahead of him and his glowing pupil-less eyes.

Hades heard the trickle turn to a rush the closer Anubis came. The noises returned to a murmur almost immediately after Anubis closed the gates to the Underworld. It would be reasonably orderly again until Beltane or El Dia de los Muertos, or later Obon, dawned.

"I have some souls to weigh," Anubis said politely from the threshold of Hades' private chambers. "I will see you later."

"Thank you, old Comrade. And thank our associates for me."

"It comes with the territory." Anubis eyed Persephone's peaceful form on the bed and withdrew.

Patient, unmoving, Hades kept vigil.

Osiris assumed his place upon the dais, filling the great hall with his somber grace and striking awe into the souls who drifted past the dais.

Hel, Wotan's somber associate in the Underworld, brought them refreshments and took a moment to check their patient.

"Well?" said Hades as she trod softly away from the bedside.

"Fast asleep. Perhaps we should send for Dhanvantari or Asclepius?"

"They lied to me," growled Hades.

"Possibly, or perhaps it simply takes a little while for the enchantment to wear off. Pixies and Sprites practice a potent sort of mischief." Hel patted his arm in passing. "Give her a little longer."

Hades sighed and nodded.

"We will continue to manage the place for the time being."

"Thank you, Hel."

"Anytime, Hades."

Time passed, eternal time, and the murmurs beyond that chamber ebbed and flowed. Light shimmered frequently as souls passed directly or finally into it, just as sunbeams broke through passing clouds. Bright Intercessors moved serenely amongst those who lingered on that plane, glowing as softly as paper lanterns in a mild night.

At last Persephone sighed and stirred, stretching with languid ease. She opened her eyes to see Hades sitting beside her with her brimming cup cradled in his hand.

She hesitated. Although it surprised her to see him and to realize just as swiftly that she was back in the Underworld, it was not an altogether unpleasant surprise. She had been cold. Now she felt quite warm and comfortable there in her marriage bed.

Half-smiling, still concerned, Hades proffered her the cup. "Hel made you some refreshments."

"That was good of her," Persephone mumbled. Groaning mildly, she moved to sit up, but her veil pulled against her.

Immediately Hades removed it with one long graceful sweep of his hand and let it float out across their bed. With his other hand, he pressed the cup into her pink-tinged fingers. "There."

Persephone frowned into her cup's sparkling contents. "How did I come to be here again?" She took a tentative taste and nodded once as the warmed spices coated her tongue. Cinnamon's aroma rose from the cup.

"I brought you here."

"In your chariot?"

"I carried you Home in my arms."

The frown that had begun to relax intensified, although she preferred to stare into the depths of her cup.

"Do you remember where you were?" he said.

Her frown took on a different complexion as she lifted her face to gaze past the great fire pit toward the back of the dais with its intricate latticed stone work partition. "Once I had done with Dionysus and my Mother…"

A sudden darkness glanced across Hades. His lips tightened. His gaze sharpened.

"...I simply wandered where I wanted. I was free you see."

"What was the last thing you remember?"

"Standing in as northern forest...it was so lovely and tranquil, so lush and then suddenly I felt overwhelmed by a craving for rest. I thought I would take a nap and found a lovely little place beside this enormous grandfather tree where I could nestle down. Now that I think back, I remember hearing music just as I dropped off to sleep. Is that where you found me? Under a large tree?"

"Yes. Dionysus told me where to look." Hades watched her expression closely and saw her brows arch ever so slightly. "He was quite specific and also quite firm in telling me to come to you.'

"Why should he meddle so in my affairs?"

"Because somehow he knew that you were being meddled with by others."

"What?"

"When I found you, it was quite clear that you had fallen prey to some malicious mischief. Sprites, they wanted to keep you under an enchantment so that Spring would linger forever in their glen."

Persephone's jaw dropped and she looked Hades full in the face.

Hades nodded and arched his brows. "Their music is their magic. It reaches out and snares you. I know because they tried to stay me too."

"And thereby keep Death from ever coming to their spring-enchanted home. I see. That's a precious amount of nerve!"

"Nature's imps have plenty of nerve. I am rather surprised Demeter never warned you about such entities."

"Perhaps because they are not native to my birthplace in the natural world. If I had come into their mortal realm in the north, then she would have said something. Those impish creatures were fortunate my Mother did not hear of their endeavor."

"I told them as much when I retrieved you."

"They put up no fight to keep me?"

"They made threats, even as they sent their insidious enchantment after me, but I threatened to inflict an early winter on them in the heart of their sweet spring. They couldn't get me out of there fast enough."

Persephone smiled into her cup.

Hades' heart filled to overflowing to see it. He basked in her silent delight. "Drink up. I think Hel brewed that especially for you."

"Then I had best consume it," she said softly.

"When you are ready, we should return to the dais. It would do everyone good to bask in your radiance again."

Persephone stole a thoughtful look at him as she sipped.

9.

In the realms of the Living, time passed swiftly. Civilizations rose, flourished, and expired.

In the Eternal realms, outside of time and normal space, time-such-as-it-was passed differently.

At equal times, twice every earthly rotation, Persephone left Hades' side to preside over the return of her season, blessing one hemisphere or the other with her energy. She returned with Hades every Walpurgis Nacht or from the opposing hemisphere when the north honored Samhain or el Dia de Los Muertos. They would usher the spirits back into the nether realms and Anubis would follow and close the gates.

More often than not Hades withdrew at once with Persephone beyond the partition, past the fire pit's eternal flames, to their private chambers while Osiris ruled from the dais, stoic and utterly inscrutable. Meanwhile Anubis and Hel had Garmr and Cerberus weed out the unclean spirits again from the throng and drive them lower. As fierce as those two were, far worse it would be if Hades had to involve himself with his deadly, soul-shattering two pronged fork and his shepherding staff.

Even worse it would be if Osiris opened his mouth to admonish for he spoke with the voice of the Source, which could shatter and scatter a soul's essence. For the most part, Osiris maintained a benevolent and meditative silence, speaking only softly, without moving his lips. Low and rumbling like the heartbeat of Gaia, his voice carried into the furthest, most desperate alcoves of the almost endless Underworld. Everything fell silent for a time, a long time, afterwards.

The realm of Hades and Hel and Osiris was far more restless than one would have thought or liked to think…

Most souls who passed through that domain were at peace and possessed such serenity that they shone with gentle warmth in the echoing gloom of the Underworld. Hades only glimpsed them again when they passed through with the shimmering speed of a prayer back above to visit loved ones on the wings of grace and compassion. They lingered among the Living only long enough to give what aid and consolation that the Living could comprehend and bear, then Hades would glimpse them again just before they disappeared into that seemingly endless passage. Sentient brilliance flooded its threshold for an instant, but then its cool, calm stillness returned. Velvety blue shadows flowed, as dense as fog, within the passage again.

There were times when even Hades felt the burdens of his office wear down upon him. It seemed that there was only one cure for that. Hades liked to extend his hands into the wake of those passing spirits and feel those shadows caress them. It never failed. He walked away refreshed and ready again to cope with the steady stream coming across his upper threshold.

Most were indeed fine. As though drawn by the very force of gravity, they passed as surely as the sun 'crossed' from horizon to horizon, from lives they had known to the Life they had ever belonged to.

The rest were another matter. The Restless, the Confused, the Traumatized, the Wrathful and the truly Poisonous souls were problematic. They required considerable help…or surveillance. These souls tended to linger, either trapped in their myopic mortal belief systems unseen among the Living or wandering aimless, distracted and a little uneasy in the Underworld.

Hades had the same advice for all of them:

"If you see a Light, go into it."

Not enough of them did…at least not right away.

If only the Dead could see themselves as their caretakers perceived them then it would be so much easier for them to remember what they truly were and where they truly belonged and pass on to the Source of All Things. In the cool near-darkness of his grey realm, they flickered like so many little candles in a vast cathedral. Softly, he trod among them, wading through a pool of souls. They murmured as gently as a stream's passage through a deep forest.

As the saying goes, *Not all who wander are lost*, so it was that in Hades' realm not all who occupied those shade populated grottos and bedrock chambers were there for any other reason than their own conscious choice. Those ones were not the same as those who lingered in the belief that they belonged in that somewhat purgatorial place. A resigned bunch, this latter group occupied themselves uttering constant prayers and mantras and mea culpas as they perambulated in wide circuits before the dais. The former assembly, to whom Hades made a point of greeting with a respectful inclination of his head whenever they crossed paths, shone brighter than the rest of the souls. Like the 'Purgatorials', these *Intercessor* spirits traversed the Underworld from end to end, up and also far into the depths uttering prayers and mantras wherever they went.

Unlike the 'Purgatorial souls', the special Intercessor souls aimed their invocations outwards beyond the confinements of the Underworld to encompass that strife-ruled realm where Time and its Seasons reigned. They were many and emerged fully determined from many places and ages of the Living.

One epoch, words – a sentence – appeared above the thrones on the dais:

The Greatest shall be the Last to enter.

Hades sensed the 'Greatest' moving between the realms, even patrolling, his realm among one of those bright Intercessors. Yamaraja, Osiris, Hel, they all felt the Intercessor's presence and yet none of them saw the 'Bright One'. Somehow that seemed redundant. The feeling was enough.

Just as the North Star shone in the night sky, Persephone shone in the whispering gloom. Her presence filled that space as powerfully as incense, spreading hope along with the recollection of days spent in sweet spring sunshine, the scent of blossoms, rain, and moist sun-blessed earth. When Patroclus, Achilles, Ajax, Hector, Agamemnon, Cassandra, Clytemnestra, Odysseus, and many others wreathed in equal or greater luster crossed their threshold, Persephone greeted them, all of them, in this, her destined role. One and all, they trembled to see her seated upon her throne beside dark, stoic Hades.

By the time Anubis and Yamaraja had weighed these restless souls, they had had ample time to wonder at the sight of Osiris, his impassive visage gazing out across Eternity, and at Baldr as he passed across the chamber as bright as Dawn itself, sending ripples through the sea of souls. In the end, Hel was good enough to escort them to Valhalla, after some appropriate detours into other regions for their purification.

Grim Agamemnon, though, left for his sojourn in the recesses of Tartarus with Persephone's voice echoing after him.

"You murdered you daughter! How could you? She went with you trusting you, believing you, and you bound her innocent voice and cut her throat like an animal." The Queen of Hades strode to the edge of the dais, her fists clenched at her sides, still shouting at the cringing mortal soul. "She crossed directly into the Light. There is mercy. Remember that while you are down there confronting what you have done. Iphigenia is at peace. Don't you wish you were, King Agamemnon?"

Heaving a great sigh, Persephone turned back toward Hades.

He looked a little amazed. "Remind me never to run afoul of your temper."

Blushing, she sat upon her customary seat and arranged her raiments. "It had to be said. Artemis was furious about it too."

Hades nodded as his lips curved upward ever so slightly. "I got the impression that he would sooner become reacquainted with Clytemnestra's ax than your tongue, my Love."

Persephone shook her head. "She'll be here soon enough. I shall arrange a reunion."

"Oh dear. That should be interesting."

In the curtained recesses beyond the restless flames, Hades and Persephone grappled. At last he gripped her head, sinking his fingers deep into her thick hair, and held her still.

"Why won't you let me kiss you?" he breathed. She said nothing, but stared over his left arm toward the far wall. "Just one kiss." His lips brushed her temple. "No?"

She sighed and would not return his regard.

He sighed and kissed her temple. "You smell like honeysuckle." He kissed her cheek. "If you will not kiss me with your sweet mouth, I will kiss you everywhere else. I have been to Kama." She caught her breath and looked at him. "He has given me his divine sutras and I mean to put them to use." He moved downward, his strong hands moving across her, followed by his lips. As his hands pressed her thighs apart, he said, "Brace yourself."

Swiftly spinning mortal time decreed Persephone make her biannual return to inaugurate another spring in the hemisphere most familiar to her from her days of maidenhood. Breathless, she swept forth to greet the Harvest Mother Demeter, who embraced her.

"My poor dear," Demeter clucked as she fussed over Persephone's purple and black raiments and the veil floating gracefully, as full-bellied as a sail in a stiff current, behind Persephone's elegantly arranged coiffure, "to have to spend so much time below in that ghastly place. How you bear it I will never know. And Hades...how do you bear him?"

"I bear him because I must," replied Persephone hastily. "Enough of him. I am here and we have our duties, do we not?"

"Yes, at Eleusis." Demeter led the way.

"Will Dionysus be there?"

"He has his own rites to attend to, so I could not say." Demeter cast a look back.

Persephone averted her blushing look toward the horizon before Demeter could see it. "I have scarcely seen him since the 'restoration'. I was wondering how he was."

"Since he found Ariadne, hardly anyone sees him around Olympus. Hera thinks that Dionysus stays away on purpose, just like Hades."

"They have that in common then," said Persephone.

Demeter looked her in the eyes. "Among a choice few other things, yes."

Persephone's face turned bright red.

Demeter squeezed her arm. "What was done was necessary – in both cases. I realize that now. Our purposes transcend us."

Although Persephone was not required after that first time to meet with Dionysus in the meadow, she and Demeter were required at Eleusis where the mortals commemorated their ordeal and honored them in sacred ceremonies. Unseen and yet felt most potently, Demeter and Persephone directed the worshippers and received their homage as they blessed them with insight into their strife-filled existence. This was the purpose that Persephone's fated union had endowed her. This was the power Gaia had invoked of her and Dionysus provoked in his turn.

Once the Eleusinian Mysteries had been celebrated, Persephone's time belonged to her and her alone for a spell. Sometimes she was content to accompany Demeter to witness the return of spring throughout the hemisphere.

This particular time Persephone lingered back as Demeter moved off toward the night shrouded fields.

Demeter paused and cast an inquisitive look backwards. There was simple, subtle lift of her brows.

Persephone stood facing the east where dawn's first blush glowed along the horizon. She turned her face, her utterly expressionless face, and stared a moment into Demeter's eyes.

"Very well," Demeter said and with a parting look of encouragement threw her shawl about her shoulders, and walked out among the furrows.

Although she was tempted to glance back at her Kore, she did not bother. She knew that Persephone had sped away to the east. She had asked after Dionysus. She had gone to find him.

"She will find what she must find," Demeter said aloud and sighed. It had not occurred to her that Persephone might have any lingering attraction or further interest in the elusive, unknowable Twice-Born One. For the first time, she considered that Gaia had created a bond between them.

How would Hades react to that? He would find out someday, for there were no secrets from Death.

A sweet, soft spring morning had arrived by the time Persephone came upon the remnants of a Dionysian ritual, along with its celebrants, naked for the most part and in a stupor or slumber. It was hard to tell which.

These were mortals.

Persephone passed among their tangled forms with all of the impact of a forgotten memory intruding upon their dreams. Some of the revelers stirred and mumbled and turned their faces away from the bright light.

A short distance away, several nymphs tenderly cared after an unconscious couple. They removed the vines and the bull horns from the young man's head as they washed his body. One nymph washed the blood from his thighs and his penis. He moaned in his deep slumber, recuperating from the after-effects of a fierce possession. The same blood another nymph washed from the thighs of the young woman just as she had washed the blood's intimate source. Another maiden combed her long black hair whilst two more washed her bruised body. She sighed beneath their care.

When the nymphs saw the figure in the flowing black and purple, her radiant golden red hair gleaming even beneath her veil, they recognized her. At once, they paused to bow their heads.

"Is the Twice-Born One nigh?" Persephone said lowly.

Her presence intimidated them into silence. They nodded and one of them pointed toward a distant grove near the hills. Their wide eyes followed her as she walked away. Then they whispered to one another...

"The Bull-Horned One is not alone."

"Should we have asked her to wait?"

"We should have sent someone ahead."

"It is too late now."

"She will understand. It is their way after all."

A battered kind of idyllic peace permeated the forest grove at the base of the hills. Persephone hesitated on the edge of the wide furrowed plain. After a Dionysian ritual, the Bull-Horned One would be resting, perhaps lounging under the wide boughs of a tree or soaking in the sacred pool, as she knew from the 'restoration'. He might want some peace to meditate. He might be resting his head in Ariadne's understanding lap with her soothing hands upon his face.

She had never met Ariadne, mortal princess rendered transcendent immortal by the will of the Twice-Born One. If she was there, Persephone thought it would be good to meet her. She felt that they might share a certain empathy based on their somewhat similar ordeals and transitions, although Ariadne would have much more in common with Psyche.

Persephone was still musing over what it must have been like to go from humble mortal to divinity as she trod calmly through the undergrowth past tall trees. Blossoms snowed softly everywhere she moved dotting her veil, nestling in her braided and coiled hair. Everywhere, life burgeoned about her.

Ahead she heard the steady tumble of water and a little ways away the trickle of a stream idling a path through the woods. His energy surrounded her and she felt herself in tune with it as she caressed a smooth tree trunk in passing or ran her fingers through a patch of wildflowers, thrilling at the softness of their petals. Their source was the same as all that surrounded them. Their purposes ran parallel, arising from the same indomitable root.

Her pace quickened.

Her glances darted ahead where the rising morning sun dazzled the bright new green leaves. She was close now to the clearing where the sacred pond and Dionysus lay.

The stillness ahead struck her like a pocket of fog in a vale. She moved more slowly, treading more carefully in her trespass.

Dionysus might be resting and she did not wish to startle him or disturb him at all, if he was asleep. Serving the ways of Nature could take quite a toll on one.

Even more deliberately and carefully she approached. A space in the foliage opened before her as though a curtain had been raised. Before Persephone stretched a cooling pond possessed of the most enticing tones of blue and green. Scarcely rippling at its heart, it reflected the sky and the brightening trees. She smiled to hear the busy birds sing and to glimpse them as they fluttered about.

A dove flew out of the trees near the waterfall and crossed the length of the pool. It shone a dazzling white in the sun's beams.

Persephone's eyes followed its progress to the boughs of the tree it landed in. Then her gaze dropped to the grassy space beneath it on the opposite side of the water, a figure, a movement caught her notice. Letting go a gasp, she took a step back. The deep shadows sheltered from ready sight, from Helios and Sunya's bright ascension across the sky, Dionysus and Aphrodite, where she knelt for the sake of indulgence.

There Persephone lingered, but only until her eyes assured her of the certainty of the act she was witnessing: Aphrodite's particular homage to the Bull-Horned One. Then she withdrew burning with her blushes, aware of the forest whispering about her, and thinking that at least she had not been witnessed herself…

…Although she had been seen.

Through half-closed eyelids, Dionysus peeked at her whose presence he felt resonating with each step upon sacred Gaia's skin.

Even with her smiling eyes closed, Aphrodite sensed her would-be rival's surprise and discreet, but hasty withdrawal.

After Aphrodite Phillomedes had finished with Dionysus to their mutual satisfaction, she took on one of her other mantles, becoming Aphrodite Peitho and idly stroked Dionysus' damp hair as she spoke, "So you say she had a vision of Hades when you coupled with her."

"She saw Hades in my place and I saw Ariadne."

"And where is darling, brave Ariadne?" Aphrodite asked without caring much what the answer would be.

Dionysus glanced at the sky's deep blue. "Safe in the other realm, shining gentle."

"Do you think Hades saw her at that moment?"

"Yes. In that moment, we were one, soul brothers as it were. Now as to whether he realized it at the time that I cannot say."

"In all these epochs since, the Queen of Hades has never embraced her King between her thighs or clasped him to her breast the way she did you at the 'restoration'."

"You know well enough why that is, Aphrodite Androphonos."

"I know also that she turns her face away from his and will not suffer him to kiss her lips, although she suffers these same lips to bite and suck on her soft flesh as he ravishes her. I know also that Hades permits the adoring succubi to make sport of his desire and satiate themselves upon his loneliness when she is absent."

"And when they are done consorting with him he lies alone embracing her pillow." Dionysus frowned. "I know how his heart aches for a kiss from Persephone – just one kiss for him alone."

"And here she came instead seeking for your intoxicating kisses."

Dionysus closed his eyes and let his tousled head rest in Aphrodite's lap.

"Ah." Aphrodite smiled in the direction Persephone had gone. "You would have covered her with kisses if I had not been here already. You might still mingle your native strength with hers before the next dawn."

Dionysus opened his eyes. "I might."

Their gazes locked for a long silent moment.

"I will arrange for you to find her tonight," said Aphrodite.

"I need no help from you there. We are connected in our own way."

"I have a notion" she smiled brightly, "a notion for a potion. We shall combine our influences. Seek her out and give her the refreshment we concoct. Seduce her gently into a conducive sleep and I shall ease Hades' path to her bower. She will be dreaming of you and be coupling with her Consort. The desire we produce in them shall work its own magic. Hades will awaken her truly and receive the kiss he longs for."

"Why are you doing this for him now?"

"Because I am the embodiment of Love and Desire. It is my role."

"It will mean only further bitterness if this precious kiss is not sincere, but you know this. What are you really up to? Persephone has not offended you and, no matter our association, is no rival to you."

"Why this tone of accusation?"

"Because Athena is correct: you are the minx supreme when it suits you, particularly when your jealousy has been aroused. Mark my words: you meddle with the Queen of Life and Death - my Consort in Resurrection, at your own peril. Do not upset the balance."

Aphrodite's expression turned grave, although still as thoughtful as before. "I promise upon the Source of All Things that I shall not upset the balance."

Dionysus smiled up at her. "Good."

"You will help me?"

"I shall consider it."

Smiling, Aphrodite leaned over and kissed the Bull-Horned One, perfectly mindful of the consequences such a gesture would encourage. But then she was clever and knew what she was doing.

Persephone wandered until her heart stopped pounding quite so hard, and then she kept wandering until her mind could resolve itself into something akin to a state of calm. By then she was content to keep to herself, her need to commune with the Twice-Born One having submerged again. It had not gone away, but it no longer troubled her.

Instead, she took pleasure in all that she was part of. As the sun began to set, she took herself to some high white cliffs and there stood to watch the sun set beyond the ocean's horizon. She would have liked to lose herself in the beauty of her mortal surroundings, but the distinct sense that she was being watched intruded and just would not go away.

Sighing a frown into being, Persephone looked back over her shoulder, or, rather, she glared.

Cernunnos paused in mid-step to incline his antlered head. "Greetings, Queen of Hades."

Somewhat surprised, Persephone inclined her head in return. "Good evening to you, My Lord Cernunnos. What brings you forth from your cherished forest?"

"You, my good Lady. We saw you pass and as we were planning a great feast this night, it seemed rude not to invite you to it."

"Ah. Is this just a feast? Or is it something else as well?"

"A simple gathering where a meal shall be shared. We shall have a bard to sing to us as well."

"That sounds perfectly lovely. I shall gladly attend."

"Very well! When you have enjoyed your sunset, I shall give you a proper escort." Cernunnos smiled as they exchanged formal nods and walked back toward the forest, whistling.

Smiling as well, Persephone resumed watching the setting sun paint the clouds in colors that rivaled Aphrodite's sumptuous raiments.

10.

Cernunnos returned with an escort of tiny Faeries to light the way for Persephone. He wore a wreath on his head. As they strolled into the forest, the Faeries who wound vines and fragrant blossoms about his elegant antlers, also alighted upon Persephone to weave a delicate and sweet-smelling coronet upon her soft, coiled hair. By the time they reached the site of the feast, the Faeries had also crafted a beautiful necklace about her graceful neck.

It was already a beautiful mild night and a full moon had begun to rise. There were twelve generous bonfires spread about the great meadow, contained in circles the Faeries made. The feast had begun. Of food and drink there was plenty. Lively music jostled mortal-immortals and divine incarnations alike, for the mortal-immortal Seelie folk loved to dance under the moon.

Cernunnos was a considerate host. He saw to it that their guest received ample portions of whatever it pleased her to consume: wine or honey mead, tea or rosewater, boiled eggs, cheese, bread, sweet cakes and honey, strawberries and cream. Whatever they had they shared with her. Her bright smiles were their reward.

Then the bard came forward from the direction of a mortal village and performed an epic of a brave hero and the maiden whose love he sought. The Seelie folk and the Faeries left off their merry whirling to crowd about Cernunnos and Persephone and listen in.

Cernunnos leaned close to his guest and whispered, "If the bard is gifted enough, these Faerie folk would listen to him sing the praises of a turnip."

Persephone covered her mouth to keep from laughing aloud. The poor mortal bard had enough to bear without the Queen of the Underworld breaking his concentration.

Without leaving her comfortable seat upon the moss where she and her host basked in the warmth of a great bonfire, Persephone flew away with the bardic music upon a great adventure. She journeyed with the Hero to exotic lands which she and her fellow listeners recognized as genuine kingdoms lost in times past, their grandeur buried beneath sand and soil beside the bones of their citizens. It gave the Hero's great deeds a bittersweet aura. Whoever he had been, he had long since gone into the Underworld, he and the beautiful, faithful Princess he braved Death to win. She had probably seen them as she stood witness and judge while Anubis and Yamaraja weighed their souls against the weight of an angel's feather.

It saddened Persephone that she could not remember them at once. She stared into the fire and attempted to conjure them up from her memory.

By the time the bard conjured up a vision of a well-deserved wedding, Persephone had conjured up their faces anew. These fierce little mortals did not live long, but these two seemed to have lived star-crossed lives. Even as the bard's audience applauded the happy conclusion to the epic, Persephone was remembering the Princess: she had indeed been beautiful and noble-spirited. She died a brave death in childbirth giving her warrior consort a son, the Hero died not five years later in an ambush.

Their son did grow up to succeed his Grandfather to the throne of that mountainous kingdom. At least he lived a long and thorough life, although their kingdom died out two generations later due to hostile forces and the effects of a natural disaster hundreds of miles away.

"You look sad, My Lady," said Cernunnos.

Persephone snapped out of her reverie with a half-hearted smile. "I am sorry, my Lord Cernunnos, but I was distracted."

"Did you not enjoy the bard's performance?"

"Indeed, it was wondrously evocative and full of romance and brave deeds, but I was lost in memories. That's all."

"Here. I shall have Puck come and recite some cheeky rhymes. He can cause a boulder to crack up."

Persephone patted his arm. "Perhaps later. I am a trifle parched and my cup is quite dry."

Cernunnos picked up her cup. "But of course…"

"No, Good Lord of the Forest," said a voice that caused Persephone to give a little start, "please stay where you are. I will refill both of your cups, if you so desire."

Cernunnos held up both cups. "If you would be so good, Lord of the Vineyards."

Persephone sat with her hand pressed over her pounding heart. At last she felt she had enough self-control that she could look up.

Dionysus smiled at her briefly as he filled their cups from his wineskin. "Thank you for inviting me, Cernunnos. I brought a special vintage just for the occasion."

"Oh dear! The last time I tasted of your special vintage even my antlers ached."

"This one's different." Briefly again Dionysus met Persephone's glance. "I have always felt the full moon most conducive for dreaming and for visions. It is a magic night when the moon waxes full. This wine aids in the production of the sweetest of dreams. It enhances one's visions too. I drink it only when the moon is full or when there is no moon at all."

Cernunnos restored Persephone's full cup to her and sat gazing at the moon's reflection in his cup for a long moment.

Persephone's gaze remained fixed upon Dionysus. When he took a long unceremonious swig from his wineskin she drank from her cup. She drained it dry. Gazing defiance, she held her cup up.

Dionysus smiled and refilled it.

Fully away of the mortal bard's quiet, astonished gaze following them, Dionysus and Persephone danced with the forest folk around the bonfires. Cernunnos and several of his chums beat out a tribal rhythm at the center of the great encampment as the moon shone directly upon them. The dancing paused only for Oberon and Titania's procession to arrive. Chaos and excitement ensured as Cernunnos saw to it that the King and Queen of the Faeries were waited upon.

In the chaos, Dionysus led Persephone away into the forest. She went easily with him. Her head nodding, she dropped her cup along the way and did not miss it.

"Where are you taking me?" she murmured.

Dionysus had to wrap his arm about her waist to prevent her from sinking toward the ground. Low and soothingly, he said, "A quieter place."

"Whatever for?" Her head snapped up in valiant, but futile resistance to the intoxicants she had imbibed.

"So that you might rest, my Consort," he whispered into her ear.

"…so sleepy," she agreed as she began to sink.

Dionysus caught her in both arms. He lifted her with ease and taking broad strides carried her far into the forest.

To the secluded, sacred site Aphrodite had recommended, Dionysus delivered Persephone. With tender care he laid her down and arranged her clothing properly about her. He spread her long purple veil over her luminous facer and down the length of her body. Briefly he stepped back to survey his work. 'Such beauteous sleep,' he mused.

At once he stretched out on his side beside her for there was yet more to do. Without touching more than her veil ever so lightly, Dionysus stroked the air just above her and whispered to her of an encounter in a meadow. He reminded her in exquisite detail of their mutual offering to Gaia.

Persephone sighed and stirred slightly. More than remembering, more than seeing the encounter through his appreciative eyes, she felt it all over again. As though feverish she stirred, but languidly, beneath the veil that shielded her.

The night air stirred about them both. Just as Dionysus had troubled Persephone with visions of luxurious desire, so had Aphrodite tormented Hades in his rest. He had visions of his Queen succumbing to an unnatural sleep again and awoke in a breathless state. Although he had not seen anyone other than Persephone, he sensed that she was not alone. When he awoke, Hades could not say which alarmed him more: the realization that his Consort was in the company of another, possibly predatory entity, or the parting view he had had of his beloved lying in state beneath her purple gossamer veil upon a bed of soft cool moss. His vision carried him to a sacred grove, but he hesitated just outside of the sacred space.

The moon shone full and direct, so there was no mistaking it. His Persephone lay in the circular clearing within the sacred circle from his dream. Once he had found her he saw nothing else, not even the dark horned figure watching from the night shadows a discreet distance away. For a moment his heart tumbled. She was not moving. He was too late to break the enchantment.

Just as grief poured into the place where his heart had been Persephone stirred and sighed as though beguiled by impatient dreams.

In an instant Hades crossed into the sanctuary and swooped down to kneel beside her. "I am here. No spell can hold you."

As he lifted her veil, Persephone stretched, so beautiful and fragrant with Life itself. Hades breathed her in and pressed the back of his dark hand to her cheek, so soft, so warm. She peered up at him through half-closed eyelids.

"You."

"Yes," he said in a soft, deep voice. "I had a vision that something was amiss with you. I had to come to you."

Already she shook her head and smiled in a way he had never seen before. She opened her eyes completely and sat up only to embrace him and draw him down close to her.

"I had such a dream," she whispered as she stirred beneath her Consort. "I want to dream some more," she said into his as she guided his left hand lower. "He was here. I dreamt of him, but you are here. Is he you? Or are you him? ...Touch me."

Hades' hand did her bidding.

Persephone wrapped her arms about him and drew him down upon her. With his other hand, he adjusted her garments and then his own. With one hand she drew his face down to meet her parted lips and her other hand traveled lower. In her dream, she had been entangled with Dionysus again and it left her in the grip of a powerful need. If her two consorts were brethren she would verify it there under a full moon that enthralled her nature.

Dionysus lingered long enough to witness their first passionate kiss and to observe how Persephone parted her legs for Hades and lifted her knees when he moved upon her. That was enough to satisfy and that would have to do for Aphrodite when he reported their success later. He slipped away.

Halfway back to the great feast, he encountered Cernunnos.

"Where is the Lady of Hades?" Cernunnos demanded.

"She is in a sacred grove. She is fine."

"I saw you lead her away."

"I took her to meet her husband. They are together now, celebrating the full moon in their private fashion."

"Ah. Well then. 'Best not to bother them. Come along, Brother Dionysus. Oberon and Titania wish to try some of your wine."

"Wish? Or need?"

"Need. For all of our sakes, need."

"'Squabbling again, eh?"

"Yes."

"Fear not. This wine should do the trick." Dionysus patted his wineskin. "Aphrodite mulled some special spices for it."

"Ah, I see. Wait! Why do I not feel affected?"

"Are you married?"

"Ah, I see...I think."

Briefly dawn peeked at Hades and Persephone in the sacred grove. Gazing quietly into one another's eyes, they lay in a warm tangle. Then Persephone drew Hades close for another kiss, a peaceful one this time, and the couple vanished from the mortal realm.

Those mortal weeks Persephone spent in both hemispheres were as a terrible mid-winter sojourn for Hades. It was during her biannual absences that Hades had the most need to visit the passage of Light and linger upon its threshold. The Intercessor souls abided a little closer to the dais whenever she was away. He was grateful for that. His loneliness for his vibrant Consort was mighty.

Sun and moon. Night and day. Life and death. Hades coupled with his Persephone in the sacred recesses of their chambers, rejoicing just as much in her beautiful essence as he did in the perfume of a living Earth that clung forever to her soft limbs, bosom, and her sun-kissed red hair.

Even the bright Intercessors seemed renewed as they ventured forth to the remotest ends of the Underworld, blessing the rest with words and the slightest of touches.

Although the effects of Aphrodite and Dionysus' mulled wine wore off eventually, as they must, something lingered, a subtle alteration as though a window had been left cracked open and fresh air and clear bright light allowed into an oubliette.

After a night spent under the full moon, Persephone emerged from her Dionysian state with her husband resting against her in their curtained bed. His thick haired head rested on the pillow above her shoulder where he breathed in the scent of her hair. Their clothes lay in a pile not five steps from the bedside. Naked they lay pressed together so closely that only the briefest of motions from a roused Hades would re-join their bodies.

All of these details Persephone observed in silence even as she noticed that she did not mind at all. She had a great deal to mull over and as long as Hades rested she had the peace to ponder.

A succubus hissed at her from the shadows. With one lightning swift glare and a flick of her hand, Persephone sent her scurrying. Then she resumed her train of thought as she caressed Hades' glossy hair. He smelled of pine. She had never noticed that before.

Dionysus was somehow to blame – or to thank, she reckoned. His appearance so far to the north had been intentional. 'He followed me', she realized, 'then he beguiled me with spiced wine.' It had seemed so real – her dream. It summoned its strength from her memory of the 'restoration' ceremony. It felt real. She had thought Dionysus with her again.

Just when it was becoming unbearable Hades had appeared. Initially she could not tell the dream apart from the reality. By the time he had eased down between her thighs she knew and didn't care. She did not mind still when Hades awoke a little later with a keen appetite.

When the after-effects did wear off entirely, Persephone accepted her place in Hades' bed. She let him hold and caress her hands when they sat upon the dais. In their private feasting hall, she let him rest his head in her lap and stroked his raven's hair as she fed him delicacies. In their bed, she received him easily and let him linger with kisses for her lips.

Hades' eyes shone so that Persephone marveled to see it. His laconic grins warmed into such smiles that from time to time she felt the need to stroke his lips with her fingertip to verify them.

Hades was happy.

Persephone was not happy.

But she was not unhappy either.

It took her a little while to put a definition to her state. It came to her with the force of illumination.

Persephone was content.

11.

Succubi do not take rejection well.

Obsessive, voracious, predatory and therefore, utterly unrepentant, the succubi, like their masculine cohorts the incubi, occupied a particularly rank and treacherous corner of Tartarus known at the Realm of Hungry Ghosts. The most deluded, confused and recalcitrant souls pooled in this realm, craving, wandering, and raging for the temporal realms where they no longer belonged.

The Realm of the Hungry Ghosts resembled a maelstrom. It took a great deal of fortitude to tread around it upon the narrow precipice that overlooked that seething well of souls. It took much more to ford it in search of some forlorn broken spirit or malevolent entity that had forsaken all connections to the Light.

Fearless Hades and Hel took their fierce hounds Cerberus and Garmr with them when they patrolled there for the souls were forever attempting escapes.

Yamaraja assumed his fiercer aspect there. The souls shrank from him as he passed through with his penetrating gaze.

Anubis they shied away from.

From Osiris they hid altogether, since he spoke with the voice of the Source and could shatter a malevolent entity with a pointed whisper. The merely lost, confused and wounded swirled about Osiris, forming a mist, for he was not cruel.

The Maelstrom of the Hungry Ghosts required almost constant surveillance. The caretakers took turns patrolling the many realms in shifts and standing vigil over the Maelstrom. When it was Osiris' turn to stand guard, the Maelstrom scarcely rippled as the dark entities and angry spirits sank far from sight. Whenever Hades or Anubis delivered a lost or exorcised spirit to the Maelstrom, the pool of souls bubbled as though a geyser boiled in its depths. As the struggling spirit resisted, the other souls surged upward and outward.

For the most part these obsessed and nearly ungovernable entities remained trapped in the vortex at the heart of the Maelstrom. Now and then one slipped free into the rest of the Underworld, but it was exceedingly rare for a denizen of the Hungry Ghost Realm to escape into the Mortal Realm. Exceedingly rare.

The Succubi and Incubi posed a particular challenge. They came from the Maelstrom, but were not *of* it. They roamed the Underworld like the harpies and their ilk amusing themselves by tormenting the inmates of the Maelstrom. It was hard to say where they came from or when they coalesced into being. They may have been among the Living once, but somehow they had turned into primordial elementals a very long time ago.

In the past Hades had ample time to contemplate the origins and nature of the Succubi even as one or another of their insidious sisterhood indulged her appetite upon his unrequited desire. They were ever so eager to please him where his Consort would not, but in the end, they were what they were...

Vampyres.

All had been well between Hades and his *concubines.* They had developed an understanding that when Persephone was away it was their time to play.

That changed after the 'rapprochement' Aphrodite had concocted and Dionysus stage managed. The Succubi snarled and wailed in the depths of the Maelstrom as sounds of genuine pleasure echoed through to them and they recognized Persephone's voice.

If they had hoped to resume their previous relations with Hades when Persephone embarked on her biannual sojourns abroad, Hades made it resolutely clear that circumstances had changed the very first time one of their sisterhood attempt to rouse him.

"Stay in the nether regions, Siren of Lust. You and your sisterhood are forbidden absolutely from these chambers from now on."

As a multitude of her kind gathered upon the shadowed perimeter of his private chambers, the lone marauder, a spectre of harrowing, dire beauty lay supine at Hades' feet. Her pupil-less red eyes swam in angry desperation.

"Cherished Lord, do not banish us your most faithful companions. We have served you without question from the moment you were given dominion over our realm. Let us continue to console and divert you in your bouts of solitude."

"My Consort contents me now. I no longer need you..." Hades saw red eyes everywhere beyond his domestic boundaries. "...or them."

"Your Consort does not love you. We worship you as the flowers worship Helios, Lord Hades."

"Such is the sorcery of Aphrodite that she tolerates you only for the pleasure you give her."

"That remains my concern and mine alone."

"Forgive us our just concern. We have cared for and tended to you as your true Consorts before Eros cursed you. We have consoled you tirelessly whilst your Queen received the Bull-Horned One in your place."

"That will be enough."

"She grants him what only drugged wine would give you under the influence of a full moon."

"Do not banish us!" cried one of their sisterhood from the darkness.

"Let us cherish you!"

"This is the domain of Queen Persephone. You are forbidden from this place." His voice rumbled low and angry throughout the passageways.

Shrieking and wailing loud enough to drown out the bean-sidhe, the succubi flooded back into the Maelstrom.

For a long moment Hades stared without seeing into the darkness, and yet all he was seeing, remembering actually, was those two unexpected dreams he had had involving Persephone. It had seemed intensely real.

"It was real," he said to the void. He turned. Persephone's imprint in their bed had scarcely cooled it seemed. "It was real."

Hades dressed himself more out of habit than conscious thought. Taking up a scythe, Hades drew his hood over his head. His eyes turned a luminous silver-white. He swept past the dais. "I shall be gone for a time, but if you need me, send Hermes."

Anubis and Nepthys exchanged solemn looks, their conversation interrupted.

"Very well," said Anubis as Osiris assumed command of the dais in all of his silent grandeur.

Hades vanished across the smoky threshold.

"Something is wrong," said Nepthys.

Anubis nodded.

From the Maelstrom in the distance, Yamaraja began uttering mantras. He only did so when there was a disturbance.

Osiris turned his formidable gaze toward the depths of Tartarus.

Seething and cursing, the Succubi whirled and stormed the length \and breadth of Tartarus. Hunger raged inside them. They starved. Hades had forbidden them from his presence. They cursed him even as they craved him. Hades and his kind kept them confined away from the Living and their delicious mortal vitality. They cursed even the mighty Osiris and the power he came from.

They formed a whirlpool above the Maelstrom, crying out of terrible hunger.

Yamaraja cast a stern glance above his head. His right hand formed the sign of karana mudra. His left hand held firm to his shining vajra as his deep voice intoned mantras. The Maelstrom began to calm itself again.

Hissing, the Succubi whipped through the vortex at the heard of the Hungry Ghost Realm where only darkness could stay.

The worst of the worst dwelled here: Primordials and Elementals, merciless and hungry entities that attacked anything weaker that fell into their clutches and fed on their spiritual essence.

Silent intent ruled here among the smoky grey and black entities that huddled in caves and crevices, forever hiding from the Light and from its watchful Avatars, plotting, forever plotting. Sullen, the Succubi muttered amongst themselves. Those, who had thought themselves favored by Hades, moaned and sobbed.

Malevolence opened its black shark's eyes and listened carefully to their miseries. Then it spoke in a potent whisper that shattered the roar of the Maelstrom, "Sisters."

The angry entities fell silent and watchful.

"Sisters, why are you anguished?" it said.

"Brother, we are starving and heartbroken."

"This is the realm of constant suffering. Why is your grief so fresh and keen?" As it fed off their pain and anger, it took a more recognizable form and crept little by little out of its narrow recess.

"Our Master has banished us from his presence."

"Why? What did you do?"

They perceived a spirit akin to theirs in appetite.

"Nothing. We answered his call and did only what he desired and now he dismisses us."

"Then why?"

"Persephone," they breathed into the abyss for fear that they would be heard.

"Ah!" The Destroyer of the Light – such a prize she would be if she could be captured and held in one's sway, a delicious means of returning torment for torment throughout the realms. "Yes," *HE* hissed, "she will be the vehicle for retribution. I will help you regain your Master's favor, but first I must escape from this pit."

"Escape is impossible," said one of the many.

"I am akin to you. If you can slip into the mortal realms from time to time then so can I."

"It has been ages since most of us have been abroad among the Living. We have the freedom of Tartarus and Erebus, but there is no escaping past the all-seeing eyes of Osiris or Garmr and Cerberus," said the Succubus.

"Create a distraction before the dais where Osiris stands vigil. All I need is for one of you to escape and prepare a mortal *vehicle* for my use."

"How is this to be done?"

"One of your sisterhood must select a worthy mortal: a healthy male. Prey upon him as is your way. Feed upon his vitality until he can no longer cling to his living shell. Then when his husk is empty I may take it for my own."

"What do we gain for your freedom?"

"I shall help you to gain your own freedom. You may feast, you and your brethren the Incubi upon your feeble and delectable pray at will, with none to stop you."

"Hades and Anubis will hunt us down. Yamaraja will assume his ferocious aspect and stalk us."

"I will hold them at bay."

"How?"

"I shall beguile and enslave the Kore whom your Master loves in your stead."

The Succubi hissed and spat at the mere mention of Hades' Consort.

"Yes, that I shall do for you. Free me and see what happens once she is within my power."

"We want Hades. We would consume him until he too is a husk, a spectre of his former might and magnificence."

"Free me and he is yours, I promise."

The great shrieks that echoed upward from the Maelstrom's all but impenetrable depths troubled Yamaraja. He knew a war cry when he heard one.

Emboldened by the Succubi and the Incubi, other inmates of the Maelstrom surged forth in mass exodus. Some of their numbers fell to Yamaraja and his vajra, returning, whimpering, to the well of souls.

More of their number fell to the might of Anubis and his staff. Garmr and Cerberus drove still more back.

The rest met with disaster before the dais where Osiris waited. Standing still and calm, Osiris uttered the sound of Creation and Destruction in a low steady hum. Their desperate malingering energies burst apart into countless particles, finer than any dust. Osiris swept them toward the passage of Light, which consumed them, returning them to the Source, for nothing is ever lost.

Of the many hungry ghosts and instigating entities from the Maelstrom who attempted an escape, two and only two succeeded. One Succubus escaped and clinging to her wild hair flew the cunning inmate from the depths of the Maelstrom.

His name was *UPIR LIKHYI.*

Hel and Yamaraja took a tally of the souls. The instant they realized that Upir Likhyi was neither among the defeated nor among the extinguished they sent for Hermes.

Only he knew where to find Hades.

12.

In the realm of the Living, times were difficult, riven with strife, devastation and uncertainty. The Golden Age was well and truly over.

Its distant descendants lived in the shadows of grand, but half-buried ruins and could not even begin to imagine how Life used to be. Even the world seemed to have grown colder. Diminished, the cities huddled behind fortified walls while lesser, scattered settlements coped as best they could with the weather's effects on their crops and with marauders driven abroad by hardship at home.

People in some corners of the world expected it to end and groups of them took to living in isolation where they prayed and waited for Time itself to end.

Plagues ravaged the numbers, raging with all the relentlessness of wildfires from one end of the civilized mortal world to the other. Following its progress in his hooded robe strode grim-faced, white-eyed Hades and maroon-and-saffron robed Apollo. They had met up at the site of the initial outbreak, summoned to a city lane littered with the dead and dying by Persephone.

"Lord of Plagues," she called the moment golden Phoebus alighted beside Hades, "is this your doing?"

Apollo Paeon surveyed the devastation with a frown. "Rats with fleas, my Dear," he said, "rats with fleas."

"Normally I would agree," said Hades, "but this time…"

Apollo continued to cast frowning glances everywhere. "Where are the cats? How come I don't see any cats?"

"Because these fools decided that cats were the minions of someone called Satan and they murdered as many as they could catch," said an angry woman dressed in robes of slate grey.

Turning at once they beheld Hecate treading carefully past the corpses in the side alley.

"Greetings, Wise One," said Hades.

"That wasn't very helpful of them," groused Apollo.

"Well, you know how it is when people get an idea in their head," said Hecate as she joined them. She met Persephone's glance. "Where is the Twice-Born One?"

"He sped off to India to see what Shiva and Kali knew of this disaster. As soon as he finds out anything, he said he would return." Briefly Persephone met her Consort's stare and felt it pierce her.

"Why India?" said Hecate.

"Because, like my husband, Dionysus also suspected that there was something different behind the beginnings of this crisis." Persephone continued to meet Hades' gaze.

His expression flickered. "Yes, Kali would know something useful."

"Let us hope she does," said Hecate as she leaned upon her walking staff. "Where is our glorified carrier pigeon?"

"Hermes is surveying the extent of the plague thus far," said Hades.

"At least the other hemisphere stands safe from this," said Apollo.

"Small miracles," mumbled Hades.

Hecate's perceptive eyes studied Hades' expression. There was a slight air of distracted concentration about him. "Is your wife, my niece, correct? Do you and Dionysus share the same suspicions…that I also harbor?"

Hades met her glance and noted Hecate's arched brow. "In my case, more than a passing suspicion."

"Two entities escaped. One helped the other," said Hades.

"What sort of nastiness were they?" said Hecate.

"A succubus and…"

"One of your concubines?" Hecate's brows arched again.

Hades met Persephone's curious look. "Former concubines." It was hard to tell whether Hades was irritable or ashamed or flustered. In that moment even he could not say precisely what he felt.

Then Persephone blushed and averted her gaze.

Hades' face turned smoky. His white irises darkened.

Apollo scratched his ear and eyed one of the plague victims.

Hecate's look passed from Hades to Persephone and back again. "One does what one must. You two can spit recriminations at one another later about him seeking comfort for what he could not have and her enjoying her duty so much that she hankered for another. Aside from the spurned succubus, who else troubles this vulnerable realm?"

"A piece of pestilence that is called Upir Likhyi," said Hades.

Apollo watched a plague victim breathe out for the last time. Mist-like, the soul rose from its wretched shell. Quickly Apollo cradled the small luminous consciousness in his hands, turning it over and over so very tenderly. Like had been harsh to this blameless soul, a young man of scarcely seventeen winters who most nights was content to have a full belly and a warm place to sleep.

Persephone watched Apollo tending to the soul. When he turned about, carefully, a thoughtful look on his face, she stepped forward and held out her hands cupped together just so.

Apollo hesitated.

"Let me tend to him. It is my domain."

Apollo relinquished the soul to her soft, pink-tipped hands.

Holding it safe in the right hand that she pressed close to her breast, Persephone announced, "I shall return to the Underworld and maintain court over the Dead." She gestured with her left hand to the terrorized and dying mortals surrounding them. "Someone must be there to help greet these souls."

"Someone who will not terrify those who have been traumatized enough," said Hecate. "Yes. Go, Queen of Hades."

Persephone met her husband's dark-eyed gaze. "Good hunting, my Lord."

Hades inclined his head.

Inclining her head briefly, Persephone turned away and in three strides vanished from that realm.

Hades sighed.

Apollo adjusted his maroon cloak. "So, am I to understand that this is the doing of your Succubus lover and a vampyric spirit?"

"The Succubus had only the power to create a useful vessel for her master Upir Likhyi to use here," said Hecate. "This disaster is but the side effect of his malignant presence."

Hades said, "He has begun to feed on the blood of the Living."

"He will be hard to catch now that he is reborn and revitalized," said Hecate.

"It isn't only a matter of combating him. First, we have to find him," said Hades.

"And what the Upir has unleashed cannot be stopped, I'm afraid," said Apollo. "It must burn itself out."

"I was afraid of that," said Hades. "The river shall overflow its banks."

For a moment all three incarnations surveyed their surroundings in silence.

"I say, we begin where Upir Likhyi began," said Apollo.

"Where precisely was that?" said Hades.

Hecate pointed with her staff toward an austere complex of structures atop a hill. "In that den of restless contemplatives."

"Or what's left of them," commented Apollo.

"Ah!" Hecate took on a cunning look. "Things are a trifle different up there. Come along and I'll explain…"

There was no moon that first night when the Brothers heard an unseen presence pacing their dim corridors. At that dead hour of night no one was meant to be out of chambers. The Order's Patriarch was quite strict about this matter, so those monks who heard the sounds knew at once that there was an intruder upon the Mount, a stranger where no outsiders were allowed.

Still, thinking, hoping that it was perhaps one of their order sleepwalking, one of the monks whispered through the door. "Go back to your cell, my Brother, before you are caught and reprimanded."

Immediately silence filled the corridor beyond his door, but there was nothing still about it. Although there had not been another footstep, the monk felt a presence gather just on the other side of the door. Crossing himself, he backed away to where his three cellmates sat utterly still and nearly breathless with fright. Clasping their crucifixes, they prayed softly.

Those who had awakened to the sounds dared not sleep and could not begin to relax their guard until dawn.

Only as dawn's first rays glowed softly upon their bell tower did a sense of peace return. Still, they took no chances. Those who had heard the sounds informed the Patriarch, who promptly utilized Holy Water on the corridor. He even blessed the doors with it.

The second night came over them. It passed seemingly without incident for dawn came, spreading its welcome light everywhere without any alarms or strangeness, and yet one of their Order failed to rise with the rest.

Brother Bonifacio lay ill.

Their apothecary came at once to his humble beside. He felt of the Brother's hands, his neck, his forehead, and pressed his hands to his chest and stomach. Brother Bonifacio was examined from head to toe. No marks were found and all the while the wretched young man lay oblivious to his caretakers.

"What is amiss with him?" said one of the senior monks.

"I cannot say, but that perhaps he has caught a chill or a sleeping sickness," said the apothecary. "I shall give him an herbal tea. Perhaps that shall revive him."

"Of course. Do what thou ought. I must confer with the Patriarch. Send to me should his condition alter."

"Yes, Father Demetrius." The apothecary turned to his case that was filled with carefully labeled vials.

His apprentice brought a pot of steaming fresh tea and watched closely as the apothecary mixed several ingredients with his mortar and pestle. He stirred the tea as his master added medicine to it and then supported Bonifacio's head as his Master poured the tea a little at a time down his throat.

Four sips gone and Bonifacio coughed and sputtered awake. Still, coughing, the young man seized the elder man so suddenly and with such force that his tea pot nearly went crashing across the room.

"Easy! Rest! Be at peace," said the apothecary.

"No. No." Bonifacio looked with wild eyes about the chamber.

"Thou art under my protection and care. All shall be well, Brother Bonifacio."

"No, Brother Ignatius, no." Bonifacio pulled him closer and hissed into his ear. "I was attacked in the night."

"I perceive no marks upon thy person."

"A demon in the form of a woman of terrible, devouring beauty…she came to me here. I thought I dreamt, but alas, I could not resist her wiles and I could not awaken once she had taken command of me." Suddenly all the color went out of his face and he sank back into the apprentice's arms. "Tell me it was but a dream."

"It was a nightmare." Brother Ignatius said with a kind look. "'Twas only a fever dream brought on by a sleeping sickness. Drink of this and rest." He handed the teapot to his suddenly pale and wide-eyed apprentice.

"No! Do not leave me alone. Do not leave me!"

"I shall not leave, but for a moment to send for Father Demetrius. Then shall I return to keep vigil as you rest."

"Yes. Bless you. Bless you. Thank God."

Informed of Bonifacio's claim by Father Demetrius, the Patriarch summoned all the weapons in his spiritual arsenal. Bonifacio's chamber was cleansed and blessed. His cot was reduced to firewood and his bedclothes burned with it. Upon the newly constructed cot and new bedding the Patriarch of their Order sprinkled Holy Water and then burnt incense as he blessed the humble cell thoroughly.

Into his refreshed cell, Bonifacio was restored, fed, and prayed over by Brother Theodosius, who would keep watch as he slept.

As the night stretched, calm and quiet, Brother Theodosius could not stop yawning. After the last of the evening prayers, when the whole monastery settled down until morning, he grappled with sleep himself. His head nodded and then bobbed back up, again and again, as waves of sleep drew him from the shores of his everyday world. At last he succumbed, there on a bench near the small hearth with his chin resting upon his chest.

As weary as he was, he did not sleep well: As though flooded by shadows, the Monastery surrounded him. He tried to move, but it was as though he waded through water as high as his waist. He shivered. It was imperative that he return to Bonifacio's sickroom. He didn't remember leaving it, but he knew the trouble he would be in if he did not return at once.

'How can I be here when I do not remember leaving my vigil?' he thought.

Theodosius struggled to return to Bonifacio's side. Doors became walls. Walls became doors. Everything that should have been familiar felt strange, off-kilter. The shadowy water turned heavy and sludge-like. He shivered and wanted to wake up.

A moan echoed through to him. Someone was in pain. He heard the sound again, more shallow, closer. Step by step from a fog-shrouded valley, Theodosius emerged from his uncomfortable slumber. He stirred and forced open his bleary eyes. "Brother?" he mumbled as he shifted in his seat and rubbed his eyes.

In sinful nakedness, Bonifacio writhed upon his bed. Sounds of agony escaped his lips as he flailed against the entity whose lascivious exertions kept him pinned down.

Brother Theodosius crossed himself and pressed himself against the wall. Sick with horror, in the grip of a truly terrible fascination, he could not tear his eyes away from the daemonic Succubus as she drew Bonifacio's very essence into her being.

Her appetite wrung a sob from Bonifacio. She made wild sounds of delight as the young man released more than his seed into her and fainted.

Brother Theodosius tore from the room shouting for help.

Nothing could persuade him to return for the next night's vigil.

Bonifacio was in a very poor state. Enfeebled and terrorized, he pleaded for rescue. The Patriarch blessed him with Holy Water yet again. It was decided that they should move him to another chamber altogether and then the next day to remove him from the monastery to their patron the Duke's villa. Father Demetrius would be his guardian.

And as for the room itself…it was bricked up as soon as Bonifacio had been removed from it. This time they didn't bother taking or doing anything to the furnishings. Whatever resided there could have the chamber to itself.

As for Brother Bonifacio, he was carried to a chamber close to one of the small private chapels. There they made him comfortable upon a cot, provided him with nourishment, and three stalwart members of the Brotherhood to watch over him until he could be removed completely.

A sense of determined optimism settled over the population as night approached. The cursed chamber had been sealed up utterly with holy marks impressed in the wet plaster over the bricks and fresh mortar. Bonifacio rested placidly where he could hear evensong.

Night came…and went.

His three guards reported with bright looks how peacefully, how well and safe Bonifacio passed the night. Neither a sound nor the shadow of a nightmare troubled the young man.

Their morning smiles disappeared though when several monks reported hearing a voice of Darkness muttering and laughing lowly from within the sealed room. Then when they discovered Brother Theodosius disheveled and unconscious in the garden, their alarm returned. Whilst Bonifacio consumed his porridge with a child's simple enjoyment, the monks delivered Theodosius to the Infirmary.

Just as before, the apothecary Brother Ignatius treated the patient.

And just as before, his patient awoke in a state of panic tempered by severe fatigue. "She came for me. I ran from her, but there was no escaping. She devoured my very vitality even as I begged mercy of her and invoked the Heavens. She means to come for me again. Save me."

A sensed of panic simmered beneath the day's activities as the elders conferred as to the best course of action to take. What had preyed upon Bonifacio and Theodosius would prey upon any or all of them given the opportunity, they realized. They prayed and meditated and consulted various texts in their library for aid.

As the sun set, they were still debating whether to purify the entire monastery themselves with Holy Water, prayers and incense, or to send for a specialist in the city.

Brother Bonifacio would rest again in the chamber beside the small chapel.

Brother Theodosius lay in the Infirmary, his bleak expression fixed toward the ceiling.

Both entered another night under close, determined protection.

The rest of the uneasy Brotherhood spent the night in prayer in the main chapel.

In the dead hour of night, Theodosius screamed. His guards shouted for help. "Demon!"

In the tumult as monks scurried this way and that, and the Patriarch himself led the charge to drive the damned entity from their premises, Bonifacio succumbed to the embrace of his unwanted lover.

Helpless, his guards returned in time to witness Bonifacio's body convulse one last time. The Succubus greedily kissed her prey as he exhaled his last breath. With a look of bright, fierce appraisal for them, the entity turned to coiling smoke and slipped out between the window's shutters.

With despair in their hearts, they interred Brother Bonifacio in the vault where two hundred years of their Brethren decomposed. They hoped that the worst was over. They prayed that the daemonic woman had taken enough and would be content.

Another night came.

The sealed room emanated silence. Brother Theodosius slept as much as exhaustion demanded of him and for as long as his nightmares could cling to him. He had a restless, but unmolested night of it, just like the rest of the monastery's inmates.

Another day and night passed without incident.

Then another and another after that.

Brother Theodosius left their monastery for one closer to his birthplace. No one blamed him for leaving and quite a few wished they had accompanied him by the next dawn's full bloom.

That terrible dawn revealed several things: the entrance to the vault had been disturbed and Bonifacio's tombstone moved. Bonifacio himself was missing, although his immaculate winding sheet remained. There was no trace of him anywhere. Brother Lucius lay in his bed at death's door with two hideous puncture marks on his neck. Young, handsome Brother Antonius had fallen victim to the entity that had killed Bonifacio and driven Theodosius away.

"...And since then," said Hecate, "your spurned concubine has been consoling herself amongst these helpless men."

Apollo, Hades, and Hecate stood before the closed doors. They sensed the furtive lives within attempting to maintain some sense of normality although they wanted to flee – to the other side of the world if only it were possible.

"I assume Upir Likhyi's first victim survived," said Apollo, "or you would have mentioned him."

"The wretch lives and is recuperating," said Hade, his gaze set on the high stucco walls.

"And Upir Likhyi?" said Apollo.

"Long gone," said Hecate. "The monk Lucius was just to give him strength to go out into the greater world. He hit the town with a vengeance. You saw the after effects."

Hades nodded.

"So what next?" said Apollo.

"Capture the Succubus and restore her to the Underworld," said Hades. "Queen of ghosts and ghouls, will you help me?"

"Why do you think I showed up?" retorted Hecate.

Hades grinned somberly for a response. "Then let's go clean house, shall we?"

"Right." Apollo waved his hand and the bolted doors flew open.

"You go in first, Hades," said Hecate. "It will be night soon and we need bait."

Only during the daylight did the assaults cease and the monks enjoy some semblance of peace. Thus far the promiscuous entity slaked her dreaded thirst on the healthy young men in their order, but as she drained them of their vitality to the point of enfeeblement, eventually, she would stalk the older inmates too.

She brought them agony and ecstasy all at once. Those who had faced martyrdom from her and yet survived bore their whitened hair or wrecked health as a badge of honor. They had endured the onslaughts from one of Satan's own whores and had not cursed God, but lived still to glory HIS NAME. Those whom the Succubus had not yet kissed meekly awaited their trial by torment as the sun set each evening.

The elders were not unaware of this, but nothing they had done or could think to do anymore could uproot the malignant being from their monastery. Therefore, it was with an aching sense of despair that the Patriarch trod alone into the great church and prostrated himself before the altar and their large poly-chromed crucifix.

The only words he spoke were, "Help us."

At that same moment Hades crossed the monastery's threshold.

The old man felt the atmosphere change around him. Groaning slightly he rose upon his knees. Fear trembled in his knees and hands. Was this shift what presaged an appearance of the dreaded daemon? It was not cold though. If anything, the enormous space felt warmer and seemed brighter.

Upon his knees he shifted as he peered about. He gasped and threw himself forward, prostrating himself before the three softly luminous figures approaching him. "Art thou angels come to deliver us from the foul daemon who torments us?" Unexpected, unbidden tears filled the old man's eyes.

Hecate, Hades, and Apollo stopped a short distance away. Looks were exchanged. Apollo held up his golden hand and nodded to his companions. They nodded back.

"Fear not, good Father," the Golden One said, "for Deliverance has come."

Raising up upon his knees, the old man raised his palms toward Apollo. "Thank, God. Praise unto him, Our Heavenly Father. Art thou an archangel?"

Apollo weighed his response carefully. "We have come to help."

"What do you require of me?"

"Summon all of your brethren here and bid them pray mightily that the malevolence be removed forever and your communal body healed of its corrupt predations. Do this now. You may not see me once you have gathered everyone into this sacred redoubt, but I shall be with you to drive back the entity."

Smiling with as much radiance as he felt in his being, the old Patriarch climbed to his feet and rushed to ring the bell that would summon the rest of their Order to the church. With more might than he had felt himself capable in years, he pulled the ropes.

As the first ponderous toll rang out, Apollo nodded at Hades and Hecate, who withdrew with Hecate sternly leading the way.

When the Patriarch paused to observe his brethren hurrying in, he noticed that the three fierce archangels...or saints, he could not say which they were, had gone. A luminous atmosphere lingered in the center of the church though. The Golden One was indeed present – with his flaming sword at the ready, the Patriarch had no doubt.

"A great deliverance has come," he declared to his breathless assembly.

"What sort of deliverance?" said Father Demetrius.

"I have beheld two fierce archangels and a saint here in our church. They have come to drive out the Evil that torments us. A great battle is about top ensue and we must pray for victory and for God to heal us."

Apollo stood between the congregation as they assembled themselves for their emergency mass and the entrance they had come through. He arched his brow to hear himself called an archangel, but shrugged. In the end, it was all the same as far as he was concerned. All such incarnations came into being only by the will of the Source, himself included.

If the Succubus came his way he would obliterate her with one blow.

Hecate sensed where the restless entity hid from daylight's activities digesting her wicked feast: the tombs in the underground vaults. She marched directly there, pushing her sleeves up as she neared the gated entrance beneath the monastery's ground level. She and Hades slowed when they saw the bewildered, furtive ghost of Brother Bonifacio kneeling at the entrance facing outward. They stopped before him and for a moment listened to his endless recitations of penitence.

"Good Brother Bonifacio," said Hades, "why do you linger here?"

Looking up, the monk's spirit gave a little start. "Because my sins brought great suffering upon my brothers. I pray for forgiveness and I pray for their safety, but…"

"But what, young man?" said Hecate in the manner and tone of a caring Grandmother.

"She…IT mocks me whenever it rushes past me to torment my brethren. I am damned. I let Evil in and I am suffering for it."

"You are indeed suffering, Bonifacio," said Hecate, "but you are innocent."

"I fornicated with it. 'Tis my doing and my fault."

Hecate looked to Hades.

Hades laid his powerful hands upon the spirit's shoulders. "It has the power to coerce submission from the unwilling. It uses one's animal nature in treachery against one's better nature. She escaped from her proper realm of confinement to wreak havoc among the Living."

"Do you see matters clearly now?" said Hecate.

"I begin to…but I must stop her."

"You have done all that is required." Hecate extended her hand to him. "Poor, betrayed soul, to suffer as you have and die so that your sacred body could be stolen. We have come to put an end to their wickedness."

Hades stepped past him to face the vault entrance. "I shall reclaim you, my willful and rebellious subject." Then he stepped through the closed gates and into the tombs.

The ghost of Bonifacio stood up and gazed after Hades. "Shall he be safe?"

Hecate patted the young soul on the shoulder. "She cannot hurt her Master, Lord Hades. He touches the hands of God Almighty, so imagine what it shall feel like for that foolish Succubus when he catches a hold of her."

Bonifacio looked intimidated and dazzled all at once. "I see. Praise be, I see."

"Come with me, my Son. Better things await you."

Nothing could hide from Hades of the White Eyes, nothing living or dead, and certainly not a wretched Succubus cowering in the catacombs. Naked but for her long, smothering tresses, the entity struggled between her desire to flee and terrified immobility.

Hades was coming for her. She felt his resolute anger. She could smell it and perverse thing that she was she grew excited even as her terror kindled.

Suddenly, Hades loomed before her hiding place with his terrible shining eyes glaring into the darkness directly at her.

A strange mutilated giggle escaped her in the darkness that no mortal eye could penetrate.

"Come to your Master," he said in a voice that rumbled into the Earth itself.

The Succubus moaned and whined. Then, snarling, she burst out into the open. She meant to escape. Glutted on mortal vitality, she was reinvigorated and craved more. She thought she could escape.

Hades' powerful hand closing about her throat forced out a shriek. With ease Hades lifted the flailing entity up and shook it. Whimpering, the Succubus clawed at his hand, but without effect.

Still carrying the vile renegade by its throat, Hades rejoined a solitary Hecate outside of the vault. "Brother Bonifacio?" he said.

"'Embraced by the Light," said Hecate as her harsh gaze settled upon the Succubus. "Now, foul vixen, lascivious thing, where is the Instigator of your Disobedience?"

"Free to roam. Free of your dominion, false one," she chortled at Hades instead.

"Why are you not with him?" said Hades.

The Succubus pouted. "He abandoned me here."

"Ha! I am sure you were heartbroken about it," said Hecate.

She snarled at Hecate, which only amused the goddess.

"My Liberator shall settle my affairs. Mark my words," the Succubus spat at Hades.

"Give her to me," said Hecate. "Let me discipline this one."

"No. No. Keep me at your side, My Lord. I shall help you find him." The entity was still clinging to his arm as he held her out to Hecate.

Hecate took a merciless grip of the Succubus' dense hair and dragged her to her side. The entity whimpered and tried to pry her hand loose.

"Where shall you go next?" said Hecate.

"To rejoin Apollo and thence to go on the hunt."

"Good hunting, my Lord Hades." Hecate gave her captive a fierce tug and, turning, vanished into the wall with it.

Hades went up to Apollo.

13.

Time passed. Nothing changed and yet things did change both above and below. Tumult upset the peace, but peace found a way to return. The cycle never stopped because the Living failed to remember and did not learn.

In what the Living later called the Dark or the Middle Ages, Hades dreaded crossing the great hall because it meant passing amongst the souls pooled there, including the new arrivals. Thanks to flea-ridden rats, a harsher, colder climate cycle, and Upir Likhyi's restless, but strategic predations, there was a surfeit of European-born souls crossing into the Underworld.

All of these wretched European souls had spent their Sabbaths feeding their imaginations on frightful depictions of Eternal Damnation - with its attendant miseries and those zealous beings who inflicted these punishments upon 'sinners'- rendered in stone, wood, or with pigments painted on plastered walls. For most of them, their lives had been hard enough. Even the Powerful and Wealthy enjoyed a precarious existence at the mercy of the Fates.

Then they died…not always peacefully and sometimes more than unpleasantly and found themselves in the Underworld confronting its exotic caretakers.

Hades dreaded his shift on the dais. "Anubis, are you sure I cannot persuade you to cover for me entirely?"

Anubis stood on the back steps leading to the dais. "No way."

Persephone waited a few steps ahead, adjusting her purple veil. "It will be fine, Aidoneus."

"How about Osiris?" he said.

"Are you kidding me? It is time for his shift to end. There is only so much shrieking that even Osiris can tolerate before he gets what the mortals call a 'headache'."

Hades sighed. "Very well." He adjusted his black robes. "How do I look?"

"Very Lordly," said Persephone with a warm look and a stroke at a crease in his garments.

"If I look so 'lordly', why do they start screaming the instant they clap eyes on me?"

"I like it when they simply keel over in massive conniption fits," said Anubis. "You should hear what they scream when they see me!" He rolled his eyes.

"Do they call you 'Satan' too?"

"Usually I get – 'It's the devil!' But I have had worse things flung at me too. Generally, they just scream." Anubis gestured over his shoulder. "I am going to take Garmr and Cerberus for a romp in the Elysian Fields. We all need a walk." Anubis gave a little wave and padded off softly.

In the near distance, Anubis whistled. Garmr and Cerberus filled the space with their excited yapping.

Hades sighed and held out his arm to his Consort.

"It won't be so bad," Persephone cooed to him as she took his arm.

After an exchange of bows, Osiris and Hades exchanged places.

Shaking his head, Osiris departed. Odds were, they wouldn't see him for a while.

Hades was pretty certain that he heard Osiris muttering as they passed one another. The word 'holiday' stood out.

Scarcely had Hades and Persephone settled into the thrones amid a flurry of murmurs from the souls lingering in the great hall when Hecate bustled in from abroad.

"Oh dear," said Persephone.

"What is it? Oh, Hecate," said Hades.

Hecate stopped directly before their dais.

"Why do I get the feeling that I am not going to like what she is about to tell me?" said Hades.

"Brace yourselves," said Hecate. "They have lost their collective minds up there. They have turned on each other and are sacrificing Innocents to their new god of fear. The first wave is imminent." She frowned over her shoulders.

Hades stood as the first shadows gathered just across their threshold. "Christ."

"And you'd be partially correct," said Hecate dryly, "they are indulging in these atrocities in HIS name." She turned to face the new arrivals as they trickled in.

Persephone stood. "HE cannot be happy about that."

"HE isn't," said Hecate, "trust me there."

Terrorized and traumatized beyond all mortal endurance, the souls huddled in familial clusters, their sight clouded by their horrible last moments on Earth. Some stared blankly and remained mute. Others moaned, remembering their agony. Some wept still from the cruelty that had been visited upon them and their loved ones.

"Drowned, burned," observed Persephone.

"Humanity has a truly astonishing gift for imagining up horrific deaths to inflict upon one another," said Hecate. "I think one of these poor souls died because she actually saw me."

"She saw you?" said Hades.

Hecate nodded. "Unfortunately, she reported her vision. Their response was that she saw Satan's Great Whore because she was in league with Satan to begin with. Nothing she did to appease them saved her. They simply changed the rules each time. They wouldn't be content until they had set her on fire in the public square. They have a rude surprise waiting for them when it's their turn." And Hecate grinned.

Persephone sat down. Her hand was pressed to her heart. "When you see her, bring her forth to me. I will help her see the Light in the passage. She should not linger here after what she has suffered."

"None of them should," said Hades, "and yet..."

"Demeter offered to withdraw her strength from their crops, but I told her that it would just give them further cause to indulge in these 'witch hunts' as they call them."

"It is bad enough that plagues and starvation deliver so many souls to our care," said Persephone, "but do they have to sacrifice good people to this 'Satan', whoever that may be."

"There is dark energy enough in the lowest realms," said Hades. "Upir Likhyi is proof enough of that. It is primoridial or was at first. It feeds on anger and pain and exists to procreate more of the same to further its existence. It has no name, nor a single recognizable face. However, if these mortals insist on bestowing so much energy into the creation of a single entity, the summation of everything they fear and despise, then they will create one."

"Indeed," said Hecate, "they should be careful that they do not create what they fear most. Devotion of that kind is poisonous."

"More work for us," said Persephone. "Where is Zeus in all this?"

Hecate snorted. "At least Apollo shines Reason into other realms, but the Sky Pater spends his time in his usual fashion. Now that no one burns incense for him in his long lost temples, he hides his sulks in an attitude of indifference."

"Deplorable," said Persephone.

"He is that and more," said Hecate. "He has had his better moments, but those happened so terribly long ago."

While they spoke sotto voce to one another at the dais, the trickle became a fairly steady stream into the great hall. Although the gentle Intercessors moved boldly into their midst, unease stirred throughout the throng.

Hades grimaced. "I do not like the looks of this crowd."

"Hmmmm. They do seem a bit jittery." Hecate took a firmer grip of her staff.

"Would you like me to address them?" Persephone said softly.

"No. Plug your ears while I get this over with," said Hades.

Persephone sighed and, sitting back in her throne, placed her dainty fingertips in her ears.

Hecate rested her staff against her shoulder and folded her ears shut and held them closed.

The Intercessors formed a luminous circle around the new arrivals.

Hades advanced to the edge of the dais. He had scarcely raised his hands from his sides and cleared his throat....

"AHHHH! Tis Lucifer!"

"The Flames. The Flames!"

These were the last coherent words the Divine Incarnations heard for some time.

Hades grimaced and then, heaving a great sigh, he plugged his ears.

It took some time for the new arrivals to stop screaming...A LONG TIME.

It took them only a little while longer for them to stop gnashing their teeth and for the chorusing pleas for mercy to die down. By that time they had recited and invoked all sorts of punishments with such masochistic fervor that Hades stood absolutely appalled.

"Why would anyone want to shove hot coals down someone's throat?" Hades mumbled.

"Gracious," murmured Persephone over a sea of weeping souls.

Hecate arched her brow at Hades. "I wasn't kidding was I?"

Hades made a face that suggested disgust liberally mixed with pity and nausea. At last though he could say, as he always did, "If you see a light, go into it..."

An orientation of sorts was required. It took awhile to get through with this lot. They startled so easily or seemed lost still in their mortal anguish and oblivious to their new surroundings. More often than not Hades had to wait for each soul to quit shrieking, blubbering or pleading before he could explain himself and the Underworld to them.

"...So you are not about to impale me on your pitchfork and broil me over the pits of Hell?"

"I'm not a farmer. I don't own a pitchfork."

In all of his existence, Hades could and would never understand the mortal obsession with darkness and death. It made no sense to him. Mortals lived surrounded by beauty that they would recognize – if only they stopped and truly saw it. How could they shun beautiful Life to wallow in ecstasies of cruelty and ugliness of spirit? He said as much to Persephone time and again.

And she, his bright, most cherished beloved, would remind him that if they had shared his existence below, they would agree with him.

"It is as though they must have something to be afraid of or something to hate or they will not be content," she had added once.

This time around Persephone and Hecate both had to assist Hades in culling the truly selfish and fiercely unrepentant souls from the humbler ones. While Hel prodded the wretched ones ahead into the less pleasant depths for an extended visit in what Osiris referred to as the 'purification' realms, the Intercessors took charge of the rest, assimilating them into their contemplative flock.

From the usually shadowy passage arose a constant, but gentle beckoning light. Souls, newly arrived from abroad, flew directly into it as bright as white doves caught in the midday sun. Now and then an Intercessor stepped forth from or into the passage to collect a spirit or two from the great hall. They guided those spirits toward the Light.

Fortunately, there were lulls. More usually though Hades' shift ended and Osiris or Yamaraja or even Hel stood upon the dais. There was time to attend to other matters, like Samhain, Beltane, el Dia de los Muertos, Walpurgis Nacht, and Upir Likhyi.

Persephone made her usual jaunts up to usher in the spring in one hemisphere or the other, but things had changed.

People the world over honored the arrival of spring in various fashions. They performed their ceremonies and held festivities more out of custom or superstition than anything else.

In that temporal realm, nothing stayed. Nothing was meant to, but still...It saddened Persephone to stand before a ruined and utterly forgotten temple alone, but for the whispering breezes playing with her veil and Artemis' beloved wild things, those that had survived mankind. She strolled amid the fallen blocks of marble and granite, the weeds and the wildflowers, caressing the inscriptions as she passed them.

Demeter was no longer there to greet her. It had been a few human centuries since Demeter had been there at Eleusis to greet her. The Living no longer came to Eleusis to honor her nor did they invoke her for aid or for insight, so Demeter had spread herself across the Earth, becoming one with Great Mother Gaia.

In a sense, Demeter was there – everywhere. Persephone felt her spirit in the welcoming breezes and felt her strength in the ready earth. She took some comfort in that, that and in the birdsong surrounding that lonely place.

She sighed. "Where have you gone, Dionysus? Where has everyone gone?"

"The Bull-Horned One decamped to India," said Hermes as he stepped up beside her, "and there he remains. Bacchus is still lurking in the civilized places, but who wants to see him?"

Persephone smiled through her purple veil. "Hello, Hermes."

"Hello, my Lady. I didn't startle you, did I?"

"No, I was too melancholy I guess."

"Ah, yes." Hermes stood gazing at the desolation. "I know what you mean."

"It is always a little of a shock to come here anymore. You know. The Underworld is such a bustling hive and then to come up to this solitude."

"How long has it been since Demeter stopped materializing?"

"Three human centuries, I think. When the New Way finally made the Old Ways taboo or obsolete, she no longer saw the point. She remains, but I can only see evidence of her when there are crops rising in the fields or fruit ripening in the trees."

"Do you speak to her?"

"To her, yes, when I stroll through the fields and orchards, but she does not speak back to me. Sometimes I hear a ghost of her whisper among the leaves or in the breeze."

"I am sorry to hear that."

"Don't be. She knows that I no longer need her, so she is free to do what she must." Persephone smiled sadly and took Hermes' arm. "Walk with me."

"As you wish." Hermes removed his gleaming helmet and tucked it under his free arm. He scruffed up his brown mop of hair to a desirable degree of rakishness.

In the distance, the plowing had begun and the fields were being sown.

"So Dionysus is in India," she said. "Where is Artemis?"

"The Huntress keeps to the wilderness, alone, but for her beloved animals."

"What happened to her companions?"

"They're all dead. I would have thought you had noticed them when they flitted through your hall."

"I probably did at the time, but it was so very long ago. Time blurs. She must be so lonely."

"She has her animal companions to run wild with in the wildernesses of both hemispheres. She speaks of the Spirit Bear and Brother Wolf from time to time. She does pop up from time to time, you see. She doesn't say much though, never does, never did actually, but she abides on Olympus for a while. When she has had enough of Hera and Zeus or Ares and Aphrodite and their dramas, she disappears again. Usually, I've run into her when she was with her brother incarnation Apollo or sometimes with Leto."

"Artemis is rather enigmatic, when one thinks about it," mused Persephone aloud.

"When you look into her eyes, there has always been a wild quality to them, rather like the wolves she runs with: intelligent, perceptive, and unknowable. She isn't quite what she used to be, but we have all changed just as the civilized world changed."

"How have you changed?"

"I have become a little more serious. I am busier, but I feel as though no one cares whether I come or go. Hardly anyone in this realm," Hermes gestured toward the farmers, "bothers to pay me any mind. Sometimes I miss the attention, but as long as the Source allows me to continue I will linger between realms."

"We have all changed."

Hermes grunted and nodded. "Indeed, although some of us in subtle ways, others in greater ways, and some are stuck in their glory days." He gave her a wry grin.

"So how are things on Olympus?"

Hermes made a few noises of uncertainty and discomfort. "I wish I hadn't mentioned them. Some things must be seen to be believed. I can take you there for a little visit."

"I shall consider it. How are affairs between Ares and Aphrodite?"

"Some things belong in a continuum all of their own. That's the best way to describe those two and their persistent influences."

"So people still pay homage to them in sacred spaces?"

"Not exactly. It's more like their actions are their homage although they no longer invoke their power by name. Ares and Aphrodite are something of an exception." Hermes shrugged.

"In other words, they are 'Primordials'," said Persephone.

"I believe you have it."

"What about Eros and Psyche?"

"Similar and dissimilar simultaneously to Ares and Aphrodite. They have become paradoxes among our kind. They *are* and are *not*. They are neither here nor there and yet are everywhere. They move between the realms, which is a little disturbing, if you ask me I blame the Tantric meditations they started a few mortal centuries ago – their little gift to the world."

"Athena," said Persephone.

"For the time being she prefers to serve as a disembodied influence. She is at her wit's end with certain corners of this particular world and feels that becoming pure spirit is the best way to help."

"Poseidon?"

"Like your court, the court of Poseidon is a busy place. Humanity may have forgotten him, but has a realm to look after."

"So does he miss the tributes?"

"Not at all. In some ways, he is like Artemis in his devotion to his assigned sphere of influence. Like her, he has begun to feel that someone must look after the humbler lives in his domain, since humanity will not."

"Hephaestus?"

"He took his cue from Athena and serves as an influence to see what he can do. These are dire times among the Living."

"I noticed. And Apollo?"

"Although he acts like Eros and Psyche, transcending the spiritual realms, him I actually see more of than the rest. I see him almost as often as I see your Lord Hades."

"You're one of the Hunters then?"

"Apollo, Hecate, Hades and myself – we form regular hunting expeditions. We'll corner that pestilential vampyr yet."

"Hecate said that Upir Likhyi's accomplice had made a pact with him: his freedom if he swore to destroy Hades through me…somehow."

"Hecate has a gift for wringing the truth out of the wretched," said Hermes. "Even the worst of the worst dread her presence."

"Apparently, the accomplice was a Succubus who was once my Lord's concubine…"

"More than one member of that dark Sisterhood attended Hades in his bed – to be frank."

"Before or after?"

"Before and after."

Persephone stopped and fixed a direct look upon Hermes.

Hermes met her gaze without hesitation. "Remember that you do not love him."

"I find that I have become accustomed to him," she said after a moment's discomfort and careful deliberation over her words.

Briefly, Hermes smirked as he narrowed his eyes. "We all have our roles to play and duties to fulfill. You must return to the mortal realms to insure that cycle of life is maintained. From our perspective, your sojourns abroad seem like a mere day in duration. For your Consort, they are a nearly unbearable ordeal. Thanks to Eros, he suffers a great passion for you."

"That I know."

"That's hardly surprising."

"Stop being condescending and get to the point."

Hermes grinned appreciatively and resumed their stroll. "I see that you've changed too."

"I was changed a very long time ago by the will of the Fates."

"Not entirely. Trees don't need tending to grow, you know."

"Hermes."

"In your absence and before your time, Hades was lonely enough…"

"Weak enough, you mean."

"Lonely, isolated, weak – they're interconnected you must admit. Need is need."

Persephone glanced off toward the hills all vaguely purple and blue across the valley.

"Since you did not love him, I expect you tolerated his embraces. Even so the toxic influence of Eros drove him to seek comfort from those who had been more than willing to give him ease. Distasteful, yes, I know, but Zeus has done much worse."

Persephone turned a darkened glance toward him. "Hecate said that their pact involved getting me out of the way so they could destroy Hades. Should I be concerned?"

"Only if you yourself are corrupted and you are so thoroughly **of the Light** that it seems highly improbable. Upir Likhyi touches you at his own peril."

"But Zeus is corrupt..."

"Ah, but he is not evil, just an Egotist, which means that he is capable of doing both harm and good – for now at least."

"He strikes me as selfish."

Hermes nodded. "And self-involved too – that is the true sign of the Egotist. Frankly, there have been times when he could put Narcissus to shame in the self-adoration department."

"Which means that there is precious little affection to spare for Hera."

"Yes, poor dear. If anyone needed Eros to provide her with a consort in the manner you 'won' Hades, it is Hera. She desperately needs someone to love her with a becoming passion."

They strolled in silence for a time.

Unseen, they passed among a good many mortals going about their chores. In the meantime, Gaia turned slowly beneath the rays of the star Helios, their sun, and gradually warmed herself.

"Will Upir Likhyi come after me?" Persephone said at last.

"I'm not sure. It's likely that he feels no obligation to the Succubus who survived the escape and provided him with a corpse to possess. She is back in Tartarus, so he can do what he pleases without any sense of obligation." Hermes took a frowning, thoughtful breath, "Or he could simply be holding back on his promise until he needs a way to stop Hades from capturing him."

"Hades is frustrated that he hasn't been able to catch Upir Likhyi."

"We all are."

"If he does come after me in the end, what should I do?"

Hermes smiled at her. "Be steadfast. Remember that you are Queen of the Underworld."

Persephone took more comfort in that bit of advice than she thought she could.

They continued their stroll.

14.

The Delirious and the Dying saw the Strangers. They were the only ones who could. Some thought they had seen minions of Satan, but some thought they had seen angels passing in their plague-ridden midst casting careworn glances upon the suffering. Then there were others who saw only Hades clearly in his robes of eternal night, his stern face and startling silver white eyes, and knew they had seen Lucifer himself...or the Grim Reaper...or the Angel of the Death. He startled them.

Others who glimpsed all four Strangers in their close and heavy hooded cloaks and robes knew they had seen the 'Four Horsemen'. Never mind that there wasn't a horse anywhere nearby or that one of the strangers had a distinctly matronly figure – the four had to be the 'Four Horsemen of the Apocalypse'. Their surprise, when they passed over and discovered otherwise, was complete and rather loudly expressed.

Fortunately, Yamaraja and Osiris discovered that simply placing their fingers over their lips and 'shushing' worked wonders with the new arrivals. The new arrivals tended to fall silent a little more readily. At last, a fragile air of tranquility returned the great hall.

For his own reasons, unknown to Persephone, Hades had begun to venture into the Living realms almost immediately after her departures abroad. While she tended to the seasonal cycle she engendered, Hades tracked Upir Likhyi or tried to.

Waiting for him were the same triumvirate of Apollo, Hecate, and Hermes. This time though, Hermes left their meeting early, but promised to catch up later.

Apollo, Hecate, and Hades stood on a wind-blasted hill overlooking a small town. They could smell the rotting mortality already. Death hovered over the place like a fog and even from their polite remove, they could see and hear the dying and the ghostly population they would soon join.

"I think I know why we haven't been able to corner your escaped fiend yet," said Apollo. "Hermes and I put our heads together and pondered the matter over."

"Hecate and I have been conferring too," said Hades, "but speak first, Apollo. We may have come to the same conclusions."

"The reason why we have lost Upir Likhyi's scent is because he has been clever enough not to leave a trail of blood-drained corpses in his wake."

Hades nodded. "He captures..."

"Or seduces," said Hecate. "The corpse your concubine chose for him was a handsome young man in life. That makes it easier."

Hades continued, "And he feeds off his victims just enough to stave off starvation and then moves on to another victim."

"Precisely," said Apollo. "Our Upir is living a precariously parasitic existence. Unfortunately for him, although he is not leaving us a tract of corpses by which to track him down, he is leaving enough pestilence in his wake to show us where he has been."

Hades gazed off at the town. "And from which we may deduce his next destination."

Apollo made a sweeping gesture toward the town. "He has been here and I think he may still be here. This burg has the air of infestation about it."

Hades adjusted his grip on his scythe. "Let us go and have a look."

Apollo adjusted his maroon cloak and led the way.

As the trio passed amongst the few Living, who moved about with cloths covering their noses and mouths as though they possessed a magic that could ward off this pestilence when they could not even keep away the stench, their strange eyes glanced upon the mortals with looks full of dispassionate compassion.

Now and then they passed within view of a mortal gifted with special sight. Invariably, the man or woman would stop and sometimes even drop what they held as they stared with an astonishment that weariness could not quite extinguish. Out of the gloom of that terrible hour three personages passed led by one bearing the soft radiance of an angel and eyes that pierced the soul.

By then the Hunters had learned what to do if they were actually seen, they made a simple gesture of benediction that such individuals understood and accepted in meek silence. That usually did the trick. The Living made some kind of reciprocal gesture and almost always knelt on the spot to pray. It didn't hurt. Rather, it helped, but more importantly for the Hunters, they avoided inflicting any further trauma on beings already overwhelmed by their worst nightmare – *the end of everything they had known and held dear.*

The Dead and Dying were everywhere. It was a familiar site which they had begun to hate, something which also quietly surprised them whenever they reflected upon the situation later.

Apollo Paeon, surefooted in his certainty, led the way directly to the church on the hillside overlooking the town. At the gate to the churchyard, he stopped to survey their surroundings. "Whence this gloom?"

Hades and Hecate gazed out upon the world with him.

"It is scarcely midday," said Hecate, "and yet the gloom increases as though it had twilight gathering behind it."

"It rises thick from the valley to oppress the Living," said Apollo," even as it creeps down through the forest from the ever-winter mountain tops. This place is shrouded in it."

"Shrouded is correct," said Hades. "Your instincts are correct, Pajawone. Upir is here."

"Even the birds are silent. He has grown potent," said Hecate as she watched the fog-like atmosphere descend upon the church. This is sacred ground and here he has chosen to hide – the brazen monster."

Hades stepped into the churchyard. "May we do what we were empowered to do."

"Aidoneus Hades," said Apollo, "we must be careful all the same. Upir Likhyi may yet do us some injury or injure an innocent to thwart our assault."

"I smell nothing alive here but the moss spreading on these gravestones," said Hades. "The church door stands ajar. This place is deserted. Whether because of the plague or our miscreant we shall discover." Hades scanned the churchyard for traces of disturbance among the graves.

"Where does one start?" said Hecate.

Hades sighed. "So many fresh graves."

"There's a mass grave over on this side. Look at the size of that mound," said Hecate.

"I shall check this side," said Hades. "You go around that side and we will meet around the back."

Hecate adjusted her grip on her staff and set forth into the heart of the southern graveyard.

Apollo stepped directly across the church threshold and peered with luminous eyes into its sacred darkness.

To his far left Hades paced soundlessly looking this way and that among the graves. Now and then he paused, tilted his ear toward one of the graves and stabbed his scythe into its earth, saying from above, "Arise."

Sometimes like mist, sometimes resembling a curling trail of smoke, a ghost would arise, bewildered, beseeching, or recalcitrant. With a short, smooth gesture of his free hand, Hades swept them off to the Underworld.

Over on her side of the graveyard, Hecate harvested a similar crop of ghosts, who could not or would not leave that plane of existence. She made a similar abrupt sweeping gesture that sped them into Osiris or Yamaraja's stoic presence. Then she resumed her patrol, stabbing at the fresh graves with her staff.

From the church's threshold, Apollo's eyes and ears strained the stillness and the darkness for any movement not of the Living.

A rat scurried out across the aisle.

Apollo's gaze locked upon it.

The animal froze and trembled.

"Just a rat," Apollo muttered, lifting his fierce gaze.

The rat fled past him. It would rather take its chances in the open churchyard than linger in the presence of the Lord of Plagues.

Apollo straightened. His gaze intensified. "Ah," he said. "I feel you – even in the darkness. Foul defilement you are. There is no tomb…no bottomless shaft into the Earth that Lord Hades cannot reach."

There upon that threshold sun-blessed Phoebus Apollo stood sentry radiating dire intent. In the crypts below the bone-achingly cold flagstones, their prey crouched and cursed bitterly beneath its rasping breath.

Beyond the stout little church, Hecate found Hades immersed in a low swooping cloud leaning upon his scythe and gazing with his white eyes into the forest.

"He's here someplace," Hecate said. "I can smell him." She wrinkled her nose at the church. "One of the disadvantages of being us: heightened senses." She waved her hand before her nose.

Hades cast a shadowy smile over his shoulder though. "There are also advantages. The forest still smells of spring and rain." He closed his eyes and simply breathed for a moment. "I had forgotten how wonderful trees smell."

"No wonder Artemis has chosen to live in the wildernesses anymore," said Hecate. "Perhaps when this is over I shall lose myself for a time in the woods. 'Perhaps find a little dwelling deep in the forest and reside there."

With a look almost of melancholy, Hades turned away from the evergreen covered slope.

When they returned to the front, they found Apollo standing quite still and quite alert in the doorway.

"The fiend left traces all over these hallowed grounds," said Hecate, "but he has hidden in here."

Apollo nodded once. His stare remained fixed ahead on the space above the crypts. It was as though his very gaze pinned their prey into a corner and if he risked a look away or even blinked, Upir Likhyi would slip free. "What is the strategy?" he said in a calm and very low voice.

"One of us goes in," said Hades, "and either dispatches the monster where he lurks or flushes him out where the other two deal with him."

"Bear in mind," said Apollo, "he knows we are here."

"Expect a fight then." Hades nodded.

Hecate stared into the darkness, her bottom lip jutted out in concentration. "Right! Hades, drive him forth. Apollo, block his escape in your inimitable manner. Then you slice off its corpse head, Hades, and I will catch its nasty little soul by the neck when the blow shocks it loose."

"I'm game," said Apollo.

"You two, stand ready. I will be back shortly." With a toss of his cloak back across both of his shoulders, Hades strode directly into the crypts.

In the crypts, the darkness trembled as it swirled about Hades. It flowed everywhere about him, washing over the crypts and tombs, pooling in the narrow catacombs. There was nothing inert about it. There never had been. Hades stood absolutely still until the darkness calmed again.

He wrinkled his nose. The stench of a vampyr was something beyond the stench natural rot. It had a special sour, festering quality, ripe with the odor – or aroma, depending on one's perspective or appetite – of fresh blood. It lingered in the nostrils to such a nauseating extent that it left a nasty taste on the tongue.

Hades grumbled. "I should have invoked Kali to come on this raid."

A foot scuffed the ground and then its owner attempted to stay absolutely still.

"You cannot hide from me," Hades declared. "I can sense you. I can smell you." Calm in his deliberation, grave and stern in his eternal purpose, he faced the correct direction and fixed his terrible bright white eyes upon a particular alcove.

Inhuman shrieks of dismay erupted from the darkness.

Shrieks.

"There is more than one," said Hades. A frown settled upon his brow.

"I heard that," said Apollo.

"Trouble," said Hecate. She heaved a great breath. "We can handle this."

"As though we have a choice in the matter," said Apollo, bracing himself.

High-pitched, human-formed, yet scarcely coherent screams echoed from beneath the church in as way that no mortal sound could carry. From Hades no sound came at all as the sounds traveled from one end of the catacombs to the other.

"Perhaps we should go down," said Apollo. "Hades is being mobbed."

The Luminous One took one step forward.

Not four paces ahead the violence below slammed against the flagstones. Dust flew up into the air, followed scarcely two rushed heartbeats later by several of the stones.

Propelled by divine might and determination, Hades burst out into the open. Caught in the vortex of a swarm of Upir Likhyi's vampyr concubines, Hades kept his grip upon the throat of their foul queen with one hand as he swept at the rest with his scythe. He resembled a dervish in his swinging black robes trapped in the heart of a nightmarish whirlwind.

Clad in their gauzy burial robes, their winding sheets flying in tatters behind them, the vampyr harem rushed about Hades tearing at his robes and sleeves when they weren't ducking his wind-milling scythe.

Already their clawing fingers had drawn Olympian blood from his hands and forearms and from several smaller cuts on Hades' face and neck. The smell of his potent divine blood drove them mad with hunger. Twice their queen had managed to twist about in his grip so she could sink her teeth into his hand and wrist. Her horrible blood-black eyes rolled over white as she sucked and slurped on the punctures. Her vampyr sisters shrieked and moaned simultaneously – in anger at Hades the tormentor and in bloodlust for their share of his essence.

Each time it had taken Hades three ferocious blows of their queen against the stone pillars and walls before he could interrupt her feeding. She wailed less from the pain of having her skull smashed finally against the flagstones than from having her feast interrupted. She clawed at his wounds and crammed her bloody fingers into her red mouth to suck the blood from them.

Over dinner Poseidon had once described the sharks' feeding frenzy to Hades. In the depths of the catacombs, Hades realized that he was caught up in one and forced an exit through the church's own floor, just as the queen and one of her sisters bit into his hand and forearm simultaneously.

Hades hissed at the pain and tightened his slippery grip on the queen's neck. She growled and bit again – harder. His grip relaxed just long enough for her to seize a firmer hold on his hand and sink her teeth deep into his wrist. Blood spurted. The queen made a sound of wild delight and guzzled blood that overran her lips and dripped easily down his arm onto the floor.

120

In that moment another vampyr bit into his other wrist. Hades winced and, scowling, lopped off her head with a deft move of his scythe. One of her sisters seized his wrist in her stead before her corpse head hit the floor. Her eyes rolling back, she locked her mouth on the wound and drank.

There were two left who growled in frustration that they had not had a taste of Olympian blood yet. One of them flew to lap up the blood that ran down Hades right arm. The last took advantage of Hades' momentary dismay to lean over his shoulder and sink her teeth into his powerful, straining neck.

Hades grimaced and growled in a voice that only Osiris could have comprehended. The force of their onslaught caused him to waver and fall backwards.

The vampyr women rushed over him, settling down to feed on his blood, content to drink from their Source for all eternity if they could keep him captive.

None of them realized their mistake until the church lit up with the force of divine retribution. When she felt her corpse skin begin to sizzle, their queen dared to look up.

Apollo reduced her to a pile of ash with a solitary touch of his warm finger.

Hecate caught the queen's startled spirit in her fist and shoved it into the sack she carried from about her waist.

Apollo's glancing slap obliterated another vampyr's rotten shell and Hecate harvested another damned soul.

Hades pried the vampyr from about his neck with his blood-stained hands and held her out to Hecate by her long tangled hair. Hecate reached into the corpse and yanked out its befouled soul for her sack. Hades let the quieted body fall.

To their eternal damnation, the last two clung to Hades too busy feasting upon his delicious blood to realize that he had picked up his scythe. In moments two more defiled mortal heads rolled upon the ground and Hecate was tying her squirming sack shut with a stern frown on her face.

"You look a fright, Hades, and I should know," said Hecate.

Apollo looked horrified. "Let me tend to your wounds."

"Upir Likhyi is not here," was all Hades said.

15.

Hermes left Persephone's side without warning. A sudden autumnal gust had passed over them and for a moment it was as though as shadow passed over the Earth. Something dire had happened. Pivoting north, Hermes donned his winged helmet and shot away toward the horizon.

Troubled, she remained for a time where he had left her. Her mind wandered instead far into the past – to day Hades stole her from the meadow, but also to the day she returned to the meadow to meet Dionysus in the sacred circle, and then to the night under the full moon where Hades awakened her. Turbulence filled her heart. Such is the nature of longing.

Persephone turned eastward. There was One whom she knew from days long past and whom she needed to see.

Hermes prepared everything at Olympus, where he waited with Asclepius upon the shining marble steps. Their wait seemed long.

A gust of stormy northern wind heralded their arrival even as a shadow as dense as a thunderhead delivered Hecate, Hades, and Apollo, who supported Hades to Olympus. The aroma of fresh blood washed over Hermes and Asclepius, whose concerned expression intensified.

Hera rushed forth from the heart of the Olympian palace to the top of the steps above them. She pressed her scented veil to her nose.

Everywhere Hades shifted he left bloody footprints smeared upon the pure marble. His black raiments had taken on a deep ruddy hue.

A dire shade of brownish red stained Golden Apollo's splendid body and fine raiments. If it was not so obvious that Hades was leaning upon Apollo, Asclepius and Hera would have thought Apollo the injured one.

"Quickly," said Asclepius, "we must lay him down."

"Bring him to my chamber," called Hera.

"No, take him into your pantheon," called someone from the gates of Olympus.

Apollo glanced over his shoulder. "Dhanvantari! You came!"

"By the power of Vishnu and the wishes of Yamaraja and Osiris, I have come with Vrinda Devi," said Dhanvantari with a nod to his right.

Lovely Vrinda Devi nodded in greeting, her eyes fixed on their injured brother incarnation Hades.

"But Persephone," muttered Hades, stirring against Apollo's shoulder. "Has she come?"

"I have brought the ambrosia," said Dhanvantari. "We must take him into the high temple." He handed the golden container to Vrinda Devi, who clasped it snug to her bosom. "Asclepius. Hermes. Lift his legs. I shall help Apollo support his shoulders. He will heal only in the temple in the embrace of the Source."

Hermes and Asclepius lifted Hades' feet from the ground even as Dhanvantari and Apollo managed his upper torso. They moved swiftly up the side steps to the High Pantheon of Olympus, a still and meditative place that opened its own tall golden doors to receive them.

Vrinda Devi trod lightly in their shadow.

The temple doors closed after them as soon as Vrinda Devi had entered at the last. Hecate and Hera lingered on the steps.

Hecate sighed. "It is in the hands of the Almighty now. We are but manifestations of Divine Will and exist or disperse by the will of Destiny," she said toward the high altar and the holy of holies beyond it. Then she regarded Hera staring at the bloodstains on the steps. "Oh dear, it is quite a mess, isn't it?"

Hera looked up at Hecate. Her expression was an unquiet one. Then she saw the struggling motions inside Hecate's sack. "What do you have there, Queen of Ghosts?"

Hecate untied the sack from her obsidian beaded girdle and held it up. "These are the bitches that wounded our steadfast Hades."

"I don't understand."

"Vampyres, a nasty surprise left for Hades by Upir Likhyi. We thought we had cornered that nasty piece of work himself. Instead, we uncovered a nest of his progeny. If Apollo had not been there, they would have kept him captive and drank him dry or till the end of the Earth itself, whichever came first. I think Hades would have preferred spending an eternity at the heart of the maelstrom in Tartarus than enduring a mortal eternity whilst a coven of vampyres glutted themselves on his divine essence."

"How horrible." Hera glanced toward the temple doors.

The smell of burning sage began to trail forth from the temple.

"What shall you do with those monstrous entities?" Hera eyed the restless sack.

"They were humble mortal souls before our villain worked his malignant necromancy upon them. There may be hope of redemption for them yet." Hecate eyed the plume of white smoke ascending from the temple roof. "I shall return once I have conferred with my compatriots in the Underworld."

"Be careful."

Hecate laughed at that and turned away.

Within the pantheon, Hades lay upon the simple marble altar. His bleary gaze remained fixed upon the round opening in the temple dome where light poured into their cool space from a perfect blue sky. "Where is Persephone? Where is she?" he murmured.

Apollo frowned into Hades' face. "We shall find her, Aidoneus."

Hades looked past his radiant head toward the heavenly blue circle. "Why has she not come?"

"He is delirious," said Apollo.

"So would you be if a swarm of Vampyres siphoned off so much of your divine essence," said Asclepius as he adjusted his sleeves well above his elbows.

Dhanvantari set his great jar of ambrosia upon a side altar and made similar preparations.

Vrinda Devi started a small fire before the altar and fed it with special incense. Murmuring mantras, she collected water from the temple's sacred font into basins made of fired red clay.

"Remove his raiments and burn them," said Dhanvantari, "for they have been stained with divine blood. They must be rendered back to the Source of our Being as an offering and sacrifice from Hades."

"Indeed," said Asclepius as he placed a sponge in one of the basins, "I fear that only the Will of our Creator can determine whether Hades remains among us in this realm or returns to the heart of the universe."

Apollo and Hermes exchanged looks over Hades' red-stained body as they removed his clothing in careful layers. Still murmuring mantras, Vrinda Devi stood beside the altar holding a great basket. Into her basket they piled his hooded cloak, his belt, and his black tunic robe.

Vrinda Devi watched Apollo peel away the blood-soaked garments which Hermes first cut open straight down the middle. At last Hermes and Apollo cut and peeled away their friend's under-tunic, but only after grappling with a moment's apprehension. The under-tunic was supposed to be white. It used to be. Instead, it was stained thoroughly a dark, malodorous red.

Asclepius and Dhanvantari drew closer to observe this last uncovering.

"He still bleeds," gasped Vrinda Devi as Apollo's wet red hands slapped the under-tunic atop the pile.

Hermes stepped back, silent and somber…and quietly horrified by the blood that had dripped onto his toes.

"Burn his blood-blessed garments," said Dhanvantari. "Make haste."

Vrinda Devi rushed down from the altar's dais to the fire and fed Hades' clothes to the sacred flames. The fire grew broad and high and smoke curled upward encircling the ceiling and filling the dome before flying upward toward the heavens. When she had dropped his ruined cloak upon the flames, she noticed the blood pooled in her basket. She surrendered the basket to the flames at once.

When Vrinda Devi returned to the altar, Hermes and Apollo were helping Dhanvantari and Asclepius to wash Hades' body. They pressed the damp sponges to his skin and wiped away the blood with long, soothing strokes.

"There," said Asclepius, "we have uncovered the punctures. Now, Vrinda Devi, bring the cup of ambrosia."

She retrieved a small gilded alabaster cup filled almost to the brim with fragrant ambrosia. She knew what to do. Dipping her fingertips into the ambrosia, she then pressed them upon Hades' raw punctures and then smoothed more of it all around the bites. As she moved from wound to wound, Hades grew quieter and calmer.

By the time she had treated the last wound only a little polluted amount remained in her cup. She stepped back as Asclepius and Dhanvantari inspected Hades' wounds.

"The bleeding has stopped and the wounds are closing up." Asclepius wiped his brow and smiled briefly.

"Now, Vrinda Devi," said Dhanvantari, "refresh the cup and give it to our friend to drink."

She did so and returned.

Apollo lifted Hades with great care and supported him as Vrinda Devi gently urged drops of pure ambrosia past Hades' lips. His eyes opened, but slightly. "Where is my Bright One?"

"Drink now so you may receive her in good health," said Vrinda Devi.

Hades drank the rest of the ambrosia, sighed, and closed his eyes.

"He will and must rest now," said Asclepius. "We must keep him quiet and let none disturb him until he awakens."

"What of his Consort?" she said. "Hades asked for her."

"If she wishes to keep vigil at his bedside, she may, but the outcome is out of our influence now. Either he shall continue with us or he will return to the Source of us all," said Asclepius. "If one of you will offer the bloodied water and the sponges to the sacred flame, I shall keep the first vigil."

"Vrinda Devi and I shall tend the sacred flame," said Dhanvantari.

Asclepius glanced over his shoulder. "Then the duty falls to you, divine Father, and to you, Divine Messenger, to inform the rest of our kind so they may organize accordingly."

"Very well," said Apollo as he exchanged bows with the Divine Healers. "I shall seek out Persephone. She must be told."

"I shall go to Osiris and Yamaraja," said Hermes. "This concerns the balance of the Underworld."

As Apollo and Hermes left through the already open temple doors, Vrinda Devi placed a silk pillow beneath Hades' damp head and then spread a silk and wool coverlet over his naked body. Both were the color of his heavenly sky.

Hermes arrived in the Underworld to find a conference already underway upon the dais. Moving carefully through the agitated pool of souls, he approached the dais and exchanged nods with the attentive Intercessors as they shepherded the restless souls.

Osiris stood at the forefront, his impassive face turned upon the souls and the Intercessor spirits. Behind him crowded the rest: Nepthys, Anubis, Hel, Hecate, Yamaraja, and that many more incarnations from cultures from everywhere, including ones lost to time, all of them Divine Incarnations, all of them caretakers of the mortal dead, and all of them acquainted with Hermes.

One presence though he did not know quite so well. Fierce in aspect, stern in expression, her powerful arms were folded over her chain necklace made of skulls, Kali Ma stood between Hecate and Yamaraja on the edge of the throng. She was associated with mortality, but her dominion lay over fields of death, funeral pyres, and charnel houses in the mortal realms. Her quick, gleaming eyes looked his way.

Hermes inclined his head. "Kali Ma, destroyer of demons, your legends precede your mighty presence."

"Quicksilver Hermes, runner between the realms, it is well to see you too," Kali Ma said in a throaty voice.

"What brings you to the Underworld?"

"Durga called me forth to take up the reaping scythe of Hades and continue the hunt in his stead." Her voice reverberated throughout the Underworld, driving the unrepentant souls into the furthest corners to hide. "How was our noble brother Aidoneus Zagreus when you left him?"

"Resting. He is being tended to by Asclepius, Dhanvantari, and Vrinda Devi."

"Nepthys leaned out of the meeting. "Osiris and Isis have summoned forth Immutef to attend to Hades. He has a gift for healing."

Hermes nodded. "I should have been there."

"Unless you had gone down into those catacombs with Hades, you would not have been able to prevent this any more than we could," said Hecate. "We thought there was only one. We were wrong."

"But surely…"

"Lad, they were ripping into him when he burst out of the floor. It was a feeding frenzy before we realized it."

Hermes sighed. "Hades kept asking for Persephone."

"I know. I hope Apollo locates her. It would do the old boy good to simply have her at his side, even better if she was there when he awakened."

Yamaraja stepped back from the assembly, his hands upraised. "There, it is decided. Kali Ma shall lead the hunt for the malevolence known as Upir Likhyi. Medusa shall be summoned and tamed for our purpose. Send to Athena for the head of Medusa. Send to Isis, for her body must be restored to receive her head. When Medusa rises from the clay, the hunt shall resume."

16.

Apollo found Persephone gazing out over the Ganges, its reflected sunlight glowing in her distracted gaze. Her expression was dreamy and there was a soft, sensual curve to her lips.

"Dionysus?" she said, turning her head.

The brightness of her smile, the eager light in her eyes caused Apollo to wince.

"Oh! I'm sorry. I thought you were my friend." She blushed as she shot glances beyond Apollo.

He could not help the stern tone that came into his voice nor the severity in his gaze. "Your regret is sincere enough, one suspects. You were expecting the Bull-Horned One to join you here?"

"We have entered dark times. I sent to him for I needed his counsel. He is indeed my friend. We have a special bond."

"The last I heard Dionysus was with Krishna among the Gopis. Not even Zeus has been able to stir him from this land. It is unlikely that he will interrupt his idyll among the lovely cow herders to fan the flames of your desire."

"Truly it was not from lust or love that I came here. I was melancholy for everything that has passed from this realm. I had been talking with Hermes, but then he left so abruptly. I could not bear the sight of another abandoned temple so I came to this place where Life still resounds from the temples. Your expression is so forbidding and yet I have done nothing wrong."

"Your heart knows what it would do and it you cannot escape, but I came not to aggravate you."

"Then what did you come for?" she said, cool and curt.

"Upir Likhyi left a trap for Hades and he was badly injured." It relieved Apollo to see Persephone's eyes go wide and her hand fly to her mouth. "He has been asking for you ever since. I came to bring you to his side for he needs comfort."

"Then I should go."

Apollo offered her his arm.

Persephone accepted his arm. Her brow remained furrowed, her gaze touching the dusty path before them. "Do you miss the old days?"

Apollo gazed off after the western sun. "You went to Eleusis."

She nodded. "It is so still there now, that is, what is left of it. Do you ever return to Delphi?"

"From time to time," he gave her a quiet little smile, "but only when I am melancholy."

Persephone smiled sadly back.

"I find," he added, "that I am just as busy now, perhaps even busier, than I was then. There are ever more people upon this Earth, ever more concerns. It takes all of my will not to have to diffuse my energy across the world as Athena has felt compelled to do. But then, these are, as you said, dark times, and greatly in need of the light of wisdom, so she does what she must."

"As do we all," said Persephone as Apollo placed his other arm about her. "Where are we going?"

"To the High Pantheon of Olympus."

"Not to the Underworld?" She placed her other hand upon his shoulder.

"The Underworld is an unquiet place and Hades needs a more tranquil atmosphere."

"Ah."

"Ready?"

"Yes."

"We're off then." Apollo sprung into the air, carrying Persephone with him.

There was a sudden glint of a sunbeam and they vanished – to the astonishment of several children playing nearby.

Apollo and Persephone alighted upon temple steps bathed in a golden sunset.

After being surrounded by all the little sounds of abundance belonging to the humble Earth, Persephone hesitated in the sudden stillness. Zeus did not mind a brisk, refreshing breeze, but upon Olympus the fiercer winds were forbidden from blowing. Ganymede, the beautiful youth, stood alone upon the palace steps. As shy as a deer, he slipped back into Zeus' domain.

Persephone gazed after him. How old had he been in mortal years when Zeus claimed him for his obedient cupbearer? How long did his mother grieve for the loss of her beautiful boy? How long did his proud father search for his precious son before his heart broke utterly? Did Ganymede have even one friend upon Olympus? Or did he spend his eternal exile from humanity serving his doting and possessive captor and trying to stay clear of Hera's jealous streak.

"Does Ganymede have any friends at all?" she said loudly for his benefit.

Apollo mused a moment. "Well, I know that Hermes and Heracles have made a point of showing him little courtesies and kindnesses when they encounter him on his own. I offered to teach the lad music, but Zeus decided against that: jealousy. Athena used to let him accompany her on her strolls and my sister Artemis took him hunting once in a while. Generally, you could say that everyone pities him whenever they catch a glimpse of him. Well, not quite everyone. Zeus regrets nothing, or if he does, it isn't for very long. Hera borrows him for her errands and for special chores, so she tolerates him sometimes."

"And yet she doesn't tolerate his other conquests."

"She tolerates Ganymede because if Zeus is busy enjoying his handsome cupbearer then he won't be off with some mortal woman. Hera doesn't consider Ganymede as much more than Zeus' pet and plaything."

"How does Ganymede feel about his circumstances? Surely, being snatched from his normal life to live at the beck and call of Zeus must have been terrifying." When Apollo's silence lingered, Persephone looked into his solemn face. "How bad was it?"

"How bad was it for you?"

Persephone's gaze returned to the palace. She could just see the youth peering out of the shadowy entrance at them. "It was devastating beyond all words. I wept. I prayed. I hoped. I despaired. Everything changed and there was no escaping it all."

"Ganymede wept too – when he thought no one could hear him. Your Mother was able to get you back. She came all the way here to get you. No one came for Ganymede."

"Does he love Zeus?"

"If he has any affection for him, it is because he must. There is no escape for him. As long as he pleases Zeus, Zeus does not care whether Ganymede's affection arises from a sincere place or has been grafted onto his nature by habit and necessity. I know that he still lives in awe and straight forward fear of us, so I believe that he chooses also to content Zeus so that Zeus will protect him."

"Take me to Hades. I cannot bear any further cruelty."

As they ascended, the high golden doors eased silently open. By the time they reached the temple landing, the doors stood wide open to the night gathering in the north. Incense insinuated itself past the threshold to perfume the Olympian air. Within the incense swirled the sounds of a sitar, a tabla, and other instruments, playing a melody that bathed one's soul in the purest tranquility.

"Ah," said Apollo with a pleased look at Persephone, "the reinforcements have arrived." He strode in, his maroon robes and saffron chlamys flying in his wake.

Persephone trod in, slower in her uncertainty as her sight adjusted to the warmth of the meditative shadows.

The only light lay at the far end. It came from the four lamps placed in the four directions surrounding the high altar and from the small sacred fire on the dais before that altar. A shadow-like curtain hung over the altar and surrounded it, a slender translucent barrier between the altar and the rest of the temple. Persephone could only just make out a shadowy form inside the improvised tent – a figure lying prone and utterly still.

Aidoneus Zagreus, Lord Hades.

Persephone stopped and stared. Suddenly she wanted to leave. She turned away only to see the temple doors closing. It took her a moment to face the altar again.

Apollo was settling amongst the musicians. Saraswati was there holding her sitar. Dionysus held the tabla and seemed halfway into a trance already. The muses Erato with her lyre and Euterpe with her flute were there. Hermes held the Pythagorean scrolls bearing the music their crisis required. Since Erato played her lyre, Apollo took up one of the instruments Saraswati had brought and joined in.

As surprised as she was to find Dionysus there, Persephone stood awed and enthralled by the whole scene. Immutef worked beside the sacred fire concocting a fluid for Hades to drink. Vrinda Devi and Dhanvantari fed special ingredients to the sacred flame and wafted the incense toward their patient. Asclepius handed ingredients to Immutef as he needed them. Other than the music encircling their divine patient, all was silence or so it seemed to Persephone.

The closer she came, the better she could hear the mantras Vrinda Devi and Dhanvantari were uttering, lowly and steadily as they worked.

Her face as luminous as the cloud-veiled moon, Persephone emerged from the temple darkness into the amber light surrounding the altar.

Immutef glanced up at her. "Ah, the Consort is among us. The elixir is ready. Let her administer it to the noble Aidoneus Zagreus." He spoke in an ancient, accented voice that brooked no refusals.

"Of course," she said.

Giving the elixir one last flourish of a stir, Immutef poured some into the spouted alabaster cup Asclepius held. This cup Apollo's sainted son placed in Persephone's hands.

As Persephone turned toward the altar, Vrinda Devi drew aside the thin curtain. Asclepius stepped into the tent and with great care raised Hades' head and bare shoulders, cradling him against his chest and shoulder.

"He must drink all of the elixir," said Immutef, "if he is to begin to recover his strength."

"I understand." Persephone stepped into the tent. She laid her left hand against her Consort's cheek.

Hades stirred and groaned. A frown surfaced on his unconscious brow.

"Speak to him," said Immutef. "It will draw him out of his nightmares."

"I am here, my Lord," Persephone whispered close to his face. "Drink this and be well."

Although his eyes remained closed, Hades turned his face toward his wife ever so slightly. His lips parted, but to whisper her name not to drink, for such was the lingering power of Eros' golden arrow.

"Give him a sip, my Lady," said Asclepius. "We took care to sweeten it with ambrosia and honey from the meadows of Elysium."

Persephone poured a little between his lips. For a moment it pooled over his teeth then enough of it seeped onto his tongue and he swallowed willingly. Sip by sip, Persephone poured it all down his throat. When at last it was empty, Asclepius laid Hades down and took back the cup.

"We should cover him up again," said Vrinda Devi as she lifted the embroidered edge of the blue coverlet from his waist. "His garments were utterly ruined with his own blood. We had to surrender them to the sacred flame."

Persephone accepted the coverlet from her, but hesitated. Although the punctures had closed, angry red marks remained surrounded by blackish purple bruises. She wondered if he would carry these scars too the way he still bore the fierce mark of Eros upon his chest. For a moment, she wanted to press her hand upon his heart's scar and then give it her most tender kiss.

Instead, she drew the coverlet up to his neck. "He is hardly there."

"He lingers yet," said Dhanvantari.

"Take his hand," said Vrinda Devi.

"Will he even feel it?" she said.

"He will feel your essence when it flows into him and that is what he needs," Vrinda Devi said.

So Persephone reached under the coverlet and closed her hand around his and left it there. Making a slight sound, Hades turned his face directly toward her, sighed and sank into an even deeper rest.

For several moments her heart had run wild at the prospect of being liberated from her incarnate union with Hades. Gazing at his becalmed, strong-featured face, she discovered herself grappling with mixed emotions.

Persephone's simple contentment had been more fragile than she realized.

17.

Athena was the last to arrive in the Underworld. A strange, excited silence greeted her. Even the souls pooled in the great hall seemed to be holding their collective breath as the Intercessor spirits staked out positions throughout the vast chamber and bowed their heads ever so slightly as mantras murmured past their lips.

Upon the dais stood the body of a strong, voluptuous woman reconstituted from red African earth, reincarnated from collective memory. Sacred symbols covered her earthen body in colors of ochre and crushed lapis lazuli. Kali and Isis stood before their recreation, examining it thoroughly. Wooden bowls containing pigments sat in a row before the clay woman as though they were offerings. Nepthys led the others in the burning of incense around the life-sized figure.

Athena had dispersed herself throughout the beleaguered world from the isle that had provided her an entrance into it in the beginning: Crete. Heeding the summons of Osiris and Isis, Athena distilled herself back into a recognizable form upon her cherished Cretan soil, took one look at the changing mortal world, and disappeared beyond its boundaries.

Shimmering, resplendent, Athena materialized upon the threshold of the Underworld. Her presence sent a ripple through the Underworld.

"The Patroness of Holy Wisdom has come," said Anubis.

Athena stayed where she was. She surveyed the assembly. When she saw the headless figure standing upon the dais, a frown glanced across her brow. "Are you certain you can bend her toward your purpose?"

"I think Medusa can be persuaded," said Kali.

"Very well, since **you** think Medusa shall prove malleable, I shall not deny you. Here, take my aegis and with it its embedded trophy – the head you require." Removing her aegis with ease, Athena held it out in both hands.

Hermes came forward to retrieve it.

"If I am needed," said Athena, "send to Olympus for me. I intend to visit Hades."

"If he awakens," said Hermes, "tell him that Kali has taken up his mantle and that Osiris and Yamaraja brought back Medusa to join the hunt."

"I shall do that. Where shall you be?"

"Running between the realms and between Kali and Osiris for the duration of the hunt."

"Take care then."

"Believe me, after what happened to Hades, I intend to take great care." Hermes turned away with the aegis held out at arm's length.

Athena did not wait to see the resurrected Medusa, but pivoted and vanished to the higher realms.

"Hold up the aegis to me," Isis said.

Hermes did as commanded.

"Ah, there you are, tormented and beguiled one," said Isis. She removed Medusa's head from the aegis. It transformed in her gentle hands from monstrous decrepitude back into refulgent beauty, possessed of high cheeks, full lips, even sensual features, and long glossy black braids arranged in elaborate coils about her head.

For a taste of her sweet lips and the delights her body would provide, Poseidon had come to land. It was Medusa's great misfortune that Poseidon found her in Athena's temple and not Aphrodite's. She had paid for his lust and her weakness twice over. Furious at the desecration of her sanctuary, Athena first turned the mortal beauty into an immortal monster of bodily corruption. Then she dispatched a mortal hero to cut her fearsome head off for his own purpose. Naturally, the grateful young man offered his deadly and dreadful trophy to his divine advisor at the conclusion of his adventure. Eventually her ruined body had rotted away, returning to Gaia, while her sad head decorated Athena's aegis.

No longer.

Cooing spells and blessings, smiling Isis placed the head atop the clay body and smoothed it into place atop the neck. With each strong, patient stroke of her perfumed and blue-stained hands, Isis pressed more of Life's energy into Medusa. The clay figure warmed and its surface softened.

Isis laid her hand over Medusa's breast and pressed once and deeply. Her heart fluttered to life, as though panicked, and then settled into a strong steady rhythm. A great gasp escaped her lips and then she breathed in deep and then out again. Beneath her eyelids, her eyes moved. Her hair coiled and uncoiled - alive.

At once Kali bound her coils about her head with blue silk.

Medusa gasped as though emerging from deep waters into crisp cold air. Her eyes flew open. Wild with panic she looked around. Her hands flew up to ward off the memory of **him** who claimed her head.

Isis caught her blue-marked hands with her blue-stained ones. "Shh…shhh." She held her hands firmly, but gently. "All is well again. All is well."

"It has been too long since you have been among us, my sister incarnation," said Kali.

"It was terrible," Medusa breathed.

"It is over," said Yamaraja. "A new eon arises around you. Your unique strength and sorcery is needed."

"I was rendered monstrous and then exiled," said the snake-tressed one with the fierce gaze. "I am still a monster in the eyes of many."

Isis held up an obsidian mirror.

Instinctively, she shielded her face and averted it from what she could not hear. "No!"

With gentle insistence, Kali pried her hands and away from her face. "Look, sister. You will be surprised I think. Look."

Isis smiled softly and held the mirror level to her face. "I know you are brave enough to confront a mirror."

Medusa turned her face toward the mirror and seized it from Isis. "But this is my long lost face. This is who I once was."

"Your beauty has been restored." Isis laid her warm hands against Medusa's smiling cheeks.

Kali dropped the blue silk's loose ends over Medusa's bare shoulders. "You have retained your unique powers. Do not uncover your restless mane unless you mean to do battle."

"I would dare Poseidon to come within a mile of me now." Medusa laughed.

"Clothe her," said Anubis. "There is much to tell her."

"So there you have it," Hecate said as she finished her soma and stood away from the makeshift table several yards from their patient's tent. "Medusa has been reincarnated and has joined the hunt for Upir Likhyi.'

"It makes sense," said Asclepius. "Both Kali and Medusa reign over fields of Death and its processes."

"As do I in my fashion," said Hecate. "Between the three of us we should be able to track down this member of the living dead."

"Are you going with them, Hermes?" said Vrinda Devi.

"I will relay between them and here so that when Hades returns to us he will know what is being done in his name."

"How long will he be between life and oblivion?" said Hecate.

"Unknown," said Immutef.

Dhanvantari poured a cup of simple tea into an even simpler fired clay cup. "I have asked that a sand mandala be made on his behalf in the Underworld. Is this being done?"

"The Intercessor spirits had begun marking it out upon the dais when we departed," said Hermes.

"Very good," said Dhanvantari.

Hecate looked past them toward the tented altar. She nodded at the familiar silhouette standing close vigil over the recumbent figure. "Has our Lady been there all this time?"

"Since she arrived," said Apollo. "I would have thought the merest touch of her hand would have awakened Hades." He sighed. "But his wounds are far worse than we realized."

"They attacked his vitality," said Immutef, "and drained him most grievously. We must monitor him till we are certain that he does not suffer some poisonous daemonic infection."

"He'll pull through," Hecate decreed with more authority than she felt. "Hades is stubborn that way. Well, I must be off."

"Good hunting," said Apollo. "If you need my help, send for me."

"Without hesitation." Hecate left the temple.

Europe convulsed with plague again and again. Apollo Lord of Plagues was summoned to determine the cause. As Kali, Hecate and Medusa waited, Apollo surveyed the devastation. Cloaked and hooded so that not even one strand of his fiery hair appeared to mortal sight, he looked as much a pilgrim as the trio who summoned him. Whenever they moved among the Living, they garbed themselves in thick northern clothes and covered their heads so that the shadows would conceal their strangeness better. They let no one come close enough to see Kali's bluish complexion, the fiery amber glow to Medusa's glance or the peculiar motions beneath her loose turban, or Hecate's unearthly majesty.

Apollo trod with careful deliberation with his hands extended slightly over the ground as though feeling for drafts. His frowning glance alighted upon this plague victim and then the next. He stopped and raised his face.

"Nothing?" said Hecate.

"How could you tell?" said Apollo.

"By the way you just twisted your mouth. You only do that when you're absolutely flummoxed."

"If Upir Likhyi was here, he is long gone," said Apollo, "and that is a big 'IF'. Rats with fleas, my Ladies, rats with fleas."

"The bastard has gone to ground again," growled Kali. "It is too clever by far."

Hecate stamped the ground with her staff. "He cannot remain in hibernation forever. Hunger will send him out into the night sooner or later to feed on these helpless souls."

"And in the meantime," grumbled Medusa, "what can we do?"

"Wait. Gather your strength for future battles with these demons of the night. Be alert. Be wary for the slightest ripple in the darkness," said Apollo. "An opportunity shall arise soon enough."

"Very well," said Hecate. "I am off to the Underworld to confer with the Caretakers."

"I shall seek out Dionysus in India," said Apollo," I am hoping that he will come with me to Tibet to see an Oracle who resides there."

"I shall go home to India too," said Kali. "You are more than welcome to accompany me, sister of mortality."

"Then I shall go with you." There was regret in Medusa's tone.

"Our day shall come and then shall Upir Likhyi regret he ever left the maelstrom of Tartarus," said Kali as she took Medusa's arm.

The four strangers vanished from the narrow lane.

Such was the misery among the Living that no one noticed.

18.

One moment Hades was in the embrace of restful, timeless oblivion. The next he opened his eyes, quite simply, and gazed up into a dark canopy. Utterly still, completely silent, he lay upon his sacred sickbed and let awareness dawn upon his senses.

No music enveloped him.

No voices echoed.

The canopy was but a veil. He perceived that all was night within the great space and beyond the tall open doors far across the sanctified space. He recognized the place: the High Pantheon of Olympus.

Hades was alone but for the night's mild breeze and the sweet fragrance of honeysuckle that washed over him. He smiled a little and breathed in so very deeply as Gaia washed him in the fragrances of spring.

That spring Aidoneus Zagreus, Lord Hades, enjoyed something akin to a rebirth.

The hullabaloo came with the dawn when Vrinda Devi found Hades lying awake gazing off through the gaping temple doors at a lightening horizon. Her cries of delight brought in the rest of his caretakers. "He has awakened! He is among us again!"

Somewhat languidly Hades smiled at the joyous jostling he received. At last a pleased silence fell over the assembly until Vrinda Devi laid her incense-perfumed hand upon Hades' bare arm.

"I am so sorry," she said.

"Why? Because Persephone was not among you to greet me?" Hades said.

"Yes."

"But she is here. She is everywhere. Her essence is upon the breezes." Hades closed his peaceful eyes as the sweet morning air passed over him again and caressed him with the perfume of flowering abundance.

A conference soon convened in the Olympian Pantheon and a consensus efficiently arrived at. Although Vrinda Devi volunteered for the duty, the rest forbade her from going anywhere near the palace of Zeus. Instead, Immutef and Asclepius went up to the palace to ask a favor of Hera.

They found her alone upon the Olympian throne, radiating calm indifference towards these mortals turned intercessory bodhisattvas.

"Great Queen of Olympus," said Asclepius as he and Immutef bowed briefly, "we beg an audience of you."

Expressionless and erect upon her peacock throne, Hera said, "Speak your piece."

"Hades has awakened…" said Immutef.

"Has he?" Her face brightened. "That's a fine piece of news!"

"Indeed, Great Queen," said Asclepius.

"The Underworld is yet too unquiet a place for him," said Immutef, "therefore, we ask whether Hades might complete his recuperation in your airy and bright palace."

"But of course Hades may convalesce here. I shall tend to him myself for I am gifted at the domestic arts."

"Blessings upon you," said both sainted beings as they bowed, also in unison.

And so Hades was moved into tranquil chambers close by Hera's royal suite. There he idled away his time in restful naps. When he was alert and neither Hera nor Ganymede were there to fuss over his comforts, Hades spent his time musing and daydreaming out the wide portico at the ever-passing cloud vistas in the sky.

Nothing could persuade Hades to let his daybed be moved away from that refreshing view. Every day he marveled at the subtle variations of blue hue the sky possessed and enjoyed the whimsical or dramatic forms the clouds assumed. Every night he breathed in with pleasure the aromas of the vital and sometimes turbulent Earth below and beyond the spectral Olympian mist. Now and then volcanic ash darkened the sky and concern would darken his brow.

Invariably, Hermes would stop by to assure Hades that everything was being taken care of. "On no account are you to rise from your convalescence until Dhanvantari or Immutef give you leave to do so."

"What happened?"

"The Earth wished to remind Humanity of its insignificance."

"It will do that from time to time." Hades sighed.

"You're bored out of your mind, aren't you?"

"Is it that obvious?"

Hermes nodded. "Do you want me to bring you something to read? Or something to do?"

"Ganymede brings me whatever I crave in the way of sedate diversions. Whenever Zeus is elsewhere, he plays chess with me. The rest of my waking hours Hera consumes. She fusses over me like a mother hen."

"She has been so much more cheerful since you arrived." Hermes winked.

"She is talking my head off."

"Well, you can't beat a captive audience, Hades. Hera hasn't had anyone around to talk to in a **LONG** time."

"I get that impression." Hades rubbed his face and scruffed up his thick black hair. "Perhaps you should ask Apollo to send me something we can while away the time reading aloud. I shall take whatever he and his Muses recommend."

"I'll pass on the request."

"How fares the hunt?"

"In fits and starts. Upir Likhyi emerges from hiding about as often as the sun goes into eclipse. He wreaks a little chaos among the Living, cuts a swift, but wide-spreading swath of terror through the survivors, and goes underground as far from his picnicking grounds as possible. Kali, Medusa, Apollo, and Hecate – they've come close to cornering him a few times, but he has had the sense to leave a nest of ravenous acolytes behind to impede them."

Hades rose up on his elbows. "Was anyone injured?"

Hermes shrugged. "A scratch or a cut or a nip now and again. Immutef or Asclepius patches them up when the dust settles. Then they're off again." He grinned and arched his brows. "The decision to reincarnate Medusa was pure genius. Whenever they suspect an ambush, Medusa goes in first to flush them out. You should see how they scramble to get clear of her."

Hades chuckled and lay back upon his cushions. "I can imagine."

"Between Apollo's fiery presence and incinerating touch, Kali's dexterity with her sword, and Medusa's particular talents, Hecate has her sack full of damned souls. They make quite a self-pitying racket until Kali snarls at them. Then they whimper and moan…all the way down to the Underworld."

Hades grunted. "Of course, by then Upir Likhyi is well away."

"Well and truly, and safe in his hibernation somewhere far away from his desecration grounds."

"We'll catch him yet. He'll get lazy or arrogant in his perceived immortality, which is all the same, and we'll catch him." Hades folded his hands over his stomach and winked at Hermes. "'Just a matter of time."

"Well, I must be off." Hermes donned his winged helmet which had been tucked under his arm for the duration of the visit.

"I'll see you when I see you," said Hades as he closed his eyes.

"Hades?"

"Yes, Hermes?"

"You didn't ask after Persephone."

"No, I didn't."

Hermes stood in silence a long moment before he turned to leave.

When Hades re-opened his eyes, it was due to the sensation of brightness piercing his eyelids. Halfway shielding his eyes, Hades squinted upwards.

Phoebus Apollo cocked his head sideways as he regarded the invalid. In his arms, he held two stout, bound stacks of books. "How are we feeling?"

"Well enough to be curious. What did you bring me?"

"A sampling of humanity's best and brightest imaginations that have crossed your home threshold since you've been here."

"Don't remind me. I hate this enforced idleness." Hades held out his arms for the bundles.

Apollo plopped them onto his lap.

Hades grunted, but was already reading the spines. "The Decameron. Orlando Furioso. Orlando Innamorato. La Divina Commedia…"

"Ah yes! The Divine Comedy," said Apollo. "You should find *The Inferno* fascinating."

"Oh?" Hades scrutinized more titles. "Beowulf. Canterbury Tales. Everyman. Sir Gawain and the Green Knight."

"Yes. I had some poetry bound for you too. Hephaestus quite outdid himself."

"La Morte D'Arthur. Icelandic Sagas – A Compilation," read Hades. "The Illiad. THE ILLIAD?" He arched his brows.

"So you know the participants, don't let that prohibit you from enjoying it. I had a copy of The Odyssey bound for you too."

"I see. These are rather fine. Hmmmm…The Lays of Marie de France. The Tale of Genji. You and the Muses have done a thorough job. Thank them for me."

"I shall. Are you sure these are enough? I can produce still more. The creative branches of humanity are ever-blooming."

"These will be plenty for the time-being. I shall take turns reading them aloud with Hera. Anything to win me a respite from the unending drama that is her marriage." Hades rolled his eyes. Leaning over, he set both stacks beside his daybed and undid the straps. "Hold on. What is THIS? Love poetry?" He winged it at Apollo.

Apollo caught it and eyed the spine with an abashed grin.

"Come on. YOU – of all of us – should know better than to give me a volume of love poetry."

"I do actually. I suspect one of my lady friends. You know how tender hearted the Muses are."

"Give it back to them as a present from me. Let them sigh over it," said Hades. He spined out the stacks beside his daybed so he could peruse the titles.

"I'll do that." Apollo watched Hades select Dante's work.

"The Inferno, you say?"

"The Inferno." Apollo grinned hugely.

"Very well then." Hades settled back upon his cushions with The Divine Comedy in his hand. "I'll give you my review later."

"'Can't wait to hear it." Apollo waved the poetry book at him and trod softly out.

When Hera entered a little while later, she found Hades chuckling and avidly turning the pages.

"What is that? Is it a comedy? Euripedes?" Hera glanced at the title as she set down the round tray bearing their luncheon.

Ganymede shadowed her, bearing another tray with their refreshments.

"I'm not sure it would be – to a mortal, but to me – it is something remarkable in its extravagance. Pull up a seat, both of you, and I'll read it to you."

Quite excited, Hera had Ganymede rearrange the furnishings so that they could enjoy this new diversion.

It wound up being quite a leisurely luncheon for all three of them.

If Zeus noticed his divine consort's preoccupation with her invalided charge, he never let on. He came and went according to his nature and seldom saw Hera at all, except in their bed, where he dallied with her out of habit and an excess of appetite that no mortal female could satisfy. Zeus knew that she spent a great deal of her idle time keeping Hades company. He knew that Ganymede had overcome his fear of Hades and spent his free time diverting him also on lazy afternoons.

Zeus was not in the least bit jealous. There was no cause to be. Hades was cursed to love Persephone. And, infamously, there were still a few surviving Succubi willing to care for Hades when his Consort could – or would – not. He hadn't seen or caught the slightest whiff of one of those lascivious entities anywhere near Olympus though. Hades had become a monastic it seemed.

Still, Hera was quite sunny these days.

"I am off on my constitutional," Zeus would say.

"Have a lovely excursion," Hera would usually reply as she was already swanning off to some other corner of Olympus, her silken robes and veil flying after her.

Once, she even called out over her shoulder, "Happy hunting, My Lord."

Zeus stood dumbfounded well after her echoing footfalls died away.

Wonderful as it was that Hera hardly ever harangued him or wept over his neglectful ways anymore, Zeus couldn't help but be curious. Whence this change in Hera's moods?

One balmy day that particular spring, after Zeus had consummated yet another seduction of yet another fresh-faced, agile-limbed maiden in some fragrant forest, he returned to Olympus – early.

It had been a couple of millennia in human terms since Olympus had bustled with occupants. Everyone had scattered with the winds, or entrenched themselves in their preferred domains. Poseidon kept to the oceans and usually sent back apologies along with his usual excuses of being too busy whenever Zeus commanded his presence at his feasting table. It used to infuriate Zeus, but invariably he discovered that Poseidon did indeed have his hands full. His dominion was being traversed more frequently by restless humanity.

Artemis preferred the wilderness and the wild animals to a humanity that devastated her virgin forests everywhere it settled. Apollo had said that she preferred more and more the Scandinavian lands or the so-called New World's wondrous expanses.

Athena has become increasingly ethereal, more of an intercessor than a formal goddess. He seldom saw his favorite.

Aphrodite was still a gadfly, forever plotting against social constraints.

Ares he saw frequently enough. Zeus made it a point to speak to him and ply him with sage advice. It halfway puzzled him, halfway relieved him that Ares couldn't get away from him fast enough. He got the distinct impression that Ares wasn't paying attention to anything he said anymore. If he cared more, that would have bothered him.

Still, humanity was restless and prone to quarrel, so Ares was quite busy. He kept council with his counterparts among their fellow Incarnations of India and the far North. Even Heracles found better things to do. He was busy too, Zeus reasoned – and accepted all too readily. One less thing to be bothered with.

When he did encounter Apollo on Olympus, the Golden One was almost invariably meditating. If he had a home, he made it elsewhere. There were moments when Zeus met Apollo's thorough gaze and saw an ancient, transcendent intelligence staring back at him. Zeus squirmed then and making some excuse, absented himself.

Much better it was to deal with Hera's sulks and tantrums than endure Apollo's potent scrutiny.

Dionysus had turned out to be a wild and unknowable entity, who preferred other climes and seldom ever came to Olympus. Perhaps that was just as well.

Then there was Hades and Persephone, and Hecate and Demeter. Demeter had become one with Gaia and Devi. He sensed her everywhere upon the Earth, but saw no obvious sign of her. Hecate dealt with moonless nights and all the unholy things that dwelt in darkness. Zeus respected and even feared her. Naturally, he avoided her.

Persephone, beautiful sacrifice, he would have liked to see, but for some reason she would have nothing to do with him. That she might have heard his role in her fate never occurred to Zeus.

And now Hades – of all of them: aloof Hades! - recuperated on Olympus. Zeus had visited his bedside exactly twice. The first had been when Hades lay in the Pantheon. The second was shortly after Hades had been settled in the palace under Hera's supervision. He had made a grand public gesture of assigning Ganymede to help Hera and then sallied off.

That spring day when he returned early, Zeus found no one waiting to greet him in the fashion to which he was accustomed. No Ganymede. No Hera. Not even a nymph with a tray of refreshments.

Only one of the Graces, whose name escaped him in his mood, moved past the Olympian threshold.

"You!"

The Grace backed up three steps and tilted her head at him. "Yes, my Lord Zeus?"

Every time he encountered the Graces, he was struck by their pure and simple beauty. Zeus softened his tone. "Where is Hera? Where is my pet?"

She motioned over her shoulder down the airy corridor she had just traversed. "Where they always are at this hour: reading with Hades."

"Oh."

"Will that be all?"

Zeus grunted and nodded.

Her slippered feet padded away.

Zeus grunted again and stomped toward Hades' sickroom.

There he did indeed find Hera and Ganymede seated about Hades on his daybed. His beautiful cupbearer leaned back against Hades' feet with his arms behind his head and his faraway gaze roaming the blue and gilt spangled ceiling. Hera sat doing embroidery.

Zeus gawked a little. He couldn't remember the last time he had seen Hera wearing such a peaceful expression. Her brow carried not a trace of its usual furrows. She looked up at some passage Hades read aloud and smiled.

Ganymede fidgeted and grinned at the ceiling.

In the shadows beyond, Zeus turned away and more softly than he had come, walked away.

Only the Three Graces saw him pass and then leave Olympus.

That evening Hera gazed out into the twilight upon the Earth's curved horizon. "But what was his mood? Was his face dark with rage?"

The Graces exchanged looks. The other two shrugged and the one raised her hands helplessly from her sides.

"I thought he looked a little thoughtful, pensive even. I couldn't tell you why," she said.

"And he left Olympus again?" said Hera, wearing a new breed of frown: a concerned one.

The Graces nodded, but one of them added, "I'm certain he shall return. He always does."

"Ah well. You are right, I expect," said Hera. "Ganymede will be pleased no doubt. He can spend the evening playing chess with Hades instead."

19.

Persephone did not return to Olympus to see Hades…and Hades did not send for her.

Although Hermes told her of his full awakening, she stayed where she was gazing at the ruins of Eleusis.

"Did you hear? Hades is among us again," said Hermes.

"Yes, I heard you. Thank you, Hermes." She gave him a quiet smile, shadowed with sadness. "You are free to course the winds between the realms once more."

"You aren't going to see him?"

"Here I shall remain until I am sure that spring has taken proper hold."

"And then?"

"Then you shall find me in the Underworld."

"If Hades sends for you?"

"I shall be in the Underworld," said Persephone in a firm manner that suggested she would go nowhere else besides.

Hermes donned his golden helmet. "Very well."

She had already turned away from him and from Eleusis and was walking out across the world.

Hermes watched her for a time. With a sigh, he caught a zephyr by its dragon tail and rode it to the east as far as it would carry him. He braced himself for the scene that would erupt should Hades ask for Persephone...It shocked him then that Hades did not ask for her, not once.

When her time in the mortal realms was done, Persephone did return to the Underworld and to the throne upon the dais. There in her turn she alone greeted the souls who did not pass directly into the passage of Light. She did not remain aloof upon the dais though, but passed amongst the restless souls.

"Mater Dolorosa," the souls would murmur and press closer about her presence like so much pale mist.

Her hands caressed the whispering mist, passing over its surface as though over a gentle stream. They grew calmer in her wake.

Anubis stood upon the dais once observing 'Mater Dolorosa' soothing their suffering charges. He held his hand out to her when she returned to the dais.

Accepting his courteous gesture, Persephone stepped back onto the dais. He escorted her to the throne and stood beside her when she sat down. Together they gazed out over the becalmed pool of souls.

"They don't scream like they used to," said Anubis, sounding immensely relieved.

"Thank goodness," said Persephone.

"And you?"

"What do you mean?"

"Well, since you've had to shoulder the responsibilities by yourself, you've managed to imbue this place with an aura that is calming and reassuring. It has made a significant difference."

"I thank you, but I am not certain my presence alone is the cause. Times have changed abroad. I get the impression from so many of them that Life is so very hellish above that coming here is akin to coming to a refuge and finding sanctuary."

"You may have something there," said Anubis.

Together, for a time, they watched over the souls and watched the Intercessors moving like lanterns through the pale gloom.

A great illumination gathered just on the other side of their threshold. So great it was that they all, even the distracted souls, turned to look.

As burnished and warm as a summer sunset, Apollo appeared just beyond the threshold. A trifle uncertain, he had swathed himself completely in his maroon cloak, covering even his fiery hair. Only his otherworldly gaze shone from the shadows concealing his face, not that it did any good.

"My my. It's Apollo," said Persephone. "What is he doing here?"

"He never comes here," said Anubis.

"I had better go see what he wants." She moved away from the dais.

"I hope it isn't bad news." Anubis leaned upon his crook.

Persephone hesitated and glanced back briefly.

Nearing the threshold, Persephone spoke lowly, but a little urgently. "My Lord of Illumination, what brings you to the Underworld?"

From the depths of his cloak he produced his right hand and opened it. In it lay but five dusty, dried out laurel leaves. His hand trembled. So did his voice. "I went to my sacred grove to pay homage and collect leaves for a fresh...The grove was obliterated...Daphne." He caught his breath. Steadying his voice, he also stood a little more erect. "Foolish mortals, they cherish destruction to the detriment of all. She's gone." The whole time Apollo stared at those five fragile, desecrated leaves.

Persephone closed his hand around the leaves and held it closed. "I am so sorry."

Apollo met her grave expression with glistening eyes. "Do you think she suffered when they ch...chopped her down?"

"Life is suffering. You know this."

Apollo nodded, but his tears darted down his face. "I never meant her any harm."

"Whatever the nature of her limbo above, Daphne is free now. She suffers neither drought, nor flood, nor frost, nor the tearing winds, nor the constancy of her exile. She is free. Keep that in your heart." Persephone wiped away his tears.

Apollo nodded, causing fresh tears to burst their banks and rush downward. "I know this. I know. It isn't as though I meant anything to her, but just knowing that she existed, however isolated in that sacred place among her arboreal offspring, it was enough for me. I made it a point to return to her, to pay homage to her...I begged her time and again to forgive me. She must have been so frightened when I loomed upon her horizon...and then when the men came with their axes..."

For a long moment, Apollo gazed past her into the Underworld. "Are you sure Daphne is free? Truly free?"

"Yes."

"She isn't here, is she?" He gestured toward the pool of souls. "She can't be. She mustn't be. She suffered enough as it is."

Persephone reached up and took his face in her hands. "She is not here, Apollo. She returned to the heart of all things where she belonged."

Apollo swallowed and wiped his face against his arm. "Good. That is as it should be."

"Yes, Apollo." Persephone stroked his left arm.

He opened his right hand again and gazed into it. His eyes widened.

In place of the five laurel leaves lay five coils of Daphne's lustrous dark hair. Apollo nearly dropped them in his surprise, but Persephone steadied his hand despite her own surprise. With his other hand, he so very gently caressed the thick, curling locks.

"I have never forgotten her." Apollo smiled sadly, but his tears no longer flowed. "I have never forgotten how her hair shone with a reddish tint in the sunlight as it flew in the breezes. It slid like silk over my fingertips and then it was gone into leaves, supple green leaves. There were so many times when I basked in her shade and drowsed beneath her whispering boughs. I blessed her for those simple comforts she had not meant to give me."

"And now the blessing has been returned, I think. Here is your proof of her release. You possess at last a true remembrance of *her*."

"I shall cherish it. Can you braid these together for me? I fear I may drop them."

"Of course. I shall braid them into a love knot that you can carry close to your heart."

"Please do."

When Zeus returned to Olympus, he went directly to Hades in the portico.

To find him sitting alone with a book open on his lap and his faraway gaze fixed upon the horizon was disconcerting. Zeus glanced about the shaded space. Hades was absolutely alone.

"What? No audience?" Zeus said.

Hades shot him a look. "Not at the moment, no."

Zeus looked back down the corridor. Only the gentlest of zephyrs idled there chasing its tail. "Where are they?"

"Ganymede is off with Heracles and Krishna. I believe Heracles said something about an excursion to the Himalayas, or was it Ankara? Anyway," Hades shrugged, "somewhere east of here."

Hades eyed Zeus a moment. Zeus was frowning, but not in any mood even remotely akin to irritation. "It's good that Ganymede gets to go off now and then. Don't you think?"

"I suppose so. Where is my Consort?"

"In the Pantheon with Parvati and Isis."

"Remind me to steer clear of there."

Hades grinned and turned the page of his book.

"What were you reading yesterday?"

"*WE* were reading the Decameron by some clever chap named Boccaccio."

"It is it a good story?"

"It comprises a good many diverting tales. Would you like to read it? We finished it yesterday." Hades reached down to the shortest stack beside his daybed. He lifted the top volume and held it out.

"Unlike you, I do not have so much time on my hands." Zeus strolled to the edge of the portico and peered out over a cloud sea.

"Oh, you have plenty of time, too much time on your hands, to be frank. The people have a saying, '*Idle hands are the Devil's playground*.'"

"Who's this *Devil so and so*?" Zeus frowned briefly over his shoulder.

Hades shrugged. "Someone they have invested a great deal of energy believing in. I get mistaken for him all the time and so does Anubis. We get a lot of screaming." He set the book down.

Zeus faced him again. There was a look of bemused astonishment upon his face. "They scream at you?"

"The instant they set eyes on me. Then they start blubbering about '*pits of eternal Hellfire*', flaming lakes, stakes up the backside...not that there aren't unpleasant places in Tartarus...but sometimes it's hard to tell whether they do or don't want these extravagant punishments visited upon them. They describe them with such enthusiasm and gusto." Hades shook his head.

Zeus settled into Hera's favorite seat and, leaning back upon the cushions, stretched his legs out. "What does happen to them? Do they get what they want?"

"It depends on their condition. We get quite a few broken spirits who believe they deserve more of the mistreatment they received in other realms. It takes a little time to get through to them. Generally, we view them as invalids, so we let them pool in our great hall where we can mind them. Eventually, they achieve some sort of realization and either fly down the passage to the Source or return to the Living realms."

"Why would they return if they suffered so much up there in the first place?"

"There are many reasons: to do it all over; to make amends; to try again...They go where they must."

"And the rest?"

"Well..." Hades sat up and arranged his cushions a little higher. "Well, the ones who were warped along the way suffer a more mundane and yet efficient retribution than their imaginations have conjured."

"Which is?"

"They confront their consciences, or rather, their consciences confront them. It is an excruciating ordeal. There are some who cannot see the light for the darkness, those who love themselves more than all Creation, and those who enjoy the pain they inflict." Hades turned the pages of his book to and fro. He did not make eye contact with Zeus, would not even look up at him. "The Selfish and the Recalcitrant ones."

"What becomes of them?"

"Those ones we keep." Hades looked Zeus directly in the eyes.

"But what do you do to them?"

"We break their egos. Every ounce of pain and grief they inflicted upon others we inflict upon them a thousand times over. The lucky ones wake up and embrace humility. The lucky ones get to leave...eventually."

"And the unlucky ones?"

"Stew and fester, wail and lament, and blame everyone but themselves. Then there are those who use it all to indulge in yet more self-pity."

Zeus sighed and stretched, oblivious to the cool constant stare coming from the Lord of the Underworld. His mind wandered after his gaze toward the dominion of mankind.

Hades shook his head and held out his copy of The Decameron. "This is just your sort of book."

"How so?"

"Lust, lechery, adventure..."

Zeus began to reach for it, but stopped. For a long moment both stared at one another, Zeus with his seething eyes like gleaming copper and Hades with eyes dark, cool, and impenetrable.

One of Hera's handmaidens began to come in, but took one look at the staring contest, pivoted and went the other way.

After a moment Zeus took the book, but did not peruse it. "You don't like me, do you?"

"I don't respect you, which amounts to the same thing."

"Fearless honesty you have."

"There is no room for lies where I come from."

"Do you mind if I ask you a question?"

Hades took on a lean grin. "Don't ask anything you don't want to hear the answer to."

Zeus hesitated. "You truly do hold yourself as superior to me, don't you?"

"Superior? No, not superior. More fortunate perhaps."

Zeus gaped. "Fortunate? What can you possibly mean by that? You live in a place of darkness surrounded by the most wretched and the damned. I live up here." He gestured at the endless sky. "I have the freedom of these skies and of the land below. I come and go as I please."

"Ah! That is the crux of the whole matter. You have entirely too much freedom."

"How can anyone have too much of such a good thing?"

"Once you stood among us as our Chief, the supreme arbitrator and lawgiver to and guardian of Humanity. As we all did, you had a role to play and play you did, more and more often when you should have exerted your influence in ways less casually destructive."

"And your point? I would appreciate it, if you would speak your piece and stop chewing on my earlobes."

"For you, the words '*freedom*' and '*idleness*' are interchangeable to a promiscuous degree. You lost all sense of productive purpose ages ago."

Zeus frowned at the book in his hands.

"And what is worse is that you have shown an utter disinterest in recovering it."

Zeus winced at that. "Meanwhile you are the paragon of responsibility."

His sarcasm made no dent in Hades. "Although my realm is neither here nor there, my sense of purpose has been my constant. You care about our charges only in so far as they serve our interests. You are just as myopic as Humanity is, but worse, because you know the Infinite Consciousness. One day this world will end, but you shall hardly notice."

His face was as black as a storm filled night and its lightning shone in his eyes as Zeus stood up. He tossed the book on the marble floor beside the daybed. "I'll send in one of Hera's handmaidens. Since your wife will not do as she ought, you could use a little attention to dull your fangs.' Zeus moved to leave.

Hades spoke to his disappearing back, "Why should she come when I have not sent for her?"

Zeus hesitated in mid-step.

"Like me, she knows her place and her duty, which is more than can be said for you anymore, Zeus."

Zeus stomped off. "The sooner you are gone the better," he snapped.

20.

It happened quite suddenly. One morning Hera came in with one of her handmaidens bearing the second of two breakfast trays.

The daybed stood empty. Its coverlet lay tossed halfway off the end onto the floor.

Hera gasped and rushed in.

A small, small sound caught her attention. Hera turned so fast several berries flew from their bowl.

Swathed in his customary colors of night and oblivion, Hades stood beside the balustrade. Wild winds reached up from the mortal realms to ravish him and play with his voluminous raiments.

In all of their existence Hera had never seen such a look on Hades' face. Hades never laughed with gusto or smiled with the sort of sensual delight that Zeus did, but she could tell by the light in his eyes that he was rejoicing.

"I'm sorry," he said, his lips still smiling. "I didn't mean to startle you."

Hera's handmaiden had recovered wit enough to collect the berries from the floor.

"Has Immutef or Dhanvantari been here?" said Hera. "Did they give you leave to get up?"

"There was no need to consult them," said Hades. "I am well."

"Oh." Hera fidgeted. She glanced at the breakfast on her trays and at the daybed with its stacks of thoroughly read books. "Then you must be leaving."

"I think I must. A few centuries have passed on Earth and all this while others have shouldered my share of the burden. It is time I took up my duties again."

"I see." Hera's shoulders slumped a little.

"I will miss our leisurely hours among the imaginary people," said Hades. "We had quite a few adventures in this place."

Hera smiled, but briefly and averted her gaze to her tray. "Yes, we had such a lovely time. What shall I do with your books?"

"Keep them or give them to Ganymede." For a moment, a look of discomfort crossed his face. "I know that Ganymede suffered a transfiguration so that Zeus could keep him, but the young man remains scarcely seventeen summers' of age, no matter the passage of time."

Hera stiffened a little.

"You know his being here was none of his fault. I know that you only just tolerate him."

"Just," Hera growled.

"I am asking you, please, Hera, do not leave him entirely at the mercy of Zeus when he is here. Do not neglect Ganymede either when Zeus is away. He should have passed on with the rest of his line a long, long time ago." Hades motioned toward the corridor. "That is the loneliest soul I have ever encountered. Have a little compassion."

Hera met his somber gaze. After a moment, she said, simply and calmly, "What would you have me do for him?"

"Keep him about you for company for you are also one of the most supremely lonely souls I have ever met."

Hera set her tray down upon the table and promptly dashed way her tears with her deft fingertips.

Still uncertain, her handmaiden hovered near the doorway, resting her tray upon her left arm.

"I am sorry, Hera. I did not mean to make you cry." Hades came back into the shade.

"Yes, of course." Her face reddened as she dashed away more delinquent tears. "Zeus does that often enough, only I never let him see it."

"You and Ganymede should be allies. He certainly needs a friend when there is no one else around. Stand between him and Zeus now and then. When he comes around craving a bit of buggery, tell him you need Ganymede to help you move the furniture or to collect fruit from the orchard."

"Ganymede goes off with Zeus willingly enough."

Hades folded his arms over his chest. "As though the boy truly has a choice in the matter. He is a hostage for whom no ransom has been demanded."

"Ganymede is a slave." Hera nodded.

"I believe you have it," said Hades.

She wiped away one last truant tear from her face. "I will see what I can do. Perhaps we shall read to each other."

"There are still adventures unexplored." Hades motioned to the second stack, recently refreshed by Apollo and the Muses.

"You were good company, Hades. You will be missed."

Hades bowed. The eager wind tousled his dark hair. It shone with a sapphire blue tint wherever the sunlight graced it.

Hera motioned to the table with its waiting tray. "Can I not prevail upon you to linger for a little breakfast?"

Hades eyed the entrees. The gleam returned to his eyes. "Why not?"

Still savoring the flavor of strawberries and sweet cream, Hades set foot on Earth again. He breathed in deep, saturating his senses with a hemisphere in full bloom. Soon enough the Underworld would reclaim him, but for now he lingered in the wild places and in pastoral places a polite distance from large settlements.

A side effect from his convalescence was a longing for quiet and tranquility. Hades had developed a preference for keeping to himself and dreaded having to end it once he returned to the Underworld.

Instinctively his sojourn turned ever northward, following spring's progress. His pace quickened. His eager glance sharpened.

On a mountain meadow radiant with wildflowers and everything that grew green in that climate, where glaciers dazzled the eyes in the sunlight high beneath an achingly beautiful blue sky, Hades stopped. His breath had been stolen away, just as his heart had been one warm and leafy green day long, long ago.

Persephone. His bright and beautiful one, whom even Helios could not outshine in his wounded heart, lay in slumber's gentle abandon amid the idly wafting wildflowers and grass. Lulled to sleep by an ocean of whispering trees and the warmth of a midday sun, Persephone had spread her cloak upon her sacred Earth and lay down. Her gilded red hair shone, more precious than the gold mankind prized. Helios took care to ward off the chill descending from the mountain peaks.

For a moment, Hades dared not move. How long had it been since she had been in his presence? How many mortal centuries had blurred together between them? Her beauty made his heart ache. As much as he longed to stroke her hair and breathe in its perfume, Hades stood away from her rather than disturb her – his vision.

Perfectly alert, Persephone opened her eyes. Even as her glance shot toward him she sat up. Astonishment shone upon her face. "Is it really you?"

Hades nodded.

A smile burst upon her face. "Aidoneus."

156

In an instant Hades knelt over her and took her face in his hands. "I almost forgot. How could I? How could I forget how this felt – this ache – and you? How could I have forgotten how it feels to be in your presence?"

Persephone smiled into his face. "You made my heart leap."

Hades kissed her face, here and there and there and finally there – on her laughing mouth. She sank backward as he leaned over her.

Helios bathed Persephone in warmth as Hades tore away her spring gown as though it were the thinnest gauze. One reciprocal tug from Persephone upon his belt, a bold hint of her desire, and Hades hauled his clothes over his head and tossed them aside.

Helios valiantly warded off the glacial chill creeping down from the mountaintops, but there was no need of such chivalry. The couple's exertions created ample heat to ward off any remote threat of a mortal chill. The vale that hosted their passionate reunion resounded only with the sounds of waterfalls, birds, and the unending sea sounds of its evergreen forests; and amid all this, Hades and Persephone abandoned all restraint.

As the tides ebbed and flowed, so did their bouts of passion. During one of the lulls, Hades and Persephone lay entwined watching bright clouds cross the sky.

"Why did you not send for me?" Persephone said as she glanced at his profile.

"Because it was not necessary."

"I would have come as I did when you were first injured." Persephone rose up on her elbow and peered into his face.

"I know." Hades looked back into her face and stroked her hair. "You did not have to be beside me for me to feel you. You smell of spring and a living Earth, did you know that?"

"Yes."

"As I lay in my sickbed, the winds would bring you to me. I would lie awake and breathe you in in the scent of honeysuckles, in the night-blooming jasmine, and even in the roses of Aphrodite. In some manner, you were always about me, no matter where you went or what you were doing."

Persephone laid her head against his shoulder. "I did not expect to miss you. At first, I didn't miss you at all. I was relieved for I was free of you, but then in so many little ways, I felt your absence. I began to need you, but first you were gone from our realm and I could not reach you. Then, later, you did not send for me. I thought perhaps that you were angry with me for not being at your side. Then I heard from Aphrodite of all those hours spent with Hera…"

Hades kissed her hair.

Persephone pressed closer, embracing him.

He closed his arms tight about her. "I wish I did not have to go back to the Underworld. If I could, I would never go back."

Slightly shocked, Persephone mused in silence, frowning. "They have not captured Upir Likhyi yet."

Hades sighed. "I expected as much. Apparently, he is my ultimate responsibility."

"Do you get the feeling that there is a reason we have not been able to recapture him yet? Kali, Medusa, and Hecate have come so very close, so many times to capturing him, and yet, he slips away each time. It is as though we are not meant to capture him, not yet."

"I suspect that is because his escape is my fault. My self-indulgence led to his escape."

"I do not like not knowing the why of things. I do not like the truth being withheld from me."

"We all serve a higher purpose, my Love, no matter its turbulent course."

"It feels ominous, Aidoneus."

Hades rolled over on top of her. He cradled her face in his hands and kissed her. "I will always return to you, Persephone."

As the sunset bloomed across the sky, they dressed. Hades replaced her ruined gown with an exquisite flowing one he fashioned from the forest shadows and the spreading twilight. Her veil he crafted from the mist rising from the waterfalls' constant spray. Then arm in arm they descended into the Underworld.

In contrast with the idyllic isolation of the Scandinavian fjords and mountains, the Underworld was a raucous hive, more of a city than Hades was accustomed to anymore.

The instant Cerberus caught wind of him, he howled – with all three heads. Soon Garmr joined in out of empathy.

When Persephone brought Hades across their threshold, they were mobbed by their associates. Even the souls and their shepherd Intercessors pressed close to the utterly revitalized presence that Hades had become.

Anubis clapped Hades on the back so hard that he lurched forward, grinning. Hel gave him a fierce hug. Nepthys gave him a gentler one. Yamaraja laid his hands upon Hades' shoulders and touched foreheads with him. For that moment, they stood still muttering mantras, while the rest of the Underworld's caretakers waited their turn to welcome Hades.

From the dais Osiris beamed with all the grace of the Enlightened One.

Hecate, Kali and Medusa waited beyond Osiris. No sooner had he exchanged bows with Kali and Medusa than Hecate seized him in a great mothering embrace.

"It is good to have you back, old son," Hecate declared. She steered him toward the fire pit. "We were having ourselves a little war council."

21.

There existed and still exist on Earth volcanoes spawned by a merciless Gaia, volcanoes that rose as phoenixes did from their own smoldering remains to devastate the Living again and again. They were so infamous that they had names: Thera, Vesuvius, Tambora, and on and on.

In the very opening of the opening of the epoch the mortals of the West would term their 19th century, there was a rash of these earthly outbreaks culminating with Tambora's explosion in 1815. As a consequence, the greater world shivered and drew a little closer to their fires, starved, struggled and had to move to distant, difficult places in hopes of survival. Chaos bubbled over.

These sorts of dire times suited the infernal interloper Upir Likhyi quite nicely. Already he had weathered the bloodthirsty tumult of various reformations, rebellions, and revolutions with their attendant wars. Long before, the foul vampyr had learned to keep close to larger populations of potential prey. All those plagues and wars over the centuries had provided him with many a fine ruined church or abandoned castle to call home, the grander the better and to those places he clung for as long possible. When he had to move on his preference was for lonely, derelict dwellings where death hung fog-like, but he was careful: too much isolation was dangerous for his survival.

The revolution in France where the blood ran in the streets of Paris provided him with a substantial smokescreen between himself and the Hunters from Hades. He gave great thanks to God for the cruelty of mankind that enabled him to thrive with so very little effort. Absolutely fearless Upir Likhyi roamed the streets among the Living as though he were one of them in his stolen body. He had long since assumed the name that had belonged to his body when a purer soul had occupied it: Sebastiano Bonifacio or Sebastian Boniface, depending upon whom he was beguiling when he introduced himself.

No longer strictly a foul nightmare, Sebastiano luxuriated in humble mortal lodgings above ground surrounded by the noisy Living. It was easy to feed. Prey was plentiful and readily available to hunt and for a few coins he could have just about anyone he craved. Courtesy of his unlamented accomplice the Succubus, the body he possessed appeared to the immediate glance healthy and strong, a young man with a hard, lean, but handsome Mediterranean face.

In the past he fallen in among the crusaders headed south as one of them so that he would have his pick among them or among the pilgrims they encountered. He was well regarded for his willingness to be on the night watch, but he always managed to slip away by the time they reached Turkey. Monasteries were always good places to wait for groups of pilgrims returning from the Holy Land.

How glad they were to have a strong knight to escort them north.

How glad he was to have a ready supply of the Living so close to hand in those dark, dark nights.

Seigneur Boniface killed none of them. He converted none of them to the Darkness either.

All it would take to bring the Hunters fierce upon his trail was one forlorn, bewildered soul crossing Hades' threshold. He had figured that out fast. It took him a little longer to figure out how not to stain his victims with contagion. Sebastiano learned caution. He survived.

The Hunters were relentless though. Nothing would stop Hades, it seemed.

They closed in on him once, but he was ready. His handsome face had charmed several women to lower their defenses and ignore their better instincts. None of them recognized what the terrible blackness in his unblinking eyes or the pallor of his gaunt face meant. None of them realized the peril until it was too late.

Sebastiano could never decide which he liked more – terrified prey struggling and pleading for mercy even as he bore down on them, or the ones who surrendered themselves, feverish with lust, eager to sin. Even the willing ones suffered that delicious moment of regret when they gasped and struggled as he prepared to render them unto the powers of the night.

The misguided and the willing he gathered into a harem in a remote corner of a mountainous region. There he taught them his ways, but he did not teach them the secret of conversion, and neither did he warn them not to kill outright in their feeding frenzy.

In a village in the Italian Alps ruled a man called Alberti, a 'Father' in more than just an ordained sense. For him the Seven Deadly Sins did not apply. Loved by some, feared by that many more, Father Alberti enjoyed his authority over the village and the comforts he commanded. He was an infamous connoisseur of spring flowers. He always made sure to pluck the first blossoms to enjoy at his leisure.

Sebastiano Bonifacio heard of the priestly despot from one of his harem...

"He watches over us all during Mass when he should be attending to his duties. He notices every little thing," she told him not half an hour before her mortal existence folded over into exile. "No one prospers without sharing their good fortune with him." Then she whispered, "No girl once she turns maiden in her first bloom stays a maid for long. No beauty survives unblemished by him."

"Come with me and together, we shall visit retribution upon him," said Sebastiano.

Her hatred of her girlhood rapist overwhelmed any frail, lingering reservations about her new seducer. She still screamed when he bit into her neck and held her down. Once she had been converted by blood to his kind, she could not lead him there fast enough. Her blood black eyes gleamed at the prospect of tasting Alberti's blood just as he had tasted hers in his fashion a mere seven years before.

She led the way through a moonless night. As dawn crept through the mountain valleys, illuminating the mist, Sebastiano and his harem hid in a cave overlooking the church and the simple village below it. From hunger their vampyr master gave them no respite. Through a seemingly endless day they prowled the cave seeking anything living to slake their merciless thirst.

"We starve, Master Bonifacio," said one of his harrowed concubines.

"So feast on rats or on bats," he retorted.

"There are none to be found," moaned another, a wife who had cuckolded her husband just once too often and would never see him or her children again – if they were so very fortunate.

His concubines gathered close about him, fawning over him in hopes that their caresses would persuade him.

"They are too smart to be caught in here with us," whined another of the defiled sisterhood.

"Trust me," he said with a smile, "Father Alberti will not be so smart. Today we fast. Tonight we feast."

Alberti was in good spirits as evening spread over their village. He had dined well, although his dinner guest had not. Despite all of his coaxing, the thirteen year old girl, a shepherd's daughter, would scarcely touch her meal even though she spent the whole hour staring at her plate.

"What you need is exercise to rouse your appetite," Alberti declared, "and I know precisely what will suit."

As his grim housekeeper cleared away dinner, Alberti led the girl to his chambers. She stumbled and shuffled every step of the way.

Sometimes the housekeeper could hear the girls. Usually they cried, but some went silent to the slaughter. Like her neighbors and relations in the village, she prayed for deliverance from this ogre and despaired that it would ever come.

Deliverance came when Alberti was still on top of the girl, grunting and smiling at her fresh tears. Suddenly he found himself on his back, pinned to the floor. Any anger he felt was lost in surprise and then horror as the daemonic women bit into his exposed flesh where his blood vessels coursed closest to his skin. The last to bite was his victim and to her, her 'sisters' left the appropriate, offending delicacy to satiate her vengefulness along with her blood thirst.

He flailed, but there would be no escaping. His blood was as vigorous as his unsavory appetites and Sebastiano's little clan drained him dry.

The housekeeper heard his groans, but cringed away from them. What a bastard he was.

As for his last victim, the girl scarcely drew breath to scream when Sebastiano seized her up into his terrible embrace. His nostrils flared. The smell of her living blood was sweet and he so seldom permitted himself to indulge. This treat he wanted to himself, so he carried her into Alberti's private chapel. There he tormented the girl. There he finished her.

Sudden thorough silence flowed throughout the place. The housekeeper became uneasy. Alberti was an unquiet man. Thinking, and indeed, hoping, that something had happened to Alberti, the housekeeper ventured in to investigate.

Full-bellied and content, Sebastiano's concubines withdrew into the crypts to sleep as dawn hinted at its return.

Their master lingered above, surveying the carnage his minions had inflicted upon the unholy priest and his wretched housekeeper. Then he lit candles about the altar where he had left the shepherd's daughter, pale and waxen in her unnatural death. He blew her a parting kiss and blew a second one toward the crypts.

Then he left.

Naturally, they went in search of him. They cut a swath of terror through whole communities.

Hades, Hecate, and Apollo found them before they could be reunited with Sebastiano. If it occurred to them that he had abandoned them, they had plenty of time in Hecate's custody to curse him even as they savored the memory of Hades' divine blood on their tongues.

From that time onward Sebastiano gathered minions about him as a rule only when he sensed danger closing in.

For a time he had hoped to enjoy a respite from their persecution when Hades could no longer lead the hunt. He rejoiced in his victory over Hades, but then that witch goddess of the Earth Hecate reappeared with fresh, fierce reinforcements. He did not know them, although one of them was legendary, but he could smell them when they were close and shuddered.

Kali and Medusa possessed qualities and strengths that rendered them nearly invincible in battle and exceedingly difficult to shake off his trail. They and Hecate were never far enough behind and he knew when they were nigh by the aroma of incense, earth and rot that preceded them – the bringers of death.

Quickly he would create minions and gather with them in some secluded place. Then he let them dispatch the living residents in an orgy of blood and slipped away, content that Kali and Medusa would liberate him of his new dependents. For a little while he was free to lose himself among the larger populations of humanity and fed at his leisure.

When he hungered, Sebastiano bought himself a warm body for a few hours or days. Then he returned them and selected someone new. None of the pimps or madams cared much that he left curious marks on their merchandise. They cared only that they seemed weaker and needed time to convalesce before they could be rented out on a regular basis. He refused to touch anyone younger than fourteen.

"Flesh is like wine," he explained, "it requires a little aging before it can be enjoyed."

When there was no money to pay for his meals, Sebastiano prowled the taverns and inns and patrolled the streets at night.

Hunting in those days was easy before modern innovations and too, too many people crowding everywhere. The night was a realm unto itself. The world became something *other*, something to be feared, something desired, or something to be endured. In the deep, star-filled nights he hunted, waylaying men in the lanes and alleys and women who walked the streets or made the mistake of leaving their windows open on a mild evening. Afterwards he roamed until it was time to retreat to his hiding place.

If it weren't for the constant threat posed by the tireless Divine Hunters, life would be perfect.

Long before the '18th' century emerged from the energetic bluster of the previous 'century', Sebastiano attained and was able to maintain an appealing and useful façade of civilized sophistication. Money meant nothing to him, but when he had access to some he made cunning use of it to conceal those aspects of his person that gave his prey pause. Powder, rouge and wigs concealed a great deal.

Such were his successful predations that he came to view that century as a halcyon time. He entered it in the guise of a priest, an identity he assumed quite randomly…

Over a simple meal in a coach house inn, idle conversation was shared.

Sebastiano occupied a corner beyond the hearth where he could bask in the shadows and observe without being observed himself. His back to the corner he watched the entrance. The recent cut on his left hand and arm itched badly, a gift from Kali's sword. That he did escape and intact gave him neither consolation nor satisfaction.

Ever the predator, not even his foul mood stopped him from observing the priest who settled at the table nearest him. Swathed in self-satisfaction, he waited for a meal to be brought to him.

Sebastiano's blood black eyes gleamed. Courtesy of his stolen body he entertained a peculiar fascination with the priestly caste. He liked his men of the cloth hypocritical and gluttonous in their pursuit of sin. He liked his brides of Christ pure and utterly unfulfilled, which gave them a blind innocence he could exploit.

"The weather is hateful and yet you are serene, Good Father," said Sebastiano in a husky growl laced with a sinuous centuries' old accent. "You must be particularly blessed to be in such fine spirits."

"I am indeed fortunate for I have gained such high esteem that the Holy Father sees fit to entrust me with the care of his flock – the Carmelite Nuns at the Convent of San S-------. I shall also perform mass for the village there."

"I expect they await your arrival with feverish impatience."

"On the contrary," he proclaimed with a tight smile, "they would do well to do penance in advance of my arrival."

In his comfortable shadows, Sebastiano smiled behind his hands.

"This order is rife with the daughters of the wealthy and privileged. They are cosseted and coddled. They indulge in luxury when they should be humble. I mean to bring them to heel."

"That sounds like a labor Heracles would hesitate to take on. Women are soft and love their comforts," said the vampyr.

"When I am done, they shall love and serve Our Lord instead."

Needless to say, he did not arrive at the Convent. He did not even leave the inn.

For some unknown reason, the priest ran naked from his room in the dead of night, 'tripped' and ended at the bottom of the stairs dead of a broken neck.

In his place, *Father Boniface* took charge of the convent. To the Mother Superior and the other elders, he presented himself as the irreproachable church patriarch, stern and unbending in his discipline. They had to accept his authority, something that pleased the vampyr to no end.

To the nuns and novices, Father Boniface was an enigma, both seductive in his exotic looks and intimidating in ways they could not name. Over time a select few were rewarded or punished with special audiences. The consequences were the same: they left his presence pale and chastened, bearing with secret pride or shame Father Boniface's little *'love'* bites in private places.

The convent was a kettle forever simmering and in danger of boiling over. It suited the vampyr Boniface so very well. He kept his female charges upon the flames, siphoning off their energies before they could boil over and act out.

For a time he was actually quite content with his arrangement.

Then one morning deep in the stillness of his cell where no light ever penetrated, the atmosphere shifted. His eyes opened. The Hunters were coming. He had mere hours.

There were four other priests who lived in neighboring cells. Unlike him, they seldom had access to the nuns and novices, except at Mass or Confession, and as Boniface kept his 'favorites' subject to his authority even in the confessional, they suspected nothing. There had been no suspicious pregnancies, so as far as they were concerned all was well with Father Boniface.

Two of these priests were much older and good men: Robert and Joaquin.

The other two were younger. One waited on Boniface. His admiration was unmistakable and had been very useful. What Boniface could not do, Brother Jacques did in his place without complaint. Brother Honore was just as willing to assist, but his motivations arose from a different direction. Whereas Jacques' gaze followed Boniface, Honore's followed the young noblewomen who made up the majority of the convent population. He was assiduous at attending the confessional when any young woman was involved.

This was also useful for the vampyr now that the Hunters were on his trail. Father Boniface had only to stand in his doorway and speak, "Come, Brother Jacques. I need you."

And the younger man dropped the quill he had been holding over the household accounts book and hurried to his cell. This time Boniface's tone had sent an unmistakable thrill throughout Jacques. "Yes, Father Boniface. What do you require of me?"

Boniface met him with an expression of quiet, fixed intent. One hand he set upon the man's arm and the other he placed upon his shoulder as he drew him within. There was always time to enjoy his victims, to linger over their self-betrayal and savor the flavor of their mortal bodies. Honore and the old men were busy in the chapel and would be busy for the next two hours, ample time for what the vampyr wished to carry out.

Brother Jacques trembled as Boniface gathered him close in the near darkness and kissed him. His mouth tasted of cheese and apples until Boniface grazed the inside of his bottom lip and the tip of his thrusting tongue with his sharp teeth. Then Jacques tasted of blood, wonderful succulent, iron laden blood. He moaned as Boniface sucked on his lips and tongue. Boniface felt the man's desire pressing against him. He pushed him down upon his humble little bed. The Hunters were coming and there was no time to lose.

"This is my communion and now it is yours too," Sebastiano commanded. "Drink."

The first moment his lover's blood touched his wounded lips and tongue his vitality returned. It was Sebastiano's turn to groan.

When it was over, Jacques arose before his master an altered being, possessed of new powers and a new awareness. He embraced his vampyr lover and swore eternal fidelity.

Sebastiano smiled with eyes as dark as an abyss. "Let us summon Brother Honore. He will be a little restless after hearing confession from all those lovely young ladies. He will be grateful for a respite other than what his hand provides him when he thinks no one is looking."

Master and minion together converted Honore to their *brotherhood*, although Jacques indulged far more in their special communion ceremony than Sebastiano did. While Sebastiano watched, Jacques completed the conversion process. It wasn't that he wasn't hungry, he was, ravenously so. But the Hunters were coming and he had every intention of feeding late into the night, him and his minions.

That afternoon Father Boniface sent for the nuns and novices under his particular authority, one by one.

None of them returned to the convent.

Darkness dwelled where Father Boniface resided and the rest of the convent gathered in their chapel. As night crept upon their remote valley it brought an ominous aura of finality with it. Unearthly sounds began to echo from the direction of Father Boniface's isolated chamber, daemonic and wild.

Brothers Robert and Joaquin closed all of the chapel doors and locked them. The Mother Superior led the Sisters in desperate prayer. Robert and Joaquin sprinkled holy water upon every door and window, and then in a wide circle around them all. Then they patrolled within their holy circle leading the prayers.

The convent and its chapel did not survive the night. Fire ravaged it.

The village neighboring it lay deserted soon thereafter too.

Not all of the villagers survived the night either, and yet those who took refuge in the chapel did, a miracle credited to the appearances of a wrathful **Arch Angel Michael**, his hair blazing with the incandescence of the sun's own celestial flames.

Once again Hecate, Kali, Medusa, and Apollo the fierce bringer of Light found a vile nest of Vampyres waiting for them. There was more this time, freshly converted and ravenous. Several of them lingered within the desecrated precincts of the convent furiously attacking the holy water reinforced doors and windows. The majority had rushed out into the village from which shouts and screams erupted.

Flanked by Kali and Medusa, while Hecate and her dreaded reaping sack brought up the rear, Apollo strode within to liberate the terrified mortals trapped there. While Kali and Medusa guarded the side approaches and Hecate collected the remnants of those hapless vampyr souls who rushed them, Apollo threw open the chapel doors.

"Spare us!" several nuns cried.

Brother Robert and Brother Joaquin thrust forth their crucifixes, but stood speechless before the radiant being standing there.

The Mother Superior knelt before him with her pale, aged hands clasped before her. "Great Arch Angel, deliver us from the demons that have destroyed our Brothers and Sisters."

Apollo gestured behind him. "Flee this befouled site and never return. Go to the mouth of the valley. You will be safe there."

Taking an empty lantern from the wall, Apollo set it aglow with a whispered word. He gave it to the Mother Superior.

"Nothing that comes from the Darkness shall dare molest you as long as you bear this," he said.

Overjoyed, they thanked him and blessed themselves as they passed him. Indeed, even as violent bloodlust stalked the lanes surrounding them, they passed safely, making certain to collect as many villagers as they could along the way.

Halfway across the valley they saw an orange glow behind them.

The convent was on fire. It burned throughout that scream-filled night and smoldered all the next day.

Two days later bands of villagers returned just long enough to collect belongings and supplies, livestock and furnishings and then they abandoned the place forever.

By the time Napoleon was turning Europe upside down, the forest had overtaken the haunted village with its cursed ruins. The people of the valley claimed the place was haunted by the damned and their victims, but this was not so.

Hecate had carried off all of the doomed who hadn't escaped the rampaging vampyres and the damned, all but their progenitor Upir Likhyi and one other misguided soul turned to damnation.

That pair disappeared into the restless Age of Enlightenment with its revolutions and continental wars.

Then when Tambora's eruption ushered in an extended period of gloom and the bloodthirsty idealism of the revolutionary era gave way to a time of introspection, Sebastiano felt that at last he was where and when he belonged. In this *'romantic age'* he felt right at home.

Then one day, in the depths of his dark, subterranean resting place, he awakened. It took Sebastiano a moment to calm his mind and stop searching the darkness with quick glances. He felt it and knew it to be true.

The Great Hunter Hades was on the move once more.

22.

Hecate had been correct, Hades discovered. Upir Likhyi had grown talented at hiding his traces and then escaping divine retribution by the proverbial skin of his gruesome teeth.

Hades began to believe that Persephone had been correct also when she expressed her intuition that they were not meant to find that foul entity. She had been afraid to utter the suspicion, but it did seem as though that destiny was at work.

"We could consult the Fates," Hades suggested once.

Persephone pressed tightly against him in their bed. "I am afraid of what they have to say."

"I will talk to Apollo when I see him again," said Hades after a moment. "He is not as intimidating."

"If you must." Persephone kissed his ancient scar beneath which his heart beat sure and strong.

Apollo listened to Hades' concerns, frowning all the while. Then he nodded, saying, "I trust her intuition. There is a destiny at work and nothing we do or fail to do will prevent its ultimate completion. It is merely a matter of when."

For a long moment they gazed out across the Italian side of the Alps. A wind rushed down from the shining peaks covered with a pure white and tugged at their thick cloaks. In such oppressive weather, the mortals in the nearby town kept behind their medieval walls, safe from the worst of the gusts, and from the discovery of two strange strangers standing openly down the road from their gates. The air had a sharpness to it and already flurries hastened down from the smoky blue grey clouds above.

"Persephone believes she can help us capture our fiend," Hades said at last.

"She does realize the risk, one hopes?" said Apollo.

Hades grunted as he nodded. "She wishes to confront it in person and dare it to come for her."

"Upir Likhyi would not be able to resist an opportunity to work his vile necromancy on the Queen of the Underworld. To captivate her, he would throw his usual caution to the winds."

"Set a trap," said Hades.

Apollo nodded.

"Upir Likhyi must be stopped. He has done enough harm."

"Persephone has power that he has not paused to consider. I think he will be in for a very rude surprise." Apollo smiled.

Hades grinned back, but it was half-hearted. "So we must meet our destiny head on."

"WE do." Apollo jogged him on the shoulder.

Her presence at the fete was a mystery. No one knew who she was or remembered seeing whom she came with. Suddenly she walked among them, passing from room to room smiling a private smile, glancing at everyone, but saying nothing to anyone.

Wondering eyes followed the auburn beauty with a face as fresh and fair as the brightest spring morning, but who wore a diaphanous gown, mantle, and veil that bespoke the hues of twilight intertwined with the velvet darkness of a moonless night. She walked with purpose, stood with strength in her straight back, and gazed everywhere with such a knowing gaze that caused those who met it to avert their eyes.

Was she well born? Certainly she carried herself like a Duchess.

Some thought she carried herself too well for as Duchess. Surely she was a courtesan.

Those few emboldened rakes that endeavored to approach the *Lady of Night* turned back, strangely abashed by the sereneness in her sudden stare. She possessed a forbidding virtue.

At last the Lady of Night came into the last of the upstairs galleries. It was quieter here. There were a few members of Parliament discreetly negotiating votes before the fireplace. A few, scattered groups chatted amiably at their tables and upon the chaise longues. A couple here and there politely courted one another in low spoken smiles. It was a little darker in here and certainly cooler. The windows had been opened wide to catch every breeze.

Long before she had entered that gallery she realized that she was being followed. It wasn't the **one** she sought, though. For a moment she lingered by the window and let the breezes caress her ringlets and fill her purple veil like a sail at sea.

"Are you mortal or divine?"

Persephone fired a wide-eyed look over her shoulder. She knew who he was at once, but not in the manner that all of London did. His was a wounded soul. Already she saw him occupying a place among the purgatorial souls adrift in the great hall of Hades.

"You swan amongst us mere mortals like the Faerie Queene scarcely deigning to favor us with your sweet glances, and yet no one knows who you are." Her arched brow compelled him to add, "I am Lord Byron."

"Of course you are," she said in a disarmingly plain tone. She looked him up and down. 'Such a fierce little peacock', she mused. "You wish to know my name?"

"Indeed all who have set eyes on you do. Only I was brave enough to approach you, for there is something strangely aloof about you, my Lady."

"My true identity is a dread secret," she said pleasantly enough, but the look in her eyes was anything but pleasant. "None of your kind may speak my name and not suffer the consequences."

Byron smiled. "My kind?"

Persephone held up her hand. "If a name you must have, let this one suffice: *Kore*."

Byron hesitated and frowned as he tilted his head slightly. "'Kore' – the 'Maiden'.

"You know your Greek."

"Indeed I am obsessed with Greece in my fashion."

"I know."

He began to open his mouth and paused, eyeing her for a moment. "Where do you come from?"

Persephone burst out laughing. "Such impudent curiosity you have, Lord Byron. Be careful where it takes you."

Although spoken pleasantly enough, her words possessed a quality of understanding that unnerved the flawed poet.

With a distracted, curt little bow, he withdrew from the gallery. Every step of the way, he felt her terrible, calm gaze on his back.

Safe within the doorway, he risked a look back over his shoulder.

She was gone, utterly, as though she were an apparition.

Alarm seized him good and hard. For a time he lingered in the doorway, oblivious to the other guests. This was impossible. If she had gone out the window anyone would have noticed and cried out for her safety. There were a number of lingering puzzled looks toward the window, but then conversations resumed.

Byron had not imagined her. In her whispering raiments of soft night wafting the sweet scents of jasmine about her person, the enchantress had stood out. None who had seen her could ignore her face's tender moon-kissed beauty or her sun ravished auburn hair. He had witnessed the other men approach her only to fall back utterly confused by her imperturbable smile and penetrating gaze. Then he, too, had braved an encounter with this incarnate paradox: a maiden with the all-knowing eyes of an ancient crone and the demeanor of a sphinx.

There was no mistaking. She had been there. Then she was gone, vanished as thoroughly as a passing whim on a busy day. Whether she was a ghost or a banshee Byron chose not to find out. He turned to leave the room with every intention of quitting the establishment altogether. He glanced off to his left and froze.

In the near shadows a tall man stood cloaked in archaic robes the color of a raven's wing. His black hair was a little wild and his demeanor just as unsettling. What caused Byron to speed away from there was the sight of the man's silver-white irises – looking directly at him.

Back in his rooms, Byron grappled with disbelief and fright. He thought of his recent travels, of the time spent in ancient lands and of Greece. Had some spirit followed him back from his journey?

The notion was unreasonable and yet he could not shake free of it once it occurred to him. It rooted there and spread shoots throughout his fertile mind. She haunted him. A full fortnight passed before he stopped watching out for her. Although he sensed her everywhere he went, he never saw her.

A year passed and then another. Living became its own distraction. Because Byron could exist no other way, his life filled to overflowing with tumult. Love came to him and he used it hard.

Finally, his profligacy became his prison and from his homeland he uprooted himself for good and all.

1816, June precisely, Byron's willful recklessness had brought him to Villa Diodati by Lake Geneva in Switzerland. Eventually, he would move on, but for now he rested among Alpine vistas and managed to keep himself reasonably occupied.

Although an exile, he was not alone. There were neighbors, chief among them Percy Bysshe Shelley, Mary Wollstonecraft Godwin with their little boy William, or 'Willmouse', and Mary's step-sister Claire Clairmont, of whom the less said the better – as far as Byron was concerned. There was also his recently hired personal physician John William Polidori, a trifle high-strung man whom Byron liked to needle. Whether his cruelty arose out of boredom or simple dislike even Byron could not say. Still, he man had his uses and was not an entire bore, so that counted for something.

The weather was more March gloom and rain than June warmth and sunshine. He wrote. He stared into the fireplace. He wrote some more. There was no fun to be had niggling at Polidori, not since two days before when he had come rushing back from a walk as though he were being stalked by a nightmare. Percy would come round soon enough and then time would not drag so much.

With Shelley he talked about nearly everything that a reasonable body could discuss. They discussed philosophy, threw ideas back and forth, investigated God's true nature, talked about poetry, life and how to live it, something Shelley had sorted out apparently. These were invigorating discussions for the most part and Mary joined in quite frequently. It was no surprise that she could hold forth as well as Percy, not when her parents were Mary Wollstonecraft and William Godwin.

As for Claire, well, any true interest he had had in her had long since dwindled into dislike, but here she was again upon his threshold, hopes in hand. Having time on his hands, Byron found a use for Claire, when he wasn't scribbling rants for his beloved sister Augusta or to his wretched, maligned and maligning wife Annabella. His mind was a crowded place.

The rains confined them all.

This was going to be trying.

Claire was everywhere, wanting him.

Mary was restless, but at least she had young Willmouse.

Shelley carried on in the certainty that only a self-possessed free spirit could manage.

Doctor Polidori's nerves did not improve. He flinched at the shadows. It was becoming an irritation.

The weather could not have been more conducive for the provoking of nightmares than if they had been in the heart of October. Darkness ruled out the sunshine. Rather than shun the unnatural and unseasonable ambience, they embraced it. Byron and company indulged in the reading of ghost stories from a book called Fantasmagoriana. It had the desired effect. It gave everyone a lovely case of the frights, not that Polidori needed any further motivation there.

That particular chill and dreary ebbing afternoon Byron observed Polidori staring with particular concentration out of the upstairs window. "Are you afraid that your lover will not come?" he said in a cool, curling tone. "Or are you content to watch the wretched wench drown in the downpour?"

Polidori flinched and looked his way. His expression was ashen.

Claire rushed to the windows and grinned as she bounced on her toes. "Where is she hiding? Is it that round German girl we saw two days ago?"

Shelley eyed Byron as though trying to read his motives. "This weather would gnaw at anyone's nerves," he said calmly.

Mary met Polidori's look and frowned. Whatever had rattled the doctor, his reaction was sincere.

Claire pouted and gave Polidori as mistrustful look. "I do not see a single soul, not so much as a duck."

Polidori turned back around at once. "Truly? You see no one?"

Struck serious all of a sudden, Claire looked again. "No."

Polidori wrung his hands and pushed himself toward the hearth.

Byron observed his every gesture. "It will be night soon enough and whoever that was will either have to go back whence they came or come inside."

"Heaven forbid IT comes in! No, night…it will be the worse for us once night falls." Polidori glanced from the windows to their walls.

Perhaps the good doctor had been imbibing the laudanum with his afternoon tea. Byron prepared to humor him. "How so?"

Polidori knew condescension when Byron inflicted it. His expression turned deadly earnest. His hands dropped to his sides. "Because IT likes the night."

If he had not been so grim, Byron would have laughed at the doctor. Instead, he watched Polidori stride from the room looking quite stern.

Claire did laugh, but without real mirth.

"We must not let the fires burn low tonight," Mary said to no one in particular.

"Perhaps we should not read more tonight," said Shelley.

"We should read only during the day," Claire agreed firmly.

"We must occupy ourselves somehow." Byron avoided Claire's quick, overeager glance.

"Let us write our own nightmares instead," Mary began.

23.

Night closed them in. Night was absolute then, oppressive, mysterious, threatening, and seductive all at once. None of them had forgotten the doctor's cryptic and unsettling comment.

Within the villa, Mary's literary challenge enlivened dinner and afterwards the place simmered with creative endeavor.

Determination gleamed in Polidori's eyes and set his lips in a firm line. His pen scratched briskly upon his paper. Now and then he paused and looked toward the night pressed against the windows. Then he resumed work.

Claire seemed determined to act oblivious to anything that might spoil her fun. Her mind revolved around Byron, although at the moment, she was elsewhere in the villa, primping and parading before a mirror in preparation. She would pop up soon enough no doubt to offer him further respite from boredom.

Byron eyed Polidori from his sofa beside the fire. On the floor beside him lay the beginnings of something which he was too distracted to continue.

Slouching on the neighboring sofa, Shelley mused into the flames. Unlike Mary or Polidori, his ideas idled with him before the fire. His glance shifted toward his companion. He leaned toward Byron and whispered, "What did Polidori mean by *'It likes the night'*?"

"I couldn't say, but his apprehension was authentic. Perhaps we should ask him to explain himself."

Shelley frowned toward Polidori.

Claire ambled in. She fixed a smile on Byron as she raised her voice, "Mary, Willmouse is crying – again."

Mary set her work aside and hastened softly from the room.

Claire watched her depart and then flung herself upon the divan at the nearest end of the room to Byron. She arranged herself to provide him with a ready view of her lightly clothed charms. Peering over her shoulder at the men, she said, "I am surprised to find you all here."

"Oh? Why?" said Shelley.

"Where else are we supposed to be?" Byron groused.

"Nowhere, I suppose," Claire sighed. "It is only that I would have sworn one of you was in the corridor upstairs."

"We have been here since dinner," said Byron.

"Only you and my little Willmouse have been upstairs," said Shelley. "Perhaps it was one of the servants."

"They are all downstairs having their dinner," said Byron as he glanced at the clock on the mantel.

"I heard quite distinctly a man's footsteps treading in the corridor. I thought for a moment that it was you, Percy, but then he moved past my door. Then it occurred to me it might be the doctor going up to check Willmouse, because the steps didn't sound familiar at all. Now, I see, the doctor is here, so I don't know who it was," she said airily.

Polidori shifted. He was looking at Claire.

Byron noticed.

"It must have been a servant," Shelley said without much conviction.

"I looked to see who it was and there was no one in sight. Then I heard the child crying, so I came down for Mary." She sighed for Byron's benefit.

Byron ignored her effortlessly. "Is something amiss, Doctor?"

"You do look pale all of a sudden," said Claire, not that she cared.

"Are you ill?" Shelley sat up.

"No." Polidori's glance shot toward the doorway.

Sudden swift footsteps heralded Mary's return. "There is a stranger upstairs. My Willmouse..."

Polidori flew from the room before Shelley could stand. Even as they rushed from the room, they heard Polidori pounding up the stairs. They caught up with him in the room set aside for Shelley's use.

The doctor stood against the encroaching darkness as though he could and would defend the child from it. His wild eyes cast about the shadow haunted chamber.

Mary rushed in from behind Shelley. She clasped her son to her bosom and checked him carefully.

Although little Willmouse no longer cried, he gazed about with wondering eyes.

"Did you see him?" said Mary as she edged toward Shelley.

Polidori shook his head. "And yet I sense a Presence."

"A presence?" Byron was the last to reach the doorway. "What sort of presence?"\

"One that lives in shadow. He has left this chamber, but not the villa." Polidori's wandering gaze witnessed the sudden guttering of the lights in the room.

Claire wrapped her arms about herself and looked into the corridor. "Did you feel that?"

"We all did." Byron turned about. "It was as though as door opened and closed." He frowned into the chamber and muttered, "Now I smell honeysuckle...or something like it."

"It is warmer here than it was a moment ago." Mary glanced about the chamber. "Odd."

Already Willmouse had gone back to sleep as though nothing had ever disturbed him.

Mary gazed into her child's face and smiled. "Percy, please bring my projects up to me. I am going to stay here with Willmouse tonight."

"Yes, of course."

Polidori stalked out past Byron and Shelley, saying, "I shall see to it that the villa is locked up tight for the night...Talk to the servants."

Byron and Shelley exchanged looks before the latter hastened out behind the doctor.

Very lowly, Byron said, "I shall interrogate Polidori...get to the bottom of this enigma."

Shelley nodded. His departing glance flew to Mary.

Mary was pacing across the far end of the chamber, humming softly to their son.

"I shall insure that these chambers are safe before I retire." Byron raised his voice as Shelley ducked down the corridor. "Claire?"

She jumped and turned toward him with her hand pressed to her heart. So, she did have enough sense to be scared of their situation after all. "Yes?" she said.

"Keep watch by your sister until Shelley returns," he said.

Claire pouted slightly and drew her shawl closer about her shoulders. "Very well."

Byron closed the door upon them.

What sounds there were came from other, more distant rooms. Byron lingered in the dim hallway, letting his eyes adjust to the barely adequate lamp lights spaced at remote intervals along the length of the corridor. Their flames burned steadily, scarcely flickering as some distant door opened and closed. Somewhere downstairs and toward the back of the villa the servants moved about. Their voices ebbed so that only a random word now and then emerged with any clarity.

He was alone....and yet, Byron knew beyond all reason that he was not alone.

'*Because IT likes the night*', Polidori had said.

What could the doctor have been talking about?

A shadow passed a doorway mere feet away. There was purpose in its stride.

That was Polidori's chamber.

Byron tilted his head. He knew he had seen the doctor rush toward the stairs. "Doctor? Doctor?"

A lamp glowed only feebly in Polidori's chamber. A man's figure shadowed between its yellow light and the far wall.

Byron moved closer, as swiftly and quietly as he could manage.

It would have been hard to say which would have been more startling: to enter the room and find it empty, or to enter it and find that pale-eyed stranger gazing back at him from across the room, as grave and calm as a Stoic. At any rate, he encountered the latter.

Instinct, nay, common sense demanded Byron give out some manner of alarm. Tradition decreed that he challenge the strange intruder with some sort of demand or a command perhaps: *Who are you? And what are you doing here?* – for starters. Certainly he stood fit and ready for the fight if the stranger made a threatening gesture. His pugilistic trainer in London had taught him what he could do, and Byron knew he could put up a fierce fight, if need be.

And yet, he stood frozen to the spot, so astonished that only a gasp had escaped him. A profounder instinct then caught and held his impudent tongue.

Where the shadows pooled between the hearth and the nearest corner, the intruder stood as though the darkness itself had distilled him into being. The tall, black robed figure looked quite solid. There was no mistaking – he was real. Whoever or whatever he was, Byron realized he would be a formidable opponent in any confrontation.

So Byron stayed where he was – in the doorway, perfectly still.

There the two remained eyeing one another as life echoed in from remote corners of Villa Diodati.

Somewhere out of sight Shelley's brisk footfalls approached the stairs. Byron let go a quick breath. He wanted to look away, but dared not.

The stranger across the room did not move, not even to breathe. Awareness gleamed in his unsettling white eyes.

Byron held his breath.

Shelley's footsteps resounded lightly on the stairs.

The specter – for what else could it be? – took on a shadowy smile and his white irises darkened as though the shadows trickled into them – the way water filled a bowl.

So close and closer still, the footsteps came up the hall, pausing before each doorway before moving onward. It took all of Byron's will to resist the urge for a glance backwards. Sweat trickled down the back of his neck. He breathed in and then out.

The short cry behind him caused him to jump and look.

Polidori stood there.

"You?"

Polidori lunged forward, his wide eyes staring past Byron. "Who - ?"

"I…" Byron turned back around.

The intruder was gone…as though he had never been there.

Polidori stumbled backward.

Shelley had to pivot to avoid smashing into the physician. His frowning gaze met Byron's for a moment as he continued on to rejoin Mary, Willmouse and Claire.

"There is another one," Polidori muttered. "A second one." He veered out.

Byron lunged and caught his arm. "An other what?" He kept his voice low.

Still frowning their way, Shelley closed his chamber door.

"***Strigoi***," breathed Polidori.

"Strigoi? Did you say 'Strigoi'?" said Byron. "What is - ?"

Polidori clasped his arm in return. "***Voykolakas. Upyrii.*** The Undead. A Vampyr. I saw one…I thought there was only the one…"

"Calm yourself, doctor."

"Polidori's grip tightened so much that Byron winced and pried his fingers loose.

"You saw it. This one…this time you saw it?" said Polidori.

"Yes, I saw it. Let us go down. I do not wish to disturb the others."

"I warned the servants, but there is not much one can do to stop revenants."

Byron steered Polidori away. "Keep your voice down, lest you frighten the ladies. We shall converse below."

"Indeed, we must not upset the ladies," Polidori muttered. He pulled free of Byron and hastened ahead. At the top of the stairs, he stopped to assure himself that Byron followed.

"I am behind you," he said.

To the room they had vacated mere minutes before, the poet and his physician returned. Only the fire in the hearth remained to welcome them to the unnaturally still room. Byron made certain to close the door quite firmly as Polidori ascertained that they did indeed have the room to themselves.

After what he had seen in the doctor's room, Byron no longer thought Polidori's behaviour anything other than justifiable. While Polidori's gaze darted everywhere, alert for the slightest inexplicable movement, Byron checked to reassure himself that the windows remained bolted shut.

Turning away from the last window, Byron said, "When you said, 'Because it likes the night', were you referring to that specter we witnessed in your chamber?"

"No, a different creature. This is all worse than I thought."

"Tell me everything you know." Byron poured out two glasses of wine and held one out to Polidori.

His hand trembled as he accepted the glass. His glance shifted toward the writing he had left unattended. It would not take him long to complete his little nightmare, but he feared that his mere writing served only to invoke what troubled him.

"I must have trespassed upon its domain somehow and attracted its notice." Polidori downed his drink.

"Tell me."

"I felt the need for a constitutional, a stroll away from this place, away from you. I wandered without caring where my feet carried me. Then I felt a change in the atmosphere surrounding me. Only then did I stop and truly perceive my surroundings. I had trespassed into a cemetery. The view before me was placid and serene. I could have taken comfort in it, but for the unyielding sensation that I was being watched by something malevolent."

"How could you be sure of that?"

"By the manner in which my skin crawled. It took me more than a moment to summon back my courage and then to survey my surroundings. I had thought perhaps I would see an irate caretaker close by. I stood fully prepared to beg his pardon and withdraw." Polidori leveled a serious glance upon his employer. "There was no other living soul about."

24.

A long silence fell between them.

Byron frowned at the half full glass he held. "If it was not 'living', what do you think it was?"

"Without a doubt I saw a denizen from the dreaded depths of the Inferno." Polidori moved nearer to the table and turned over several pages of carefully inscribed prose. "For a time I thought myself in the grip of a hallucination, but no longer – not after I saw that second specter." He frowned to himself. "This last one strikes me as different somehow."

"You have yet to describe the first creature you saw," Byron prodded. "What did it look like?"

Polidori gazed back at him with dread lying dark in his eyes. He spread his left hand over his manuscript. "A vampyr."

Byron tilted his head. "I've never seen one, so..."

Polidori shuddered, but straightened again. "What I saw staring out from the depths of a mausoleum looked like a living corpse. It was male, but with a lean, hard face, and sickly white as though it came from the moon."

The doctor raised his hands before him and regarding them, flexed them. "This daemonic being had terrible long fingernails, more like claws or worse, like talons. It looked directly into my eyes as it flexed them. It had blood black eyes, and thin grey lips."

Byron frowned toward the ceiling. "What we saw upstairs looked nothing like that."

"No. Except for his white eyes, he looked almost mortal. What I saw in the mausoleum was feral. What we saw tonight looked rational." Polidori shuddered again. Abruptly he downed the remainder of his wine and set it down. "Perhaps it was just the ghost of medieval monk."

"More wine?" Byron reached for the decanter.

"No. Tonight I must keep my wits about me."

Byron filled his own glass again.

Both mused in a silence disturbed only by the fire's crackling in the hearth. Its warmth filled the room and there was nothing out of the ordinary.

Polidori sighed and sat down. "The oppressive atmosphere has evaporated. Perhaps we are alone now. Shadows are but shadows once more. No cowering behind bolted windows and beneath blankets tonight."

Byron wondered at that as Polidori collected his writings and headed for the door.

"I am exhausted after all. I shall see you at breakfast, my Lord," Polidori said.

After three more glasses of wine, which he scarcely tasted, Byron retired as well. The soft warm glow of mild inebriation cured him of any malingering unease as he climbed the stairs. He couldn't resist checking to see whether Polidori lay awake grappling with a night terror. It disappointed him a little to see the doctor sleeping quite soundly by the light of a single, guardian taper.

When he settled at last in his own bed – alone for a change thanks most likely to Mary's unintended intervention with Clare – Byron gazed for awhile at his windows.

There in the dark Byron half-feared, half-craved a glimpse of the Vampyr that had so terrified Polidori. Only the miserable weather pressed against the glass.

Vaguely relieved and decidedly disappointed, Byron closed his eyes and sank into sleep.

Although daemonic vampyrs did not visit him in his bed, dreams did, whispering to him along with the rain. He dreamt of Home, but a jumbled one where different times and dwellings sat in close quarters, like a series of connecting chambers. It both troubled and beguiled him for everything cherished and familiar seemed somehow altered, off-balance even or half-sprung from another realm altogether.

Everywhere he went he met family and friends. Those who still lived he could not see clearly. Those whom he had lost stood stark before him. At last, everywhere he moved he met only the Dead.

And then he found himself in a great dark cavern.

He dreamt, but it felt real enough when a draft chilled him through and through as it grazed his cheek. His own hand felt real enough too when he touched his cheek.

Only after his eyes had adjusted did he realize that he stood in an enormous and ancient Hall deep in the heart of the Earth. He sensed more than he could see others – the Deceased, he realized with a jolt and a catch of his breath. He wanted to awaken, but could not. He stirred or thought he had, but his body slept on, solid and still.

Am I dead? his mind wondered.

"No," came a strong, resounding voice.

In his vision, Byron flinched and in its slumber, so did his body. Still, he did not awaken. There would be no respite.

Across the great hall he saw a pair of thrones illuminated as much by a great pyre behind it as by the luminous mist that pooled and rippled before their dais. Byron gazed at the flames.

'At last, I see my true destination', Byron mused.

"No, this is not *hell*," said the same masculine voice just as Byron saw its possessor upon one of the thrones as *He* stirred beside a more petite figure. "And I am not Lucifer. Neither am I Satan." This last was both firmly and wearily stated.

In his living moments Byron had never felt such astonishment. A sense of dismay accompanied it. His most fleeting thoughts lay naked before these two beings and their ghostly court.

Scarcely had Byron's dreaming gaze set upon the petite figure than recognition seared him. 'Kore', he gasped.

She shifted a little, relaxing out of her formal pose. Her expression warmed a little.

Her consort made a small gesture. "As we have met previously, there is no reason to keep such a fearful distance. Come closer."

Where the resolve came from, Byron could not be certain, but it had not failed yet in life and it did not fail him during this strange sojourn. There was a mosaic before the royal dais. He stepped directly upon it, studying it as he did so.

At the mosaic's heart Medusa's ferocious visage stared back, her eyes wide and her blue tongue extended. To the left Dionysus marched, accompanied by a young faun. To the right, Hades commanded his chariot. With one hand he gripped his reins. In the other he clasped a young woman with radiant hair, who leaned out away from him – Persephone.

The instant recognition lit his face, the austere man upon the throne commented, rather dryly, "Yes, indeed, and in person no less."

Byron caught his breath as he gaped at them. Their eyes cut deep into his soul. He bowed his head. 'I meant no disrespect.' He glanced up. 'Have I intruded?'

"On the contrary," said 'Kore', "we summoned you."

"But why, Lady Per-"

She frowned abruptly.

Hades' hand shot up. "Do not speak her name. You are mortal."

It was Byron's turn to frown. 'Her name is commonly known and pronounced in my world. I have read of you.'

Hades leaned forward. "All the same, do not speak of it. Not here, and certainly not casually."

'And yet surely you address her,' said Byron.

Hades leaned further forward. "I am her Divine Consort. I can call her Lizzie May if it suits me. You are mortal. Remember that. It is unwise to invoke my wife by name."

'Yes, of course.' Byron looked at his feet.

Hades exchanged lively looks with Persephone. "Petulant, fractious little lump of clay isn't he?"

She propped her chin atop her pale elegant hand. "Yes. He is that most frustrating and intriguing paradox: a flawed mortal who is also special. Ah, look. See? There goes his surly little brow and now his eyes are smoldering. I have offended his sensibilities. I would apologize, my Lord Byron, but I am not in the least bit sorry." She smiled over her knuckles at him.

"Fine. You summoned me here. What do you desire of me?"

Hades' quite normal looking eyes were bright with amusement. "A better look at you, considering that you have seen the both of us, it seemed the polite thing to do."

'I remember you. Your eyes were white when I saw you this evening."

Hades nodded. "Only in the realm of the Living do my eyes shine white. Here, I am myself."

Byron glanced at the shadows pressing close along the edges of the mosaic.

Earlier, en route, he had been able to see his friends' faces quite distinctly, but now they dared not enter the rectangular mosaic, and for as long as he occupied it their faces seemed shrouded by veils of fog. He heard their murmurs.

"…living soul, a living soul."

For a moment, he felt certain that he had heard his name breathed across the inviolable boundary. Then he recognized it. It was the voice of a schoolmate – and lover – whom Byron had outgrown and neglected in the end.

"Yes, HE is here," said she whom he dared not name. "Do you feel guilty?"

Byron glared. His affairs were his own business. He did not care for her implied reprimand.

Hades grinned and exchanged glances with his cool-eyed consort. "If he does, he does not like to and resents the imposition of youthful regrets."

'Do what you desire with me and have done with it,' Byron grumbled.

"Ah, you see, there's the rub. There is nothing we could do that you would not and have not willingly and heedlessly, I might add, done to yourself already." Hades shrugged.

"We are simply enjoying the spectacle," said Persephone without any trace of amusement whatsoever. Her unblinking stare beat down on him worse than any fist.

'We have seen one another. Now, unless you have further use for me, may I depart?'

"Go where your mind takes you," said Persephone. "We are not holding you here."

'But you summoned me.'

"True, but only you are keeping yourself from leaving," she said.

'But you are the rulers of the Underworld, surely...'

Hades gave his head a mild shake. "Caretakers. Guardians."

"And judges," added his Consort in a voice of iron, "when it is required." She tilted her head and dropped her hands into her lap. "You should not be so in love with damnation."

Byron's retort died in his throat as Hades stood and came to the edge of the mosaic. The Lord of the Underworld's dark eyes looked straight into his and calmly, he smiled. "We have no jurisdiction over you...YET. In time however...Oh! Be so good as to tell the good Doctor Polidori not to fear. What was troubling him and stalking your villa I have driven off."

Persephone resumed a more formal pose. "Have a simple journey back to the land of sleep."

Byron began to bow.

She added, "And do give my regards to your compatriot Mr. Shelley. Tell him that I foresee a birth in flames."

Byron shuddered.

His eyes shot open. He looked everywhere. His chest hurt and then he remembered to breathe more deeply. "I am back," he announced to his quiet room.

Already, a gradual pale light illuminated the room. Morning had come. Byron sighed.

By the time he encountered Shelley and Polidori, he had forgotten what he had been instructed to relay to them. Surely it had been something akin to an opium dream, and after such a strange evening they had experienced, Byron thought it best not to speak of his dream at all.

By the time Byron remembered the cryptic message for Shelley, it no longer made any difference…

1822, July…Smoke and flames roiled high above the sea washed sands near Viareggio, Italy.

Six years had passed since Byron's exile began and now Shelley had gone to join his beloved little Willmouse, whom malaria had carried off in 1819. Poor Mary, she grieved elsewhere, a proper remove from that sorry place, which perhaps for the best.

Even Byron had found it hard to observe and absorb what the hungry sea had done to Shelley's face. It was a cruel desecration. Their mutual acquaintance Leigh Hunt huddled in the coach. He was too horrified to bear witness when grief alone was hard enough to bear.

When he sprinkled salt and incense upon Shelley's funeral pyre, Byron remembered with the force of a blow and understood.

'I foresee a birth in flames.'

Her name, forbidden from speech, escaped Byron's lips. He turned away. The sea beckoned.

Not much longer, not much longer at all, and Byron sped through his life and straight into the merciless teeth of destiny in Greece. In April of 1824 a fever aggravated by the dubious practices of the medical profession delivered the poet from the realm of the Living onto that familiar threshold.

This time his perception had altered. Byron saw everything with absolute clarity. His fellow Dead paid him no special mind, none whatsoever, except for one.

Across the great hall a figure turned his way.

Shelley.

Smiling wanly, he beckoned to Byron.

Byron crossed to his side at once.

"I wish I could say I was glad to see you here, but…" Shelley began.

"Mary is strong," said Byron, "stronger than we thought. Would that we had the resilience of our ladies."

Shelley nodded, but his gaze reverted toward the thrones behind him.

There sat dark-eyed Hades and smiling Persephone.

"Your compatriot was reciting poetry to me. When he is done, then it shall be your turn perhaps?" she said in a voice that was more command than request.

"Is this his sentence?" said Byron.

"He lingers here," said Hades, "because he will not go forward without his loved ones. Nothing will convince him to move. However, if you see a light, a light so bright that you would expect to be blinded by it and yet find that you can still see clearly, feel free to enter it. Suffering is not obligatory."

And so it was that Byron joined Shelley in the Underworld.

25.

Once again Sebastiano and his minion that wretched renegade monk Jacques had gone to ground again. They were a *contented* pair for the time being. In the pursuit of their debauches they had inspired a great many nightmares and suckled well from the many victims they had seduced along the way. After preparing a nest of voracious vampyrs for Hades' benefit, the pair vanished to the Carpathian Mountains where isolation and fearful superstition could be best exploited.

The **battle of 1821** had been brutal. It had raged from one end of that forgotten ancient cemetery in Bavaria to the other. This time there had been five Hunters: Hades, Kali, Medusa, Apollo, and Hecate.

Jacques insisted on going back to see whether any of his favorites among their conversions survived the fight. "If Manfred escaped, I should like to bring him back. I liked him."

Sebastiano sighed his impatience. "And if you find that Gerda survived instead? Will you bring her back?"

Jacques' handsome cherubic face turned ugly. "Her I do not care for. She can fend for herself."

"Ah, but Gerda I did like. Her I should enjoy having close again." Sebastiano lounged upon the tomb of a dead knight. He let his fingernail trace its dulled outline.

"I serve you abjectly. Why do you insist on hurting me?"

"Because I can and because I have an appetite for suffering and corruption. It is so easy to cause you pain, especially when I lack for entertainment."

"I have followed you everywhere, done everything you wanted…"

"And with gusto too, I have noticed. Corrupting your better nature has been a pleasure."

"I love you beyond life."

"Which has been quite useful as well."

For a moment, a long hard moment, Master and beguiled minion stared at one another.

"I meet your every whim. I have tolerated your favorites…" said Jacques.

"Do not deny that you have had your own favorites. I have seen you with your pretty ones, those delicious youths and Adonises."

"And I shared them all with you."

"You could have had a taste of my trembling maidens and ripe ladies at any time."

"You know my preferences."

"Yes, how did you think I was able to seduce you into this existence? All of you are so easy."

"I am going for Manfred."

"Since I cannot dissuade you, then I shall command you. Although as you well know, it is exceedingly unlikely that the Great Hunter left any survivors, should you find any of our converts clinging to life then you must bring them back. Any survivor. I will not leave one of my kind at the mercy of mere peasants. This is understood?"

"Yes."

"Fine. Off with you and do not let the Great Hunter find you." Sebastiano laid back upon the tomb and arranged himself over the knight's engraved form. "Ah, this one suits me perfectly."

Jacques slipped away as Sebastiano pushed the lid back. Soon the knight's remains lay in a heap behind the tomb and Sebastiano was climbing inside to clear out it out completely.

The stench greeted Jacques long before the sight of the carnage did. It had taken two full nights of flying upon great bat wings to return to their last nesting site. Dawn was yet three hours off when he alighted in the forest nearby.

Until he was certain that none of the Hunters lurked among the gravestones, he let the forest conceal him. He watched with owl eyes, utterly still, thoroughly silent. Other than the natural creatures of the night scuttling and swooping about, nothing stirred. Jacques ventured out into the cemetery.

Almost immediately he found the bodies. Most lay an impolite distance from their heads. Several bore exotic arrow shafts embedded deep in their hearts as well. In those five days since their abandonment to the Hunters, their mortal remains had been left to endure Nature's predations. Bloat, rot, sunshine, rain and scavengers had been industrious in their turn.

Jacques let out a cry of dismay when he found what remained of his Manfred - beautiful, submissive Manfred. Three arrows stood embedded in his chest. His left arm hung by only a tendon where Kali's sword had sliced it. Manfred had been only 18 winters old, tall and splendidly formed in the Grecian mold. He had resembled a Viking with his crisp blue eyes and shining blond hair. His strong, supple body had been ruined. His head was missing.

Jacques darted everywhere. He found many heads – and kicked them aside with a growl. "Manfred. Why can I not find your beautiful head?"

"Because THEY took it," said a vaguely familiar female voice.

Jacques fired a venomous look toward the same forest that had concealed him.

In mortal life her name had been Margareta and she still suffered from the divine wounds she had received in battle. She had also been one of Sebastiano's mortal concubines, the first he had converted in advance of this last assault. She should have healed up entirely, but her bones flashed white where Kali's sword and Hades' scythe had struck flesh and sliced deep. The broken shaft of an arrow stuck out of her right thigh. She was still a vampyr, still immortal, but her wounds were putrefying.

She had been beautiful.

She looked a ghoulish color of grey and her skin hung flaccid from her bones. Although she had escaped the Hunters, she was still dying, or rather, her body was. Once it finally dropped from rot she would become a pure nightmare, something worse than any Succubus.

Jacques wrinkled his nose at the stench of her, but he took some glee at the prospect of bringing her in that state back to Sebastiano. The look on his Master's superior face would be a joy to see.

"What do you mean they took it?" he snapped.

"The one they called Kali claimed Manfred's head as her trophy. She caressed it lasciviously and said that she would add his head to her necklace."

The bitch. Jacques glared at Manfred's ruined splendor of a body. That he should have perished and Margareta survive was beyond endurance. "How is it that you are still here?"

"I fell down a well when the Fiery One shot me." Margareta pointed at the arrow in her thigh. "I entered an underground current and wound up in a cavern a ways away."

"Lucky you."

"I do not feel lucky. Death is consuming me. I feel myself rotting and it is torture. I do not know what to do."

"Neither do I, so spare me your precious complaints."

"My Master would. Does he live?"

"Of course he does."

"Please take me to him." She limped nearer and reached out for him. "Sebastiano can help me."

"What makes you think he cares about you, especially in your pungent state just now?"

"Because he knows I love him."

Jacques snorted.

"And because I live to serve him."

"Sebastiano loves no one and servants are cheap and plentiful."

"Please take me to him." Her hand caught at his sleeve.

Jacques knocked it away.

Margareta whimpered and slapped at him. "He would want you to take me to him."

Jacques snarled and kicked her down. Bile spit out of her mouth as he plunged his hand into her rotting chest. From it he tore her heart. As her dying eyes bled he ripped her heart to pieces.

Several nights later Jacques returned to the crumbling castle and Sebastiano.

"Were there no survivors?" said Sebastiano.

"None." Jacques moved past him without making eye contact.

"Too bad about your Manfred."

"Yes, isn't it?" He headed down to the tombs to pick out his sleeping place.

Sebastiano smirked. He knew a lie when he heard it.

26.

In between hunting raids with the rest of his war party, Hades divided his time between his duties in the Underworld and sojourning in the realm of the Living tracking Upir Likhyi.

During one of his early autumnal sojourns among the earthbound, early in the so-called *19th century*, Hermes went searching for Hades. He found the night-robed Lord of the Dead by the seashore.

Hades wore a quiet smile as he peered into a very sheltered nook in a tidal pool. A wary little crab peered back up at him.

"No, it isn't your time yet, little soul."

The crab stayed put. It wasn't taking any chances.

Scarcely had Hermes alighted upon stones so rough that they could bite and gouge humbler feet when Hades spoke up, "What is it now?"

Hermes tilted his wide-brimmed helmet back and propped his hands on his hips. "I know I didn't make a sound. How did you know?"

Hades looked over his shoulder. Broad smiles and huge laughs never disrupted his stoic demeanor and yet, he was not immune from amusement. His thoughtful and usually somber eyes would light up and the corners of his lips would curve upwards. It helped that Hermes, their 'resident' trickster, could provoke mirth from even the most stern-faced among them.

Hades shrugged. "I just do. What do you need?"

Hermes opened his mouth.

Hades frowned. "Wait. Zeus isn't holding another of his wretched banquets is he? Those always turn out badly."

Hermes sighed as he surveyed the ocean shimmering under the sweet spring light. "And yet he wonders why we are forever coming up with excuses to leave early."

"Or to not show up at all," said Hades.

Hermes snorted. "You're the lucky one. After your convalescence, Zeus would just as soon never have you around for so much as a cup of tea. Hera is the one who insists on extending you the courtesy."

Hades arched his brow. "I have not spoken with Zeus since that time. I hadn't realized that I had burned any bridges."

"I get the impression that Zeus does not care for any comparisons between the two of you, which naturally tend to arise when you're in the same room.

'   "He feels he comes off rather badly, eh?"

"In Hera's eyes, yes. There may be a little jealousy on his part. Hera speaks only kindly and affectionately of you anymore. He has forbidden Ganymede from mentioning you at all."

"Poor Ganymede."

"Do not be surprised if Ganymede dons proverbial wings to spread himself upon the winds."

Hades shot Hermes a sharper glance.

Hermes nodded. "He despairs of his lot."

Hades looked up at the seagulls. "Poor Ganymede. So what brings you here?"

"I could ask you the same thing – standing around on the South American seashore on such a bright and benevolent day."

Hades sighed. A gentle breeze had just ruffled his hair. "We all have our bouts of restlessness. Apollo spends his among his lovely Muses, catching up on the latest developments."

"Except for today."

"Oh?"

"He's brooding at Delphi or what's left of it."

"Ah, well, and Zeus has his mortal conquests and his lightning storms.

"And what do you have, Zagreus?"

"I go for strolls and simply soak up all the lovely energy everywhere."

Hermes stood silent and attentive for a moment. "It is a splendid day."

Together they gazed out across a fragile world.

Hades turned his back on the ocean. "You do want something, don't you?"

"There is a *Mother* spirit in the northern hemisphere who will not go willingly. The Fates have decided her destiny, but she would cling to her life and risk becoming a ghost. She does not deserve that."

"How many children does she leave behind?"

"Six young ones and fortunately for them, a strong, doting husband."

"I see." His irises turned white. "We should go then."

Hermes sighed. "Let's get this done with."

In less than an instant they stood before a sturdy two story house that sat resolute astride a steep hillside.

For a moment, Hermes let Hades absorb the view of the small suburb of gravestones before the house, arrayed between it and a grim grey church. The wind that blew here rushed mercilessly down cobbled streets from higher and wilder elevations. Hades observed the residents on the lower lanes forcing their purposeful way past the shoving gusts.

As his gaze settled again upon the village of graves hard beside their destination, Hades mused, "Six children you say."

"Six," Hermes nodded with a frown for the rude wind that pulled on his chlamys. "The oldest is but seven and the youngest is only one."

"I have seen worse," Hades muttered to himself, then more loudly, "Shall we go in?"

"I shall linger by the doorway if you don't mind." Hermes eyed the village with an inscrutable expression that bordered on serious.

Hades looked up at the windows. "She is easy to locate?"

"Yes, and you should have no difficulty conversing with her. She is between realms and delirious as a result. She can see us readily."

"Very well." Hades moved toward the door.

Hermes looked sharp over his shoulder. "Do not come to her with 'white' eyes. It will frighten her."

"I will show her my normal Olympian eyes then." His silvery white irises turned as dark as volcanic soil and he passed through the door.

Hermes stood sentry before the doorway. He watched as a few stalwart souls scuttled into the church, just as eager to get out of the September currents as they were to pray away their troubles. Hermes pulled his cloak closer about himself, more as a reflex than out of genuine need for warmth.

Hades was right. Hermes had seen places far worse to live in, much, much worse.

Very briefly, Hades glimpsed the six children – five girls and one boy, and so very vulnerable as all younglings were. They were subdued and no wonder there. The anguish within that household was as thick and palpable as smoke. It swirled around the Lord of the Underworld as he passed through, following a silver stream no thicker than a thread to its anchor – a mortal, careworn young woman dying in her bed.

Upon that threshold, just where the door met its frame, Hades stopped and politely inclined his dark head.

Those few other souls gathered about her bedside grieved and prayed and saw him not.

She, though, did.

"Madame, it is time."

Her lips trembled, but only her mind spoke up pure and clear. "I cannot leave them. Not now. Please let me stay."

"These matters may not be re-arranged. The time is now. I have come to escort you in all safety."

A weary tear slipped from beneath her right eye as she closed them both. "My children...who shall watch over them?"

"Their father shall. This you know."

"He has his duties and he is heartbroken."

"Your sister Elizabeth shall remain here."

"Shall she?"

"This is certain."

At last she calmed and began to relinquish her hold. "Shall I be allowed to see my children from time to time?"

"That is not forbidden."

"They will need my presence. I wish to watch over them."

"There are limits, but you will remain aware of them, their joys and their sorrows."

"I want to stay here."

Hades shook his head. "It is time to go."

"Please let me haunt."

"That I cannot abide."

"Why not?"

"Because you do not merit such a fate. Rise and come away with me. There is only suffering for you if you remain."

"Will you watch over my poor, dear children when I cannot?"

Hades paused. "You do not realize what you ask of me."

"Act as their protector when you can. Befriend them if need be."

Hades frowned. "You do not know who I am."

"You are the *Angel of Death*." Her soul, still confined within its frail shell, smiled.

His face clouded as Hades bowed his head. When he raised his face and lifted his gaze, her soul, shining so soft and pure, had sat up away from her barely breathing body. She regarded him fully, buoyed by trust.

Hades bowed more formally. "For you I will keep a weather eye upon your little ones."

"Bless you."

"Will you come now, Madame?"

She looked about her at her beloved husband and her redoubtable sister on either side of the bed where she had suffered until the final respite had arrived. They gazed at her cancer-harrowed body with grim realization. She had gone utterly still.

Her children stood there under the stewardship of a nursemaid. Solemn, they gazed at their Mother's body as her soul whispered past them, reaching out, but unable to embrace them one last time.

"Yes, I see that I must leave now," she said as she tore her caring gaze away from the Living and toward the dark, wingless angel in the doorway.

His grave expression softened as he extended his large hand to her.

She smiled as she accepted his hand. She looked back one last time upon her be-stilled body, but already her Guide had spirited her into the After Realms. There, she passed directly from his gentle stewardship into the passage of Light.

True to his word, the Lord of the Underworld took his restless constitutionals where he might also observe the six children. If they sensed his presence at all, it was as a passing shadow or a hesitation in the wind that ruled the wild hills above their parsonage home.

Hades kept a distance from their bright little souls, but then their father Patrick, who meant only for the best, sent the girls to a place where unfortunate conditions gave HIM reign. It grieved Hades to witness what the Fates had decreed. Perverse creatures of irony the Fates could be. It would not be unlikely for them to bind this innocent family to His realm from the moment their Mother had urged that promise upon him.

Unseen, Hades accompanied the two eldest daughters, the mother's namesake Maria and the aunt's namesake Elizabeth, on their final journeys home to the parsonage. He watched over them and when it came time to cross over, he brought forth their radiant Mother so that she might greet her daughters and escort them herself.

Both times their joyous reunions with their Mother were Hades' only and best reward for his diligence.

During those long spells afterward, Persephone sat beside him on her throne quietly wondering at the thoughtful grace softening his somber features. She did nothing to disturb his meditations. The Fates did that well enough among the Living without any prompting whatsoever.

For a little while though, there was a lull in their lives during which Hades fulfilled his promise from what he considered a prudent remove – the moors and hills above the parsonage where the four surviving children liked to roam as they grew up. Hades found that he liked the isolation of their wild playground. When he knew they were coming, he took to waiting there for them.

More often than not the wind carried their voices ahead to him. As they drew near, he turned away from the view to observe their progress. Sometimes he shadowed them, smiling at their little exchanges and found an unexpected consolation and enjoyment even in seeing the world through their vivid young eyes. Their restless little spirits passed in and out of his presence without any notice of him whatsoever.

Or so Hades thought.

As they matured, their subtle differences began to estrange them in telling ways. The only son developed other *outer* interests and pursuits and as was expected of menfolk he ventured out more deeply into the workaday world. He took part in his sisters' amusements less and less. They missed him, but life was difficult and they were poor. Eventually even the three sisters found that their destinies carried them far from Home and Patriarch too.

Hades did not follow them on their sojourns. There was no need to. In calm voices the Fates had whispered beneath those northern winds, "They shall return in time, Hades. 'Best wait for them in their cherished northlands."

So Hades occupied himself collecting errant souls, herding victims of disasters and plagues into the after life.

One day, one of the two sisters who had ventured across the Channel returned. This one considered herself the strongest in her sense of independence, but this last European sojourn had shaken this conceit. Even though she would not fully admit it to anyone else, not even herself, the recognition that she did possess limitations after all to what she could endure would never leave her again.

Still, deep down, it piqued her that she had the precious vulnerability of a hot house flower. In the end, once she stood safe again in that parsonage she embraced it for it had returned her to where she had wanted to be all along. It gave her an able excuse never to leave again. Up went her sleeves, for there were chores she could do. There was bread to bake and the German language to master all at the same time. With so much to do of a practical nature and so much going on in her restless mind, there simply was no time left for loneliness for her sisters.

Still, Loneliness was an insidious disease. It had a way of creeping up on one. When its baleful influence could no longer be ignored, she took to their favorite haunts to commune with nature and the spirit that commanded it. It did the trick.

Even in such remote solitude high beyond their town and the mills and factories farther down hill, she did not feel lonely. Rather, contentment suffused her.

Whenever she set forth from the parsonage, she expected and desired absolute solitude. Now and then it bothered her to spy some stranger in the near distance.

It was a relief though to witness that he wanted as little to do with society as she did. One moment he stood with his back to her, gazing off across the unforgiving hills and the next he had gone – utterly. Initially, she was relieved. She craved only her own thoughts for company. Interruptions were a bother.

However, there were more sightings. Each time she came upon him it seemed to startle him. Always he stood with his tall back toward her, allowing the wind to course over him, whipping at his strange voluminous black garments and running icy fingertips through his black hair. By the almost electric look of awareness in his eyes when his head snapped in her direction, she knew that she had startled him. Their gazes would lock: hers wary and unwelcoming, his calm, penetrating and not unfriendly. Every time something off in another direction, a bird or some imagined movement seized her attention. By the time she looked around again he had moved off.

Rather, she assumed he has simply marched down the slope's crest, this stranger who reminded her of a raven, for he had disappeared from view so swiftly and absolutely. Surely the *Raven Man* had just slipped away down the other side of the slope. One moment he had been there and the next it was as though the Earth had swallowed him up with one eager gulp.

Not two weeks had passed when a dream came to trouble the young woman, a dream like no other, for it felt more real than life itself. Although she did not remember leaving the parsonage at all, she found herself standing in the same spot where she would first catch sight of the aloof stranger. Everything looked as it should and yet something felt a little off. She felt the chill wind, saw the heavy blue grey clouds rushing across a pale cerulean sky. She did not see the stranger in his usual haunt. Her horizons were unbroken, infinite.

She did not see him, but he was there somewhere…somehow.

'Who are you? Where are you?' In her vision she spun about, thinking that he was behind her.

'I am everywhere and I am here.' His voice was somber, but deep and careworn instead of stern.

'Who are you?'

'It is for the best that you do not know my name. Even better as you must not speak it, but rest assured – I mean you no harm.'

'Why do you leave? Are you afraid of people?'

'Nothing of your realm frightens me. Nothing can frighten me.'

'You do not have to leave. I will not disturb your reveries.'

'That would be wise. You must never speak to me, Emily.'

With those ominous words echoing strong in her mind, she awoke to see the first hint of dawn outside her window.

That day she did not embark on her customary march, nor the next day, or the one after that.

On the fourth day Emily deemed her trepidations as foolish and set off on her walk. The closer she came to the crest of the path where she had always viewed the stranger the stronger her uncertainty became. For a moment, Emily hesitated, but the strength of spirit she had from her father sent her marching forward.

From the spot where the stranger always lingered, she enjoyed a full view of the steep hillsides and the deep vale below. There was no place to hide she realized.

There was also no sign of the *Raven Man*.

Then, for the first time in her life, Emily fled that beloved landscape for the snug confinements of the parsonage.

The weather turned particularly unforgiving after that. For some days afterward, Emily could only look out the windows now and then and wonder.

By the time more reasonable weather returned, her fear had given way long since to ferocious curiosity. Nothing could hold her back from making an excursion. If he was a ghost, she wished to verify it. She would verify it!

Well-swathed against any malingering elements of nasty weather, Emily set off upon her solitary walk. Eagerness hastened her sure stride all the way until she crested her side of the hill. There she faltered.

Except for the ungentle breezes tugging at her clothes, she was alone. Disappointment raged deeper than any sense of relief as she looked everywhere about herself. She was absolutely, resolutely alone out there.

At last Emily had to accept that there was nothing to do but continue her walk. That she did, although at a decidedly more thoughtful pace. She took her usual path. By the time she reached the other side her mind had gone off in pursuit of other notions that informed her pencil.

Then, at the very last moment, she felt it – a change in the currents or was it that subtle shift of light causing everything to brighten just a little? Whatever it was, it was palpable. She stopped to take in the pure white quality of the light. In turning to wonder and admire the seemingly supernatural tranquility, she froze and gawked.

Standing in the near distance, exactly whence she had come was *Raven Man*. He gazed directly at her. She had had every intention of engaging him in some purposeful conversation. Instead she stood rooted to the spot, startled mute.

The stranger inclined his head in greeting, turned away, and descended toward the town.

The instant she lost sight of his tousled dark head the light changed and the breezes resumed their rude prodding. That startled her. She hadn't noticed the sudden, unnatural stillness that had belonged to the pale celestial light. Emily thought to run after him. She wanted to quite badly, but she knew he would not be there. There wouldn't be so much as a footprint in the ground.

A great sigh escaped her. She resumed her familiar walk.

The next day and the next and the whole week beyond that, Emily ventured out with eager eyes. Her solitude remained unbroken. Perhaps the specter appeared at only certain times of the year. Perhaps he would not manifest again to brood in his favorite spot until the next year.

Eventually, Emily stopped looking for him. Her sisters Charlotte and Anne were home at the parsonage again, so she forgot about the stranger in the midst of other concerns and preoccupations. She might have forgotten him entirely, but for that one day when she and her sisters were out taking their customary walk.

Anne let out a cry and stepped back so suddenly that it startled both of her sisters. Inadvertently, she interrupted Charlotte's relentless barrages of persuasion, giving Emily a brief respite from their older sister's ambitions.

Directly ahead stood the *Raven Man*.

As disconcerting as it was to find him so boldly regarding them, looking for all the world as though he were waiting for them, Emily grinned to see him again. He looked as he ever did, resembling more one of her *creations* than he did a being of the natural world. Emily dared march several steps closer. She tilted her chin in greeting.

Silent and agog, Charlotte and Anne hung back, caught in the stranger's serious gaze.

To their immense surprise, Emily addressed him as familiarly as she spoke to them within the safe confines of home, "Where have you been? I had become used to NOT seeing you."

For a moment, a look of bemused surprise illuminated his darkness and he seemed about to respond. He stopped himself. Instead, he drew himself up to his full and formidable height.

Emily faltered backward two steps.

Then he smiled a grave, but kindly smile, bowed, and departed swiftly from sight.

"Who was that?" said Charlotte, once she was sure that he couldn't possibly hear her."

"Someone who is more retiring than we are." And Emily resumed walking, a triumphant look on her face.

Anne and Charlotte could not leave that site fast enough.

"Did you notice?" Anne whispered. His eyes turned from silver to brown as he looked at us."

Charlotte's persuasions won out, and so Emily and Anne also applied their imaginations in an effort to engage the greater world. Against all odds they did do just that and took some satisfaction in their endeavors.

Unfortunately what had been hard won was forever balanced against an unenviable destiny that decided to take more than it had ever bestowed. As the three sisters found ways to flourish in the face of an indifferent society, their only brother began to rot from the inside out. Wounded already by impetuous and naïve conduct, his spirit fell victim to self-pity and its toxic appetite for any means to dull its pain, whether alcohol or narcotics. Then illness beset him as it had his long-departed elder sisters Maria and Elizabeth. By then he had neither strength nor the will to fight mortality.

The *good son* his family had despaired of ever seeing again resurfaced in those last hours. His was yet another desperate, flailing life finding its footing when it was too late to do any good. This was the way of things, as Hades knew from long experience.

As Hades had four times before – for the matriarch, for the elder daughters, and for the aunt Elizabeth, - so now he stood just beyond their embattled family's mourning circle watching the precious only son Branwell during his last morning of mortal existence.

Directly behind him stood, as she had done three times before, the Mother who had extracted that promise from Hades. Luminous and serene she waited to embrace her beleaguered son.

In their very last moments sometimes the dying saw those who awaited them and so it was for the wretched young man in the bed. His dying eyes perceived both Hades and the unexpected, and yet astonishingly familiar woman flanking the *dark angel* with the silver eyes. He *knew* them both at once. His soul leapt forth at the sight, pulling his wracked body upwards.

Immediately, he stood in his Mother's embrace and his husk fell back into his Father's grieving embrace. They vanished from the mortal threshold and appeared at once in the Underworld.

As Hades shifted to follow them, his gaze locked with Emily's.

She saw Hades. She saw HIM.

Emily had witnessed her brother's spirit pass his way, as a shadow passed along a wall. Then she looked above Hades' head.

Hades glanced too.

An ominous smoke-like veil gathered there and rolled outward over the simple room and over the survivors. This was how the Fates forewarned Hades. Unfortunately, the young woman saw it too. She didn't understand what she was witnessing, but she could intuit its meaning in time.

Hades withdrew a step. Darkness weighed heavy upon his heart.

Emily shot a glance his way.

The stranger had gone from her mortal sight.

Hades witnessed her surprise and then the terrible and sudden realization in her eyes. This he had not meant to happen, but it had. Worse, to his life-loving mind, she had embraced the realization, without fully comprehending what she was about to endure during her final passage.

Hades knew he would be trespassing into that bleak household again all too soon.

"Why do they love death…obsess so over oblivion so much more than life?" Hades mused aloud beside his warm, radiant Persephone.

"It is their ultimate destination," she said. "Naturally it should fascinate them."

Hades shook his head and wound a length of her rippling hair about his fingers. "But not to the point that they should love it more than Life."

"Their true tragedy is that they look and seldom ever *see*."

In a sense Hades never fully left that household in Yorkshire. As Emily entered her last autumn, her last season, she carried on with her daily existence in a kind of defiance. Even though she did not see her old acquaintance, she felt his melancholy presence. There were times that she felt him watching her, watching over her actually. When she dared look, her mortal eyes could not perceive him. No sooner did she wish that she could than she felt grateful that she couldn't.

Alongside her sisters Anne and Charlotte, Hades witnessed Emily's relentless decline. More than his prey, he regretted that she was so stubborn in her denial of aid and comfort from her family. It did not have to be that way.

"Who are you punishing?" Hades mused aloud as he watched her gaunt figure stumble and falter. "This perverse obstinacy serves no purpose," he whispered to her although he knew she would not listen.

Her sisters would help her but she would have none of their interference until it was too late.

Not many hours later Hades gestured the way and her willful spirit passed by him in silence.

Hades did not follow, not yet. His gaze had landed upon the one named Anne, whose gentle soul burned a little too brightly all of a sudden.

In the spring, early on a Monday afternoon, Hades attended the next deathbed of that blighted little family. He greeted Anne's bright, brave little soul with a simple inclination of his head. As he peered up at her with his silver white eyes, he extended his hand to her. There was wonder in her eyes as she accepted his hand.

Already a fog rose between them and the Living realm. As her Mother's figure grew brighter ahead, her arms outstretched, Anne looked back. "My sister...What will become of Charlotte?"

"She is not yet done with Existence."

"Will you...? She will be so lonely."

"That I have already sworn," Hades said as she disappeared with her Mother.

For a spell, Hades wandered.

Persephone saw precious little of him. When she did, he seemed preoccupied. He gazed at her with a distancing sort of thoughtfulness.

It was not as though he was being cruel or cool towards her. Rather, Hades seemed to be regarding her through a veil of another perception. He spent less time upon his throne or within his private chambers.

Upir Likhyi and his minion Jacques seemed to have gone into hibernation. The Hunters were at a loss. Hades knew that it was only a matter of time. The Fates weren't talking, but Hades didn't need to hear what they had to say.

Nearly a full six mortal years passed before Hades returned to escort the last of the six children across.

There had been no mercy in her death. Just as her siblings before her, Charlotte suffered for having a spirit more vigorous than what housed it. Just as stubborn and defiant in her way as her uncompromising sister Emily, Charlotte took a firm hold of what Life had offered her by way of consolation at long last. A fuller life lay within her grasp. It should have been within reach. She should have caught it and held it close, but there was cruelty in the Fates' impartiality.

204

So it was on a morning in March that the expectant mother was reborn herself into the After Life, as regretful as her own Mother Maria had been. She inquired after her husband Arthur, her bereft father Patrick, and after her child who would have been.

"Your men folk will come in their turn," Hades assured her. "All will be well, Madame."

"My child…"

"'Has returned whence it came, for nothing and no one is ever lost."

Charlotte sighed and let go.

Six more mortal years later, Hermes brought the lonely patriarch Home.

Hades watched with a peaceful smile as they – all of that humble family – were reunited. The Light opened up about them and in less than a heartbeat's time absorbed them. As their joy echoed around the vast cavern, a great weight lifted from Hades.

Persephone took his hand in hers and drew him away with her.

27.

In Hades' search for that pestilence Upir Likhyi the Spiritualism Movement that the 19th century spawned did not help matters. Rather than spreading the clarity of Enlightenment into the Underworld, it clouded the proverbial waters. All that energy the Living focused on the Dead turned that domain into a veritable dustbowl of restless spirits.

Eventually things did calm down, somewhat, although a steady stream of dabblers pulsed the currents of the Underworld in search of insight or loved ones. Frankly, Hades was ambivalent about psychics and ghost hunters. They did little, if any harm, although Hel blamed them for her migraines and Anubis disliked how the psychics' energies unsettled their inmates. Hecate found herself overwhelmed by ghosts and seldom could visit Hades and Hel at their court. It took the combined efforts of Osiris and Yamaraja to restore calm anymore, however fragile and fleeting.

During that time wars broke out, flared hot and consumed nearly whole generations. As a civilization consumed its own, from the north of the western hemisphere, a flood of dazed, brutalized men began to pour before the steady stream of First Nation inhabitants became a tragic trickle.

"Heavens!" said Anubis. "What now?"

Persephone added more incense to the burner. "That smell. That new sulfurous smell is all over them." She and Nepthys wafted the incense out over the new arrivals.

"Valhalla is about to get mighty crowded," said Nepthys as she noted the variety of uniforms these new arrivals wore.

"I had best go abroad to see what is happening," said Hades and vanished across their threshold almost at once.

Battlefields, one after another, Hades traversed with a grim set to his mouth. Everywhere the stench of rot filled his nostrils. Bodies lay everywhere he went where once flourished virgin forests, placid meadows, and farm fields.

It did not take him long to encounter Hecate squinting out across some recent field of carnage. "Insanity, old son," she said without turning to watch him approach. "I must be losing my touch. More and more souls escape into this landscape than I can capture."

"Do not blame yourself. Chaos has swept them up. We shall bring them Home in time." Hades drew up alongside her.

Hecate shook her head. "I cannot restore these forlorn souls to the Underworld. I could not drag Upir Likhyi back to the Maelstrom where he belongs. Something is amiss."

"There is a destiny at work, Hecate, and it we must accept."

"I don't like the sound of that."

"Neither do I."

"That bastard bloodsucker has to surface sometime."

Hades frowned at the Earth. "He will in good time. I can feel it."

"I don't like the sound of that either."

"Neither do I, but I've developed a sense where that pestilential entity is concerned. It is fitting. He is my fault when it comes down to it."

"Hmmmm."

"Now, I didn't like the sound of that, Hecate."

"You shouldn't," she retorted. "'Don't like your tone. 'Don't like it one bit, old boy."

"Me neither." Hades shrugged. His gaze roved, but then he stopped to stare. "Is that - ?"

"Bless me for a maiden aunt," said Hecate. "That's Ares and Athena."

"And they're actually conversing."

"Will miracles never cease?" Hecate bustled forth to interrupt them.

Hades followed, only mildly curious, and treading more deliberately across the despoiled land.

Both deities leaned upon their spears. Ares held his blood hued golden helmet under his arm. Athena had popped hers up a little and tilted it back away from her face.

Hecate hailed them. "I hope you two are happy with yourselves. Look at what your demand for valor on fields martial has wrought."

"You know bloody well, old witch, that we did not instigate this slaughter," Ares said.

"Ah, but you participate in your unenviable fashion readily enough," Hecate chided. "Mortal millenniums may have passed since those seasons before the walls of Wilusa, but none of our natures have altered THAT much."

Ares smoldered.

Athena's expression turned arctic. "We do not delight in these occasions." She gestured with her spear across the fields filled with ruined humanity. "How could anyone when this sort of relentless slaughter is possible?"

"Their ingenuity at destruction and mass murder increases by the day," Ares commented.

"You cannot stand before me and claim that your hands are unstained," said Hecate.

"No," said Athena, "but we ally ourselves in the cause of Providential Destiny."

"Where there is true valor," said Ares, "there I shall be. To those who express courage in the face of oppressive odds I shall lend resolution."

Athena nodded all the while. "And to those spirits of Enlightenment who face down the forces of oppression itself, I shall lend Courage itself. Zeus may still be a philandering peacock, but we who remember whence we came have evolved as the times have required."

"The Source is All," said Ares solemnly. "Those souls have sacrificed themselves for the nation's destiny."

"Once they find their way there, Valhalla will be quite loud again," said Hades.

Athena and Ares spied him off to the side and inclined their heads to him. "Greetings, Aidoneus Zagreus, Lord Hades."

Hades bowed his head back. "Greetings, Atinija, and to you Ares." Then he set off across the battlefield.

They could hear him muttering mantras over the corpses he passed.

"He seems preoccupied," said Ares.

"A cloud hangs over him," said Hecate. "Frankly, I'm concerned."

"If you need my strength," said Athena, "simply call out."

"I will come too if you need me," said Ares.

Hecate nodded and leaned on her staff.

They watched Hades disappear in the smoke and fog.

Hades did not come back to the Underworld, so Persephone arranged her veil of shadows over her fair face and went abroad. She had never gone to look for him before. She had never had to. It had always been the other way and he always seemed to come directly to her no matter where she was. Just like that. It had to be a simple matter of concentrating and lo – she would come upon him.

Persephone could not find Hades. She couldn't even find where he had been, which would have enabled her to track him down.

"Kali! She would know where to look," Persephone realized aloud to the night air. Perhaps he was with her and the other Hunters.

She rushed to India.

She found Dionysus first.

Seated in the lotus position atop an earthen mound, the Bull-Horned One gazed out over the Ganges with eyes that saw Infinity. Before she could draw near, he called out, "Greetings, Beloved. What brings you to this sacred land?"

Suddenly, Persephone realized the terrible absurdity of her search. Of all of their kind, she should have been the one who knew where Hades was, and yet, she stood at a loss, helpless and bereft. Soft and low, she replied, "I cannot find Hades."

Dionysus turned to look at her. His look of astonishment caused her to hang her head. "I have not seen him and if you cannot find him, then I do not know what to tell you.'

"Do you know where to find Kali?"

"She is not abroad with the Hunters, so she must be meditating in her temple."

"Then she cannot help me."

"She might know the places Hades likes to haunt."

"When Hades goes abroad from the Underworld he wanders. He has a restless mind and he tends to follow it."

Dionysus faced the Ganges again. "In his stead, there are two places where I would be: where there is death in abundance or where there is peaceful life."

"That could be anywhere."

Dionysus nodded as he glanced over his shoulder. "And everywhere."

"I should know these things. I should have known." She pulled at the hem of her sleeve, worrying at the embroidery.

"Calm your mind and your insight shall arise."

"I've been concentrating."

"Yes, but you're overwrought now. Why are you upset?"

"Because something feels wrong. It is as though a darkness gathers on our horizon and something is coming that cannot be prevented."

"Fear is a waste of energy. What happens must happen. What does not happen does not. No sense in wasting energy dreading and worrying about what may or may not come. The Tibetans north of here have a saying, *'Hope for the best. Prepare for the worst.'*"

Persephone nodded, but plucked at her veil. "Walk with me, Dionysus? Until I can calm my mind, walk with me?"

"Certainly." He climbed to his feet and rearranged his colorful robes. "Where shall we go?"

"Wherever our feet take us." She held out her hand.

Dionysus laid her hand over his arm with a little caress. "Let's go find Krishna, shall we?"

She nodded. "How is Ariadne? We never see her."

"She resides in her special place. I go to see her quite often."

"Why do you not live with her?"

"I do."

"You love her then."

"I do. Do you love Hades?"

"Hades loves me."

"You're being evasive."

"Do you love Aphrodite?"

"Ah!" Dionysus grinned and shook his head. "Aphrodite *loves* me."

"But you – "

"Let's just say I love what she does. Aphrodite is a power unto herself. She has her own flexible rules and will not be bound absolutely – to anyone. We both have our purposes, she and I, and it is never anything but a pleasure when our purposes meet."

"I see."

Dionysus fixed a serious, but not unkind look on her. "Do you love Hades?"

She reddened and drew her veil closer about her head. "Why do you ask?"

"Because I think therein lies the crux of your problem: if you loved him – no, let me rephrase that – if you admitted that you loved him, you could find him."

Persephone paused in mid-step. "You think so?"

"Get out of your own way and see what happens."

After two cups of soma with Krishna and Dionysus, Persephone set off again. She went west by northwest.

Lost in thought and frowning as a result, Hades returned to the Underworld. Scarcely past the threshold, his frown intensified. He stopped short and raised his face. Looking back, he said, "Where in Hell is Cerberus?"

Hel sat upon the dais. Garmr lay at her feet, his head resting atop her soft moccasin- like shoes. "You've come back!"

Hades motioned behind him. "Where is my dog?"

Hel sighed. Garmr whined and rubbed his head against her leg. She reached down and patted his head. "'Long story short: Hera has him."

"What? On Olympus?"

Hel nodded.

"Why?"

A few things have happened since you went off on shepherd duty in the Americas." Hel motioned to him to come nearer.

Hades eased through the pool of souls. Their murmurs were louder than he recalled.

Garmr crept over to him, whining.

"He misses Cerberus," said Hel. "I'm thinking about getting a puppy."

Hades crouched down and rubbed Garmr's ears. Garmr rolled over, offering his belly for a consolatory rub. "What happened?"

Hel considered the situation a moment. "Did you know about Ganymede?"

Hades' look sharpened. "What about him?"

"He couldn't stand his existence anymore. He threw himself from the very highest pinnacle of Mount Olympus."

Hades stood up and let the energy of their realm enter him. "Ganymede is not here," he said after a moment.

Hel shook her head. "No, he is not. We think he haunts Olympus."

"What does Zeus - ?"

She shrugged and waved her hand idly. "Long gone, his base instincts rule him now. Zeus is off somewhere fornicating as though he still mattered. Who knows the monstrosities he's begetting upon an unsuspecting humanity."

"So why did Ganymede jump? Zeus wasn't there to bugger him anymore. He could do as he liked."

"We've been mulling that over. Yamaraja thinks it's because without Zeus around to distract him, Ganymede felt the full force of his Olympian exile. He had no real freedom and certainly no power to leave. The rest of us can come and go. Even Hera's handmaidens the nymphs could come and go as it pleased them, but he is unlike everyone else."

"Poor boy. Who told you?" Hades stroked Garmr's head.

"Hera, of course, when she came to see you. You weren't here to reassure her and she said she felt uneasy up there all alone, so she begged to take Cerberus back with her. We let her borrow him. That was probably a bad idea, but she said that you would understand."

"I do. I wish she hadn't taken my dog, but I do understand."

"Hecate tried to find Ganymede and bring him back, but he was too scared of her to come out of hiding."

"Be fair. She is intimidating. I'll go find him. Ganymede and I became rather close when I was convalescing up there. He knows that I would never hurt him."

Hel patted her knee.

Garmr crept over to her and laid his head upon her knee. He sighed and moaned.

"I think you had better get that puppy," said Hades. "Send Anubis."

"He has already offered to find you another dog. I'll tell him."

Hades began to turn away. "When you see Persephone next, tell her where I have gone. Tell her I will be back as soon as I have had a talk with Ganymede."

"I'll do that, but I think she's out there looking for you already."

Hades frowned as he walked back across the great hall. "She's never done that before."

28.

Hera greeted Hades with only slightly less enthusiasm than Cerberus did. While Cerberus leapt up and down, his three heads licking and barking and vying for the place directly beneath his hand, Hera embraced Hades.

"It seems an eon since you last visited, Hades." Hera stepped back and adjusted her shawl. "I only wish that the circumstances were pleasant ones."

"So do I."

"I found his ruined beauty. Poor thing. His body was smashed on the rocks, and yet he hides here still. Zeus still doesn't know. He hasn't been home in so long." Hera wrung her hands. "He will be furious."

Hades reached out to bestill her hands and held them firm and calm in his. "If he is, send to me and I shall deal facts with him. Zeus may have command of the skies, but he has never held command over me and my dominions."

Hera laughed bitterly. "He hasn't even command over his own nature. Every day he spends away from me is a repudiation and a punishment. He cares nothing about my pain or loneliness, just as he cared nothing about poor Ganymede's loneliness and terror. He will care very much though that I allowed Ganymede to destroy himself."

"Calm yourself. Send to me and to Apollo and we shall temper Zeus' mood. Now, I have come to tend to our poor young friend. Ganymede should not linger in his chosen purgatory."

"Will you restore him to his family?"

"I hope to. First, I have to find him and persuade him to come with me." Hades kissed Hera's left cheek and moved past her into the palace.

Panting contentedly, Cerberus padded along beside Hades. The head closest to his master caught the hem of his garment and walked along tugging at it.

Olympus had changed. Silence reigned where once Zeus and his court used to wine and dine and fuss at one another. Invisible zephyrs whispered throughout corridors that music once idled in. As softly as he trod, his steps carried ahead of him.

The few nymphs who remained had all collected upon Olympus to serve their great Queen and live out their days. Shy and solemn, they paused in their activities to watch the Lord of the Underworld pass. One of them struck up a doleful song after he had passed. Hades recognized the language as Spanish and the subject as one of lost love, a song from nearly 400 mortal years past.

When he returned home, he would catch his Consort in his arms and hold her close until the ache went away.

The palace stood neat and clean, in perpetual readiness for company. It stood as lonely as its Queen.

When he was done helping Ganymede, he would send to Kali and have her get Shiva and Parvati to invite Hera over for a prolonged visit.

A young nymph emerged abruptly from a side chamber, nearly walking into Hades. "Oh! Sir! Forgive me." She curtseyed.

"There is nothing to forgive, Lady. Have you seen the forlorn shade of Ganymede?"

"It is difficult to. He hides more in death than he did in life."

"Where is he seen most often?"

"In the gardens. He loves the gardens still. They were his refuge from Olympian powers, especially when they were in a tizzy."

"Thank you, Lady." Hades bowed his head.

She curtseyed again, her eyelashes fluttering as she stole glances at Hades, whom they seldom saw. Then she swept swiftly and softly past him, too scared to look back even once.

Upon the edge of the gardens, Hades lingered. The leaves stirred in idle breezes. In the distance a bird trilled. Seemingly alone, Hades stood still. He knew he was not alone. The Great Hunter of the Living and the Dead could sense whenever any of his wards was near.

His dark gaze shifted to his right, toward a wildly overgrown little garden temple. "Ganymede, you know me, son. Come out into the lighr."

The vines rippled as though someone passed behind them.

Ganymede's elusive voice emerged, "Are you alone?"

"Yes. I have come to take you home."

"Home to where? I have no home except for Olympus." Bitterness tightened the tormented soul's voice.

"There is the ultimate home, son. It stands ready to receive every being who has existed or who will exist for the duration of time and beyond. Its portals never close and it awaits your return."

"You make no sense. My home was among the Trojans and they have left me behind in the purgatory you call Olympus. There is nothing else for me." His voice began to drift away.

Hades entered the garden and moved directly to the little temple. "You remember me. You remember our hours spent as friends? Ganymede, do you remember those peaceful days?"

"Yes, Lord Hades." His voice had moved a little nearer.

"You know that I would not lie to you or hurt you. You know this."

"I do." His voice hung heavy with anguish. "I cannot leave."

"Indeed you can. Come with me now."

"No. I can't. I no longer know the way home. And what if I return and my family does not recognize me? What if I don't recognize them?" Ganymede wept.

Hades pressed through the leafy barrier. In the cool, shaded space within he found the slim pale form of Ganymede's ghost, more mist than shadow, so wounded, so fragile that even the slightest breeze could have dispersed him.

Ganymede cringed as though he would withdraw so far into himself that he could withdraw out of existence altogether.

Hades stood quite still and radiated calm concern. If he moved, he knew Ganymede might vanish and he did not want to pursue him all over Olympus.

"I should not have done it. Zeus will be furious. He will be so angry. Where can I hide? When he comes back, he will beat me and then he will - !"

"Ganymede," Hades kept his voice calm and firm, "he can no more lay a finger on you than he can his own breath. Zeus has no power over you now."

"This is true?"

Ganymede stood on the cusp. He might go either way. He might succumb to the perceptions of his tortured existence and stay a prisoner to a life he no longer belonged to. Or he might step out of the prison of his own mind, free to return home with Lord Hades. Half-fearful, half-hopeful, Ganymede's eyes glistened as they met Hades' somber dark gaze.

\   "This is true," said Hades.

"How can you be sure?" Ganymede trembled and looked toward the palace. "He is Zeus. His power is everywhere."

Hades extended his hand. "His power ends when and where mine begins. I am your master now."

Ganymede wiped his face. He stood a little straighter. "Truly? You can stand between Zeus and me?"

"I stand between you already. Not even Zeus can deny my authority, no one in the living realms can. Now come along and I shall take you home."

Ganymede seized Hades' hand. "Home! Please. Home."

Ganymede passed directly from the protection of Hades just across the threshold through the brilliant passage.

Hades lingered there for some time listening to the distant echoes of the young man's reunion with his family. Even after the light had dimmed to the softest of afterglows Hades stood there, his eyes closed and a peaceful smile curving his lips. Neither Hel nor Anubis nor any of the other caretakers disturbed him.

Whining softly, Cerberus padded back to Hera's side for consolation.

With only a full moon for company, Persephone's pace did not falter until she found herself deep in the remote Alps, on a forgotten Roman road, when a sudden fog rose before her. She paused and drew her veil over her face again. There was nothing natural about the phenomenon. The air felt electric and full of presence.

The boundary of another realm loomed directly ahead. It might be a Faerie or Seelie folk realm, but it felt like none she had encountered in her many millennia of existence in any realm.

First one, then another, and then a third form shuffled forth from the murk. They were a little on the short side and on the stout side in their voluminous robes. She could not see their faces for the hoods that sheltered them from the air, but she did not need to.

They had never met before but Persephone knew them at once. Recognition hit her with all the force of a kick to the stomach: the Fates had come to see her.

As she bowed to the trio, Persephone trembled as they arrayed themselves across her path. They stopped and waited for her to lift her eyes again. "Greetings, terrible ones," she said.

"Greetings, Queen of Hades, great Mater Dolorosa," said the eldest.

They wore smiles that were not pleasing to see, for their eyes were cold with impartiality, or just as likely, Persephone realized, indifference.

"Do you require something of me?" she said.

"We require nothing of you," said the eldest of the dreaded trio.

"Surely there is something you have come to impart to me, or you would not have left your fateful loom."

"Simply this," said the eldest with a nod, "go home to Hades. Take him into your warm embrace and bear his passion in your marriage bed. You will find him gazing off into the infinite heart of all things. Take him by the hand and take him to your bed."

"He would do these things without any encouragement from me."

"In the past this would be true. This time you must command him."

"Why?"

"Because he needs that from you and…" The Fates exchanged looks.

"And what?"

"Because there may come a time all too soon when you shall want what he has lavished upon you and it shall not be forthcoming and when that day comes the throne of Hades shall be ruled by another."

Persephone felt a jolt. "Answer me this. Is there a reason we haven't been able to capture the foul one?"

"Yes."

"Yes, and nothing more? That's all you have to say? Yes? Can you do nothing more?"

"This is not of our doing. This is out of our hands. Do as we suggest. That is the best we can do for you or anyone."

Already the spectral fog was dissipating. One of the Fates turned to look into the forested shadows.

"One matter more," she said, "leave this place at once."

The Fates had gone. Persephone stood alone. She looked into the surrounding forest.

Startled from his concealed rest in that forest, Sebastiano had witnessed the strange interview from the impenetrable shadows. His eyes feasted on the otherworldly beauty dressed in the colors of night and eternal shadow. He saw the three crones appear and listened to their voices crossing eternity with great interest.

When that weird trio vanished, Persephone seemed to stare directly at him with eyes as bright as a moonlight dazzled pool. His hungry eyes were still feasting on her beauty as her form turned to mist and vanished from that realm.

Sebastiano mulled the incident over.

Nearby, Jacques groaned in his sleep. He was hungry.

Sebastiano eyed his minion, his resentful lover whose most recent Italian conquest slept in his embrace, still mortal and utterly devoted to both strangers. Eventually Jacques would convert Giovanni to their ways and then they would have to find fresh prey to sup upon.

From centuries past, Sebastiano remembered, with fresh interest, his promise to that gullible Succubus. He had promised to take Persephone away from Hades so that she and her voracious sisters could have Hades to consume at their leisure. Once he had gained a body to traverse the living world, he had forgotten his promise – entirely on purpose.

Now, he felt obliged to fulfill his promise, even if only so he could sink his teeth into Persephone's succulent flesh and drink the nectar that flowed in her divine veins. The Fates themselves had just forewarned his prize of a dire event that would place a new master upon their throne. Sebastiano – Upir Likhyi – lay back, pillowing his heads upon his arms. He smiled into the shadows.

He would fulfill his promise...for his own reasons of course.

29.

In the so-called Modern Age, wonders bestrode the land hand in hand with horrors, one after the other as humanity seized all the power its intelligence could concoct – and then used it. It was breathtaking to witness, but terrible too for it seemed as though all of existence were sliding downhill towards a collision with a destiny that wasn't desired.

Apollo and the rest applied their influences where they might do the most good. To one another they showed faces of stalwart determination. Privately they showed faces lined with anxiety to the shadows – an unnatural state. Even Ares observed the civilization-devouring wars with an air of grim horror. However, for as long as Hope coexisted wherever Despair attempted to take root, they all kept their proverbial sleeves rolled up, influencing and even interceding, subtly, on an individual basis.

The Underworld seethed and boiled from the chaos the Living caused. Zeus might have abandoned all sense of responsibility for a life of sensual indulgence, but Hades had no such luxury. He dared not relinquish his obligations for even an hour unless Osiris, Anubis, Hel, Yamaraja, or one of their many other incarnate associates covered for him.

Hades stayed clear of Olympus and Hera dared not send for him to visit, not after Hades delivered Ganymede to the After Life. Zeus blamed Hera, but he despised Hades more for taking away his beautiful young man. Even though he knew Hades desired only his consort Persephone, Zeus still simmered with wayward bouts of jealousy. Ganymede had come to love the kindly Hades more than he had ever managed to like his captor Zeus. He had regarded Hades as a father figure of the best sort and Zeus as one of the worst sort. That stung Zeus, so he spent his time indulging himself, neglecting Hera, and ignoring humanity's plight.

When she was not abroad communing with her Mother's energy, Persephone went most places where Hades went. Hades wondered a little at her behaviour, but did not question it. Upir Likhyi was still out there somewhere and Persephone was the key to his capture, so it made sense that she should accompany him abroad among the Living.

Big wars, little wars, they were all the same. Each produced a vast influx of traumatized souls into the Underworld. Each left spirits adrift among the Living like so much debris. Hecate, among others, had her hands full finding and then coaxing these souls to let go of their surroundings. Naturally, the ones who did not realize or believe that they had died were the hardest to dislodge. The guilt-ridden and the 'hungry' ghosts were only slightly less problematic.

For as many people who died that many more were born to replace them. The world had become congested with the Living and Death was everywhere. This suited Sebastiano just fine and Hades knew it, for this was also the age of Kali, who grumbled at the blameful honorific even as she presided over the fields of death with a stern and wary gaze.

One hazy night in the heart of an over-baked metropolis Sebastiano loitered atop a tall mid-century apartment building. A harsh harvest yellow moon hung full just above the eastern horizon. A mere century ago its light would have been brilliant enough for mortal men to travel by. If mortals noticed its polluted light anymore, it was because they were lycanthropic or moon-worshippers of some sort. The lights of the civilization diminished la Lune's glory as it had already diminished the sensuous totality of Night.

Suddenly, Sebastiano mourned Night's lost power and hated the modern age with its ugly unnatural brilliance. When Jacques joined him, wiping his bloody lips on a towel that he simply dropped behind him, his Master was in a sour mood. But Jacques being Jacques, he had to prod him.

"What are you sulking about? We've feasted to our hearts' content with none the wiser. The Hunters won't have a clue and we're free to do as we please." Jacques stretched and smiled out over the glowing city – their abundant hunting ground.

Sebastiano's lips curled at the first airily unconcerned syllable out of Jacques' mouth. "You didn't kill any of them, did you, glutton?"

"Of course not! It's a veritable smorgasbord downstairs and they're all eager for the bite. I even drank of those young harlots' blood tonight."

Sebastiano's brow arched. "Did you now?"

"I was famished and they fought to offer me their flesh. What wondrous days these are!"

"I suppose they are," Sebastiano grumbled.

"What's the matter now?" Jacques straddled the ledge and let his right foot dangle over the long drop below. "You were in such avid spirits when we arrived at the blood orgy. Now here you are skulking about like something out of a bad Gothic novel."

Sebastiano folded his arms over his chest and turned his back on the city lights. "I find that once I have slaked my thirst and gratified my bloodlust, a poisonous sort of dissatisfaction creeps in. Once it sets in, it will not leave, not for a long spell."

Jacques seemed to sincerely contemplate his master's conundrum. "Does nothing excite you anymore?"

"Less and less does and even then not for very long."

"Not even the thrill of the hunt? The lust for fresh conquests?"

"You are kidding, right? They hunt us now and not even to destroy us. These mortals give themselves over so readily to the Darkness that there are times I want to fight them off just for a moment's respite."

"I rather enjoy it myself – the way that they vie for my attention, fight to be my favorite...I have quite the harem these days. You can't possibly miss the old days."

Sebastiano gave him a sullen look and faced the despised city lights.

Jacques carried on, appalled, "The filth of the squalor of those hovels we had to hide in. The stench of those bodies...no, give me the present. Daytime even into the night. An ample supply of prey that has actually bathed and who offer themselves to us with a smile. Give me these dissolute modern times over those years spent hiding and sleeping in crypts and ruins. We have everything we've ever wanted and you're pining for the past?"

"It is all too easy with these creatures of easy virtue. It is something else altogether to work upon another's defenses. To wear down their resistance and persuade them in the end to surrender entirely not just their physical, but also their spiritual integrity. To see the regret and the perfect realization in their eyes as they plead ever so softly, ever so breathlessly for consummation is a bliss that none of these casual wretches are capable of inducing in themselves let alone an old soul such as myself."

Jacques snorted. "I had enough of the games of seduction back in the powdered wig days. All that flirting behind fans and fondling of private parts before I can dine, it was maddening really. Give me a young buck with high cheekbones, a long lean neck, and a ready zipper, or even some collar-wearing minx with bold black eye-liner and her plump apples propped high up under her chin – and I'll feast the whole night through."

"I believe they call that 'fast food' in these parts."

Jacques retorted, "And what would you prefer, Monsieur Connoisseur?"

"A trembling pure-hearted virgin in her Sunday best. A love-starved young woman, no, even better, a Bride of Christ who has found her '*marriage*' unfulfilling after all. A stout-hearted young man without a fear in the world who craves a little adventure in a wider world. People who think themselves invulnerable and beyond all reproach. Such an indecent delight it is to gain power over such souls and watch them do what they know is wrong, to betray everyone they ever cared about with abandon, and in the end to abandon them by the wayside once they have served their purposes." Sebastiano fixed his black eyes upon Jacques, who would have paled if it were at all possible. "Betrayal is sweet and of it I can never have enough."

"Betrayal you say," Jacques muttered feeling more uneasy than he ever had since Sebastiano converted him to malevolence.

"It was never just about Blood, you fool. Blood is mere sustenance. But corruption – ah, that is how empires are built."

"What did you have in mind? And do I have a place in it?" Jacques added quickly.

Sebastiano smiled.

Jacques trembled as he had not since his last mortal moments.

As Hades and his cohorts in the Underworld observed, the modern age brought about some unexpected and not altogether unwelcome developments.

Osiris and Anubis held the dais. It was their shift after all. The lower realms churned, seethed, and wailed. The upper realms, like the vast chamber before the dais, moaned, rustled, and whispered, sounding more akin to the vast mortal forests abroad whenever the air moved.

For the moment, there was a lull. The general ambience was a peaceful one and the souls moved calmly about, guided and shepherded by the many Intercessor spirits. Hades, Hecate, Persephone, Kali, Yamaraja, Hel, and a good many others of their kind collected on the opposite half of the dais for a rare, leisurely repast about the fire pit.

Yamaraja surveyed the many platters and bowls of savory entrees and in-season delicacies. "Who do we have to thank for this banquet?" He picked up a plate and it solid with vegetables, rice, and fruit, pausing to inhale the scent of the fresh strawberries in particular.

Hecate gestured from herself to Hades and back again. "We had to make an emergency run above ground."

"Oh?" Yamaraja said just as he popped a berry into his mouth.

"It wasn't - ?" said Kali.

"No, not HIM," said Hecate, "just a couple of malingerers or was it one?"

"Two." Hades wiped his mouth on his napkin. "Apollo said that they needed a ghost removed from some house they were renovating…"

Persephone paused over her meal. "Apollo was renovating a house?"

Hades nodded. "Apparently he, Ares, Athena, Aphrodite, Hermes, and Medusa were sent on a particular little mission."

"So that's where Medusa went?" said Kali.

"Who sent them? Not Zeus," said Hel.

"Not him, he could care less about mortal concerns these days," said Hecate.

"For all intents and purposes, Zeus has abdicated," said Hades.

Nepthys poured herself some tea. "That explains some of it."

"Explains what?" said Yamaraja.

"Olympus looked deserted when Isis dropped by. She said there wasn't a soul in sight. It gave her the creeps, so she left," said Nepthys.

"Ah, so Hera must have gone to visit Parvati after all." Hades looked pleased.

"Actually, no," said Persephone.

"Oh?" said Hades. "Then where did she go?"

"'Off to an Empowerment Seminar that Artemis insisted she attend," said Persephone.

"Really?" said Hades.

"Truly. Artemis showed up one day. She had been sojourning with our kindred Incarnations in the Americas for so long that the nymphs said that Hera didn't recognize her at first. Apparently, word had gotten around to even the most remote wildernesses about Hera's reclusive tendencies. Artemis marched right into Olympus and said, 'You're coming with me.' And that was that." Persephone shrugged. "The nymphs took off right after that. No one wants to hang around Zeus anymore."

Hecate and Hades exchanged wry looks.

"They needn't have worried," said Hecate.

"Zeus sped off too, probably the very instant after Hera left," said Hades.

"Getting into trouble no doubt," said Hel. She fed Garmr a samosa.

"To say the least," said Hades.

"All right, you know where Zeus has scampered off to. Tell the rest of us so we can avoid him," said Kali.

"You tell them," said Hades. "I'd like to be able to enjoy my meal."

"Zeus has plopped down in the middle of our 'gang of six's' project. When he isn't underfoot, he's rutting noisily with the soiled widow next door," said Hecate. "None of them are happy about it, but you know Zeus. So long as he's getting his jollies rocking everyone else can hang."

"I think they have a plot underway," said Hades. "Hermes snatched Cerberus as soon as Hera left Olympus and has him with them for now. Maybe when they're done I can have my dog back."

Garmr looked plaintively at Hades and whined for emphasis.

"Anyway, I got Hecate. We went to Essex, rousted out the ghosts: an ax murderer who snuck in there when the place was derelict and some cranky pitchfork wielding old farmer; and on the way back, detoured to some markets for treats." Hades gestured at their feast. "Let them deal with Zeus."

"What's an Empowerment Seminar anyway?" said Hel.

"Something that is redundant where you're concerned, love," said Hecate. She sighed. "Let's hope it does the old girl some good."

Hades held up his goblet. "To Hera's empowerment seminar."

One and all held out their drinks. "To Hera."

"If it works," said Persephone, "Zeus will never know what hit him."

Hades grinned, widely.

Jacques had to rush to follow Sebastiano on his effortless descent into the building. Those they had left waiting in the club waited there still. For a long moment Sebastiano surveyed his as yet modest legion of followers with cold, thin-lipped smile Jacques had seen enough to respect.

Gradually the realization spread: the 'Master' had returned into their midst. Even those wearied from submission roused themselves enough to turn their feverish eyes toward him. Whatever he commanded they would do. Whatever he desired they would give.

"Yes, it is time," Sebastiano said more to himself than to Jacques.

"Time for what?" Jacques muttered.

"Time to create a great host, an army...my army."

"Why?" Jacques glanced back the way they had come. "Are the Hunters nigh upon our lair again?" He half-expected the Golden One, his hair aflame, to descend feet first through the skylight with his terrible immortal bow armed for slaughter.

Golden Apollo ruled his nightmares and haunted his dreams as an object of fatal desire. Jacques would willingly let Phoebus Apollo be the vehicle of his demise if he could have a taste of his divine blood first. He fantasized licking Apollo's blood from his hands, sucking its precious droplets from his radiant fingertips with worshipful kisses, drinking deep as the Divine Incarnation thrust one of his golden arrows into his rotten heart. Long ago, Jacques has sworn to himself that he would die by the hands of splendid Apollo and none other.

"Are you afraid?" Sebastiano sneered.

"No, but we only create colonies when Hades has come for us."

"Never say that name in my presence!"

Jacques flinched away.

"To say it is to invoke it and we are not ready to summon him."

"Summon? You mean to summon the Great Hunter here? On purpose?"

"It is time to end the Hunt." Sebastiano plunged into the crowd.

The next instant Jacques saw his Master seize upon one of his favorites, who hung weakly in his powerful grip. Sebastiano licked at the still fresh wounds on the young man's neck. Blood trickled out, but instead of drinking him dry Sebastiano opened himself up and pressed the mortal's mouth to the wound. His snarling laugh announced the creation of another of his kind.

Jacques had long since stopped observing and had already begun his second conversion.

As Sebastiano and Jacques begot vampyres, so did the new converts beget others to their kind. A feeding frenzy resulted from which no mortal in that building escaped. Not until the dawn approached did calm settle upon the old brick edifice.

From a peaceful sleep, Hades awoke as suddenly as though doused by a bucket of water. Persephone lay safe and close in his embrace. He forced himself to lie still so as not to disturb her. Their bed was warm, her body sweet, but he relinquished her ever so tenderly as he sat up and stared into the fire pit's flames.

Standing just beyond the pit waited Dionysus, his bull horns laden with vines, his chlamys draped about his body. The flames seemed to burn in his eyes as well.

They stared into one another's eyes for a long moment.

"Apollo will know what is coming," said Dionysus.

225

Hades nodded. He kissed his Consort upon her heart and softly left her side.

30.

Dionysus and Hades found Apollo in the likely place: Delphi...

There had been a party of tourists to Delphi, among them new admirers, pilgrims, of Apollo, who had come there in hopes of communing with the echo of his spirit. Utterly unaware that on that particular day he did occupy the ruins, fully aware of their sincere, if innocent hopes for a divine connection, they entered Delphi. In the midst of his meditation touching the infinite impermanence of the world, he still sensed and knew their minds.

Where the Oracle once sat, Apollo sat still and utterly calm. The visitors trod everywhere before him, excited, but still respectful of the power Delphi once held. He listened to everything they said with a quiet mind, but there was One among them...

She moved everywhere in exhilarated silence. To her bright eyes Delphi seemed magical. She felt its power in the very molecules of her being. Her heart pounded, although she couldn't quite figure out why she should be so affected. She knew only that she had to come to this ancient site and simply be there as a living being. She followed the group everywhere it shifted and took pictures for the folks at home to enjoy.

At last though, she lingered behind.

Everyone scattered, but she remained standing before what had been the site of the Oracle's chamber. She froze to the spot. Her breath caught in her throat. There was no one there and no one near her, but she felt a presence – and knew it to be a powerful intelligence.

Apollo had opened his eyes. He saw the young woman from the far North, saw her completely. "I know you from long ago," he said lowly, half in wonder, half in pleasure. "The Fates have brought our paths together once more. Such is their sense of humor." He tilted his head as he studied her form. Her new incarnation was as lovely as her previous, ill-starred one. "Or their perverse sense of justice."

Her eyes widened. She looked wildly about herself and grew fearful.

No one stood anywhere near her.

Apollo sat up straight. "You heard me! So, your curse has transcended along with you...or is it a gift this time around?"

She backed up a step, stumbled on the uneven ground, and fell backwards. Her camera flew from her hands.

The young woman never hit the ground although her sleek silver camera did.

None of the tourists noticed her absence as they regrouped to listen to their guide. Eventually, one of them found the ruined camera and wondered at it. Then, remembering, the man cast frowning looks about.

Breathless, too startled to yell, she found herself in the protective embrace of a radiant being – a golden-hued man formed from Perfection with hair like the healing warmth of the sun after an age of ice. That he had appeared from nowhere and had prevented her from falling and hurting herself was only slightly less surprising than the fact that her recognition of him was instant – and intimate.

"You," she gasped as he set her upright upon her own feet and stepped back. "But how do I know you? How can I be so certain?"

Apollo smiled a strange smile as though the situation beguiled him too. He circled around until he stood before her in his tunic and cloak of saffron-bordered maroon.

"I know you. How do I know you?" She trembled. She pressed her hands to her heart as though they could calm it somehow.

"Because we met before, a very long time ago in human time." An unearthly light resided in his eyes, as though the sun shone through the Mediterranean itself instead of the azure sky.

"Don't hurt me." She saw her companions gathered a very short distance away.

"It was never my intention to hurt you back in Wilusa."

"I will scream if you try to touch me again."

"If you scream, they will think this place haunted and most likely run." Apollo glanced at the group beyond her. "Someone might get hurt. You wouldn't want that, would you, Cassandra?"

A retort had begun to form on her lips, but the instant Apollo uttered that name – her name of old – a jolt shook her. She felt stricken. She would have collapsed utterly before ancient Pajawone, but for his catching her arms and bearing her up.

The sob that escaped her shook them both. When she lifted her face, tears flooded down her face. She clasped her hands before his face and slid from his grasp to her knees. "No more. Not again. I suffered enough. My family too – they all suffered so. Did I not pay the price then?"

"Karma works in its enigmatic fashion," he said calmly.

"For refusing to give myself up to you, you deemed it fitting that I suffer Agamemnon in your stead?"

Apollo knelt before her and as grave and calm as ever, said, "Cassandra-*Anastasia*, you suffered because you rejected your true purpose and realization." She shook her head, but he continued, "You were meant to receive of me the divine gift of prophecy. I was but the vehicle of this gift and that is all I ever was. Understand this now and at last: to receive such a gift of divine providence you must surrender your Will – your very Self – to the Divine Will – to 'God'. You were meant to serve the Greater Good, but you chose to protect your Self and serve your provincial interests. You refused to relinquish your Will. Your attachment to yourself damned you. Not me. It is from attachment to Self that so much malevolence arises, my Precious Soul."

Cassandra-*Anastasia* wiped her tears on her sleeves. Her breathing calmed.

"Do you understand?" said Apollo.

She gulped and nodded. "Yes," she breathed. "Is that why you were waiting here today for me?"

"I come here often. I knew I awaited a vision. I knew there was a reason. When I saw you, I knew why I had to be here."

"To see me?"

"That…and to bless you as you were meant to be, but that depends on you. Are you ready to relinquish your Self for the greater good? Are you ready at last to surrender to Divine Will? The Age of Kali is ending. Your gift will be needed by every sentient being you encounter." Apollo held out his hands to her. "Are you ready?"

Cassandra-*Anastasia* gazed at his palms and breathed deeply. "Yes." And she placed her hands in his.

Apollo closed his hands – such warm hands – about hers and rising, lifted her to her feet. He withdrew with her a short distance from her oblivious companions. She watched him spread his brilliant cloak upon the ground. He knelt upon it first and held his hands up to her.

"Will this hurt much?" she whispered, hugging herself.

"Have you ever been so joyful you thought your heart would burst?"

She shook her head. "I have never been anywhere near that happy."

"Well then, I think it's about time, don't you?" Then Apollo's tone softened. "Take my hands and I shall take care of you. All shall be well. You'll see."

She took his hands and settled before him on his sacred cloak.

Apollo took her face in his hands, looked deep into her soul and began, "May you speak only Noble Truth." And he kissed her mouth.

By the time Hades and Dionysus arrived at Delphi, Apollo and Cassandra had transcended realms and returned to the boundary of her mortal realm.

Her eyes stared wide, dazzled, into the night sky beyond Apollo's warmly glowing head.

Apollo placed his hand beneath her head and lifted it slightly. "Don't forget to breathe."

Cassandra-*Anastasia* gasped and then heaved a great breath. Her unfocused gaze settled upon his face.

"Just breathe," Apollo told her. "Breathe in. Breathe out. It is time for you to return to your life and to your destined path."

"The universe…I never realized." She grabbed his arms and sat up in his lap. "I don't want to forget. I won't forget. I can't forget, can I?"

"You will not forget." Apollo stroked her hair. He glanced over her shoulder at Hades and Dionysus.

A somber aura hung over the two, although Dionysus eyed Cassandra with an intrigued gleam in his eyes. "And here I thought only I communed thus with mortals," he said.

"Don't start," said Apollo. "Help me. Her clothes are over there."

"Ah." Hades looked about. Promptly he stooped to collect them.

"So this is how you create an Oracle," said Dionysus. He passed on the rumpled clothes that Hades handed to him.

"Oracles are born, not made," said Apollo as he removed her hands from his arms and placed her clothes in them instead. "You know that."

Shrouded in his night-colored robes, Hades hung back from their exchange.

"She was wearing sandals of a sort, I think," said Apollo as he glanced about.

Dionysus cast his gaze about. "I see one." He stooped to collect it."

Hades gestured off to the side. "There's the other one. Way over there."

Dionysus went to collect it. "Jehosaphat, Apollo, that must have been quite an ecstatic little act of communion you two had! Her clothes over here. Her shoes over there and there. Don't tell me you didn't enjoy your task." He handed the shoes to him.

"Don't be crude," Apollo grumbled at Dionysus. Then he looked into her face as he pressed her shoes into her hands, saying, "My task was to enable her to attain the realization of the true nature of all things so she could see clearly. This was destined many lifetimes ago."

Cassandra sat upon his lap as though it were the safest place. Her glance traveled to Hades a polite distance away. "Destiny is forever moving and we rush to meet it."

Dionysus exchanged looks with Hades. He gestured to the young woman. "This is why we had to come."

Hades stood perfectly straight. "The Oracle has returned."

Cassandra shivered. Her eyes rolled back into her head.

Apollo reached past her for his cloak and wrapped it about her nakedness. All the while he held her safe as she writhed. Suddenly she bucked and arched her back with such violence that she jerked free of his grasp.

Dionysus swooped behind her and caught her before she could strike the hard ground. Together Apollo and Dionysus steadied her and preserved her from injury. She clenched her teeth.

"This is a mighty vision," said Dionysus.

Apollo nodded. "She serves the Great Will now as she was meant to." He looked relieved, but still a little concerned as he took her face in his hands. "Breathe, Precious Soul. Oracle of All, breathe."

A deep sigh escaped her and her body calmed and relaxed against Dionysus' chest. Dionysus adjusted Apollo's wool and silk chlamys about her for she was too warm and might catch a chill.

Apollo stroked her face. "Speak. What have you seen?"

Cassandra seized a hold of his shoulders and laid her head against him. "A nightmare of angry blood and vengeance – *IT* saw me. I know it saw me."

"Upir Likhyi,' said Hades.

"Yes! The foul undead one." She shivered. "I was in his sleeping place. It was cold and dark, an unending death. There were shadows of such evil about him and they reached for me."

Dionysus and Apollo soothed her with gentle caresses as they exchanged serious looks.

"It opened its hollow, soulless eyes and looked right at me. It smiled...such a terrible smile. He will not come after me?" She looked to Apollo.

"No, I am your Protector now," said Apollo. "Upir Likhyi fears the Light too much to hunt for you. If he does, he knows he will find me too."

"What else did you see?" Dionysus stroked her hair as he would a child's.

"A legion of newborn devourers of life – they are merciless towards all. It is an army this monster has prepared," she fixed her gaze upon Hades, "for you."

"That's hardly unexpected," said Hades. "I have been after him for centuries."

"Make no mistake, Lord Hades," she said quickly. "This is not about his vengeance. I sensed a poisonous appetite in the monster for something much more than blood."

Hades laid his hand over one of his scars, his unholy souvenir from that first ambush. When he raised his dark eyes, he met the looks of his companions. "Again, this is not a complete surprise."

"To defeat him he must first succeed," she said. "The Life you love he wants also. That which you craved for so very long he craves also, but it will be different for him. This he does not realize."

Hades turned his face aside so they could not see the emotions they knew he suffered.

"I am sorry, my Lord Hades," said Cassandra-*Anastasia*.

Hades gave her a sad, but kind look. "There is no cause to be sorry. What I have heard from you is what I came to learn."

"What will you do?" said Apollo.

"Upir Likhyi has raised his forces. I shall summon every Hunter." Hades turned away and disappeared into the darkness.

After a thorough search of their group and of their lodgings, the tourists rushed back to Delphi with several locals to search for the missing woman.

They did not have to go far within Delphi's precincts to find her. She sat before the Oracle's seat with her clothes and shoes in her lap and a exotic and luxurious saffron bordered maroon cloak wrapped about her. She was dazed, but unblemished except for some mysterious symbolic markings on her hands and over her heart.

They took her back to their hotel. She was examined. They prodded her with questions and when at last she spoke, she proceeded to congratulate one of the locals on the birth of his son.

The man gaped at her. His wife was not due for two weeks and when he left her side she was fine. A quick phone call confirmed the good news. By the time he turned to ask simply 'How?', she had turned to someone else and was advising him about something that apparently was a surprise to him as well.

31.

Persephone awoke.

The place beside her lay exposed and had long since gone cold.

She dressed at once.

Emerging onto the dais she found Yamaraja and Hel conferring.

"Where is Hades?"

They exchanged looks. Yamaraja motioned toward their threshold. "We went abroad with Dionysus."

"Are the Hunters gathering?" Persephone arranged her purple veil.

"I believe so," said Yamaraja. "There is a feeling of a storm gathering." He motioned toward the direction of the ever-churning maelstrom.

"I had better go join them."

"Be careful," Hel called after her.

Persephone could tell precisely where her otherworldly realm ended and the mortal realm began. The atmosphere thickened and grew richer in sounds and aromas. One could sink one's proverbial teeth into the mortal atmosphere and taste it down to its atoms.

This time she knew she had met the boundary when she perceived a trio of gently shimmering and familiar figures just ahead. Hera, Athena, and Aphrodite stood watching her emerge from the shadows. A fourth figure stood next to Hera wagging his tail.

"Cerberus!" Persephone rushed forward to caress his three heads and rub his ears. Each head vied for its share of affection. "Have you brought him back to us?"

Hera handed over his heavy leash. "Yes. I no longer feel the need for a guard dog. It is time he returned home where he belongs."

"Garmr will be overjoyed. He has missed having Cerberus to play with." Persephone vigorously rubbed all three heads.

Cerberus groaned and clawed the ground with pleasure.

Persephone felt their seriousness. "What is it you have come to tell me?"

Brief looks of astonishment flickered between them.

"Nothing," said Aphrodite.

"We were talking," said Athena. "We are all uneasy, but we cannot quite sort out why."

"Hades has gathered the Hunters," said Persephone.

"Are you going to join him?"

"Yes."

"Ares has gone too," said Aphrodite.

"Really?" said Hera.

Aphrodite shrugged with a game smile, "*'All for one and one for all'* – to quote Alexandre Dumas."

"So has Apollo," said Athena.

"Has Dionysus?" said Aphrodite.

"No, I haven't." As four faces turned his way, Dionysus came down the path toward them. The leaves crunched under his feet. Like them, he was heavily swathed against the seasonal winds. "It was decided that – as I have a special kinship with Hades and his realm and with Apollo as well – I should remain behind to assist Osiris and the rest. To hold down the fort if need be."

"I don't like the sound of that," said Hera.

"Believe me. They didn't like the sound of it either when they were deciding the matter." Dionysus held out his hand for Cerberus' leash.

Persephone pressed it into his palm. "Is Hades expecting me?"

"No."

"What?"

Dionysus shook his head. "Not this time."

"But - ?"

"You and I must remain here with the others who share Hades' authority and power. Upir Likhyi must and will come to us."

Persephone felt stricken.

Hera caught her arm and held her tight. "Does that mean - ?"

"We hope not. We sincerely hope not," said Dionysus. "Kali wants to add that monster's head to her collection and Hecate has a special place of oblivion prepared for his nasty soul. They have a strategy."

"It will be a terrible battle then," said Athena.

"We expect so. I have already sent to the appropriate Incarnations – Dhanvantari, Asclepius, and the rest to prepare." Dionysus turned to Aphrodite. "Eros has gone too."

"Eros! Why should he go?"

"He is an excellent shot and he possesses arrows that shoot other poisons than desire."

Hera took her hand. "Eros will come through fine."

Aphrodite steeled herself. "Of course he will. Eros has a fierce warrior nature. He is merciless."

"Where is Psyche?" said Hera.

"Weeping – from what Eros said," said Dionysus.

"I will go to her." Aphrodite disengaged herself from Hera.

"Bring her here," said Hera. "We shall wait this event out here."

"In the Underworld?" Aphrodite gaped.

"There is no safer place to be," said Dionysus. "Osiris alone could defend you with a cough."

"All right then." Aphrodite gathered her shawl more closely about her shoulders and slipped away into the sunset.

"Is Zeus going to help out?" said Athena.

Dionysus shrugged. "Hermes went off to talk to him about the situation. He hadn't returned yet when they sent me here. He may not be needed. Hades has mustered quite a volunteer corps. Wotan, Thor, Freyja, Horus, Anubis, Shiva, Kali, and Medusa too of course, among others have shown up. She so loves this world that Artemis has brought the whole far western contingent. Shiva has mustered the East."

"I shall go too," said Athena. She pulled her great shining helmet forward and down over her face so that only her pale grey eyes shone with her eerie intelligence. "Victory or death." She saluted those who remained and dissolved into bright light and vanished.

The twilight pressed closer about them. Night pushed the winds ahead of it.

Dionysus frowned at the gathering darkness. "Let us go down and prepare." He ushered Hera ahead.

Persephone lingered behind. She entrusted her prayer to the wind in a whisper only it could hear. Then she returned below.

A not entirely unexpected sound rose up to greet her. "Ommmm."

Yamaraja was leading the chant.

What was unexpected was that she heard Osiris' deep, earth-trembling voice joined in.

Persephone trembled also.

32.

This time, Sebastiano left no doubt where to find him. He and his plague of minions left a swath of unnatural deaths and virulent illness everywhere in their wake. They usurped the daylight with the terror of nightfall until it felt as though darkness had infiltrated every aspect of life. Some, too many, embraced the notion with fear, or worse, an unnatural jubilation, that the ultimate oblivion had come. A good many others hung onto Hope and saw those days as something they could and would survive – damn it. The rest simply kept their sleeves rolled up and went into each day doing what they could for however long they could.

Sebastiano reveled in the fear and the blind emotions that fear spread like wildfire. They sustained him in ways he had not expected, but they were still not enough to satisfy him. Soon, very, very soon, he would have what he wanted most – all the power and authority he had ever dreamt of. Then and only then he saw himself attaining contentment.

Briefly, Sebastiano grappled with the quandary of staying in the heart of a metropolis and letting the Hunters come to him there. In a great urban setting he would have had ample prey for conversion or sustenance. Turning the whole city vampyr had its appeal, but his prey was proving resourceful, individually and also in small war parties.

When the mortals realized what they were dealing with, the foolhardy ones sharpened up an arsenal and turned marauder. At first, his minions claimed more of the mortals than the mortals claimed of them. The vampyres took great delight in converting their would-be assassins to their power and then using them against their mortal allies. They gloated. They had the upper hand.

Their prey waited until daylight and upped the ante.

After a third nesting site went up in flames courtesy of several Molotov cocktails, Sebastiano recognized that it would be best to confront Hades and his Hunters someplace where his enemies would not have such a ready supply of reinforcements.

Far out in the west they found a ghost town an equal distance from several small towns, and a national forest. In its boom days the mines overlooking the town had produced silver and its fair share of vices. In its current state, the dark ever descending passages provided abundant shelter for Sebastiano and his horde.

Unaccustomed to their new way of life, the converts complained about the caves and the bats and the other cave denizens that did not care to make way for these colonists. Sebastiano shut them up by having them construct a network of tunnels from the mines into the old town's basements. The prospect of having an underground settlement to enjoy even at midday reduced the grumbling and whining from the new converts.

Sebastiano chose the ample basement belonging to the Silver Queen, the largest of the fine old hotels left standing. There he settled with his favorites to plot, to survey, and to wait.

The Hunters were mustering somewhere. Sebastiano sensed it with impatience. He had formed his strategy. He was ready. He let his minions rampage across the neighboring rural towns converting or killing outright, knowing full well that the stench of their riotous indulgence would carry far and wide – and bring Hades directly to him.

Terrified beyond all endurance by the nocturnal predations, the surviving townsfolk of Placerville packed their vehicles with one eye on the bleak sun tipping in a steep arc toward the horizon.

"Hurry it up," said an old man, a veteran of the horrors of Vietnam who wanted no further part of any nightmare.

His daughter handed up her suitcase. "Kids, get a move on. We want to be a hundred miles away by sunset."

Her father slid the suitcase to the front end of the trunk bed. He squinted in the direction of the hills where the ghost town stood. "I'd just as soon not set eyes on your sister again, not now that she's been 'turned'."

Across the forty-year old cracked pavement lane, the last three members of what had been a family of seven were loading their mother's van. The ten and eight year old girls brought out their last cherished belongings under the restless eyes of their sixteen year old sister. Under the circumstances their eldest sister was lenient about the youngest sister's insistence on bringing her stuffed toys along.

"Okay, do we have absolutely everything?" the teenager asked her sisters.

They looked at their sand-colored stuccoed house.

"Don't forget your provisions!" their old neighbor called.

"We got 'em, Mr. McAllister," she said. "We loaded up everything we could and I got my parents' bank cards."

"Did you charge up your phones?" his daughter yelled across the lane.

"Yes. We found Dad's car re-charger too. It was in his truck," she called back.

"You should go now. Wait for us at the truck stop outside of Gilbert," said the old veteran. "We're all meeting up there to gas up and form groups. Caravans, remember?"

"Right. I'll see you there." She picked up their little terrier and put him in the van. "All right, get in. We're going to Aunt Margo's."

"Will she still be there?" said the ten-year old.

"She was there when I talked to her ten minutes ago."

"Is she still normal?' said the youngest.

"It's daylight. She's normal. Vampyres don't talk during the day. Now get in. We have to go."

Her sisters climbed in.

Their sister was still barking at them to put on their seatbelts when she backed out of the driveway and roared off.

"Come on, kids!" shouted their mother. "Daylight is literally wasting."

Her teenaged son herded his brother and sister ahead of him. They lugged out backpacks and duffle bags stuffed so full that the zippers threatened to give out.

Their shepherd mix dog sprang up into the back of the truck as they added their last bags to the pile. Their grandfather secured their belongings.

"Anthony, sit back here with Bart," said his mother. "You two are sitting up front with Grandpa and me."

"Do we get to sit in the little seats behind the big people seats?" The little boy hopped up and down.

"Yes."

"I sit behind Grandpa," he shouted and rushed toward the front.

"You always get to sit there," his sister whined.

"Just get in back," snapped their mother.

"Is that it?" said her dad.

She surveyed the boxes and bags and then their sun baked little ranch style house. "It had better be. I ain't comin' back."

"Right." McAllister climbed out of the back with a grunt and a grimace and a little assist from his grandson, who helped him close the tail gate.

Then Anthony climbed into the back. He wrapped Bart's leash end around his hand and settled with him beside one of their old camping coolers next to the rear cabin window.

As both moved to the front, grandfather and daughter hesitated as they looked at the skyline.

"I didn't hear about a storm coming, did you, Dad?" she said.

"Nope, and this one's roaring in faster than any I've ever seen."

"They look like tornado clouds, don't you think?" said Anthony.

"And they're coming on like the wrath of God. Let's get going. Annie will be worrying that something happened to us." McAllister climbed into the truck and slammed his door shut.

His daughter lingered. "I don't think we locked the doors."

"Does it matter?" said Anthony.

"That's right," she muttered. "God, I don't know which way I'm going anymore." She climbed into the truck and slammed her door shut.

As they pulled away from their front yard and her mother's cactus and rock garden, she looked back in the rearview mirror at their abandoned street. There were still cars and trucks parked at some of the houses, but the gaping doors and windows told an ominous tale. Of all those plain everyday folks who had lived on that street, the Morgan girls and themselves were the only ones left. She grieved, but did not cry. The night had been too long.

Then she saw several exotic figures standing in the center of the lane beyond their house as though they had been there the whole time. She slammed on the brakes and stuck her head out of the window.

Her father spoke for them both, "Where did **they** come from?"

"I don't remember seeing them in front of the neighbor's house when we were loading the truck," she said.

Whoever the throng of strangers were they seemed to be holding a meeting.

"Should we warn them to clear out?" she said.

Anthony had sat wide-eyed and pale faced the whole time. "No," he said, recovering his voice.

A man dressed in raven's black robes turned his face their way and lowered his hood. His eyes were shining white.

"Drive," said Anthony. "Go. GO!"

His Mom hit the gas and no one looked back, except for Anthony, but that was only because from his seat he had little choice in the matter.

The truck was the last to join up with their town's few other survivors at the truck stop. The strange weather promised to lock the valley in premature darkness, so they formed little caravans, filled up their vehicles, and left without any time for regret.

At least we need not worry about anyone innocent getting caught in the middle," said Wotan, his gaze following the truck.

Hades surveyed the crowd arrayed before him.

Each and every one of his fellow Incarnations were armed to the teeth with their preferred weapons.

When she wasn't blithely handing out extra swords, Kali concentrated with loving dedication on sharpening her own blades while Shiva looked on.

Standing close beside her, equally focused, were Lord Ogoun, checking the edge of his saber and his machete, and Hadak Ura, unsheathing the *'Sword of God'* to polish it.

Perun and Thor were testing each other's hammers. Their freshly sharpened axes shared an unearthly gleam in the strange afternoon light.

Parashuram and six-faced Skanda stood among the other divine archers Eros, Artemis, Takemikazuchi, and their cohorts preparing their bows and their ever-ready quivers,

Artemis had assembled quite a company from the Americas, foremost among them Huitzilopochtli and Mextli, and also Teoyaomicqui, who stood with Hecate, Trebaruna and Medusa, and Tezcatlipoca, who stood a little apart with his ominous-looking obsidian mirror and a fearsome obsidian blade in his grasp. Tezcatlipoca stood nearer to Apollo with whom he exchanged somber looks, and to Surya, who stood with his eyes closed in meditation next to his shining chariot.

Horus stood conferring with the lioness-headed Sekhmet and Wotan, upon whose shoulder Babd in her crow form sat, whilst Hugin the raven sat upon his other shoulder. Muninn, Wotan's other raven associate, sat upon Horus' shoulder, his bright black eyes casting about the assembly.

Kukailimoku had brought the Pacific contingent, but at the moment he was admiring Perun's war chariot along with Resheph and Andraste.

Ares's quiet, at the moment, berserker sister Enyo stood near her brother as he spoke with his fierce sons Phobos and Deimos and his equally belligerent daughter Eris. "Do not feel obligated to join in this battle. Our foes may be immune to your influence," he told his offspring.

"True enough," said Phobos.

Eris spoke up, "But that doesn't mean we cannot impale and decapitate as well as any of the rest."

"Very well," said Aries.

Athena swept in from the far south-east accompanied by Nike. The duo fell in at once with Tumatauenga, Freyja, and Tyr. Andraste turned from greeting Athena and Nike to greet Anubis who arrived with Anu, the leader of the Celtic platoon, at his side.

Hermes dropped into their midst last. He shrugged at Hades. No Zeus.

"Well then," said Hades loudly.

His comrades fell silent but for the sounds their hands made readying their weapons.

"It is time to decide our strategy," said Hades. "Night is only two hours off."

33.

From a state of half-hearted rest, Sebastiano's eyes shot wide open. He sat up. As cool and dark as it was in the cellar, he could tell by the tinge of warmth to the sunlight touched air that pushed downstairs through the door cracks that it was but a late afternoon out there. As long as the sun still reigned above, his reign remained restricted to their underground hive. This was a problem.

The Hunters had arrived.

Off to the side Jacques lay oblivious – as usual, when he should have known better by then. He had his arms wrapped around his new favorite: a high school senior, tall, good-looking, athletic, and now one of them.

Sebastiano shot to his feet. He eyed the cracked and decaying ceiling. There were too many gaps where he could see the floor boards above them and the swirls of dust descending between the slats.

He had created an army of vampyres, but they would be useless to him if they slept through the ambush. With his sharp fingertips he prodded those favorites who shared his cellar.

Lips drawn halfway back into a snarl, they awoke. Their Master's grim expression and swift glance upwards silenced them. He motioned toward the other 'sleepers' in that spacious cellar and then toward the ragged hole in the wall. They spread out, waking the rest as soundlessly as possible.

Sebastiano withdrew to the hole in the wall. Through it wound one of several interconnecting tunnels, all of which went back into the deep, dark mines. There he lingered watching the dust descend, but then, gradually at first and finally with alarming certainty light dawned across the floorboards overhead.

"Ah! The sun is setting," declared one of his minions.

"No, not the sun itself, but it might as well be where we are concerned," grumbled Sebastiano.

The modern vampyr looked puzzled at his ancient master. "What do you mean?"

"An Incarnation that shares and wields its power. Into the tunnels! Quick!" Sebastiano ducked into the cool darkness. He knew not to look back.

Jacques liked his rest, especially when his appetites had been satiated to the utmost. He and his favorite were among the last to be awakened. They were halfway to the tunnel when three mighty stomps sent their ceiling crashing onto them and those few others who had not moved quite fast enough.

The basement of the ruined hotel filled with light and heat. It also filled with the horrible screams of those trapped in the presence of Surya in all his radiant solar glory.

Down the rough hewn tunnel, Sebastiano recognized Jacques' unearthly scream of searing agony. Then that smell of scorched rotting flesh smoked down the tunnel. He covered his nose and pushed past his horrified minions.

"What is that?" they were asking.

"A sun god. Keep moving or he'll cremate you too."

"A sun god?! There's no such thing," shouted one of them.

"Feel free then to linger behind and tell him that he doesn't exist," said Sebastiano, "but I'd run if I were you."

They obeyed him. It was a stampede.

Already a shaft of almost blinding light cut into the tunnel's darkness, causing those lagging disbelievers to smolder. Then they believed even as they burst into flames. Smoke filled the entrance, dulling Surya's brilliance just enough for the last of Sebastiano's group to swerve down a side passage and out of sight.

If they thought that comfortable, silent darkness awaited them, they discovered otherwise immediately.

From the direction of the cellars beneath another dilapidated row of shabby structures that had been a mercantile store, a boarding house, a saloon and a brothel, places already whispering with echoes of the past and the memories of ghosts came fresh howls of terror and anguish. A separate mad scramble accompanied the unearthly cries.

"The Sword of God!" went the cry, for Hadak Ura had crashed through into their midst taking heads right and left with his shining sword. Ogoun, Perun, and Thor led a war party directly behind Hadak Ura that sent vampyr blood flying with each stroke and blow.

The rest of their prey could not flee fast enough.

From the direction of the outlying structures, Sebastiano and his surviving court could hear another slaughter and stampede taking place. Grimly, their Master considered the one thing that he failed to teach his new converts. It had not occurred to him to tell them of the existence of such incarnate beings as Hades and Anubis or Ares and Apollo. An army of vengeful mortal vigilantes they would have instinctively attacked, but these warriors' mere auras struck terror in his modern-born converts. The irony did not escape him. These mortals believed so readily, so eagerly in his kind, and yet they did not believe in much else.

Sebastiano stopped those first of those vampyres to reach the great cavern near the mine shaft. "Who did you see? Who came after you?"

"Don't you mean what?" said a male vampyr. "It was a squad of them – fierce bright beings."

"Describe them!"

"They wore these strange ancient styled helmets that gleamed with a golden light. They were men and women together and armed with lances and swords and shields."

"Did you hear any names?"

"Athena…Ares…Enyo, but there were too many of them and it was all going down too fast."

Sebastiano released the vampyr with a shove. "So you brought your kindred, every Incarnation the Almighty could spare," he grumbled at the darkness. "Coward, Hades. We shall meet nonetheless."

"Where shall we go? They have come underground after us."

"Go down into the mines," he told them. "They will not hesitate to come after you. There though you can attack them in the eternal darkness of the Earth. There is power in their blood. Drink it."

They rushed ahead of him into the mineshaft, where many more of the recently converted were just waking to the crisis.

Unfortunately, they discovered that they had intruders in their midst already.

The distant echoes of trouble carried through to them first. They could smell the fear and poisonous stench of vampyr blood. Scrambling from crevices into the main shaft a hissing growl greeted them, accompanied by a pair of eyes the color of fire opals peering out from a single shaft.

"Ah, I knew I'd find you here,"came a low female growl.

"We are many. You are alone."

An exotic living aroma drifted out to them, whetting their appetites and drawing forth their fangs. *SHE* smelled of spice dust and sweet oils rubbed into warm skin. But those unnatural fiery eyes…

"You may be many, but I am *MEDUSA*..."

Fear tremored through them, but so did confusion. A few kept their distance, but others couldn't help themselves. They drew closer to the strange eyes as those eyes came nearer to them.

"...And I fear nothing," said Medusa as she emerged into the open and into full view.

Too late they saw her quicksilver scimitar and the flash of red as her left hand yanked the cloth from about her clearly writhing hair. Too late they realized that the myth of their mortal reading was true and that Medusa the Gorgon was real.

Those nearest her had their breath stolen from them as they tried to catch it. Those who opened their sharp maws to scream felt their voices die in their throats and then nothing else. They began to crumble before their corpses could finish solidifying. Medusa sped their disintegration with a blow from her scimitar.

Those farther away ran away.

They ran up or they ran deeper.

It was still waning daylight beyond the mine entrance. They dared not go out to scatter across the desert landscape. They discovered also that they could not take refuge in their tunnels beneath the ghost town. The tunnels were clogged with their kind stampeding toward the mines.

The call went up, "Where is Brother Jacques?"

"The Sun God burned him up alive," someone replied.

"Sun god? What are you talking about?"

"Precisely what I said, a blazing god came through the ceiling like a fireball and set everyone aflame without even touching them. If you run that way, you'll get a good enough look at it."

"If you run *that* way the Gorgon will get you."

"What the fucking hell?"

"A Gorgon – with snakes for hair and glowing eyes that can destroy with a glance. It's down there."

"How about *that* tunnel?"

"No, there are warriors with shining helmets and flashing swift swords coming up from there. If you go that way, they'll cut your head off like that!"

"Where is our Master Sebastiano?"

"He said to come here."

"Where is he?"

"He was with us."

"No, he was behind us."

"He isn't here!"

"Listen! Sebastiano said to attack them here in the mines."

"He did. He said that there was power in their blood and to drink it."

"They're coming. The earth shakes under their feet. Can you feel it?"

"If you want to panic, take your panic back into the tunnels. If you want to fight, gather here. Let them come. We'll ambush them. We'll bathe in their blessed pagan blood."

Down the mineshaft, Medusa stood with Anubis, Kali, Anu, Sekhmet, Tezcatlipoca, and Hades looking up and down and listening to those who had fled and those who were regrouping.

"That was a war cry," said Sekhmet.

"We expected this," said Tezcatlipoca. Strange flashes of light appeared in his obsidian mirror, almost spectral in their fleeting forms, as though they emerged from his heart into the black stone.

"Which way do we go?" said Kali.

"We stay here," said Hades. "We keep the cowards who ran into the Earth from reinforcing the rest."

"Expect to catch hell from both sides then," said Anubis.

Between Surya's single-handed efforts and the collective assaults from Ares' squad and the squad led by Hadak Ura, the mineshaft filled with the undead. The sounds were deafening.

At the main entrance, Apollo and the archers waited on the slope with their gleaming bows ready armed with diamond-headed arrows.

Artemis cast a look toward the sun that sank already behind purple clouds over a hazy mountain range. "Remind me again, Brother Incarnation, why we are not doing this in the heart of the day?"

"Because our comrades will squeeze them in pincer movements," said Apollo. "They will resist with all their might…"

"But in the end," said Hecate with a grim, but eager smile and a nod, "they will feel Night's first breath and rush to meet its embrace."

"Only, they will find us waiting to greet them first," said Eros with a terrible look of delight in his face.

"Ah.' Artemis smiled a little herself.

246

Six-faced Skanda kept one of his faces turned toward the sunset. "With the sun disappearing beyond that cloud bank, they will anticipate an early evening."

Parashuram aimed at the mine entrance. "Nonetheless, they will find us ready."

Eros chuckled.

At their respective underground entrances to the mineshaft, the besiegers paused to listen to the anger and terror boiling up from the depths. They waited for a signal.

Out on the ghost town's boundary, Hermes paced as he waited for the outcome. The sound of wings caught his attention. Glancing swiftly, he relaxed at once.

Materializing as he landed, *Michael* alighted behind him. "There is much more at stake than anyone realizes," he explained to Hermes' stare.

"So I see," said Hermes.

"Indeed, Divine Messenger, if our warriors fall and fail to extinguish this plague of all consuming darkness and its creator, you shall have to make Godspeed to Shambhala. An army stands ready there to ride out and do battle."

"'Good to know," said Hermes.

Together they turned to watch the outcome.

He had to admit, these new converts were a bold bunch. By the time Sebastiano arrived in their midst, or, rather, was discovered among them, his minions had regained more than their self-control. They had formulated a plan of resistance. He credited their defiance to too many action movies. They had barely considered the nature of the forces rallied against them and yet already they considered themselves equal in power to the entities bearing down on them.

Romantic fools, Sebastiano observed, whose misguided imaginations and misplaced desires had brought them under his power and then to their dire fates in a forgotten ghost town. What he had exploited would doom them again. They rallied as he looked on, certain of their impending victory. They hailed him, their great creator. He urged them on to their destruction and moved to the rear. They might fail and yet in their failure give him his path to victory over Hades.

"Soon we shall drink the blood of gods," their volunteer warlord shouted.

Then the first breath of Night rolled over them.

The sun had set.

A great war cry went up.

In the pale twilight the archers braced for the onslaught.

Emboldened, the vampyres in the depths of the mine rushed up to join forces with them.

Tezcatlipoca stood directly in their path, armed simply with a shield and his terrible obsidian blade. At once he displayed his remarkable talent for striking absolute terror in his foes, even the undead ones, as he met the first one head on. With one thrust he drove his blade into the vampyr man's heart, twisted the blade and withdrew it with yet another precise flourish. Impaled upon it was his heart, which Tezcatlipoca ate.

What had been a charge turned into a panic as vampyres attempted to scramble past the Aztec incarnation wearing the bloody smile. Their would-be escape met with merciless retribution as Hades and his Hunters slaughtered left and right and Anu collected their souls in her sack.

Their black blood trickled into ever quickening streams down the mine shaft. The Earth drank their rotten blood as Death turned their bodies to ash. Anu's sack squirmed.

Violence whirled around Hades and his Hunters and the vampyres could not escape it

Sebastiano could not tear his eyes from the spectacle. It dazzled him and yet he watched Hades' movements at the heart of the skirmish, mindful of any possible opportunity to strike. He could feel Fate turning his way. Even when his wretched minions scrambled up the mineshaft he remained close to the battle.

The passages beneath the ghost town reverberated with battle until the old wind-blasted buildings shook as ominously as leaves in an autumn wind. Not one vampyr clambered out though.

That left the mine entrance as their last venue for escape.

In the distance the harvest moon had risen, great and glorious. Artemis rejoiced to see it.

A great cacophony massed in the mine. Its ominous noise roared out into the desert air. Then the hillside exploded.

Any mortal standing on far opposite hillside, across that desolate valley, would have witnessed a spectacular event. They would have been dazzled by what looked like a relentless arcing cascade of flames flying toward the mine entrance and the dark figures rushing out like angry ants. Then they would have been puzzled by the silence through which nothing but a forlorn wind passed. If any mortal had been foolhardy enough to linger still longer, they would have seen the sort of battle that only ancient bards sang paeans about as the ghost town lit up as if it were on fire and yet did not burn although its fiery glow reached high into the night sky.

As it was, Hermes and Michael had moved closer, silent with awe. It took them a moment to realize that Asclepius and Dhanvantari had arrived with their corps of healers.

Apollo and the divine archers cut the night air with arrow after arrow. They shot into the raging horde as they hurtled out or shot them down as soon as they attempted to take flight. Their prey cursed and screamed.

Their corpses were still twitching with their second death throes as Hecate and Perun collected their souls from opposite ends of the battlefield. During her gradual ascent behind Kali and the other hunters, Anu collected the other malingering souls.

Surya blazed from one building to the next, hunting down those who had escaped Ares and Hadak Ura's hunters in the tunnels. From a distance he resembled a white hot ball of light passing behind the thinnest of curtains. Crashes and shrieks preceded him. Sultry silence followed.

In the ghost town, floors collapsed. The buildings themselves fractured. Several tilted ominously on their foundations from the forces demolishing the labyrinth of tunnels beneath the structures.

At last, the fighting burst out into the night air.

Ares emerged first, bloodied. His punctures still dripped down his arms as he closed his hand around the vampyr's neck that drank the blood pumping in his sword arm. Now that it had tasted divine blood, the vampyr gripped tight, drinking with vicious appetite. Perhaps it thought it could weaken the war god before Ares could retaliate.

It thought wrong.

Ares crushed its neck in his fist and snapped its head backwards. As it fell away with a shocked look, Ares sliced off its head with one sweep of his sword. Cursing it for the blood it had taken, he kicked its head out into the middle of the dusty road. He clenched his fist, willing his wounds to close, but they would not.

The tide turned. His blood smelled sweet and its aroma was strong. Athena and Enyo met the onslaught on one side. The ferocious children of Ares guarded him from the other side.

"Get clear of here, Ares!" Athena shouted over her shoulder as she impaled a vampyr woman.

"They smell your blood," Enyo shouted. "We've got a feeding frenzy on our hands." She ran her sword through the mouth of a male vampyr and cut its head in half.

"I can't leave you to face this horde alone." Ares stood in the center of the circle they had formed. Dust flew up around them. He could smell his own blood mingled with the sickeningly rotten smell of their blood on his sword and breastplate.

Another vampyr was climbing up the length of Enyo's impaling sword. Its drool rolled down its sallow chin onto her blade and then onto her gloved hands. There was a precious little stretch of uncovered skin on her forearms. Its blood black eyes glanced from one arm to the other. So close. So very close. It could see her rare blood pulsing in her arms.

"Yes, you can leave us!" Enyo kicked the vampyr off of her sword.

It leapt up and flung itself toward her.

As its head bounced against her breastplate, off her left thigh and rolled across the soiled dirt, Enyo kicked its gushing torso aside. "Their hunger surpasses their fear of us, Brother."

"Go before you are overwhelmed," said Athena as she lunged to meet another clawing assailant.

Ares frowned at his blood leaking steadily in streams down his arms.

Another vampyr broke through the circle. Its face met Ares' fist, and that was enough for the war god.

The North Wind swooped past, heading for the southern orchards. Ares caught it by its mane and let it carry him beyond the ghost town. He clung only until he caught sight of Hermes standing beside Michael, whose tall wings shone as bright as starlight and snow. Then he dropped down beside them.

By the wide-eyed look on Hermes' face Ares knew. "That bad, eh?"

"You look a fright. Are you feeling weak?" said Hermes.

"No, but I expect that'll change soon enough." Ares marveled at his steady flow of blood. His blood rolled down the edge of his sword. Its droplets blackened the dull yellow sand.

Asclepius swooped down on him. "We must stop this bleeding. Come with me."

"No, attend to my wounds here," said Ares. "I must bear witness…see this battle out. Do what you can, only leave me to wait it out here, where I might still lend a hand."

Asclepius sighed. "Very well, but you will sit for the duration."

Ares did as he was told. His solemn eyes remained fixed on the battle.

Fierce Mextli joined them next with one hand pressed to a terrible bite in his shoulder. Several vampyres attempted to continue their assault on him. Scowling, Mextli summoned his native born power and obliterated them with a single bolt of lightning delivered via his bloody index finger. The gust of western wind that scattered their startled ashes was an afterthought. He fell to his knees at last, dropping his shield and weapon upon the ground.

Dhanvantari rushed to tend to Mextli at once.,

Vrinda Devi stood by with the rest of their corps, ready for more of their wounded.

Ogoun emerged from the fray next. He stomped into their midst and stopped abruptly as though he had emptied his last reservoir of strength. He wavered. His body gleamed with fresh blood, his and his preys'. A tremor went through his mighty body. His saber and machete fell to the ground.

Ogoun collapsed into Hermes' swift arms.

Vrinda Devi rushed forward as Hermes laid him down.

"We are prevailing," he whispered with weary, but defiant smile kindling in his dark eyes.

Sekhmet's roar sent more vampyres rushing into the night air and into the shooting gallery.

Tyr and Thor lurched into their midst next, each supporting the other with dust-caked smiles. Both had endured a ferocious mauling and had responded with appropriate retribution.

"I'll race you to Valhalla," Thor said to Tyr.

"As though Hel would let you so much as wipe your feet on the welcome mat on the way through," Tyr responded.

Both laughed and on seeing the full moon saluted it with wolf howls.

On the firing line, Artemis smiled a little more keenly and shot another arrow.

Another of Sebastiano's vile followers fell truly dead with the goddess' arrow embedded in her heart.

Hecate seized a hold of its moaning spirit and shoved it into her sack. All the while she collected she hummed her potent mantras under grimly smiling breath.

34.

The fight below had ended. All was silent and dark in the depths.

Above, all was clamorous strife and even that receded more and more into the distance.

Medusa and Tezcatlipoca lingered behind with Hades surveying the already rotting corpses.

The rest of his fierce little squad drove the malingerers ahead into the archers' range. Sekhmet's roar echoed down to them.

"Oh dear," said Medusa with a wry, breathless smile, "Sekhmet's mad now."

"Someone must have bitten her," said Tezcatlipoca. "It will not have occurred to them that she can and will bite back."

The scarcely human shriek that followed confirmed his observation.

"We should go up. They might need a little reinforcement," said Medusa, "if only to shove those creatures outside for the archers to tend to."

Tezcatlipoca responded by setting forth toward the night air.

Medusa fell into step alongside him.

They had ascended a good distance before they realized that their Leader was not behind them.

Hades waited until their footsteps softened in the distance, then he turned and stared pointedly down a side shaft. "I know you are there, Upir Likhyi. You reek of the charnel house...where you belong."

"It was foolhardy of you to linger behind." Sebastiano's blood black eyes radiated red from a safe distance.

"Was it?" Hades said. "I know what I'm doing."

"Are you sure about that?" The foul revenant moved with a calm and deliberate pace like a side winder.

"I have come to deliver you to the Underworld. This age is ending and you with it."

"At last!" he snorted. "It certainly took you long enough to catch up with me. How many centuries has it been since I escaped? Eight? Nine mortal centuries? Are you sure you were 'meant' to capture me?"

Hades' silver white eyes took on an unholy gleam. His lips curved in the shadows. "I will be the vehicle of your defeat."

"You're so cocksure of yourself." He moved closer and closer.

Hades did not move. "I knew that you would be easy to catch this time."

"You do not have me in your custody yet."

"To catch you all I had to do was show up, Pestilence."

"That I was counting on." From a position of near stillness, Sebastiano rushed out.

They hit the opposing mine shaft wall. The old timbers shook. Rocks ricocheted down the shaft. Dust and dirt cascaded over their struggle.

Sebastiano clawed and ripped at Hades wherever he could catch at him. His fingernails scraped against Hades' black clothing. It was hard to get a grip on him. Everything about Hades was smoke and shadow it seemed and yet his hands clasped about the vampyr's straining neck felt all too solid and possessed of great strength.

This strength he could not hope to match with just his strength alone. He craved this strength for his own. He could smell Hades' splendid immortal vitality. He breathed it in so deeply that he could almost taste the Olympian's blood.

Sebastiano tugged and pulled, pushed and kicked, bucking his whole body so violently that for a moment he was amazed that he didn't snap his own neck. His only chance lay in somehow upsetting Hades' balance, so he writhed and clawed and punched.

"Break my neck and be done with it," he hissed.

Hades frown intensified.

If it weren't for the Olympian's hands about his throat, he would have laughed. He settled for hoarse gloating. "You can't do it. It isn't as easy as you had thought."

Sebastiano bucked with his whole body.

Hades stumbled.

They dislodged a beam. Its fall toppled them both.

In that instant Sebastiano saw his opportunity. Hades hit the floor just as Sebastiano's teeth found his neck.

Hades cursed the Fates. "Damnation." He gritted his teeth and gripped the vampyr's head in both hands.

The evil one spread his body across Hades' torso and clasped him in his fatal embrace. He bit down even harder. Warm vitality, true ambrosia gushed into his mouth. Divine energy spawned directly by the Source of All Things flowed from Hades' wound into Upir Likhyi's being.

Hades grimaced. His hands trembled. Such pain…he had not expected such searing pain. He pushed. He kicked. He punched, but once Sebastiano had anchored to feed, he was incredibly difficult to dislodge. The sound of his own blood being suckled from his own body, the smells of it and that entity's corrupted body mingling made Hades' stomach wrench.

Upir Likhyi drank without restraint, without any fear although he heard the approach of his enemies.

"Release him!" Medusa's voice ebbed strangely.

Hades could not see her, but he thought she sounded alarmed and beyond furious. He realized that – briefly – the pain in his neck had dulled.

"There is nothing you can do for him now."

Medusa must have said something more for Upir Likhyi spoke again, "His power lives in me now. What was his is now under my dominion." Then he hissed into Hades' face, "And that means **everything**."

Digging his sharp fingers through Hades' clothing into his body, Sebastiano bit again.

Hades yelled.

Sebastiano snarled. He could always tell when his victims reached the point of no recovery. His body thrummed with Hades' essence as he felt Hades begin to go limp.

Suddenly, Hades clasped him.

His strength caused Upir Likhyi to frown. He looked into Hades' eyes and saw them darken.

"Home," said Hades in a gravelly voice, but then he sighed, "Persephone."

Victor and victim vanished from that plane of existence.

The Hunters knew at once something had altered. The archers lowered their bows. The battle in the passages subsided. Led by Surya, his light calming, the Hunters emerged into the open night, examining their fresh bruises, gashes, cuts, slashes, and gruesome punctures. They helped each other up and slapped each other on the back or supported one another as they limped away from the ghost town.

The very few vampyres who lingered did not do so for long. Between Kali's merciless sword work and the patient diligence of Wotan, Athena, Enyo and the rest of the Hunters, they left that plane of existencel.

"Is the fight over?" said Dhanvantari.

"Not here, not quite," said Michael as he flexed his wings and watched Medusa and Tezcatlipoca climb hastily out of the mine.

"Where's Hades?" said Hermes. Then he met Michael's serious gaze. "Oh. Uh oh."

"Be ready to fly to Shambhala."

Hermes stomped his foot once hard and vanished from the Earth.

The archers led the hunters toward Michael's position.

"So," Apollo said to Artemis, "what now? Are you going back to your dog walking and your tree climbing?"

"My wolves are perfectly capable of walking themselves," Artemis retorted with a wry grin. She rubbed her dusty face against her buckskin sleeve and stretched her neck. "I run where they run. As for the trees," she sighed and frowned more than a little pensively, "humanity will insist on putting a price tag on the Divine Creation."

"There will be an awakening, mark my words," said Apollo, his face radiant with a mysterious smile.

"I would that it began yesterday," she said.

"Patience, sister."

The smell of incense, warm and sweet, washed over Hades. Smiling as he breathed it in, he released his grip on Upir Likhyi. "I said I would deliver you."

The Vampyr lifted his dripping mouth from Hades' wound. For a moment he gazed about with uncertainty.

The gentle murmuring souls withdrew from the mosaic upon which the two had appeared.

Sebastiano could see the dais and the solemn figures arrayed upon it: Osiris, Hel, Yamaraja, Nepthys, Isis, and moving forward from beyond the thrones, Dionysus, Hera, Aphrodite, Psyche, and Persephone, who looked wraithlike in her black gown and enveloping purple veil. The others made space for Persephone to stand between Osiris and Yamaraja.

Garmr and Cerberus shoved forward to stand on either side of the mosaic. Cerberus sniffed the air with one head, the second one whined, and the third growled.

"You will not leave here again," Hades whispered.

Sebastiano climbed to his feet. Divine blood had a rich after taste and he had consumed more than his fill. Only when the bitterness of Death curdled in his mouth did he stop drinking. All of Hades' vitality was his. Energy pulsed throughout him as he placed himself before the dais.

"This is as I planned," he told them all. Then his blood black eyes settled on Persephone. "This is what I wanted."

Persephone's chin tilted upward ever so slightly. Her veil trembled although she did not. Concealed in the folds of her gown, her hands curled into fists.

Anubis, Medusa, and Kali arrived on the threshold a mere instant after Hermes did. Hecate bustled in after them and Anu with her, their sacks writhing with wretched souls. They stopped at once to see what would happen.

The Underworld had never been so silent and still.

Hera stepped to the very edge of the sacred dais. "Would you dare to claim our Brother's place here?"

Hermes saw a strange smile appear on Hades' pale face. After eons of coping with Zeus, nothing intimidated Hera once her temper was up. Nothing.

"I have taken his essence into my being. He is now me." Sebastiano stepped calmly toward the dais. His white-less eyes saw only Persephone's veiled radiance. "So, yes, I have come to take his place amongst you. His dominion is mine…as is his Consort."

"Mater Dolorosa," the spirits in the great hall moaned. A shudder passed through the pool of souls.

Isis rushed around him the moment the vampyr exited the mosaic's special space.

Already Hermes, Kali, and Medusa knelt beside Hades. Lifting his head, Isis knelt and placed his head upon her lap. Whispering prayers, she placed her hands firmly upon his neck wound. Perun, Teoyaomicqui, Babd, Huitzilopochtli, and more of their kindred Incarnations crossed over and gathered about Hades. Perun glared at Upir Likhyi's back. Teoyaomicqui and Huitzilopochtli exchanged grim looks.

Isis sat with her face bent over Hades, praying steadily, softly all the while, seeing only his dark eyes gazing softly up into hers.

Upir Likhyi stopped directly before Persephone. Hades' blood still dripped down his chin as he smiled at her, oblivious to Osiris and Yamaraja on either side of her.

Aphrodite trembled. Psyche buried his face against her neck rather than look a moment longer at that monster.

"Is she a prize to be claimed just so?" Hera shook with fury.

256

Dionysus stepped down from the dais and moved between the mosaic and the vampyr '*god*'. He looked straight into Persephone's eyes. "From the beginning Kore has been the eternal sacrifice. That is her purpose as the Incarnation of the Eternal Union between Life and Death."

A terrible awareness kindled bright in Persephone's eyes. Her beautiful mouth curved as she held out her hand. "Come, husband of old reborn. Come to our chamber."

Upir Likhyi seized her hand. Its soft warmth was too much to resist. He pressed her hand to his mouth and breathed in her aroma. Then he bit into it.

Persephone gasped, but bit on her lip before any other sound could escape. Hades' precious blood was now smeared upon her pale, pure hand. Tears rushed into her eyes, but they dared not fall. She would not let them.

Psyche wept against Aphrodite's shoulder.

Aphrodite gazed at Persephone's face with anguish and rage warring for supremacy.

"But come, my Lord," Persephone said distantly, "this is not the place for a proper reunion."

Sebastiano's mouth relinquished her hand with a lick of his tongue. Her smile sparkled as she backed towards hers and Hades' private spaces. She drew him along with a hand wet from her own blood.

"Your blood is as sweet as nectar," the vampyr '*god*' said in a low, breathless voice as they disappeared beyond the partition.

"Horrible," said Aphrodite.

"I don't understand," Hera said. "How can you all stand by?"

Isis kept her gaze locked with Hades'. "It will be all right. Persephone will not betray you. Persephone…"

" – Knows what to do," Hades breathed. "Persephone…"

Hecate looked to Dionysus.

Dionysus crouched down beside Hades and took his right hand in both of his. "Persephone understands her purpose, Brother. Rest easy. Rest in peace."

Isis looked up with alarm electric in her golden amber eyes.

"What are you saying?" said Hera.

Anubis rushed onto the dais and then crept to peer into the chambers beyond.

Beside the eternal flames in the heart of that pit, beyond which Sebastiano could appreciate the sight of a luxurious royal bed, the vampyr 'god' tore away the twilight colored veil that had denied him the full pleasure of seeing the goddess' beautiful face. He tossed it into the flames. The veil shimmered as it flashed out of existence.

"You do not avert your face. You do not lower your gaze. You are bold," he said. "I like that." He brought his smiling face mere inches from her skin.

Persephone could smell her Consort's blood souring on Sebastiano's breath. "What now, my Lord?"

His roving gaze locked with hers. "Bare yourself so that I might feast." He pulled at the gold brooches holding her bodice in place. His breath scraped across her cheek as his fingernails pierced the fabric over her breasts. He dug them in deep until he felt her blood warming his fingertips. Breathing in that fresh, injured scent with an expression of bliss, he nicked her neck with his fangs and rolled his tongue over the wound.

Pain shimmered across Persephone's face the way lightning passed through a cloud bank.

Upir Likhyi thrust his fingernails still deeper into her soft flesh. "Delicious, isn't it? This exquisite pain. Your blood is a perfume. Bare yourself. I command it. I will consume you unto Oblivion, Queen of Death."

"You must kiss me first," she breathed.

"I will do as I please." He withdrew his bloody fingernails and seized a hold of the gold brooches instead.

Persephone stilled his impatient hands with caresses and a smile. "You must kiss me first, because all unions are sealed with a kiss." She raised her face to his, close, closer still.

"Ah! I see blood on your lip!"

"Your desire caused me to bite my own lip."

"Yes," he murmured. "Blood is all."

"Taste me."

Sebastiano ran his tongue slowly across Persephone's bottom lip. A soft groan escaped his bloody mouth. "I will savor you."

"Kiss me."

A short little sound of delight escaped Upir Likhyi as he pressed his sharp mouth to her plump, pomegranate lips. His horrible bottomless eyes gazed fully upon the goddess' beauty, enjoying the prospect of seeing her delicious torment as he drank her essence from her soft mouth.

As she would a lover, as she did at last for Hades that blessed spring, Persephone closed her eyes and accepted his kiss. He cut her lips and tongue with his fangs and sucked on her mouth, a vampyr's kiss which the goddess returned. Sebastiano savored this kiss and lingered over her swelling lips.

When she pressed her fragrant body close, the life that throbbed throughout her caused Sebastiano to growl, "I will bite your sacred secret places first."

Persephone opened her bright eyes, as bright as the sky on a perfect day, and drew his mouth back upon hers. Her eyes did not close, not this time. Her arms enclosed him in an embrace as her blood filled both of their mouths. She stared directly back into his eyes.

He saw no fear in her eyes.

Neither was there pain…nor desire.

Warmth flowed from her everywhere their bodies touched. Her life was pouring into him.

Sebastiano began to exult. This was better, so much better than he had imagined. The power of Hades that was his met and merged with the power of his new, divine Consort. A tremor went through him such as he had never enjoyed before. It surprised Upir Likhyi to feel weak at the knees all of a sudden.

Still cradled in Persephone's embrace, her lips upon his kissing as though she would never stop, Sebastiano sank down toward the fire pit. He was helpless as she leaned over him. Then her eyes crackled with delight, no, something worse – jubilation. He saw it blaze across her face, recognized it and recognized too late his mistake.

Licking the blood from her lips, Persephone laid him out beside the fire pit and gazed into his wide eyes.

"I should have drained you, no, converted you on the spot," he gasped.

"The result would have been the same. I embody the rebirth of all living things. I harmonize the eternal cycle of Life and Death. I am Life, defiant and unstoppable Life." Persephone let him absorb the enormity of her revelation for a moment. "It is time now for you to become One with Life and all of its suffering.'

The vampyr 'god' squirmed. He shook his head wildly.

Persephone took his face in her hands. "How warm you are, Sebastiano that was and is. Come, my bridegroom, and become my husband." She closed her mouth upon his.

Sebastiano groaned and closed his eyes. No more blood passed his lips. He was mortal, a mere human at last.

Anubis turned away.

Small sounds emerged from behind him, so fleeting that they scarcely carried as far as the partition behind the dais. Anubis watched the strange shadows lurching on the wall.

Only one strangulated, agonized cry carried out past him. Anubis turned to look.

From the heart of the flames Persephone rose as the red-hot orange flames blazed a white-hot blue and that which was poor Sebastiano the humble monk and the vile spirit that had occupied him vanished into nothingness.

Purified and unblemished, Persephone paused beside the pit to coil her lustrous long hair. Flames gleamed from within her eyes.

Anubis rushed to her side. He picked up her gown and helped her into it.

Persephone was still pinning her brooches in place as she hurried back out onto the dais.

Slumping, Isis knelt upon the mosaic. Hades' blood stained her creamy white gown and her hands, which she held out helpless from her sides.

Persephone stopped. "He is gone forever. I fed him to the Eternal Fire, purified this realm of his evil with my own hands," she announced to the room. "I did it, Hades, my Love."

Isis looked at her hands and then at the mosaic.

It was empty.

"Wait," said Persephone. "Where is he? I did as I was meant to. Upir Likhyi is gone. Where is my husband?"

Isis glanced at Osiris.

"No. No," Persephone muttered. She flung herself upon her knees on the mosaic and ran her hands across its surface. Her fingertips paused over Hades' face in the mosaic. "Is there nothing of him left?" She looked up into Isis's face. "Not even a scrap of his robes?"

Isis looked at her hands. Where there had been blood her hands were indigo blue. Tears poured down her face.

Hermes removed his helmet.

Persephone pressed her cheek to her husband's portrait. "But where?"

Hel motioned toward the passage of Light. "He has returned Home."

Persephone sat up, desperately rubbing away her tears, trying to see clearly. "Did you see it happen? Are you sure he's gone?"

Hermes turned his helmet over and over in his hands. "He dissolved into light. It was the most beautiful pale blue light I ever saw."

"And the passage lit up so bright, and yet so soft," said Hera, her own face wet with grief. "It looked like a pair of hands reached forth. He flowed into them and now he's gone." She sniffled. "He's gone completely."

Persephone knelt with her hands pressed to her face. She gasped and heaved after one solid breath.

Dionysus moved nearer. "Persephone?" he whispered.

Persephone's scream shook the eternal night. Her sobs shook the Underworld…until Dionysus caught her rocking body in his arms.

For a time, he rocked with her and stroked her hair.

When she wept a soft, but steady rain, Dionysus bore her up in his arms and carried her to her bed. Hecate covered her and stroked her hair twice before she withdrew. Dionysus stretched out beside Persephone and held her hand even after sleep finally came to give her some ease.

Life went on until it didn't.

Mater Dolorosa reigned on, gracing her wounded charges with her kind, but sad smiles. She passed throughout the Underworld dressed in the color of a beautiful spring sky, her sun-kissed auburn hair forever wreathed in a veil that possessed the soft brilliance of a gentle sunrise.

For a time, she bore her duties with quiet, grave resolve.

Then, one 'evening' Persephone withdrew to her chamber. As she lay back upon her pillow, an old forgotten scent washed over her. Memory made her wretched once more. Tears rushed into her eyes. She wanted to grab the neighboring pillow and just breathe in the smell of her lost consort. Instead, pain drove her from her bed completely.

Weary beyond all endurance, heartsick beyond any relief, Persephone dressed in the colors of night and donned her veil of twilight. She returned to the dais, but she did not sit. She could only stand and stare across the distance down the passage of Light.

Yamaraja and Osiris had assumed the dais. They observed her for a moment. Then Yamaraja leaned nearer to her.

"Whenever you were away, Hades suffered such pain that it became an abiding ache in his very being. It ate at him like a cancer."

"He suffered when I was away?"

"Your absences were as winter to him."

"I wish I had never left his side, not even for a moment."

"That cannot be changed. Be content to know that you loved him and that he knew it."

"I am worn down, Yamaraja; so much that I can scarcely bear myself up."

"When it all became too much for Hades to bear, he would go to the very edge of the passage of Light and simply reach his hands inside to touch its subtle shadows. Sometimes he would linger there for only a few moments. Other times he would stand there for the longest time. He never failed to come away at peace again. He was able to go on."

Yamaraja peered at her profile. "Go on. Go and let the Source of All Things wash away your sadness."

Persephone wiped at her tears without much success. She nodded and crossed the length of the great hall, oblivious for the moment to the souls shifting in her wake.

Before the gentle passage, she caught her breath and composed herself a little. She gazed into it, trying to see all the way to the Infinite Light, but at that moment the passage was calm and still.

It felt as though she ached everywhere in her being as she closed her eyes and extended her hands into the passage. She sighed. It was so soothing and warm, not chilly at all. Her head tilted back as a weary tear eased down her cheek. She had felt it, a gentle caress of pure love reaching out through her pain.

First one touch soothed her left hand and then another, simultaneous touch for her careworn right hand. "Thank you." She felt her weariness rising as gently as mist in bright sunlight and then that warmth reaching into her.

Hands closed upon her hands.

Persephone opened her eyes. A cry escaped her.

The other hands held on strong and steady.

There, in the shadowy passage, formed from the most softly luminous blue shadows that she had ever beheld stood Hades. He did not speak. There was no need to. Instead, he stood smiling peacefully and held her hands.

"I wish you could come back," she whispered.

He shook his head ever so slightly.

"I want to come to you."

Again, he shook his head, but he pressed her hands to his chest.

"If I could but kiss you one more time, what I would give..."

Hades kissed her hands. His lips lingered over the place where the vampyr had first drank her blood.

"Will I see you again...like this?"

Hades kissed her palms and pressed them to his heart.

Persephone felt her fingertips penetrate his being. She caught her breath.

Hades' heart pounded as it ever did. It pounded for her.

Persephone laughed and the Underworld was filled with Light.

Someday, finally, all Existence would cease.

At that moment, Persephone knew she would be standing upon the dais. Before her would stretch that infinite and yet brief passage. She would be waiting, but not for much longer.

From it Hades would re-emerge.

Persephone would reach out her hands to him. It would take only five flying strides for him to reach her. It would be easy then, for at long last they two would be utterly alone, the very last of their kind, until the whole universe gave birth to itself – an eternal Phoenix.

Hades would kiss her hands, and then, as he had in their beginning, he would take her into his arms and take her away whence he had come – to the Light and Source of All Things.

THE END

A Few Afterthoughts…

Well, there you have it: the epic love story of Hades and Persephone.

Yes, I took liberties.

For example: Charon and the river Styx – Omitted.

They simply didn't figure in the narrative. You can assume they are out there although they don't appear in the story. The omission was a simplification – to save time in the plot when the characters came and went.

Another example: Ganymede – and his 'Fate'.

I'm sorry, but I just couldn't get beyond the fact that he was abducted in the first place and with no greater or higher purpose than to 'serve' Zeus as his cupbearer.

I left out Ploutos as well, again, no space in the dramatic narrative.

When you are dealing with some over-familiar subject, you pretty much need to find a way to refresh it and perhaps open up a new perspective to make things vital and interesting.

In order to be able to take liberties with your subject matter, you need to know the territory, which requires RESEARCH. Man, did I do a lot of research! If I could find it and it applied to the subjects in this novel, I read it.

By the way, I recommend highly Karl Kerenyi's book on ELEUSIS. It gave me some very interesting ideas to play with and some eye-opening associations. There is so much more to Hades and Persephone than can be found in the likes of Edith Hamilton, so many themes to work with. In the end, I chose a compassionate path of universality and inclusion, not exclusion.

That instinct I applied also to this novel's fictional culture. It seemed to make sense to depict an inclusive universe where Hades would co-exist with Anubis, Osiris, Hel, et al. It also made for a more interesting Underworld.

However, it's pretty obvious: I don't like Zeus. Sorry, Zeus Fans, I can't stand him. He's a swine. My apologies.

In general, I've tried to be as inclusive as possible when it came to including various other mythological and sacred figures. If however I failed to mention a particular favorite or appropriate divine Incarnation, no slight was intended. It came down to the stringent rigors of plot and narrative space, and I was trying hard to avoid dry roll calls in the middle of the action. Still, just because you don't see these extra figures in the background waving at the 'audience' doesn't mean they aren't there somewhere – going about their business.

No, I don't hate Vampires. Since everyone else seems to be taking the sympathetic route, I decided to go against the flow by going back to older depictions and staying pretty close to what exists in legend and in the works of Bram Stoker, Polidori, and so forth.

A villainous adversary was needed and I took my cue from Hades: he didn't like it when someone tried to break the rules of the Underworld. And when you think about it, vampires would be among the worst rule-breakers around. Hades would have it in for them – big time.

I also broke my own rule about using historical personages as characters in my work. Polidori, Lord Byron, the Misses Bronte, I salute you. And I promise never to do it again.

At last, on a personal note, I thought I was done with writing. I wanted to be done with writing. It takes a lot out of me and it is a very lonely occupation. Unfortunately, an event in July 2008 brought this narrative forward and I could not ignore it.

I have never felt as though I had all the time in the world. In my family, bad things can, do, and will happen. They certainly happened to my generation of the family. From the age of thirteen onward, I have been keenly aware of the presence of death. It has taken three of my generation already, taken them young and taken them suddenly. The third of us went in July of 2008 and this story came to me. I knew I had another story – this story – to write.

I did not want to write it. Call me superstitious, but I was afraid to get too close to Hades and Persephone because they are such potent figures. I have dealt with the themes of love and loss before when I wrote THE JINNIYAH, but this time it felt different. It was different. I had to find a way past fear, past grief and pain, and the path to Hades and Persephone was through compassion. It was the only way and once I found that route, the fear went away.

I hope I am done with writing. It takes so much out of me. I hope the voices subside, but they will chatter on sometimes.

In the meantime, I will revel in color and symbolism: I will paint.

And I will continue doing something positive and constructive with my energy.

Maria Aragon
September 2, 2009

www.ingramcontent.com/pod-product-compliance
Lightning Source LLC
Chambersburg PA
CBHW022006010726
47494CB00003B/912